THE FORGOTTEN HUES OF SKYE

THE FORGOTTEN HUES OF SKYE

OF SKYE

A HUES NOVEL

BOOK ONE

J. L. JACKOLA

Library of Congress Control Number 2022920623

Paperback ISBN 978-1-954175-77-8
Hardback ISBN 978-1-954175-84-6
Electronic ISBN 978-1-954175-78-5

Distributed by Tivshe Publishing
Printed in the United States of America

Cover design by Dark Queen Designs

Visit www.tivshepublishing.com

It's never too late to start over...

AUTHOR'S NOTE

Dear Reader,

Welcome to another world in my fantasy universe. The Hues series began as a standalone book, but I quickly discovered that there was more to this world and Skye and Mark's journey than one book could cover.

While I absolutely adore this series, it is not for the faint of heart, nor is its content on the same level as books I have written in the past. While fantasy and romance are at the heart of this series, it is dark at times and contains scenes that may be unsettling to some readers.

The Hues series consists of characters who are mature and sexually confident. It is a blend of fantasy romance, epic fantasy, and dark fantasy. *This series contains intense and explicit sexual scenes, language, non-consensual sex, reverse harem situations, violence, and death.*

Enjoy Skye and Mark's journey and remember—I may torment my characters but I do love a happy ending!

J. L.

KANTENDA
DRANTH MOUNTAINS
FETTERRED FOREST
CHENTHOM

ELTANDER
NENOCHIN
APENDIA

SKYE

Skye turned the ring over in her fingers.

"It really is beautiful, Sam, but you didn't have to."

"Nonsense," he said, keeping his eyes on the road, a smile filling his face. "It's our anniversary, and not just any anniversary. This one is special."

Twenty years. She remembered the day he'd proposed while hiking the Adirondacks. He'd dropped to his knee as they reached the mountain top, the view below perilous but breathtaking. Now they were no longer young kids but mature adults who had weathered the storms that marriage, kids, and life had brought them.

They were driving to their favorite Mexican place two towns over after having dropped their son, Alex, off to stay with Skye's cousin Mark for the night. They had a night to themselves, a rarity.

Snow battered the windshield as Sam drove with his grip tight on the wheel, keeping his eyes focused on the slick roads.

"Remind me why we picked a February wedding?"

"Because we're New Englanders and the cold keeps us strong," she replied, laughing.

He grabbed her hand and squeezed it. "I love you."

"I love you, too," she replied.

The tender moment was interrupted as an SUV swerved into their lane, careening into their car head-on.

Time stood still, glass particles hanging mid-air as the screech of metal against metal invaded her senses. Within the fragments of glass, sparkles of color bled out across her vision—blues, reds, and violets, brilliant and warm. They swirled around her, tingling her skin. Then they were gone, the airbags exploding, the world crumbling with the impact before everything faded to black.

SKYE

Skye woke with an abrupt breath, quickly sitting, her heart racing. Drawing her knees to her chest, she held them tightly as she leaned her head on them.

"A nightmare," she told herself as her breathing calmed.

Eventually, she let herself drop back to her pillow, looking over at the empty space next to her, running her fingers across the cold pillow. Five years had passed since the accident, yet the nightmares continued, and the other side of her bed remained empty, even though her mind continued to imagine him there.

She laid still until she could no longer; the threat of overwhelming sadness was too close. She squinted at her phone—four in the morning, too early to be awake. Knowing sleep would not return, she dragged herself from bed, trudging her way through her morning routine, and started the coffeemaker before cleansing her emotions and mind with a treadmill run. By the time dawn peeked its way across the horizon, Skye was in her office, sipping coffee.

An hour later, she made her way back to the kitchen for a second much-needed cup of coffee when Alex stepped in, rubbing his eyes.

"Early class this morning?" she asked.

He grunted what she assumed to be a yes and pulled the milk from the fridge.

Sam's insurance policy had covered the house, but there'd been little left to save for Alex's college tuition. And on her salary, they weren't able to afford the tuition without taking student loans, so Alex had decided community college would be his path instead of racking up an immense amount of debt.

Part of her wondered if he had made that decision to stay close to her. After his father's death, he'd assumed the role of man of the house. It hadn't been something she'd asked him to do, but he'd taken it on anyway, assuming a burden he shouldn't have carried at such a young age.

He kissed her cheek after gulping down a large glass of milk and left for school. She stared at the empty space where he'd been, wondering how she'd lost the little guy who had once snuggled with her.

Sighing, she put his glass in the sink, and walked with her coffee to her office, ignoring the still silence of the house around her.

Skye worked for the next few hours, trying to avoid the urge to walk away and take the rest of the day off. It would have been an act of avoidance, and one she couldn't afford. The work would continue to pile up, regardless if she was there or not.

After three hours, her head began to hurt so she looked away from the computer, figuring she'd strained her eyes again. Closing them, she leaned back in her chair; the discomfort growing until, just as she thought she could take it no more, a burst of color showered behind her lids. Startled, she reopened her eyes to find spectrums of color flooding the room as well. Colors she hadn't seen since the night of Sam's death—the only time she'd seen them since she was a small child.

Skye backed out of her chair, stumbling, trying to escape the unrelenting onslaught of her vision. Holding her head and blinking furiously to free herself from it, but to no avail, she finally squeezed her eyes shut, praying for her constant companions of blue and gray to return.

Her phone rang, and the colors fled, flooding her world back into darkness. Opening her eyes slowly, she welcomed the calm shades that made up her color-free world, letting the call go to voicemail. She slid down the wall, landing hard on the floor, her shaking legs too unstable to hold her any longer. She blinked several times, but no colors returned.

What had it been? An anomaly? A return of her vision? They'd said it wasn't possible. She'd been color-blind most of her life, a rare kind, unheard of before her. The only shades discernible were dark ones—blues, grays, blacks, and a dirty white that tended toward light gray.

She remembered colors, the beauty of them, the way they tumbled in the air as if waiting for her to grab them. Remembered the moment they had disappeared vividly, like a light had been turned off, and she'd been left in the dark. It was the one thing she remembered from her early childhood. She couldn't remember anything prior to that day, but then who really remembered their toddler years other than through pictures? Pictures that did not exist for her; she always wondered why.

The phone rang again, bringing her back to the moment. She pushed herself from the floor, taking tentative steps to the phone.

"Hello, Mom," she answered, seeing that the first call had also been from her mother and knowing if she didn't answer, the calls would continue.

"Oh, Skye, there you are. I was worried when you didn't pick up. Are you all right?"

There was something to her mother's tone, an urgency, a concern that bordered on hysteria.

"Mom, I'm fine—"

"What's happened, Skye?"

How did she do this? It had been the same when the accident had occurred. She'd known something had happened. Had flown to New England and been by her side when Skye woke up.

"I'm fine, Mom. My vision's bothering me, that's all."

"How so, dear?"

She didn't know how to answer the question. Admitting that prisms had overtaken her vision, leaving her incapacitated, sounded mad. It was mad.

"Skye?"

Sighing, she said, "Colors. Strange flashes of color like I had the night of the accident."

Her mother was quiet

"Mom?"

"Go see Mark. Have him look at your eyes."

"I don't need to see Mark. It was a onetime thing. My color vision isn't coming back, you know that."

"Call him now. He'll fit you in."

"Don't be ridiculous, I'm fine."

"Skye Langford, call him now."

Her mother rarely got angry. She was a sweet little woman in her seventies who bided her time crocheting scarves for the local orphanage. Skye was taken aback by her change in tone.

"Call me after you've talked to him. I expect a call today. Now, I've got to go. Your father is rummaging in the kitchen for something to eat, and he'll disturb my organization if I don't stop him. Goodbye, dear."

Skye stared at the phone, wondering what had come over her mother and why it was so urgent that she see Mark. He wouldn't have an answer.

She dropped the phone to the desk and sat staring out her

office window. The world of blues and grays had returned, no colors to be found. What remained, however, was a dull throb in the back of her head. Her eyes felt strained, like they wanted to be closed.

"Dammit, Mom," she grumbled, knowing her mother was right. Skye grabbed her phone with irritation and speed dialed Mark.

SKYE

Mark Brownson was Skye's cousin. He was a tall, handsome man with sandy brown hair and hazel eyes. Growing up, he and Skye had always been close, and that had not changed as they'd aged. He was Alex's godfather and had become a surrogate to him after Sam had passed.

When Skye and Sam moved to the states, Mark had followed, setting up an optical office in the same town where they had settled. He was a regular part of their life and, following in his father's footsteps, had taken over her vision care when they'd moved.

"Well, if it isn't Skye of the Isle of Skye," he said, coming to greet her with a gorgeous smile that she knew melted all the women in town. He'd loved to tease her about her name ever since they were children. Her parents had loved their homeland so much that they'd named her after it. A source of constant teasing as she'd gone through primary school.

"Hello, Mark," she replied with a smile, kissing his cheek in greeting.

"Come on, let's look at those eyes."

"You didn't have to see me right away. Don't you have other appointments?"

"Nonsense, it's lunchtime. I'm all yours."

She waved to Nancy, the receptionist, on her way back to the exam room.

"You know the drill," he said, pointing to the chair. She took a seat and met his hazel eyes. His eyes had always fascinated her, the way they would shift in subtle ways from brown to green depending on his mood. They were the one spot of color she now realized she could still see, a bit of brightness in her dull world. When they were younger, she'd fallen in love with him, wishing he weren't her cousin, that things had been different. The desire had never waned, even after she'd married Sam, but she'd accepted the fact early on that craving her cousin's touch was beyond the norms and deeply disturbing.

There were times she'd thought he felt the same, that his love for her went beyond the familial obligation. Her mind drifted to that moment when she'd been twenty-five and he in his thirties already, still not married. She'd been preparing to take her vows with Sam, and Mark had come to wish her luck. He'd seemed stricken by the sight of her in her wedding gown, his eyes releasing the longing that had lived in her for many years. Somehow, their lips had touched. A kiss meant for the cheek but slipping with the fear of marrying Sam, a man she loved dearly but only second to Mark, and a need to tell Mark her true feelings before it was too late.

He'd kissed her back, the passion nearly bringing her to her knees. In that moment, she'd almost turned from her future with Sam, almost thrown the norms of society to the wind to be with Mark. Almost.

But then it was over, both of them awkwardly apologizing. He blamed the shots he'd taken to calm his own nerves, although she'd tasted no alcohol on his lips.

He'd dropped his head, mumbling about rules and breaking his oath. Then his hazel eyes had met hers, the sadness she'd seen in them, matching her own. "You look beautiful, Skye. You always do. Sam is a lucky man. I'll envy him for the rest of our lives, but you need to marry him today."

"But Mark—"

"Don't, Skye. Don't say the words. We can take back a kiss, but we can't take the words back."

They'd stood there in heavy silence until her mother had interrupted them, the moment lost with the flurry of wedding day activities.

"Skye?" His voice broke through the memory. "Still with me?"

She gave him a smile. "Sorry, my mind wandered."

"I'd say. You just ignored everything I said. Not reminiscing about Sam, are you?"

She gave him a small shrug, unsure of what to say or why the memory had surfaced after all these years.

He patted her leg. "Let me take a look."

He went through the motions as she told him about the flashes of color that had overtaken her vision earlier that day. When he was through, he sat back and studied her, crossing his arms—strong, muscled arms that were not hidden below his white coat during this visit. Had he always been so built? She supposed he had. She hadn't looked at him in that way since the day of her wedding, closing off her feelings for him.

"Are you certain you didn't hit your head?"

Startled, she met his eyes. His brow furrowed and there was a twinkle to his eyes, as if he knew her thoughts. What were her thoughts? She didn't know herself. It had been five years since the accident. Five years since she'd shared a kiss with another man, her bed with one. She hadn't even thought of touching another man...until now. It was as though something had awakened the desires she'd imprisoned deep within her for the past twenty-five years.

"No, no, I didn't," she answered, rubbing her clammy hands on her jeans. "Did you see anything? Do you know what's happening to me?"

"You're fine, Skye. Nothing's happening to you."

He kept his distance, no comforting touch like he usually gave her. "It was just a freak incident. Nothing's changed. You're still color-blind."

She sighed, chewing her lip. "I can see the color in your eyes."

His eyes narrowed, his expression changing to a serious one that frightened her for just a moment.

"My eyes are brown, Skye. There is no color in them."

She laughed. "They've always had color, Mark. They're hazel, don't be ridiculous. I think I've always seen it. Isn't that strange? Why didn't I realize that before?" She rose from the chair, her mind confused as she opened the door.

Mark came up behind her and turned her around. "You can see color in my eyes?"

He was close, too close. Whatever was happening to her liked the closeness. She brought her fingers up to touch the corner of his eye. "Yes, your eyes are hazel, Mark. They've always been hazel." Her hand lingered, tracing the contour of his cheek.

He grabbed her hand, removing it from his face. "Don't," he said softly.

"You look just as you did that day. Still young, as if we were standing there now, that fork in the road looming before us." She laughed. "Look where it's led us. Both alone, both—"

"Skye, go home. You need to rest. Take the day off, and I'll check on you later."

He pulled the door open the rest of the way, the light from the hallway spreading in, casting a light gray shadow to the space and pulling her from her trance.

She dropped her hand, backing away.

"I...I'm sorry. I don't know what came over me."

"Come on, I'll walk you out." He led her out to the lobby, saying nothing more about her behavior. "I'll call you later to see how you're feeling."

She shook her head and wandered out the door, rubbing the hand that had touched his cheek. She felt his eyes on her, watching as she made her way to her car and pulled out of the parking lot.

Somehow, she made it home. Sitting in the driveway, she dropped her head to the steering wheel.

"What is wrong with you?" she chastised herself.

Closing her eyes, she tried to push away whatever it was, but she couldn't. Lifting her head, she rested it on the seat, staring at the ceiling, before making her way into the house. Was there something wrong with her? She went into the bathroom and splashed cold water on her face, then looked back at her expression.

Dark blue eyes stared back at her. Sam had always told her how they popped against the brown of her hair, but her limited vision kept her from seeing that. Her face was still pretty, soft, and youthful. She hadn't developed that thinned out mature look her friends had when they'd hit their forties. Instead, she could still pass for early thirties, or late twenties, even though she'd celebrated her fiftieth. Just like Mark, who looked no older than thirty-five, no one ever believing he was his age.

Her mind wandered to him again. Why had her feelings come rushing back to her? She hadn't thought of him in that way for years, forcing herself to see him as nothing more than he was, her cousin, the uncle and godfather of her son. But secretly, subconsciously, those feelings had remained.

Would it be that bad to acknowledge them? At her age, half her life was over. She was alone, no longer mourning the husband she'd lost. She was a mature grown woman, who was lusting for her cousin.

"Ewww, even the sound of that is gross, Skye!" She threw the towel at her reflection and walked away.

He'd told her to rest, but she needed something to pull her mind from him. Returning to her office, she plunged back into her work, forcing all inappropriate thoughts away.

MARK

Mark watched Skye drive off, then turned to Nancy. "Cancel the rest of today's appointments."

"But Mark—"

"Now Nancy."

He stormed past her, back to his office, hating the hurt expression on her face, but knowing it needed to be done. Something was happening. He could feel it. Skye's experiences with the colors confirmed it. Slamming his office door, he tried to pull himself together.

What had happened to her in there? It was like everything the two of them had turned their back on the day of her wedding had resurfaced. He remembered that kiss, and the hunger he'd sensed from her. The need had matched his, and part of him had wanted to steal her away, screw societal norms. Instead, he'd done his duty, and turned away from her invitation, knowing it was wrong for her. She needed to marry Sam, to stay hidden in domestic suburbia. No matter how much it hurt him to watch Sam take everything that should have been his.

All of it was for her, the sacrifices all necessary. But now? He was no longer so sure.

They'd built the world around her, a safety net that kept her protected. It had been fifty years. He'd argued that it was time to tell her, time to crack the façade. Sam was dead, and she was alone. She was mature and old enough to know the truth. They'd said he was being selfish, knowing his feelings for her.

If the truth came out, he could finally have her. But would she still want him? After a lifetime of lies, pushing her into the arms of another man, and pretending to be something he wasn't, something none of them were. Would it make a difference that he wasn't her cousin? That it had all been a story concocted the day they'd stolen her away to this world. An army of protectors whose only job was to ensure she lived.

He sat, rubbing his hands over his face, and looking over at his phone. It didn't matter now. Something was happening, and the others needed to be alerted. Picking up his phone, he called the woman who had taken the role of her mother the day they'd stepped onto the shores of the Isle of Skye.

"Mark, how is she?" Elspeth answered immediately.

"I don't know, but I'm worried. Something's happening. If she's seeing colors, there can only be one reason."

"But she described something similar after the accident."

"It wasn't the same. That was a quick burst, a shifting of the spell from the force of impact. This was intense and drawn out. There's only one explanation."

"Mage magic," she whispered.

"Someone's here. Only the presence of true mage magic can trigger the breakdown of that spell."

"Camin."

"God, I hope not," he replied, a rush of emotion taking hold of him. Camin was the threat they'd hidden her from, the reason they'd fled their world.

"But there are no other mages. The Mage Warriors gave up their power to save her, the full mages all suffered a loss to our magic. No one else has the power to call her magic forth."

The breath clenched in his lungs as fear gripped him. If Camin was here, it was only a matter of time before he found Skye.

"Call the others. We must be on full alert," Elspeth blurted out.

"We need to tell her."

"No!" she snapped.

"Elspeth, you're being ridiculous. Skye needs to know who she is."

"You will not tell her."

Mark gritted his teeth. "You may have magic, Elspeth, but I still outrank you as an Elite."

"And you swore your allegiance to all of us when you took this assignment. You are not the commander of the Elite who remain. You are the youngest, and do not forget that. The only reason you are here is because your age is close to hers, and you served a purpose. Now alert the others. Thomas and I will catch the next flight. If Camin is here, we need to be there for whatever fight he brings."

"He will kill us all, then her."

"You forget that his magic was weakened as well."

"I wouldn't count on that being the case still, Elspeth. You're a fool if you think he didn't find a way for his magic to return. How else do you explain Skye's awakening?"

"Summon the others." The line went dead.

He slammed his phone down. Stubborn fool. She would get them all killed. If Camin had magic once more, if he'd somehow found his way to this world, then everything they'd done would be lost.

What had they done, though? It should have been temporary. Hide her away, keep her safe, then one day they would be called home.

Home. He'd been young when they'd left. A mere ten years and in their long-life spans, ten years was but a babe. Elspeth was right. He'd only been chosen because his age was close to Skye's, and he'd been marked as an Elite—the guard to the Mage Warriors.

His hand subconsciously went to the back of his shoulder, rubbing his birthmark, the half-moon that lie dormant, a mere brown stain on his skin now. He remembered how it had shown a bright silver in the power of the Mage Warriors, their magic bound to the Elite. Just as the Mage Warriors were marked with their own birthmarks, called to their status in life, so were the Elite.

Skye had a crescent moon under her hairline, only noticeable when her hair was up. If they were home, it would glow a bright violet, but now like his mark, it lay dormant, powerless. Camin had forced them all into hiding. Mark didn't know if any were left of his kind. Had anyone survived or were they doomed to live in this world forever? Living life with the blind humans who were unaware of the sheer power that walked among them.

He picked his phone back up. The others needed to be alerted. If Camin was indeed here, it could only mean one thing: the war had been lost and his magic had returned. A chill ran through Mark as a memory of Camin surfaced.

He was like a void of darkness that snuffed out the light of other mages, taking it from them, manipulating it until the beauty of it no longer existed. In its place was a toxic shell of what had once been, manipulated to fit the man he had become—a vengeful, power-hungry scourge on their lands.

And he was coming for Skye.

Mark opened the group chat and typed the word they'd all dreaded seeing. The one word that had been chosen to put their emergency plans into action, calling the Elite for duty after a half a century of dormancy.

Skye.

SKYE

The doorbell rang, breaking the silence that surrounded Skye in her concentration. She heard shuffling feet outside her office and looked away from her work to the time. Seven fifteen. How had it gotten so late? She remembered Alex coming in after classes and running off to play video games with his friends but hadn't realized so much time had elapsed since then.

She stood and stretched, then made her way to the kitchen to find out who was at the door. She heard Alex jabbering away and found Mark in the doorway with pizzas in hand. He eyed the direction where she'd come from with a raised brow.

"I figured the kid would be hungry since I told you to sleep it off the rest of the day. I see you did not take my advice," he scolded her as he set the pizzas down. "And you worked late?"

Alex and the few friends he had over dove into the pizza. "Hey, manners!" she snapped. "At least get plates out, you scavengers."

They scattered, knowing she wanted them at the table since Mark was there. Even Alex's friends knew when to listen to his mother.

"You were told to rest, doctor's orders."

"Eye doctor's orders," she teased.

"Won't ever let me live that one down, will you?" he replied, a playful tone to his voice.

He'd wanted to be an emergency room doctor but had decided instead to follow in his father's footsteps and become an eye doctor. She knew it wasn't the exciting career he'd wanted and had suspected he'd chosen it for her. When he'd followed her and Sam to the states and set up his practice here, her suspicions had been confirmed. Always looking out for her, always her protector.

"Go shut that computer off and come join us."

"Yes, doctor."

She did as instructed, stopping by the bathroom to freshen up. She noted her tired eyes, heavy and slightly bloodshot, a sign that she'd spent too much time in front of the monitor. She pulled her hair up, wondering why she was suddenly self-conscious of the fly-aways that Mark had seen for years.

"Fool," she muttered as she exited the bathroom.

Something caught her eye, the corner of her birthmark. She looked closer. She could have sworn she'd seen a sparkle from it. Shaking her head, she pulled her ponytail to the side of her neck, covering the mark.

"Delirious and foolish."

They ate dinner together, Alex and his friends chattering to Mark about various topics. Alex had always been close to him and as the years had passed since Sam's death, he'd grown more attached to him. Skye stayed quiet, listening to their voices, trying to ignore the melodic baritone of Mark's voice and how it appealed to her. It baffled her how one incident with her eyes had suddenly hit the "ON" switch for an unstable onslaught of hormonal overdose.

"You all right, Mom?" Alex asked.

She blinked, startled from her thoughts, and realized she'd been unconsciously rubbing her birthmark.

"Fine. I'm fine. Just tired, I guess. Let's get this cleaned up. Who's up for a movie night?"

They all stared at her, remaining awkwardly silent before a mad chaos ensued. Alex and his friends had plans. They whisked him away, fleeing the table with a flourish of goodbyes and thank you's. The house was empty save for her and Mark.

"Huh, it's like a bunch of cats with the threat of a bath. Is that normal? Were we that way at their age?"

She laughed. "Yes, we were and yes, on a Friday night, that's typical."

Mark helped her clean up, then grabbed his jacket.

"Stay," she said suddenly. "Look, I made it awkward today. I'm sorry. I don't know what came over me. Stay and watch a movie with me. Alex says there's a good horror movie I should see. You know how I hate watching them by myself. Unless, of course, you've got a date already."

Mark put his jacket down. "No hot date waiting for me, and I would love a cheesy horror movie and a glass of wine right about now."

She laughed. "You've got it."

~

THEY SHARED a bottle of wine and a few jumps as they watched the movie. By the time the final scene played out, her face was hidden in his chest, just as she'd done when they were younger.

"God, Mom, you are such a wimp," Alex said, coming in to join them.

"Early night?" she asked. "Or did you come home early just to taunt me?"

"Eh, they were just drinking at Keith's place, since his parents aren't home."

"Drinking?" Mark said with an eye lift.

"Don't give me that, Uncle Mark."

"I can give you that," she said.

"Let's go back to talking about how wimpy you are with these movies and forget what I said."

"Mhmm. So, you came home just to tease me?"

"Yup. Why do you bother watching these movies if you miss half of them?" Alex asked.

"It's a sick obsession."

She pulled away from Mark's chest, suddenly conscious of how close she was, but still hid her eyes until the credits rolled.

Mark pulled her fingers down. "It's over. You can come out now."

She peeked around her fingers.

"I hope you never have to face post-apocalyptic zombies, Mom. You'd be the first one down."

Alex said goodnight and left them alone.

Mark's eyes were on her, evaluating her in a strangely serious way. Worry creased his forehead.

"What?"

"Nothing. I should go. You need some sleep."

She eyed the bottle of wine they'd finished and followed him to the kitchen.

"I don't think so. You'll stay here. I'm not sending you out on the road after you've been drinking."

"It was two glasses of wine, Skye, and I live right around the corner. I'll be fine."

"Two large glasses of wine, so nope. The guest room is made up, so you can stay the night. Alex will be happy to see you here in the morning. You guys can chill."

He raised a brow. "Chill?"

"Whatever it is they do these days." She laughed.

"I think you just aged us both with that one word."

His laugh filled the room, sending her heart fluttering. Until it stopped as their eyes met.

"Are you sure?"

"Yes, besides, it's started to flurry, and I'd feel better if you were here."

"In case the power goes out and a horde of zombies rushes the house?"

She crossed her arms, trying to hide her smile.

"Fine, I'll stay and fend off the snow zombies."

"Always my protector.

"Always."

There was something in the way he'd said the word that touched a part of her consciousness, sparking something she couldn't quite put her finger on.

"Night, Skye."

"Night, Mark."

They hit the lights and made their way up the stairs. As she turned to go toward the master bedroom, she stopped.

"Mark?"

"Hmmm." He turned, his hazel eyes dark in the dim light of the hall.

"If we..." She hesitated, knowing it was the wine talking. "If things were different—"

"It would have been me marrying you that day," he said.

Her heart pounded loudly, but only the sound of his words echoed through her mind. She wanted to reply, to tell him to hell with it all. That she didn't care what anyone said, that she'd loved him since they were children, that it was him she'd wanted when he'd pushed her into Sam's arms. But she didn't. She left the words unspoken.

"But they're not different, Skye. Maybe they will be one day... but they aren't now."

He turned away and went to his room, the door softly closing behind him. She could see the shadow of his figure at the door, as though he were regretting his words, his decision to walk away from her.

She stood there for a long time, until she finally willed herself to move, his shadow still against the door. The distance between them forced once again.

SKYE DREAMED AGAIN THAT NIGHT, not of the accident but of colors. Prisms of color that coated the world, filling the sky until she could barely see. There was warmth to them and something else, something that tingled against her skin.

Waking, she opened her eyes to a world of shadows, missing the warmth of the colors she'd dreamed. She yawned and checked the time. It was ten in the morning. How had she slept so late?

Rubbing the sand from her eyes, she rose, doing a long cat stretch to wake her still sleepy muscles. She thought back to the night before, shaking her head at the wine's loosening of her senses. She blamed it on the wine but wasn't convinced the wine was truly at fault. She'd acted similar earlier in the day with no alcohol to blame.

She cast her eyes to the quiet side of her bed, the side that had remained untouched all these years. A hint of guilt slid into her conscious. She'd loved Sam, he'd been a good husband, a wonderful father, and he'd loved her. For the twenty years they'd been married, she'd been faithful, her mind never straying to another man, to Mark. She'd put her foolishness aside and loved him the best that she could. But it had never been a hundred percent, no matter what she'd told herself.

Sighing, she turned away and headed to the bathroom. She piled her hair up in her version of a messy bun and rinsed off, the warmth of the shower washing away her grogginess.

When she finally made it downstairs, she found Mark in the kitchen scraping freshly scrambled eggs into a serving bowl. He raised a brow and gave her a crooked smile.

"Nice of you to join the land of the living."

"I didn't realize it was so late," she replied, suddenly aware of the ripped leggings and oversized sweatshirt she'd donned, and wishing she'd made an effort to look more presentable. Maybe it was better this way. There was no way she looked attractive like this.

"I thought you'd be gone by now."

"Kicking me out so fast?" He placed a hot cup of coffee in front of her.

Moaning, she grabbed it and took a long sip. "Thank you. No, of course I'm not kicking you out, but it's your weekend. You've got things to do."

"I took next week off. I'm fine. Besides," he gestured to the deck, "I don't think I'm going anywhere. You're stuck with me."

Her eyes wandered to the direction of the deck and widened at the snow that had accumulated. She put her cup down and ran to the front of the house, sitting in the window seat that overlooked the now buried street, staring at the thick flakes that were still falling.

"After all these New England winters, you'd think the excitement of snow would wear off, yet you're still like a small child each time."

He handed her the coffee, and she wrapped her hands around it. "There's something about snow that fascinates me. It's like this brightness in my dark world, each flake a tiny glimmer of light in the shadows."

"Huh, you never told me that."

She took a sip of her coffee and looked up at him. "You never asked."

"Whoa, where did that come from?" Alex asked, emerging from his room in the basement, his shaggy blonde hair tumbling in his eyes.

"Aren't you a little old to go back to the basics of science, Alex?" Mark teased him.

Skye couldn't help but giggle.

"Funny, Uncle Mark. Are you old enough for dad jokes now?"

He winked and headed to the kitchen.

"I'm not old enough for those, am I?"

She nodded. "Afraid so. You may still look like a thirty-year-old, but to him, you're an old man. And the numbers tell the truth."

"Need I remind you, you're pretty far up there yourself?"

"I'm still younger than you," she replied, sticking her tongue out and making her way back to the kitchen.

She smiled as she heard him grumble in response.

"So, the roads aren't passable?" Alex shouted from the kitchen as she entered.

She shot him a look, her head suddenly a little sensitive. Perhaps she'd had too much wine after all.

"Sorry, Mom," he whispered.

"Looks that way," Mark answered, opening the front door. She turned to look and in that moment as a beam of stray sunlight hit the snow, her head felt like it burst open. Colors bled from all sides of her vision as she distantly registered the crash of her coffee cup. She took no notice, overwhelmed by the colors that were searing her eyes, the pain that ripped at her head as she collapsed.

MARK

Mark knew he should have left when Skye had insisted he stay, that he shouldn't have answered her question in the hallway. He'd almost given in, almost taken her in his arms and kissed her, but he hadn't. Instead, he'd forced himself to walk to his room rather than to her like he'd wanted. He had a job to do. Her safety was worth the heartache.

Upon waking the next morning, he'd intended to leave early, but the storm prevented it. An unbelievable amount of snow had fallen and there was no leaving until the storm abated and the roads were cleared.

Thankfully, Skye had slept in, allowing him to check on the progress of the others. The other Elite had taken position throughout the neighborhood. The storm wouldn't bother them, they were well trained even after so many decades. They knew the drill and had practiced daily to stay prepared, to stay strong. Even Mark, who was positioned closest to her, rose most days before dawn and trained for hours before starting his day.

They'd all been chosen because they were the best of the Elite. He the only one who'd yet to reach the formal age when they'd fled with Skye. An older Elite had been assigned to play his father, and they'd concocted a story about his mother dying, although Mark knew it was likely the truth now. He had been training rigorously through the years so that today he was as fit as, if not more fit than the others. The thought of any harm coming to Skye was always pushing him.

Elspeth and Thomas, Skye's parents, were the only ones with magic, although most of their abilities had disappeared after Skye's true mother had cast the spell to hide Skye.

Mark remembered that day, watching in awe as she'd weaved the colors of the castle room, pulling the power from the hues, the room filling in a haze of light and color. It was the last time he'd seen a Mage Warrior in action.

He'd watched as the magic had flowed from her, then from the others in the room and those on the battlefield outside the castle. The magic of their world called to form the protection spell and the portal. Skye had been a small babe, too young to know what was happening as the spell had weaved around her.

It had taken a few years for it to completely bind her powers, her ability to see colors fading until it disappeared on her second birthday. They'd all seemed surprised that it had taken so long, expecting her to be bound as her mother and the other Mage Warriors had been that night.

As Mark had held her tiny hand that night, he'd seen the reason in her small eyes—she was powerful, stronger even than her mother. She'd soaked the colors in as they'd swirled around the room, claiming them and their power.

No one had believed him. Even Mage Warriors could not use another's power. But she had.

He stared at the snow, knowing the Elite were hidden out there, waiting for the first sign of danger. Would they be enough? They needed magic to fight Camin, needed the power of their Mage Warriors to be at their full potential, but the Mage Warriors were gone, except for Skye. Elspeth and Thomas would be of some help. They had once been full mages but not Mage

Warriors. If Camin was really here, Skye would be dead. The thought terrified Mark.

He turned his gaze back to Skye. She looked so innocent sitting in the window seat gazing excitedly at the snow. Her beautiful dark auburn hair was piled atop her head, wisps of it grazing her cheeks. He imagined what a sight she would be in their home world. The Mage Warriors had lived like royalty, treated with the finest the kingdom had to offer. She'd be dressed in a gown of the finest fabric draped across her skin, jewels sparkling in her hair.

His phone buzzed, but Mark ignored it as Skye returned to the kitchen. He opened the front door, grumbling at her quip about his age. If she only knew how young they both were in their world she'd be in shock.

Turning, his eyes met hers and he saw it, the color flashes in her eyes as the cup tumbled from her hands.

"Mom?" Alex said, rushing to her as she backed into the island, the stools screeching with the force. Mark ran to her.

"Back away Alex!" he yelled, catching Skye right before her head hit the ground. Her eyes were scrunched up as if she were in terrible pain. The binds of the spell were fracturing.

"What's wrong with her? Should I call 911?"

"No! No, she's okay, Alex."

But she wasn't. He could feel the tension in her body as she fought the escaping magic. God, why hadn't they listened to him and told her? She opened her eyes, throwing her head back, and screamed.

"Get back and get down Alex, now!" he commanded, but Alex hesitated. "Now!"

He scrambled away just as the colors bled from her eyes filling the room with heat. The empty wine bottle shattered on the counter. Flakes of paint and plaster fell from the ceiling onto them. The patio door shattered as the commanding Elite, Noah, flew through it. Behind him, Mark registered the front door slam open and the stomp of feet. Alex screamed. The colors faded, the intensity with it as Skye's body relaxed in his arms.

He looked up at Noah, the others all standing around them coated in snow, in fight stances.

"I think the cover is up," Mark said. "It's time to tell her."

MARK

Listening to the others, Mark paced in the front room. He'd taken Skye, still unconscious from whatever had just happened to her, to her room, and told Alex to stay with her.

"We should wait for Elspeth and Thomas before we do anything," Noah said.

He was their leader, the eldest, and decades older than Mark.

Mark balked at his words. "She needs to be told now. There's no more waiting. It's no longer an option."

Noah stood. "You may have taken the assignment closest to her Mark, but I still command you."

"I wasn't given a choice."

"Would you have chosen differently?" Noah pushed, knowing how Mark felt about Skye. They all knew. Too much time had passed for it to go unnoticed.

"As her closest Elite, I argue that we can no longer wait. Camin is out there somewhere, and her powers are breaking free. Are you waiting for him to come here and kill her, or for her magic to take out this entire town?"

"And what happens when you tell her? What then? Her magic

is still bound, she's still vulnerable. If Camin is indeed here, he will kill her. We will die protecting her but that is all we will do against him. We were sent here to keep her safe, not fight Camin."

"Tsk, tsk."

They all turned, weapons drawn.

"A mage," Noah muttered, his weapon still ready to kill.

The man lowered the hood of his cloak to reveal himself.

"Trent?" Noah said, not lowering his weapon.

It was impossible. Trent had been the leader of the full mages, higher in rank than even Elspeth. He'd stayed to fight as they had fled with Skye. Mark didn't understand how he was here, but his presence couldn't be a coincidence, and from Trent's concerned expression the reason for it was a serious one. The thought was unsettling, and Mark worried that Camin had indeed found where they'd hidden Skye. Trent, however, allowed no time for questions.

"Noahem? Where's the girl? Where is the Mage Warrior?"

"What's a Mage Warrior and why are all these people in my house?" Skye said as she descended the stairs.

Trent stormed over to her, and she took a step backward.

"This is she?" He took her face in his hands and studied her as she tried slapping his hands away.

"What the hell are you doing? Mark, what is going on?"

"Hey, get your hands off her!" Alex yelled, coming behind her.

Ignoring Alex, Trent turned abruptly, and walked over to Mark, his eyes appraising him. "Markhem? Son of the mighty Fedhem and Alina. Your father and mother died bravely. The king would be dead if not for their efforts."

Mark's heart sank. He'd suspected it, but with no contact to home, he had no confirmation. His father had been commander of the Elite. He had led the charge to save the kingdom alongside the Mage Warriors. He had died the night they'd fled, Mark witnessing it. His mother had sent him away with Skye, saying her goodbyes as Skye's mother weaved her spell. He'd never known if she still lived, but he had suspected she'd given her life for her kingdom, just as his father had.

"Would someone please tell me what is going on here?"

"She doesn't know?" Trent turned on Noah. "She doesn't know who she is?" he roared.

"There was no need," Noah argued. "She's safer not knowing."

"Well, she's not safe anymore. Camin has returned. He was gathering forces and waging a full-scale attack on Nenochin when I was sent here to find her."

"So, it's true," Noah said. "But he was rendered powerless. Lyra's spell bound them all."

"For a while," Trent answered sadly. "Our magic has been minimal, drained to mere parlor tricks, but no Mage Warriors remain. Camin destroyed them before his magic faded. Then about five years ago, he resurfaced."

Five years. Mark's head spun.

"The accident," he whispered, "it woke the power."

Mark's anger flared. He rose, moving closer to Noah, staring him down, for the first time realizing he was taller and broader than Noah. The flare of his blood stirred within him.

"Five years ago—I warned you. All of you," Mark said.

"We couldn't have known," Noah argued.

"But I did," he growled. "I told you we needed to tell her, and try to remove the spell, but you wouldn't listen!"

His blood boiled, muscles tightening as he started Noah down.

"It was Elspeth's order. We follow the full mage's orders. We do not stray. You were not in charge. Elspeth made the call and we obeyed," Noah replied, the anger clear in his voice and stance.

"The Elite do not take orders from full mages!" Trent yelled at Noah. "Elspeth was wrong. You should have listened to him. You have doomed her. You have doomed us all."

SKYE

Skye's frustration mounted as she tried to grasp what was being said. Her home was full of strangers, talking about her like she wasn't there and about things that didn't make sense to her. Mark seemed aware of what they were saying, and this strange man had called him a different name. All of them were dressed oddly, except for Mark. The one who was speaking looked as though he'd stepped out of a *Lord of the Rings* movie.

Finally, she'd had enough. "Someone needs to tell me what is going on before I throw you all out of my house!"

The one dressed like a fantasy figure turned to her. She thought she'd heard someone call him Trent, but her mind was too addled to be sure. "You, my dear, are the last of the Mage Warriors."

"Warrior?" Alex laughed. "You must be joking! My mother can't even kill a spider."

"Mother?" He stepped closer so that he was nearly on top of them and grabbed Alex's face and turned it, looking at Alex's neck.

"Hey!" she yelled.

Trent dropped his hand and turned to the others.

"He is not marked, and I sense no magic in him."

"No, he's half human," the man Mark had been arguing with said. He'd had an odd name that reminded her of the name Noah. Not remembering the rest of it she decided he'd remain Noah until she figured out who he was, who any of these people were.

"You let a non-Elite touch a Mage Warrior of her bloodline?"

"It's a long story," Mark muttered.

"You were supposed to protect her not breed her off like some whore."

Mark rose to his feet quickly and got in the man's face. "You weren't here! Decisions were made beyond our control. Elspeth wanted her to blend in. Elspeth made the decision and if you call her a whore again, I will strangle you, regardless of what magic you hold."

Skye had never seen him this way. First, he'd almost attacked Noah, now he was screaming at the robed man. It was a far cry from the quiet lab coat wearing man she knew. There was something forceful about this new testosterone driven side of Mark. Something that stirred that need in her again.

Not now, Skye, she chastised herself.

"It's clear to me the Elspeth lost her way. I will deal with her when she arrives. For now—"

"For now, you will tell me who you are and what a Mage Warrior is," Skye said, crossing her arms.

"I believe she outranks you, Trent," Mark snarled.

"You are the daughter of the most powerful Mage Warrior our world has ever witnessed," the man said. "Lyra was a legend, the leader of the Mage Warriors. All of your kind marked at birth. You hail from the strongest, purest line."

He moved to her and went to touch her hair. Instinctively, she grabbed his wrist and his brow raised in reaction.

"May I?"

She let him go and he picked up the stray hairs that had fallen across her neck, running his finger over her birth mark. A tingle ran through it.

"That's just a birthmark," she said, shaking off the strange feeling.

"That is the mark of the Mage Warrior. Their births are rare and special. Yours was powerful. We all felt the flare in our magic the day you were born. The call of our magic to yours. Your power is greater than your mother's and every Mage Warrior before her. Now you are the only one left."

Her legs were weak. "I don't have magic," she whispered, her world falling out from under her feet.

"Don't you? The colors you see shine brighter at times, do they not? Like prisms that overtake your vision?"

"I don't see color. I'm color-blind."

He turned swiftly to the others.

Noah addressed his perplexed look. "The spell. At least we think that's what it was. She had color until she reached about two years of age, then nothing."

"So that's why they lost. That's why the rest of the magic faded."

"Trent?" Mark said.

"They lost. All of them slaughtered. Camin was powerful, the shadow magic he used pulled from the other side of the color spectrum, something none of them had ever done."

"But they knew they were losing. That's why Lyra sent her here."

"Yes, but it happened swiftly. We knew the spell would lessen our power. The mages all agreed it was the only way to preserve our kind. To bleed the power so that Camin would finally be defeated. But it took longer than we thought. The novice mages faded first, then the full mages, our gifts no more than parlor tricks by the end of the moon. Over the course of the next year, the Mage Warriors fell until Camin finally killed Lyra. The kingdom was lost, but then Camin disappeared. He pulled his forces back and hid away as the power finally fled from him as well."

"Then it worked," Mark said.

"There was a flaw in Lyra's thinking. She'd forgotten Camin's magic was unique. It pulled from the light and dark hues of our world. We all thought she'd made a mistake, but perhaps she didn't." Trent turned to Skye.

"What colors do you see, child?"

Child? This man looked younger than Skye, but she bit her tongue. "Blues, grays, blacks, muted whites almost like a dirty cream."

"Like a world of shadows," he said. "The spell didn't just funnel the power of the Mage Warrior to her, it tied her to the Camin's magic."

"I'm really confused. Why do you think I'm this person's daughter and—"

"When you were born, Lyra was concerned that Camin had grown too powerful. They'd lost two Mage Warriors already, something that had never happened. She sent you away to ensure the line continued. You see, Mage Warrior magic is connected. As long as they live, others will be born to fill their ranks as the others age. If none exist, no new ones can be called. Here you would be protected until our kingdom decided it was safe for you to return," Mark answered.

"And you?"

"I am an Elite as are these men. We are the king's guard, the protectors of the Mage Warriors. We were sent to guard you."

She swallowed, her knees shaking. "And Elspeth and Thomas?"

"Full mages sent to protect you, posing as your parents."

"So, they're not even related to me?"

He shook his head sadly.

"And you? Are you even my cousin?" The word stuck in her throat as he shook his head again. The world came crashing down around her, like a piece of Jenga had been pulled from the bottom of the tower.

She pushed Trent aside and ran through the house, out the patio door, which was smashed completely, and into the snow. She heard Mark call her name, but she ignored him, trying to grasp some thread of reality, something that was real in her life.

The storm howled around her. Each step she took becoming harder, the soft snow almost to her knees. She ignored the cold, pushing forward until Mark's hands grabbed her.

"Are you crazy? Put this on."

He thrust a heavy coat around her as her teeth chattered. The white snowflakes shone brightly against the darkness of her world.

Anger surfaced and she pushed him away. "You knew? All this time you lied to me? All these years?" A sob escaped her before she could bite it back.

"I couldn't tell you, Skye. I'm not in charge and I swore to protect you."

"Protect me? You lied to me! You let me believe... God, I am so angry at you right now! Leave me alone."

"I'm not leaving you out here to freeze, and I'm not leaving you alone."

"Why didn't you tell me, Mark?" She heard the desperation in her voice.

"I couldn't."

She brought her hand to her mouth to stifle the pain. "All those years you pushed me away. You made me marry Sam...you..."

"You loved Sam," he said.

"Not like I loved you." She'd said the words. They couldn't be taken back.

He pulled her to him and kissed her. The heat of it was enough to melt the snow around them. The intensity almost knocked her over, but his strong hands held her up. It felt good, perfect even, and she wanted more until she remembered.

Pushing him away, she cried, "No! You don't get to do that, not after all you did to me!"

"Did to you? Do you have any idea how much it hurt to see you with him? To spend time with you both? To pretend I was happy when another man was making love to the woman I wanted? That you were bearing his child and not mine? To watch him kiss you and touch you when I couldn't?"

"You turned me away, Mark."

"I had to, just as you did. The part had to be played to protect you, to hide you. I didn't choose to be named as your cousin. It was given to me. I was a child, I had no say. You don't think I would go back to that day and change their minds if I could?" He ran his hands over his face. "It killed me, Skye. Every day for twenty years, it killed me."

She didn't know what to say. There was a distance between them that contradicted the opening they'd just been given.

"I gave you the opening that day, a final chance," she whispered.

"And I did what a good soldier does, Skye. Sam meant safety, a chance for you to blend in. He was a good man who treated you well. If it had to be anyone then I was glad it was him."

"But I loved you. You were who I wanted to say those vows to. You were the one I imagined touching me. You were the one I wanted making love to me. No one else."

Her teeth chattered and the cold affronted her, the fire of her anger dissipating.

"Did you really come out here with no shoes?"

She laughed. "Of course I did." Her smile faltered. "Where do we go from here?"

"We stop this lover's quarrel and release your power," Trent said, appearing from nowhere. "Mage Warriors and Elite are drawn to one another. It's not often but when it happens it's unstoppable. The magical and the physical linked. Elspeth should have known better than to keep you separated. Your father was an

Elite. Second in command only to Markhem's father. The two were good friends and died on the battlefield together."

"We should get her inside. She's too cold," Mark said, his voice with an edge to it. Had he known his father? She'd thought his father had been the man she'd known, but from the way this man talked, that had been a façade, too.

"You stood out here confessing your love to one another with no heed to the cold. Stay. She needs to recognize her magic and you need to explain why you have not challenged Noahem for command."

Noahem. It was a strange name and she decided she'd stick with Noah.

"It's not my place," Mark said.

"Oh, but it is and deep down you remember that. Even if Noahem has let that fact slip. You are a purebred Elite. You come from a line of Elite commanders. You have every right to lead those men and the ones at home. As wise as you seem compared to Noahem, who bowed to the will of a full mage over the safety of a Mage Warrior, you should be in command."

Skye was trying to keep up with everything he was saying but she was lost.

"She's always been safe."

"Has she? Would she not be prepared had they heeded your warnings five years ago? Would she not have been safer in your arms than another's?"

That stung and she could see it in Mark's expression.

"Elspeth has gone soft, become complacent. The safest place for Skye is with you, the strongest of the Elite. Keep her close. You will stand guard while I begin her training."

"It's probably better that I don't. Noah is in charge."

"And why is that? Your father was the commander of the Elite. You were meant to lead, Markhem," he said, the anger evident in his tone. "Noahem was given that role due to your youth. You are no longer that child. Take back what is rightfully yours. Take back command of the Elite. Challenge him and he will have no choice but to let you lead. If you had done that when you warned them, she would be safer than she is today."

Mark stood proud, then stuffed his hands in his pockets and began to walk away. "She's better off with Noah."

"I don't know Noah. I know you," Skye said. "I'm lost, Mark, and afraid. I don't know what the hell is going on. I may be pissed at you for lying to me, but I still need you."

Her teeth were chattering violently now, and she'd lost feeling in her toes.

"She needs to go inside."

Mark stopped talking and Skye looked to where his eyes had drifted. The snow was melting around her feet, the ground drying, warmth traveling to her body.

"Whoa," she uttered.

"That is child's play. As your power returns, so shall ours."

"You don't have your full power yet, Trent?"

"No, the only reason I found her was the burst of magic I sensed. Thank the gods I laid a false path for Camin on the other side of this land mass, otherwise he would have been here first. I traveled via the wind along with her magic flare. I connected to the waves of it and found her."

"That was magic?"

"Yes."

"But it hurt like crazy."

"Only because Lyra's spell has it locked inside of you. It is trying to escape. It has been since it sensed it could those years ago. Now that Camin is in this world, it won't stop. Magic attracts magic."

"Then he'll find her if she uses it."

"He'll find her if she doesn't. I'm hoping we can open a portal back with this." Trent pulled out a large amulet. "Then we can train her there. This brought me here, the last trace of Lyra's magic in it, a safeguard in case something happened and Skye couldn't return."

"Why didn't you use it to bring us home earlier?" Mark asked, an edge to his voice. "Why wait so long to find us?"

There was a moment of hesitation before Trent answered him. "It was meant as a failsafe. Lyra entrusted me with it and told me to wait. Saying Skye would find her way home but if she didn't and things grew dire, the amulet would lead me to her. Knowing we needed to find her if we had any chance of defending ourselves, I brought it to the king once Camin resurfaced and began his attacks again. Now, we need to get her home and train her."

"Wait just a minute. No one said anything about going anywhere. I have a son, a job, a life," Skye interrupted.

"The child can come with us. The rest you will leave behind."

"Are you serious? Mark, tell him this can't happen."

He lowered his eyes. "It was always meant to happen."

"Now, tell me what you've been seeing. When it happens, what is it you feel?" Trent asked.

"What is going on here?" She heard her mother's voice break through. But she wasn't really her mother. It had all been a lie.

A beautiful woman who looked to be in her late thirties came trudging through the snow, a man about the same age following her. Skye realized the snow was still falling, the storm hadn't abated, she'd simply forgotten it in her confusion.

"Elspeth, I am freeing her power," Trent declared.

Elspeth? But that was her fake mother's name. This woman was not a seventy-five-year-old woman.

"Skye, get in the house. Mark, take her."

Mark crossed his arms and didn't move.

"I said to take her inside while I talk to Trent."

"No."

"How dare you. Mind your place—"

"I have minded my place and look where it's gotten us.

Besides, Trent reminded me of something. Only Mage Warriors command the Elite. You have assumed rank here for too long and Noah has allowed it."

She looked as if he'd slapped her and turned instead to Skye. "Skye, go inside—"

"No. I don't have to listen to you either. I don't even know who you are."

"I'm your mother, dear."

"First of all, my mother is apparently dead and second, the woman who claimed to be my mother is seventy-five years old."

"Four hundred and seventy-five to be precise, my dear. We may not have had much magic left but we had enough to properly age ourselves."

She waved her hand in front of her face and there was the wrinkled and hunched woman Skye had known her entire life.

"I admit it's nice to be free of that spell," the man said.

"Dad?" Skye asked.

He waved his hand and aged as well, then they both merged back to their younger versions. Skye felt as though her head might explode. She didn't think she could take anymore.

"Now, Trent, we have this under control."

"Under control? You call this under control? Camin is loose, her magic is attacking her, and she and her Elite are struggling against their natural attraction? You are a fool, Elspeth!"

"You were not here! We did what we thought was right. You left us here for fifty years. It was only supposed to be a temporary stay until Camin was defeated. Our magic disappeared, we had no way of knowing if all was lost or saved."

"You should have made her aware and coaxed her magic forth."

They continued to argue, and Skye couldn't take anymore. She stormed off, ignoring Mark's attempts to stop her, leaving the others to argue. The warmth faded from her feet, and she was suddenly aware of the bitter cold. She burst into the house, cursing the broken door, and aware that Mark had followed her. In the living room she found Alex with the other ones they'd called Elite. She still wasn't sure what that meant.

"Mom! You won't believe this—Grandmom has magic! Did you see her? She looks young like you. It's crazy!"

He was talking at a fast pace as Skye took in the empty beer bottles.

"Did you give my underage child alcohol?"

"He's nineteen, he's not underage in our world."

She stomped her foot. "We are not in your world!"

"Mom, it's okay," he said trying to rise and falling back to the couch. "It's not my first drink."

"You'd be wise to stop talking young man. I want all of you out. Now!"

"We're staying. We're here to—"

"I don't need protection. Now leave, all of you!"

"Come on guys, she's being nice. I don't think you want to see her when she's really mad," Mark said to them.

"Damn, guess it's back to the cold and snow," one muttered.

Noah rose and came closer to Mark. "This isn't a good idea."

"Well, it's what you're going to do."

He glared at Mark as if he wanted to say something to challenge him but he didn't. They all started shuffling out, Mark with them.

"Mark, please take Alex to his room so he can sleep this off."

"I don't need to sleep, Mom, I'm fine."

"You want me to stay?" Mark asked.

"Yes, I'm not done with you yet."

"Great," he mumbled.

She heard the three arguing outside, their voices coming closer. Running back to the kitchen, she blocked their entrance.

"Skye, let us through."

"No, the three of you are leaving. I want no more talk of magic, or arguing. I need time to digest."

"You don't have time," her father said.

"I had fifty years. I think one day will be okay."

"We're not leaving," her mother said.

"We don't even have a place to stay if we leave," her father added.

She looked over at the basket on the counter, ran to it, then pushed them back out as they tried to sneak in.

"Here are the spare keys to Mark's place. You know where it is. Stay there until I'm ready to talk to you."

They stared at her, but Trent laughed. "I like you, Mage Warrior."

"How are we supposed to get there?" her father asked.

"You managed to make it here. I'm sure you'll figure something out with your fancy magic."

"We only made it here on the wave of your magic."

She shrugged. "He only lives a few blocks away. I'd start walking."

Crossing her arms, she stared them down.

"I believe you have been commanded," Trent said. He put his hand out, fingers spread. "You should have enough magic to transport yourselves there. I will be just within reach. Call for me if you need me."

Muttering a few quick words, he disappeared. Skye caught herself from stumbling back.

"Skye, please," her mother pleaded.

"Leave now," she said, her anger surfacing. The years of lies, the life she could have had with Mark, the trauma that could have been avoided if she'd just been told—all of it surfacing.

"Come, Elspeth, give her some space."

Her mother's kind eyes hardened. "If Camin comes, you'll regret sending us away."

"I'll be dead whether you're here or not."

Elspeth glared at her, then turned and walked off, Skye's father following.

Skye's tension subsided only slightly as she struggled to calm her breathing. She grabbed a bottle of wine from the cabinet, opened it and, not bothering to get a glass, chugged it straight from the bottle. Staring at the broken glass door, she remembered they'd kept some tarp from a previous year when a wicked nor'easter had broken the same glass and pulled several tiles from the roof.

Bottle in hand, she trudged to the basement, drinking as she went, letting the warmth of the alcohol take the physical and mental chill from her.

MARK

Mark settled Alex, answering his questions, and trying to calm his excitement. As he was climbing the stairs from the basement, he heard rustling from the storage room. Changing course, he headed to the far corner to find Skye digging through bins, a wine bottle in her left hand. Every few seconds, she'd take a slug, then turn back to her search.

He couldn't help but smile until reality returned.

With a sigh, he asked, "A little early to be hitting the bottle, isn't it?"

She jumped slightly before turning to him.

Taking another sip, she replied. "Not when you've found out your entire life is a lie. A big fat lie."

He walked closer. "Give me that," he said, taking the wine from her. He was relieved to find she hadn't drunk much more than a large glass. "I don't think a bottle of merlot is the best bet for getting drunk quickly."

"It was the first thing I grabbed," she replied, reaching for the bottle.

"I don't think so. You need a level head, Skye."

"No, I need to forget all this happened for a little while."

"And what good will that do?"

"It will take away the pain."

Her words stung, but the sadness in her eyes hurt worse.

"What are you looking for down here?" he asked, ignoring the pain that was gripping his heart.

"The tarp. The stuff we used after the last storm. I know it's down here somewhere."

She started looking around again, and he was relieved her focus had turned from him.

"Ah ha!" she cried happily, dragging a rolled-up tarp from behind a set of metal shelves.

"Here," he said, reaching for it. "Go on, I'll do this."

"I can do it myself."

"I know you can, but let me help."

She gave it to him, and they headed up the stairs. He went about covering the broken door as best he could before turning to find her eyes on him.

"When did you become so muscular?"

He raised a brow. "I've always been this way, Skye. I've spent years training, waiting for this day."

He thought about all his four a.m. workouts and hours spent staying in form, working his skills before the workday started.

"I guess I did see that and just avoided it. Can't be caught eyeing your cousin's muscles."

She sulked over to the sink and got herself a glass of water.

"Not gonna let that go, are you?"

She eyed him. "Should I?"

He shrugged. "I suppose not."

Placing the water down, she leaned on the counter, her navy-blue eyes shining. "You don't have weird appendages, do you?"

He couldn't help but smirk. "All my appendages are normal, thank you."

A slight blush filled her cheeks. "No! I meant like wings. Do you have wings?"

He laughed. "No, why?"

"Because magical guys have things like wings."

"You've been reading too much fantasy. And I'm not magical, you are."

"Do I have wings?"

Laughing again, he replied, "No, no one has wings."

Her face dropped. "Elf ears?" she asked, a sparkle of hope in her eyes.

Shaking his head, he answered, "No. Elves don't exist."

"Well, damn, that's no fun."

She stared off, and Mark knew her well enough to see that she was trying to come to terms with it all.

"So, there are different wizards—"

"No, no. No wizards, mages. Wizards exist, but the Mage Warriors drove them to the Fettered Forests long ago. Wizards are nasty men who steal girls, and well...they're just foul. Even their magic is foul. Camin is half wizard, half mage, which is why he was so hard to defeat."

"Half wizard, half mage? How does that happen? Did a mage fall in love with a wizard?"

"Hardly. Camin's father captured a Mage Warrior and kept her until she bore him a son. Then he slit her throat and fed her blood to Camin—pure magic."

Skye's jaw dropped.

"Sorry, as I said, wizards are a nasty bunch."

"Your world sounds terrifying."

"It's not in most parts. And it's our world."

She was quiet, her eyes drifting to look at the counter.

"Skye—"

"This is a lot, Mark. My entire life has been a lie."

"No, it hasn't. Alex isn't a lie."

"No, but how he came to be is a lie. Who he is, that's a lie because who I am is a lie. All a façade to keep me safe, but I don't feel safe. I feel betrayed."

The choice of words didn't surprise him. He'd always expected she'd feel that way.

She pushed a loose strand of hair back and walked away. He grabbed her wrist as she walked by him. Stopping, she lifted her deep eyes to him and that same flood of emotion he had each time he looked into her eyes poured back. The secret was out, the lie no longer separated them. But the truth created a bigger divide.

She looked down at his hand, and he let her wrist go. Bringing her eyes back up, she searched his. The blue in them was intense, a misty layer of tears shadowing it.

"What do I do, Mark?"

"About what?"

"About you."

A tear slipped down her cheek, and he reached out to catch it.

"I'm so hurt, angry, confused, but part of me...that part that's been pushed away and ignored since we were kids is relieved, happy, hopeful."

"I can't tell you what to do with those feelings, Skye. All I can tell you is that we've both been used in this battle and that I can't remember a time when I haven't loved you, or dreamed things were different, when I haven't wanted you desperately."

She stopped his words with a kiss. The warmth of her lips against his stirred his desire for her. He pulled her close—his one hand brushing her stray hair from her face, his other gripping her waist. The years of longing for her drifted away as her hands moved slowly over his chest, exploring what he'd longed for her to explore with every passing day.

Moving his own hands to find the bottom of her sweatshirt, he raised it so that his fingers found the warm skin below. He felt her heart quicken as she pressed her body into his so there was no distinction between where she started and he ended.

He was about to lift her and move her to the table when he heard Alex's disgusted voice.

"There is something so terribly wrong with this. I can't even… there are no words."

They pulled apart quickly, Skye's cheeks turning a beautiful shade of pink that brought out the blue in her eyes.

"I thought you were asleep," she said, hurriedly adjusting her shirt.

"I wish I were. Then this," he gestured to the two of them, "would not be engrained in my mind for eternity. You can't purge stuff like this."

"Alex—"

"Mom. I know you're not related any more but still. I mean, you're Uncle Mark. There's no erasing that."

"Alex—" Mark tried.

"Nope, nope. Uncle Mark implies something. It says we're close enough that my mother should not be swapping spit with you. Now, I came up to get some water. Oh, food," he said with excitement, spotting the food Mark had made earlier that morning before the day had turned to chaos. He grabbed a glass of water, and they both watched as he took the plate of eggs and all the bacon, piling the plates like a restaurant server.

"Look," Alex said, on his way out of the room. "I'm happy to see you getting some action, Mom."

"Alex!" she yelled.

"Seriously, Mom, it's been five years. But this is not exactly what I expected." He turned, muttering as he left them alone.

They looked at each other and laughed. It was a laugh filled with a mixture of relief and embarrassment. Mark reached out and touched her cheek.

"Hungry?" he asked.

Her eyes twinkled. "Famished. As if I haven't eaten for decades."

He understood her meaning and forced himself not to kiss her again. A lot had happened in the span of a few hours, and she was vulnerable. As elated as he was that it was all out in the open and that she wanted him as badly as he ached for her, it would be wrong for him to act on that in her current state.

He grabbed the bottle of open wine and took a few deep swallows. "Let's eat and talk."

"Talk?" She raised her perfectly arched eyebrows.

"Talk. The rest can wait," he replied, turning to pull sandwich meat from the fridge now that breakfast had long passed, and Alex had taken it with him.

Something stung his back and an apple hit the floor. He shot her a look, placing the meat on the island. Her arms were crossed and even below the baggy sweatshirt, he could see the swell of her breasts.

"I've waited countless years for that kiss, and you want to make sandwiches? Decades and you want to talk?" She made air quotations when she said the word talk.

"Skye, it's for the best." Her lips pouted slightly, and he fought the urge to cross the island and bite her lower lip. "You're emotional. This is all new. Your entire world just turned on its head. It wouldn't be right to take advantage of that."

"Wouldn't be right for whom? Me? Or you?"

He sighed, not sure how he'd been put on the defensive suddenly. He walked over to her. The closer he came, the harder it was not to take her as he'd wanted for so long.

"For both of us," he said, tilting her chin up.

"But we're free now," she whispered.

"We are, but we need to let that sink in and figure out what it means for us."

"It means that I can finally love you freely, without the guilt. That I no longer have to pretend it's you making love to me—"

"Skye—"

"No, Mark. It means so many things for us. I feel like my heart was imprisoned unfairly for forty-some years before finally being freed. Don't you feel that way?"

He pulled her into his arms. "Of course, I do. God, Skye, I've loved you, even though it was inappropriate for me to do so. You don't think I'm still single for a reason? There has never been anyone but you. When you married Sam, I tried, but none of them were you. Every time I made love to a woman, it was you I saw. It's always been you."

Her fingers traced the contours of his face, and he closed his eyes to her touch.

"Why did we have to lose so much time? Why were we forced apart?" she asked.

He opened his eyes to see the sadness reflected in hers.

"Because that's what was decided for us."

She touched the corner of his eye and smiled. "The hazel in your eyes is sparkling."

"I still can't believe you can see color in my eyes."

She nodded. "I've always seen it. It's been the only color in my life forever."

He dropped his head to hers. "When this is all over, I will take you away so that it's just the two of us, and I will make love to you every day—"

"Two times a day?"

He grinned and kissed her forehead. "Three times a day." He felt the shiver of excitement that ran through her. "Until then, we need to make sure you can defend yourself and eventually defeat Camin."

Reality crashed back upon him as he realized the danger she was in. He pushed her back to look at her. "I will not risk losing you now that I have you. If you won't train with Trent, you will at least learn who you are and where you come from. The rest can wait, Skye."

She sighed. "I'm tired of waiting."

"You? Stop pouting and let's prep you for war."

SKYE

The word "war" was enough to suck the desire out of her.

But Skye fought against it. Mark was so close; she was in his arms. And he wanted her as much as she wanted him. He'd confessed it twice now. That last kiss had been everything she'd dreamt it would be from the softness of his lips, to the strength in his jaw, and the muscles below his shirt.

How had she never noticed how built he was?

But she had, turning from it as she'd been forced to turn from him and ignore how beautiful he was. Handsome in a rugged, military way. The opposite of Sam, who was unathletic, nerdy in a way but still had his own strength. She'd loved Sam, she truly had, but under that love laid the fire that burned for Mark, a flame that could never be dampened. She'd always suspected Sam knew her feelings for Mark, but he'd never said anything and continued a friendship with him. The three had been close, even if a distance had always lain between her and Mark—a forced distance that could never be crossed. Until now.

Now she was free. Free to have Mark, to touch him, to experience him like she'd always wanted. And she wanted him now, the years of dreaming of his touch building to this moment. But instead of touching her like she craved, he was pushing her away again, insistent on talking war, the reality she didn't want to face.

"You promise to make love to me when this is all over?"

He laughed. It was a sound she'd always loved. "I can't promise that." Her heart dropped, and he must have seen the disappointment in her eyes. "I can't because I may not be able to wait that long."

She reached up and kissed him again. "Are you sure we can't talk later?" she asked, nipping his lip.

"I'm not sure, but we need to slow down, Skye."

She pulled back and shot him a look.

"Don't give me that look you give Alex when he's in trouble."

"I feel like we've been on the world's longest date."

Laughing, he took her hands from his chest and kissed them. "More like the world's longest foreplay."

He walked away and returned to the lunchmeat, fixing them both sandwiches.

"Fine, we'll talk." It was then that she realized her leggings, and socks were still soaked from the snow. "But first I need a hot shower. I'm still snow soaked."

"Well, if you hadn't foolishly gone running out into a blizzard, that might not be the case," he said, opening a can of soda

She shot him a dirty look and headed out of the kitchen. Then, to be mean, she added, "You know my shower fits two easily."

He stared at her.

Shrugging, she made her way to the stairs. "Just a thought."

She heard him mumble "gods woman" as she made her way up the stairs, wondering why he'd said gods instead of God. That was new, but she vaguely remembered the others saying it as well and made a mental note to ask him about it.

∾

THE SHOWER WAS FANTASTIC. She hadn't realized how chilled she was, the warmth of the wine and Mark's touch keeping it at bay. Feeling refreshed yet still not quite ready to step into this new life that had been thrust upon her, she pulled on a pair of jeans and a long-sleeved shirt that Mark had once told her brought out her eyes. She had no idea. It looked navy to her, like everything else in her world that wasn't gray or black. Checking herself in the mirror, she noticed how it emphasized her still perky breasts.

She stopped and thought about that. She was fifty years old, yet she remained youthful as if time hadn't forced its aging spell on her. Her mother, Elspeth, had said she was four hundred and seventy-five years old. She pondered if that was normal and made a mental note to ask Mark about it. The idea of living that long was both thrilling and fear inducing.

There were so many questions rolling around in her head. Brushing her fingers through her hair, she could still feel the heat from the hair dryer in her long locks. She rarely bothered to dry her hair, usually letting it air dry before tying it up, but today seemed different.

Staring at herself, she asked. "What are you doing, Skye? Trying to impress a man you've known your entire life, who's seen you at your worst?"

Grabbing a clip, she piled her hair up, noticing the slight shimmer of gray on her birthmark. Strange how in a matter of hours, something as mundane as a birthmark had changed her entire perspective on things.

She found Mark at the table, staring at his can of soda. A sandwich sat across from him with a glass of water ready for her, but she wasn't certain she had much of an appetite.

"Feel better?" he asked.

"Definitely. Did you need to—"

"Nah, I rinsed off before you woke up. Thank goodness for

the spare clothes I had here from all the nights I watched Alex while...well, you know."

"I'd forgotten they were up there," she said, sitting across from him.

His eyes met hers, the beautiful hazel of them shimmering in her world of darkness. It had always seemed strange that she could see their color, yet nothing else.

"Tell me about your...our world."

He smiled, and she listened as he told her of a world that sounded like something from a fairy tale. Castles and kings, towns that traded with one another, a people who were straight from another century. Countryside that spanned as far as the eye could see and mountains that towered so high they touched the sky. It sounded backward and intriguing at the same time.

"You said Camin and these wizards live in another part of the world?"

"Yes, they were forced to dwell far outside of the kingdom in the Fettered Forests. The mages and Elite guard the kingdom from them."

"How many kingdoms are there?"

"Six, although when we left, Digremile and Nenochin had fallen. From what Trent said earlier, it sounds like Nenochin was rebuilt, but I don't know if Digremile ever was. Each has its own Elite and mages. In times like the war with Camin, they come together to fight."

"Tell me about the mages," she said, still uncertain why there seemed to be a differentiation between Mage Warriors and mages.

"There are levels of mages. The novice mages have a small amount of magic. They offer their services for a variety of things, but they cannot fight, they're too weak. They're the most common. Full mages are powerful, when the order of magic is in place, that is. They are a first level of defense and are treated with great respect through the kingdoms. They go on missions for the king, lay protection spells, and fight when necessary. Mainly they're a benign protection, behind the scenes, not engaging in any physical threat but using their magic to avoid that threat. Sometimes they use it to find the threat or even to see it coming."

He took a sip of his soda and she noticed how his demeanor had changed as he talked about his world. There was a melancholy there, and that's when she realized they had all given up everything they had known, come to a foreign world, and started new lives for her. It suddenly seemed a heavy burden to bear.

"And then you have Mage Warriors. These are the rarest and the most coveted. They're treated like royalty themselves and housed in the castles with the rulers of each kingdom. They're the strongest of the mages in magic and physical strength, weapons that are the last line of defense. They fight the beasts of our world and send them to the Fettered Forests and battle the wizards who dare attack the kingdom. Where the full mages are the shield of the kingdoms, the Mage Warriors are the sword."

She stared at him, knowing her mouth was agape. He laughed and reached over to shut it.

"Mark, I can't even kill a spider. I'm the wimpiest person—"

"You are one of the strongest people I know."

"That's saying a lot from a man who knows about five people."

He shook his head, smiling.

"How long do Mage Warriors train for this stuff?"

The smile faded. "Their entire lives. As soon as they can walk, then every day after, they train."

She sat back, knowing her hands were shaking, her entire body going limp.

Change the subject, Skye, she told herself.

"What about you? What did you call yourself?"

"Elite. We are the royal army and are also marked at birth."

"You have a birthmark like mine? I never saw that."

He turned on his chair, lifting his shirt so that she could see a similar moon shape on his shoulder blade, large and distinct. But instead of her crescent moon, his was a half moon. She couldn't help noticing the muscles that lined his body, the firmness below the shirt, catching a glimpse of his abs as he lowered it.

She swallowed and averted his gaze, thinking of anything other than how her body was now tingling in places it shouldn't be.

"When do you have time to go to the gym?" she whispered, her voice strangely hoarse.

"I don't, but we train every day. When we were young, the Elite trained and conditioned me, continuing the training I'd started with my parents. When we moved here, I improvised. Let's just say my mornings begin a lot earlier than yours."

All these years he'd been training. "Who are you?"

He laughed. "The man you've always known, Skye."

She wanted to argue that he wasn't that man anymore. He'd raised an infinite number of levels above the man she'd already put on a pedestal.

"Wait, you said your parents trained you? I thought...well, I don't know what I thought."

"Both my parents are—*were* Elite. There are women Elite. It's rare for them to marry, though. Usually, the intense personalities of the Elite don't make for good matches. My line is what they call true blood. It dates back to the original Elite. That's why command of the Elite has always been my family's. The pure blood makes us the strongest."

"So, if you'd stayed, you would have married another Elite?" She didn't know why the thought hurt her so badly, but it did.

"No, those marriages were not forced. They came naturally. I suppose I'm the first in my family to break tradition."

Her heart quickened, her breath catching in her throat.

"If we'd never come here—"

"I would still have broken tradition."

She smiled, then remembered something Trent had said. "My mother was a Mage Warrior, but my father was an Elite?"

"Yes. It's not often it happens, but it does. Joinings of Mage Warriors with an Elite always produce a Mage Warrior, or so I remember being told. Your line has always been from Mage Warrior and Elite joinings. I think the last time it happened to any Mage Warrior outside of your line was ages before your birth. But history was never my strong suit."

"Okay, so there are castles, kings and queens, magic, mages, strangely strong Elite, and wizards. Am I missing anything?"

"The dragons."

She spit the water from her mouth in an embarrassing unlady-like fashion, which sent Mark into fits.

"Dragons?" she squeaked out as he reached over and wiped the drool from her mouth.

He nodded, still laughing.

"Dragons? Oh my God, what am I doing?" She rose abruptly from the table. "This is ridiculous. I am a financial planner from Connecticut, a widow with a child. This," she said, gesturing to him, "this stuff is not possible. I don't think I can do this."

She was pacing the kitchen, pulling at her hair, which had spilled from her clip. Anxiety was taking over her grip on reality. No, her grip had already slipped.

Mark stopped her motion, taking her arms in his large hands.

"Skye, calm yourself. You are doing this. You have no choice."

"The hell I don't. I can turn my back on all of this." As she said the words, she read the hurt in his eyes. "All but you, maybe," she said in a calmer voice.

He pushed her disheveled hair back with a gentle touch.

"You can do this, Skye. I'll be by your side every step of the way."

"I can't. I don't know your world. I don't have any magic. Let's run away. We can sneak off. They'll never find us, and all of this will blow over. I have enough money to live on for a few months at least."

He brought his fingers to her lips to silence her.

"You can't run, Skye. There is no hiding from this. If I could take you from all of it, shield you from it, I would. Trust me. But Camin is here, and he is coming for you. He will find you, no matter where you hide, and he will kill you and Alex if you are not prepared to accept this."

"Alex?"

He nodded. "Camin does not discriminate. He will kill you both."

Her legs gave way, but Mark caught her.

"You are the daughter of the strongest Mage Warrior, your father the second in strength only to my father. You are armed with what you need to defeat him. All we need to do is release it."

She searched his eyes for any sign of doubt, finding none. Nodding, she found her footing. Taking what inner strength she could muster, she brought her hand up to touch his face, feeling the strength of his jaw below the stubble.

"You'll stay with me?"

"Never leaving your side."

Her lips found his, and she kissed him deeply. The urge was too great to resist. The fact that she could touch him so freely was exhilarating. His arms wrapped around her, pulling her close, his hands pushing her shirt up so that they were on her skin. Her stomach did flips as if she were a teenager once again.

It was too fantastic to stop. The need that had burned in her, simmering for decades, was ablaze.

"Skye," he mumbled.

"Mmm," she groaned back, his lips making their way down her neck.

"We need to stop," he said between kisses.

His lips brushed along her neck, coming back to meet hers, his hand skimming the lacy material of her bra.

"I don't see you stopping," she whispered, running her tongue along his lips, her own fingers finding the muscle below his shirt, the heat of his skin sending waves through her.

"God, we need to—"

His hands dropped to her hips, squeezing them tight and pulling her hard against him so that she could feel the extent of his desire for her.

His hands moved further down and in one quick move, he picked her up as though she were light as a feather. Wrapping her arms around his neck, she let her fingers roam through his thick hair, pushing her mouth harder against his. He began walking with her in his arms, then the wall pressed against her back. It was like one of those romantic movies she'd watched, the passion too great to make it further than wherever the characters were.

He pulled at her shirt, and she lifted it above her head, their lips parting for just that moment. His hands lowered to her waist again, scooping her pelvis forward as she grabbed at his shirt. Skin against skin, the heat blazed. Her legs wrapped tightly around him as his kisses lowered, grazing along the top of her bra. A moan escaped her, the strap of her bra slipping, butterflies flapping a storm within the pit of her stomach.

It had been five years since she'd felt a man's touch and even then she'd envisioned it was his touch, his body, his kisses. He brought his mouth back to meet hers and she noted the slow, fiery passion in his kiss. It burned through her like an inferno that couldn't be tamed, and she didn't want to tame it. Drawing his lips from hers, he lowered his forehead, his breathing ragged, matching her own.

"We need to stop, Skye," he said hoarsely. The desire still layered his voice, but it was coated with seriousness.

Disappointment swept through her and she rested her head back against the wall, loosening her legs, and letting them drop. He held tight to her waist a moment longer, his head dropping to her now exposed chest. They remained still for several minutes, the silence of the storm outside broken only by their slowly calming breaths. His grip on her loosened as his hand moved her bra strap back in place with a drawn-out caress.

His eyes lingered, following the path his fingers took as they traveled delicately up her neck and through her hair. They were heavy with desire as they met her eyes, causing the need to flare within her again.

"We've waited this long; we can wait a little longer," he said.

"Just enough for us to make it to my bed?"

He gave her a long smile. "As much as that idea appeals to me, no."

Grazing her fingertips along the muscles of his chest, she said, "Saving the world can wait a few hours, right?"

He raised an eyebrow. "Hours?" Then he pulled her in against him. "I haven't touched a woman in five years, Skye. I have dreamed of touching you for longer than I can count. Definitely won't be hours the first time."

Her heart flipped at his words as those butterflies stirred again.

"Five years?"

"I know. It sounds dumb. I tried, Skye. For years while you and Sam were together, I took every woman I could, but none of those women were you. It never felt right. When Sam died, I couldn't bring myself to even look at another woman, but as the years went by and you never even dated, well, neither did I."

"I couldn't," she said, her eyes dropping as her fingers traced the contours of his stomach. "It had been hard enough loving Sam while my heart belonged to you. The thought of anyone but you touching me after that...I just couldn't."

He kissed her forehead, then lifted her chin. "I promise you. When this is over, I will make love to you every single day for the rest of our lives."

Smiling, she snuggled into his arms. "Maybe a few times a day? I mean, we have a lot of time to make up."

"You are going to be a test on my stamina, aren't you?"

"Guaranteed."

"Good thing in our world we're still exceedingly young."

She giggled. "Like teenagers?"

"Very much so."

He looked like he was going to kiss her again, then drew back, letting her go. Losing his touch let the chill in, and she missed it instantly. He picked her shirt up and handed it to her, his eyes wandering to take her in one last time.

"You're beautiful, Skye."

She didn't know what to say, so she leaned over and kissed him once more. It wasn't a passionate kiss, but one that tasted of the years of love they'd had for each other.

She drew away and put her shirt on, her own eyes lingering on the defined chest he was covering. How had she been so blind to how built he was? Years of forcing herself to look away, to see something different when subconsciously she knew how attractive he was. Saw the looks he garnered when they were out together, felt the jealousy stir as women flirted with him, knowing they would eventually go home with him. She'd had no right to be jealous. She'd married another man, shared a bed with that man for twenty years, but Mark had pushed her into Sam's arms, even though she was looking back at him the entire time.

"What are you thinking so intently upon?"

"The past." His smile dropped. She took his hand, saying, "Let's leave the past behind. We have a future now—one I don't think either of us thought could happen. Let's start it now. Can you call the others?"

"Are you ready?"

"The only way I can have you in my bed is to get this asshole out of my way. Damn right I'm ready."

He laughed and picked his phone up from the counter.

"I can call the others, but you will need to call Trent."

"How do I do that? I don't have his number, do you?"

"There are no phones in our world, Skye."

Of course there aren't. Such an idiot, she thought.

"No phones. That will take some getting used to. Alex will go through withdrawal."

"Ha, I have no doubt. No television, movies, or video games either."

"What do people do for fun there?"

"I think you and I will find a way to keep ourselves occupied," he said with a wink.

"No electronics?" Alex said, entering the kitchen cautiously. "Good, you two are clothed and gross to that last comment."

"Alex," Skye scolded.

"I told you, Mom." He gestured between the two of them. "This is going to take some time. Have you two really had the hots for each other all this time?"

They nodded.

"That's messed up." He stopped and looked accusingly at her. "And Dad?"

"I loved your father, Alex."

"Did you two ever?"

"No!" they both said firmly.

"Alex, I'm the one who pushed them together. Your father was my friend, and for all intents and purposes, your mother was my cousin. She was off limits, which is why I encouraged them. Neither of us would have done anything to hurt him. Hell, neither of us did anything, even after he died."

Alex eyed him. "Okay. Still weird though." He grabbed the milk and poured himself a glass. "So, do I get any cool powers like Mom?"

"No, of course not..." she started, but Mark shook his head to her.

"Not the same level as her, but you will."

She blinked. "Wait. What?"

"He's half human, but he's still your son. All Mage Warrior births have magic, although rarely do they create another Mage

Warrior. That's reserved for your line. Remember the Mage Warrior and Elite thing I mentioned?"

She did and wondered what that meant about the two of them. Had they no choice but to fall in love? Their attraction for one another undeniable because of who they were? Was her child supposed to have been his? It was all so overwhelming and in the mix was a son that she hadn't been meant to have. What did that mean for Alex?

"I am so confused. He doesn't have my birthmark."

"No, he wasn't the product of you and an Elite. Because of that, Alex wouldn't have the mark of a Mage Warrior. Just like mine is different, he has the mark of a full mage."

"A full mage? Like Trent?" she asked.

"Yes."

"But he doesn't have a birthmark."

"Yeah, I do. Remember? It's on my ankle on the inside. It looks like a full moon," Alex said excitedly.

"Correct. It will be dormant until your mother's powers are released. We think the binding spread to you when you were born, thankfully."

"Yeah, that would have been hard to cover up with lies," she said with an eye roll.

"Oh, that's not good. She's acidic," Alex teased.

Skye crossed her arms. "Anything else I should know?"

"Plenty, but that covers the basics."

She sighed, knowing she had mixed emotions about finding out what was beneath the basics.

"How do we call Trent?"

"I don't, you do."

MARK

Mark was finding it hard to focus; thoughts of Skye's skin, lips, and body kept clouding his mind. He'd wanted to take her, and by all accounts, he could have. They deserved it. He'd craved her for far too long and having a taste of her left him wanting more. But more would have to wait.

She was in danger. They all were. He'd given her the time to digest, the time to ask questions, but they were running out of time.

"What do you mean, I'm the one who calls him?" she asked.

"Magic senses magic. That's how he found you in the first place."

"But if he senses me, doesn't that mean the bad guy will, too?"

"Yes, but you have to release your powers, or we'll never get home."

"This is so frustrating," she said with a pout, "and confusing. I thought my magic was locked away. How do I use it if it's hidden from me?"

"You have fun figuring that out, Mom," Alex said. "I'm going to watch some television before I'm forced to live in the stone age."

Alex trudged off to the living room while Skye remained. Her shoulders were slumped, and she wore a defeated expression that made Mark want to take her in his arms and protect her.

"Your magic is trying to break free," he said instead. "Whatever your mother did to bind it inside of you must have fractured during the accident."

"The accident? What does that have to do with anything?"

"It's the first time you saw the flashes of color."

She stared at him, her blue eyes intense and dark.

"You weren't always color-blind, Skye. The spell took away your ability to see color. You're color-blind because you needed to be."

"I know that, but I don't understand what that has to do with it."

"You had to live in a world without color to keep you protected. It was part of your mother's spell. A Mage Warrior's power lies in the colors that the world holds. When the accident happened, you saw flashes of color, and yesterday, before you came to see me, you saw them again."

"I live in this dull world because of a spell?"

"Yes, when the color returns, so will your magic."

"Uh, hey, guys, you might want to see this," Alex called from the attached room.

Skye turned and went to look. All Mark could do was sigh. He'd fought with Elspeth to tell Skye the truth, to educate her, and to train her as best they could, but he'd caved to her wisdom, knowing in his heart she was wrong. Now they were in crisis mode and stymied by questions. They didn't have time for this.

"Oh my God," Skye said, a distinct level of fear to her voice.

He went to join her, to find out what would cause that reaction, and stared at the screen. A news reporter was talking, but it was the images that held Mark in a state of terror. California was under siege. It looked like San Francisco, but it was hard to tell from the chaos. Water in the bay churned in high waves. The bridge had been decimated. Plumes of smoke filled the air, and the morning sky was dark with it.

"Is that him?" Skye asked softly, her voice shaking.

In the center of the chaos stood a man. The camera zoomed in on him as the reporter's voice grew in excitement. Mark was young when Camin waged war upon the kingdoms, but he remembered him distinctly. Remembered the madness in his eyes as he'd slaughtered Mark's father and Skye's.

Mark had ignored his mother's command to stay inside and keep safe, sneaking to the castle wall. She'd found him after the Mage Warriors pushed Camin back. It had been their first devastating loss. He remembered the feel of her arms around him as they'd cried together. Camin's face was forever etched in his mind.

The robed man, who stood defiantly in the cloud of debris on the screen while his magic left yet another path of destruction, was Camin.

"Yes," Mark answered through gritted teeth.

Skye backed away, and Mark tore his eyes from the television. She was shaking, and her eyes filled with tears.

"I can't...I can't fight that. What are they thinking? I can't even kill a bug. I run from conflict, Mark. You know this. That man—that thing—is way beyond my league. He's crazy."

"Skye, you can—"

"No," she said, shaking her head. He could feel her anxiety rising. "No, I can't. He'll kill me before I even say hello. God, what am I doing? This is madness."

She had backed to the kitchen, her voice getting higher as her fear increased.

"This is like something from one of those superhero movies. You need Iron Man for this, not some wimpy mother from Connecticut. I can't do this, Mark."

Color filled her eyes but then he saw something else—flickers of light. Her breathing was rapid, and he wanted to calm her, but he didn't, the changing hues of her dark blue eyes mesmerizing him.

"No, no," she said, stumbling back and grabbing her head. "Not now. He'll find me."

The room burst with color. Everything in the room became more vivid until she squeezed her eyes shut.

Trent appeared in a swirl of mist, followed by Elspeth and Thomas. Quickly, Mark sent a text to the others, knowing if the full mages could sense Skye's magic, Camin would, too.

Right on cue, Alex said, "Shit. That can't be good."

Mark turned to see him pointing to the television. Camin stood in the aftermath of his chaos which was hanging in stasis around him as he lifted his head to the air, listening for something.

"He's found her!" Mark yelled.

They'd managed to calm her, and everything had returned to its normal color. Noah ran through the house to the television as Mark crossed the room to Skye. The other Elite took position around her, ready to protect her at all costs.

"We need to get out of here, now," Noah said.

"He disappeared...where did he go?" Alex said.

An explosion echoed through the quiet of the storm.

"He's here," Noah said, quickly returning to the kitchen. "He couldn't determine her exact location, but he's close enough. Trent, get us home now. Our only chance is to get to our world and lock him here."

"He'll find his way back. He jumped on the trail of magic that brought me here," Trent said.

"Not if we hold him off. Mark, you stay with Skye. My other Elite, ready yourselves for battle."

Mark grabbed his arm. "Noah, don't."

"We all knew what we were signing up for, Mark. We knew we had to protect her and raise you to take command when you returned home. Let us finish the job." Noah gripped Mark's arm. "Your father would be proud. Now keep her safe. We'll hold Camin off as long as we can. Trent, you three help her find her way home."

With that, he and the other Elite spread out to the front of the house, acting as a temporary shield.

"They can't hold him off long without another mage, and not without Skye's power," Mark said.

"None of us have the power to fight Camin," Elspeth said.

"Then use what you have to help, Skye."

Trent pulled a heavy orange amulet from his robe. "This is what Lyra left for us to find Skye. I think it's also the key to getting us back."

"And the key to unlocking your magic," Elspeth said. "I was with your mother when she created it with her own magic."

Skye gingerly touched the orange stone, then pulled her fingers back as it started to glow.

"Take us home, Skye," Mark said.

A thunderous crack resounded through the air, the ground shaking.

"He's found us. The battle has begun."

"Grandmom," Alex said, moving closer to Elspeth. She pulled him in tight.

"She's not your grandmother," Skye mumbled.

"Worry about semantics later, Skye. Whatever you did to wake your power a few minutes ago, you need to do now!" Elspeth snapped.

The bay window in the front of the house shattered, pulling Mark's attention from Skye momentarily as Noah's body came tumbling through.

"I can't. I can't," Skye cried.

Mark grabbed her shoulders roughly and forced her to look at him. "You can, and you will. You are a Mage Warrior. It's in your blood whether you command it or not." He grabbed the amulet from Trent. "Now, set your magic free and take us home."

He shoved the amulet in her hand, and it began to glow.

"I'm scared, Mark," she whispered.

"I know, but imagine how scared you'll be when Camin breaks through those men who are giving their lives to save you and kills Alex."

Her eyes flew up from the amulet, and he saw the fractures of color in them. Fear had triggered her last episode. Could it trigger another?

"That's it. Grab it now and show Camin who you really are. Save us, Skye. Save Alex."

The colors grew as she closed her eyes, scrunching them against the magic.

"Embrace it, Skye," Trent said. "Own the colors and make them bend to your will."

She opened her eyes again, and the kaleidoscope within them intensified. Trent tried to pull Mark back, but he stayed, knowing she needed him close to her. Her hand dug into his fiercely.

Slowly the color in the room brightened, intensifying until long stretches of color could be seen.

"Now command it to your will. Make it come to you then tell it what you need it to do," Trent continued.

The colors bled from the room to surround her, everything in the house now in shadows.

"Go away. Go away," she mumbled through gritted teeth. the surrounding rainbow unleashed, and every window shattered as the front of the house burst open with the force. Mark didn't look, but he knew she'd stunned Camin, likely throwing him far enough away to bide them a few more moments.

"Excellent, now bring it back and command it again."

The colors flooded even faster as Skye brought the white of the snow, the green of the evergreens, and the colors of the sky itself in. The room was awash in hues, hot with power. The amulet crashed to the ground, and Trent inadvertently let his shock show. It was their way home, or so they'd all thought. Perhaps it was only a key to unlocking her potential, and Skye had always been their way home.

"Take us home, Skye. Command it," Elspeth said.

Mark noticed motion behind him as the remaining Elite ran in. The colors were circling now so fast that a wind had picked up. Mark's breath was forced from his lungs.

"Hold tight!" Trent yelled.

The world became a flood of color that blinded Mark. He was tempted to turn away from it but instead held tight to Skye.

The colors receded. He was weightless, as if he were falling. Darkness engulfed him, then he hit something hard; the wind knocked from him. He was on his back, the hard ground below him. Blinking, Mark tried to adjust to the surrounding darkness. Skye. Where was Skye? His hands were empty. Scrambling to his feet, he noticed stars above him—a night sky.

"She did it. Is everyone all right?" Trent's voice emerged from the darkness. With a flurry, scones lit around them. He spotted Skye, Alex beside her, shaking her.

"She won't wake up," he said, his eyes filled with fear.

Mark knelt beside her and checked her pulse. She was breathing.

"Halt! What are you lot doing out here?" a guard yelled, approaching them. A king's guard. From the corner of his eye, Mark noted a slight movement in the shadows—the Elite.

Trent moved forward to greet the guard.

"We need to see the king immediately."

SKYE

Sunlight forced Skye's eyes open; the warmth of it welcome after the chill that penetrated her body. She snuggled deeper beneath the thick down comforter, hating the thought of facing another day. Was it Monday or did she have the ability to sleep in? As she searched her mind, memories flooded back. Sitting up quickly, Skye scanned the unfamiliar room.

It was spacious, larger than her master bedroom. What looked like balcony doors stood to her right, the source of the morning sun that had woken her.

It might have been morning, but she had no idea, she was simply assuming since she'd just woken.

A massive stone fireplace lay on the wall across from her, the fire crackled as if someone had been tending to it. The bed she was in had four posters that reached high above her, a deep blue canopy pulled taut across the top matched the blue and silver that lined the bedding.

Tentatively, Skye pushed the bedding back. Someone had changed her clothes and replaced them with what looked to be a nightgown but not one she would ever contemplate wearing. It was a heavy, coarse material that covered every inch of her up to her neck.

Disgusted, she tried climbing off the bed, the long material tangling around her uncoordinated legs as she tumbled onto the floor, a thick fur throw rug barely softening her landing.

"What the hell?" she grumbled, yanking at the gown to free her feet and legs.

Finally standing, Skye tried to orient herself to her surroundings, wracking her brain to remember how she had gotten here. The last thing she remembered was being in the kitchen with everyone as the lunatic madman came to kill her.

Had Camin captured her? This claustrophobic nightgown, some sort of torture device? No, he was planning to kill her, not kidnap her. Besides, Mark wouldn't have let him steal her away.

Where was Mark? Where was Alex?

She grew frantic, running to the door, As she ran down a short hall, then steps and more steps, her bare feet oblivious to the cold stone below, Skye twisted and turned until she reached a hallway. She took a moment to look up, seeing that she'd been in a tower.

Locked in a tower as if she were trapped in some fairy tale. She ran on, passing a few doors—all locked to her attempt to open them. It seemed that she weaved her way through the hallways and stairwells forever until she reached a wide-open space, the grandness of it stopping her in her tracks. The high vaulted ceiling was lined with paintings of battle scenes, different people in battle gear depicted wielding what looked like magic. Skye drew her eyes to one woman in particular—her long auburn hair flowing around her, blue eyes rich with power. Her appearance was very close to Skye's.

"My mother," she whispered, taken aback.

She stared at the image until it dawned on her.

Color. She could see the colors. Just as she had in the room when she'd been too disoriented to realize. That's why the room had been so overwhelming to her. The colors screamed to her; they were vivid and beautiful. Her color-blindness was gone.

She backed away, the color suddenly disorienting to her, her eyes trying to take them all in.

She hit something solid.

"You shouldn't be—" The voice stopped as she turned to him. He squinted, glancing at the painting, then back to her.

She disregarded his reaction, taking in the beauty of his green shirt that peeked below the metal that lay upon his chest. Then the golden hair that met his shoulders in thick waves. She reached up to touch it and he gave her a startled look.

"Blonde," she said, laughing. "I remember. That's what blonde looks like."

His brown eyes evaluated her.

"Where's my son? Where's Mark?"

"Markhem is with the king, and you should be resting."

Markhem? Why did they keep calling him Markhem?

"I don't need to rest. I need to see them."

"Very well. Are you certain you want to go with so little covering you?"

She looked down at the thick, cumbersome nightgown.

"You're joking, right? I've never worn so much material. Not an inch of my skin is showing."

He shrugged. "Suit yourself."

Then he turned and walked away.

"Wait. Aren't you going to argue with me more?" she asked, catching up with him.

"You are a Mage Warrior. No one disobeys your command."

She was too stunned to respond, instead taking in the colors that now filled her world—her new world. The guard greeted the two guards standing in front of a massive set of doors. They both gave her a disapproving side glance before opening them for her.

She spotted Mark right away. He was standing with her parents and Trent. Fake parents, she corrected herself. Noah was with them, as well as a man she could only describe as regal. They were deep in discussion.

She was tempted to run to Mark, but as the doors echoed their close behind her, she restrained herself.

"Skye, what are you doing?" her mother asked.

"I'm finding you all. Where are we? What happened? And why am I dressed like I belong in one of those PBS masterpiece movies?"

Mark laughed, then stifled it as the regal man spoke. "You are in the kingdom of Chenthom. My kingdom."

"You're a king?" That explained the look.

"King Theodore," he said, giving her a flourished bow. His green eyes stood bright against the light brown of his hair. Skye couldn't help but stare at their hues.

"Shouldn't I be bowing to you?" she asked.

He gave her a beautiful smile that would have left her on her knees if her heart hadn't already been claimed.

"Even I bow to a mighty Mage Warrior."

She gave what Alex would have referred to as her "dorky mom laugh," accompanied by what could only be called a snort. *Completely ladylike move for an introduction to royalty,* she scolded herself.

"Mighty is stretching it. Diminutive might be a better description," Trent said.

"Yes, so I've heard. Which leaves us in quite a perplexing situation."

"We left the bad guy behind, though, right? It worked, didn't it?" she asked.

"Temporarily," Trent answered.

"Indeed. It won't take Camin long to find his way back here," the king said.

"What does that mean?" Skye interrupted.

"It means we start training now. The magic is returning to the mages. Your arrival seems to have re-awoken it. That means we have a wealth of teachers," Trent said.

"None of whom are Mage Warriors," Mark said, frustration in his voice. "No one knows how her magic works. She's color-blind for god's sake."

"No, I'm not."

They all turned to her. Mark's eyes spoke for him, the hazel sparkling.

"I can see everything. It's all so bright and beautiful, no longer shadowed."

"Lyra must have linked the spell to our return home."

"Then we have hope," the king said. "You will train with Trent, Elspeth, and Thomas."

"With all due respect, Sire, I'd like to oversee the other mages. With their magic returning, it's bound to be a bit chaotic," her father said.

"Good point. We've had several come of age while you've been away. They'll have no idea how to control it. Then it's settled. Although, see that you're modestly covered before leaving your quarters in the future. I don't need you setting the guards in a frenzy."

"Covered? I feel like I'm in a cocoon," Skye said, confused by his reaction to her attire.

He waved her off. "Markhem, head to the barracks. It's time you step into your father's duties."

"Sire, thank you, but I'd like to remain with Skye as her protector. I'm sure Donakin is doing a fine job, or Noah, for that matter."

"Markhem," Noah said before the king could answer. "It's time. They've been awaiting your return as well."

"No more talk. The kingdom's safety is still in jeopardy. Make sure she's ready for battle." Theodore walked from the room. The others bowed as he walked past, but Skye was still taking it all in.

"Where's my son?" she asked.

"He's fine. We sent him to a room to rest. He has a very pretty handmaid attending to him. I'm certain he's very content," Mark answered.

"Let's get started," Trent said.

"No, can I have a minute or two with Mark, please?" Skye asked.

"Make sure she dresses, and then bring her to the training grounds with haste," Trent ordered.

"Will do. Come along, let's get you into something more decent," Mark said with a wink, taking her elbow and guiding her out of the room.

"If this is indecent, I'd hate to see what counts as scandalous around here."

He gave a hearty laugh. "You know there's nothing underneath that, right?"

Her stomach did a flipflop as her cheeks grew flush.

"I hadn't thought about it. I just needed to find you."

"I'd say it's a sexy thought, but the dressing gowns in our world are anything but flattering."

"Designed to keep men at bay?"

"You could say that."

They made their way through the hall, then up the stairs to her tower. When they reached her door, she stopped to catch her breath. "Why do they have me locked away in a tower like Rapunzel?"

He opened the door, laughing again. "This was your parents' quarters."

She stopped at the threshold. "Really?"

Nodding his head, Mark reached for her hand, the warmth of his touch enveloping her. She looked around the room with fresh eyes, wondering at the thought that parents she'd never known had once had a life here. That they'd loved each other and, for a brief time, had loved her. Her eyes fell on the chairs placed in front of the fireplace. Had they sat there together, talking, perhaps holding her? Had they made love in this room, the very act creating her life?

"Skye?"

Her eyes fell on his. "It's just strange. This room once held a life I never knew. It's a life I'll never know with people who are a mystery to me—an unknown among all the other unknowns that now make up my life."

He tilted her chin, his finger brushing her cheek softly.

"There are plenty of people here who knew them and can fill in the blanks for you."

His eyes lingered on hers for just a moment before he dropped his hand and walked toward the door.

"Get dressed. I'm sure Trent and Elspeth are waiting for you. I apparently have to go claim some right over the Elite that I don't want."

She reached back, trying to figure out how to get out of her matronly nightgown and circling like a dog to determine just where the ties were and how many there were.

"Do you think you can help me out of this contraption first?"

She stopped her dance and looked at him, noticing his tight grip on the doorknob and his shortened breaths.

Had she just invited him to undress her? Knowing damn well she wore nothing below the gown? Her heart quickened as he closed the door, pausing momentarily before slowly walking to her. She had invited him, and she hoped, despite all the madness, he would take the invitation.

He stepped behind her. Untying the lower ties first, his fingers grazed her back as it slowly revealed itself. The intensity sent butterflies somersaulting through her. She lifted her hair so he could reach the last tie, but he didn't. Instead, he moved so that he stood before her, his hazel eyes filled with the same need that was currently assailing her.

"You forgot one," she whispered, letting her hair fall.

His hand moved to her neck, tracing the shape of it as it

slipped below her hair, his eyes never leaving hers. She didn't know if she'd stopped breathing. Her body was so alive that she could feel nothing more than desire for him.

He pulled the last tie and the heavy material fell. Her hand caught it just as it fell to expose the top of her breasts. His breathing quickened, his hand drifting through her hair then tracing the curve of her cleavage.

He kissed her, the passion of it nearly knocking Skye over so that she grabbed his arms, the gown falling the rest of the way. He drew her closer and let his hands slip to her exposed backside, his touches sending sparks through her body.

Pushing his shirt up, her hands found the contours of his stomach then his back. Her body responded as his hand moved to her breast, slowly caressing it until his thumb found her nipple, a slight gasp slipping from her mouth. Her reaction offered just enough time for him to pull away and take his shirt off the rest of the way. It fell to the floor with her gown, soundless in its descent.

His needy eyes devoured her body, his lips finding their way to her breasts, sending waves of desire through her. His mouth found hers again after ascending her neck in a smooth motion of his lips, the stubble on his chin only stimulating her more. She was hungry for him. She pressed against him, reveling in the feel of his warm skin against hers, the solidness of him, the strength.

She didn't think she could wait any longer. She wanted to feel him inside of her, finally experience their bodies as one, just as she'd imagined all those years. She reached to his pants and teased along his waistband, eliciting a groan from him that stoked the fire within her. She unbuttoned them and they fell to the floor, leaving only his boxers standing in her way. Skye could feel his need for her as he pulled her tight against him, stopping the hand that was about to explore beyond the material.

"Skye, wait," he said, his breathing rapid.

"No, not this time, Mark. I'm standing here completely naked, aroused entirely too much to turn back now. There's no more waiting. We've waited too long, and I need you too desperately."

He slid his hands over the curves of her body, then back to her waist where he gripped her hips tightly, moving her against him so that she cursed the material that separated them, his erection firm and waiting. Warmth surged through her, and he scooped her up, bringing her to the bed, their fervent kisses never parting. His hand slid down her body, along her leg, pulling it up. His fingers traced the inside of her thigh as his mouth lowered to her breast. Every touch, every lick of his tongue only furthered her arousal. Skye arched her back as his fingers slid between her legs, stopping momentarily to play before slipping between her folds and meeting the moisture she knew had built there. He moaned as they sank into her, his head dropping to her chest.

"God, I want you so bad, Skye."

"Then take me," she replied, her body on fire from his touch.

Slowly, he pulled his fingers away, lifting himself to look at her. She pushed at his boxers, and he let her until he kicked them off completely. His need was pressing against her, waiting to enter her, but he didn't and instead dropped his lips to hers. Her mouth parted, letting his tongue in to meet hers as he slipped further into her space, pressing for entry, her body quivering with anticipation. His left hand cupped her breast, his other hand finding the small of her back, pressing him further into her moistness. Her breath caught as he teased, ever so slowly moving along her entrance until she could almost take no more.

Just as she thought she would break, he entered her. A cry rushed from her as her head fell back in pleasure. A grunt of satisfaction fell from his lips, and he dropped his head, taking her nipple in his mouth, his hand pushing against her back, bringing her further to him. With each thrust, pleasure assaulted her. With each flick of his tongue, electric currents spread through her like flames of fire. She clung to him, pulling him in deeper with her legs, wrapping them tighter around him.

He brought his hand to hers, their eyes meeting as the wave crested within her. Her body was alive with pleasure, her need for release too great to withstand. As she felt his body tense she broke, her climax ripping through her just as Mark's did, his cry meeting hers, his hand squeezing hers in the moment.

He brought his lips to hers with the final thrusts of his climax, kissing her passionately. Then he held her until their bodies settled and he collapsed against her. She could feel the small shakes of his body as his orgasm dissipated, her own sending small quivers to match his.

They laid there, catching their breath, until Mark finally pushed himself up to look at her. His eyes were heavy with satisfaction, her body reacting with another quiver. She brought her hand up to trace the curve of his jawline and gave him a small smile, which he met with his own before kissing her again.

Dropping his head to the crook of her neck, he ran his tongue along her skin.

"I need to stop, or we will never leave this bed," he mumbled drowsily.

"And that would be a bad thing?" she asked playfully, her hips moving in motion against him.

He groaned. "That would be a very bad thing."

But instead of lifting himself, he caressed her breasts, a move that helped neither of them as he grew within her. She continued to move her hips until he grabbed her waist to stop her motion.

"Skye, you're playing with fire."

With a throaty laugh, she brought his lips to hers and whispered, "I already played with fire. Now I'm ready for the afterburn."

It had the effect she'd desired. His body responded completely. He made love to her a second time; this time slower, more precise. She took the time to explore the places she'd missed the first time, touching and kissing until she'd memorized every bit of him. As the intensity increased, the cresting wave of desire rose again, her body succumbing as her climax met Mark's in one breathless moment of ecstasy.

THEY LAID TANGLED below the sheets like they were old lovers and not new ones. Skye supposed, in a way, they were. They'd loved each other longer than most, desired each other just as long.

As Mark's fingers skimmed her stomach playfully, she asked, "Was it how you imagined it would be?"

"No, definitely not," he answered.

She turned to her side, frowning.

He laughed before saying, "It was better. I couldn't have come close to imaging how that would feel, how you would look and feel."

He brushed his finger down her arm.

"You've seen enough of me to imagine how I'd look naked."

He groaned. "That bikini you wore to the beach that time when Alex was young. Sam forced me to come along. Huge mistake. I was afraid to get up for fear he'd notice my reaction to all that skin."

"Is that why you let Alex bury you in the sand the whole weekend?"

"Exactly."

She laughed. "I had no idea I was turning you on so much."

"Yes, you did, and you enjoyed every second. You know, I almost gave in that weekend. Sam had passed out, and you and I had one too many drinks."

"I remember that. I would have let you, you know."

"No, you wouldn't have done that to Sam, neither would I, which is exactly why I went for a walk instead of kissing you like my drunken body wanted to do."

The thought saddened her. "You gave up so much for me."

"We all did, Skye."

"But you—"

He brought his finger to her lips. "Shh. It's in the past, where it needs to be left. We have a future now, a lifetime together—several in human terms."

"Several?"

"You know how Elspeth is four hundred and seventy-five years old?"

"Yeah."

"Well, that's still relatively young. Our people lead exceedingly long lives," he said.

"How long is long?"

"Well, Theodore celebrated his eight hundredth year just before we left."

Her mouth fell open. "Eight hundred? He looks our age."

"We don't look our age, Skye. You could easily pass for twenty-nine, and I look like I'm in my thirties. We'll stay this way until we get close to our passing."

"And when is that?"

"Eh, depends. Maybe a thousand, maybe fifteen hundred."

She sat up suddenly. "Years?"

Laughing, he pulled her back down. "Of course I mean years, silly."

"People here live that long?"

"The different races live different lifespans, but yes, most are exceedingly long. The gods blessed us."

She didn't want to contemplate what living that long would be like so she asked another question, one she hoped wouldn't provide an answer that would boggle her mind even more.

"Gods? Why do you say gods sometimes? Is it different here?"

He gave her that beautiful smile she loved. "It is and I was raised both ways. Here we have multiple gods, not simply one like the human world." Her tactic hadn't worked, and now she was feeling even more in awe. Multiple gods? The idea was one she couldn't grasp. Religion had never been something she'd been raised with, but Sam had been, and she'd dutifully attended church with him every Sunday. Even without a consistent religious upbringing she'd founded her beliefs on the one god concept. To now hear that her world had multiple gods was unsettling.

She hoped her eyes weren't wide with shock as Mark continued to talk. "Where we say God or Jesus or anything similar in the human world, they say gods here to refer to all the gods in one reference. It took me a while to adjust when we first left here, but after so many years, I tend to use the human references. I still slipped from time to time and was always surprised when no one called me out on it."

"I never noticed until recently. So, I have to say gods now? That will take some getting used to."

"Eh, the other terms are too engrained in us. Might as well keep the enhanced vocabulary to spice it up. When you're going down on me, I can assure you I won't be thinking about deity names and a Christ will slip out."

She leaned into him. "I do like it when you swear like that."

"Mmm, well I can swear all day if that's all it takes to turn you on."

Her body responded, arousal drifting through her, but a hard knock on the door interrupted her thoughts of exploring it further.

Mark yanked a blanket over them as the door opened. She'd always wondered about his quick reflexes, and now she knew it must have been something to do with his status as an Elite; although, she still wasn't completely sure what that meant.

Her mother barged in.

"Good gods, you two couldn't wait, could you?"

There was that term again.

"Well, you made us wait a half a century. I figured you could wait a few hours," Mark grumbled back to her.

She put a long wooden staff against the wall. It was decorated with black markings all along it. Skye noticed she'd changed her clothes. The dress she wore was something out of a movie. It was long and flowing, with a bodice that cinched her waist, emphasizing her chest and her long graceful neck. It was a deep shade of green that complimented her sage eyes. She was lovely and enchanting, a far cry from the woman Skye knew as her mother. Once more that disoriented feeling overcame her. Everything she'd known was coming unraveled and she didn't think she'd ever grasp an understanding of this new life.

"We don't have a few hours. You're lucky Trent and Noah convinced me to let you have this long."

"Thanks. A few hours versus how many years?"

"Enough, Markhem. Get dressed and meet Noah—"

Mark sat up, and Skye could see the tension in his muscles. He rose from the bed, grabbing the loose throw to cover himself, but Skye could still see his backside, her eyes having trouble not staring at his defined ass.

She bit her lip hard and looked away as Elspeth backed up a step.

"Too many years I've had to take your orders—let you and Thomas make the decisions. I'm done. You do not have rank over me, Elspeth."

"You are not commander of the Elite—"

"I am as of today, which means you are now my inferior rather than my equal."

Elspeth straightened. She was a tall woman, but Mark still towered over her.

"Get dressed and see that Skye dresses for training. I'll be on the other side of the door," she said indignantly before storming out and slamming the door behind her.

"Nice to see her stern ways weren't part of the façade," Skye said.

He turned and flashed her a smile that sent her heart cartwheeling.

"She's got a soft side under there, you know that. We're home, though, and she's seen as a leader here. She and Trent, along with Thomas, are the strongest full mages. It's one of the reasons she was chosen to go with you."

Mark glanced back at the door, and Skye watched as the relaxation fled from his body, more tension replacing it.

"She's right. We need to get dressed."

Skye groaned and rolled her eyes as Mark dropped the blanket and picked up his pants. He raised an eyebrow at her, a sly grin forming as he pulled his boxers on, then his pants. She couldn't help but watch, taking him in—every inch of him that she'd always fantasized about, more inches than she had imagined.

"Fun's over, Skye."

"Is that all that was?" she asked playfully, regretting the words when his face fell.

"Is that all it was for you?" he asked, a serious expression reflected on his face. "That wasn't some rebound thing, was it?"

She threw a pillow at him.

"I'm serious, Skye."

"I can't believe you would ask that," she responded, the hurt in her voice clear.

"I didn't mean any offense by it, but it's a valid question. You were with Sam for a long time. You haven't dated since."

"You haven't either."

"That's different."

"Why?"

"Because I was desperately in love with you. When Sam died, I could no longer hide my need for you in taking other women. No one ever came close, no matter how many there were."

She knew his past. He'd been a player most of his life. He'd always had someone new, his one-night stands more than she could count. She couldn't complain. She'd married another man and slept with him every night.

"There is no one else like you out there. Trust me, Skye, I've looked. For years."

Her temper calmed. Sighing, she said, "Mark, you are not a replacement for Sam. If that were the case, I would have been in your bed right after his death. Sam was my replacement for you. I loved him, but he was never you. And I didn't date after he died because I didn't want anyone else, just you."

He crawled onto the bed, pushing her back and straddling her.

"I love you, Skye Langford."

"And I love you, Mark Brownson."

Drawing his lips to hers, she kissed him. The passion she felt from him burned through her. Her body woke to him instantly, but he pulled away before she could even react.

"Let's get you dressed before I lose control."

She wanted to complain but he looked determined and was halfway across the room by the time she came to her senses.

"Wait, is Brownson really your last name?" she asked instead, ignoring the let-down that was now coursing through her.

He was rummaging in a massive wardrobe, only to emerge with a handful of clothes. "No, we took surnames when we arrived there. We don't really have them here."

"You don't?"

"No, it's more a reference to where you're from."

"Is that why you always called me Skye of Skye?"

"Exactly," he said, plopping the clothes on the end of the bed.

"So, what would yours be?"

"Ah, since I was born here in the castle, I am Markhem of Strantril."

"Strantril is the name of the castle, and Markhem is your full name?"

"You're a quick study."

Laughing, Skye asked, "Why did you shorten your full names?"

"Not all of us did. Only those with names that didn't fit in did. Either that or we kept part of our name within the name we chose. It was a way of holding onto our identities. We weren't supposed to be there that long. Besides, Markhem is a bit unusual for that world."

He motioned her to get out of bed, holding up a pair of what looked like very form fitting pants. His eyes left the pants, perusing her body as the blankets fell away.

"That was not a good idea," he said hoarsely.

She pushed the pants aside and leaned into him, reveling in the feel of his bare chest against hers. His hand explored her curves, and she could feel his desire for her grow, pressing against her.

"We need to focus," he whispered as she nibbled on his earlobe.

"I am focused."

She wasn't quite sure why she was being so aggressive, but something within her had released when they'd made love. The hunger she'd kept clamped down for so many years could no longer be tamed.

"God, Skye."

His hands gripped her waist, his lips finding hers again. She didn't want to leave the room, leave his arms, didn't want to trade the pleasurable sensations for training. With him she was safe and protected. Outside the room, an unknown future awaited.

There was a hard knock at the door.

"I'm losing my patience!" Elspeth yelled.

Mark dropped his forehead to Skye's, loosening his grip on her waist.

"You're going to be the death of me, Skye. How am I supposed to concentrate when you do this to me?"

He let her go, picked up the pants and shoved them at her before walking away to calm himself down.

"I can't help it."

"Well, we both need to help it. Camin is coming, and he's not going to wait patiently on the other side of the door for us to fulfill our sexual needs."

She stuck her tongue out at him, then started searching for her underwear.

"What are you looking for?" His eyes averted from her still naked body.

"My underwear. Someone took them off me, but where did they put them? Do they even wear underwear here?"

He sighed, then rummaged through the bottom of the wardrobe, emerging with her lace thong.

"Is that what you wear?"

Snatching them from him, she said, "Just because I wasn't getting any doesn't mean I didn't want to feel sexy." She pulled them on, then held the pants up, trying to determine which side was the front.

"Christ," he mumbled, looking away and running a hand over his face.

She ignored him but couldn't help but smile at his reaction to her underwear—or perhaps it was the fact that she was still topless. The pants slid on like a glove, snug and soft. They were a soft suede that hugged her skin and were the perfect fit.

"How did they know my size?" she asked, staring at the small piece of cloth that served as a shirt.

"They didn't. The clothes were your mother's."

"My mother's?"

"I imagine so. They left the room intact and I remember seeing her once in that blue gown in the wardrobe."

Her eyes glanced through the open door. A variety of dresses hung within. One deep royal blue dress stood out among the rest. Her mother had worn these clothes, slept where she'd lain, made love to her father under the same blankets. It should have disturbed her, but as she didn't know her mother, it instead brought on a sense of nostalgia.

"Here," Mark said, taking the top from her, his eyes avoiding her chest.

He pulled the top over her head, his chest pushing against hers. "It would help if you'd put on a shirt," she mumbled through the top as it passed her face. His eyes were deep with need.

"It would help if you weren't so damn hot, but that's not gonna change."

She kissed him before he could stop her. The shirt was still around her neck, and he used it to pull her closer. His hand slipped down to grab her ass, his heart pounding in his chest against hers. He gripped her waist tight, bringing his bulging hard-on against her. She melted at the thought of it, her hand reaching down to feel it.

"Damn, woman, what you do to me," he grumbled.

There was another rap.

"If you don't stop knocking, I will take your hands off, Elspeth!" he yelled through his kisses. "I don't care if Camin is crashing through the gates of the kingdom. I'm going to take Skye again, and you are going to leave the tower!"

Her heart raced as he ripped the top back off her, his mouth ravaging hers. His hands found her breasts, squeezing them, his thumb rubbing against her nipple until she was breathless from the sensation. She fooled with the button of his jeans, but he pushed her hand away and undid them. Her own hands pushed at the tight pants that hugged her too well.

He walked her across the room until her back hit the wall. The breath knocked from her, his mouth lifting from hers as he shoved the pants down, peeling them the rest of the way. His mouth met her breast first, pausing to lick her deliciously, sucking on her hardened nipple until she squirmed. Then as his lips traced her stomach, he pushed the pants further so that her feet could take the rest of the work. His hands caressed the inside of her thighs before spreading her legs apart. She gasped in anticipation as they moved to her ass and tipped her pelvis to him. Threading her fingers through his hair, she dropped her head back in ecstasy as his mouth met her dampness, his tongue sliding through to further her rapture.

She moaned loudly, not caring if Elspeth had ignored his command. Mark warned her. Skye grasped his hair with her fingers, arching her back. His tongue slid deeper, his fingers pushing through her seam and plunging into her.

God, what he was doing to her. It was like nothing she'd ever experienced. His tongue moved to let his fingers probe, slipping to her clit, and sucking it until she was shaking with desire. The climax was building like a fire within her, one she didn't want to extinguish. Higher and higher it burned until finally, with one quick move of his fingers and tongue, it soared. Her climax hit so hard that her body shook uncontrollably, her pelvis pushing against his mouth as he continued his assault. She was breathless when he rose, wiping his hand across the back of his mouth and pulling her leg up.

She was limp as a rag-doll, but as he drove into her, she came back to life.

"You taste delicious," he whispered against her ear, kissing her neck until he found her lips again. Shivers of desire tore through her like a hundred butterflies.

She kissed him hungrily, tasting herself on his lips, his tongue thrusting with the thrust of his hips. He brought her other leg up, slamming into her, her body pressing hard against the wall with each push. The slight pain of it only intensified the pleasure. Dropping his head to her breasts, he licked the skin around her nipple, sending quivers through her. With each touch, each lick, her desire climbed further. She forced his head back up to kiss him, knowing if he continued his assault on her breasts she'd come undone again. It didn't stop the sensation, instead the fire continued to burn in her. His thrusts increased, his breathing growing ragged as he furthered his grip on her ass, tipping her toward him so that he went deeper with each move. The need built, hanging on the precipice until she could take it no more and she came. His own orgasm hit him within moments, his body tensing as he filled her with several long thrusts. All she could do was cling to him until her body calmed, his own finally relaxing against hers. He loosened her legs and let her feet slowly hit the floor.

"I don't want you to let me go," she said against his skin.

"I won't ever let you go again; I promise you. Never again," he said, kissing her.

He stepped back, wiping his hand over his face as his eyes devoured her.

"I could take you for the rest of the day, but—"

"We need to stop," she continued for him, her own eyes perusing him, realizing she'd seriously underestimated the size of him, both muscles and girth.

"You keep looking at me like that, and I'm never leaving this room," he teased. "You look like a hungry wolf, and that doesn't keep me from wanting you."

She saw the evidence as he grew firm again, quivers rushing through her. God, his stamina was unlike that of any man she'd been with. Her own heightened as she realized she, too, could do this delectable dance all day.

"Yeah," she said, her voice coming out breathless, "we can't make up fifty years in one day."

"We could try."

"If there weren't people waiting to pull us back to reality."

"Damn people," he mumbled, dragging her over to him and kissing her once again. She let her hands explore him, memorizing each muscle, before sliding down to the erection that pulsed against her again. Her fingers stroked him just as she'd imagined doing every time she'd pleasured herself.

"Stop that."

"Why?"

"Because I will take you again."

"And that's a deterrent why?" she asked, wrapping her hands around him and firmly moving with more intent.

"Jesus, you are something."

"You have no idea. For years, I've been fantasizing about what I want to do to you, Mark, and now I finally can."

"Fantasizing about me? What were you doing while you were fantasizing about me?"

"The same thing you were doing while you were fantasizing about me."

"Ah, that's a mix of things, Skye," he answered with a groan, his hand covering hers and moving with it. Her stomach fluttered. "This was one of those things. Other times it was with women I wished were you. Every time I came, I wanted it to be inside of you."

"I'm not sure if that should turn me on or anger me, Mark," she replied with a raised brow.

"I know I'm quite turned on again."

"Well, then I suppose you'll have to wait to get that release," she said, loosening her hand, his stopping it and forcing it back in place. The desire that had been simmering in her flared back to life.

She wanted him again, in some insatiable way that she'd never experienced. Encasing her hand around him again, she brought his head down to hers, wrapping her other hand through his hair.

Kissing him, she resumed her motion, feeling the heat of him. The moisture that greeted her at the tip sent a flood of warmth between her legs at the thought of tasting him. Desire driving her, she let her kiss linger on his chin, then his neck, then down his chest. She took her time, reveling in the thickness of his muscles until her mouth reached his erection that was prominent and waiting.

She took him in her mouth, her tongue tasting the remains of their sex upon him. He exhaled a sigh of pleasure, his fingers wrapping in her hair firmly. Hips pushing forward, he thrust himself deeper in her mouth. He was huge, bigger than Sam had been. It was an effort to take him, but she took as much of him as she could. She grasped his shaft, working it with her hand then her mouth, alternating in a precise rhythm. His moans grew louder each time she took him further until she adjusted to his size. Her own body responded with each rise and fall upon him, and she squeezed her legs together in response. The muscles in his thighs tightened when her own groan escaped, and his hand pushed her to take him further, his climax rising steadily until he came, the warmth of it filling her mouth as she tasted him, welcoming it until he'd finished. As the final drops of him landed on her tongue she licked them away seductively.

"Holy shit," he grumbled, his voice hoarse, his breathing short and heavy. "Where the hell did you learn to do that?"

"Did you really have an innocent view of me after all these years, Mark?" she asked, licking the last bit of him from his tip.

"Yes, I did," he replied. Skye stood and picked up her pants, pulling her underwear on, then her pants. He was still standing there, mouth agape, trying to catch his breath.

She handed his pants to him. "Well, you were wrong. I may have been married, but that doesn't mean I was dead."

"But you were a virgin when you married Sam—"

"Was I?" she said seductively.

"What? Who?"

She leaned in and kissed him. "You weren't the only one who imagined we were together."

Picking up her top and walking away, she left him there, knowing he was going through all the boys she'd known, all the ones from college before she'd met Sam. She'd taken her need for Mark out early, unable to stand the burning between her legs that never ceased when he was around.

"Shit, you didn't sleep with that dork, Tommy, did you?"

She shrugged, trying to find which way the damned top went as he pulled his pants on, leaving his boxers on the floor.

"No boxers?"

"Don't change the subject and yes, I want you to know my dick is free and hard for you when we're out there." There was an edge of anger in his voice.

"I'm not changing the subject—"

"Then who did you sleep with?"

"Are you serious? You can't even count the number of women you've slept with and you're hounding me about who I've slept with? I was not a virgin when I married Sam. I had numerous boyfriends—"

"All of whom I vetted and threatened."

"Really?" It irked her that he'd threatened boys she'd known, although there was a possessiveness to the action that also turned her on.

"I wasn't about to let just anyone go out with the girl I wanted."

"Well, that girl had to satisfy the wetness that you brought to her on a daily basis with someone since you weren't available."

He groaned.

"I wanted you, Mark. It hurt so bad that some days I couldn't even look at you without coming. Christ, you were like a piece of candy sitting just out of my reach."

"And you don't think you were the same for me?"

"I was, but you got to fuck everyone who even swayed their hips in front of you! I was locked down by you and my parents, so I rebelled and fucked them as much as I wanted to fuck you!"

He drew a breath, glaring at her.

"I should be really pissed by that comment, but something about the way you say the word fuck turns me on too much to argue about it."

She sighed. "We both did what we had to do, right?"

"Yes, but it would have been nice to know you were a delicate, innocent flower like I thought you were."

"What would the fun have been in that? It was much better seeing how fast you just came when I went down on you. Surprising you was worth every drop of you."

He gave her a crooked grin. "God, I love you."

"Sordid past and all?"

"I doubt it's as sordid as mine. Here," he said, taking the top from her again. "Let me help you with that, or I'm just going to strip those pants off you again if you don't put those breasts away."

"Aren't you out of energy yet?"

"Hell no."

"Is that normal for you? To go so many times?"

He pulled the shirt down, eyeing her. "Is it normal for you?"

"No, but—"

"Something about us makes it different?"

"Yes," she answered breathlessly as he pulled it over her chest, his fingers tracing the swell of her breast under the material.

"Exactly," he answered. "I have quite the stamina, but nothing like this without a break."

"Hmmm, we'll have to test how long it takes to wear you out."

He laughed. "At the same time, we'll test that on you, my dear." He stepped around to her back, adjusting a few straps.

"How do you know how to work this contraption?"

"I remember seeing the warriors train in these clothes when I was young. I would sneak away from my training to watch them cast spells with the mere movement of their hands. It was mesmerizing."

"It's soft," she said, running her fingers along the material. "And it has a built-in bra." She pushed her breasts up to demonstrate, only then realizing how much chest it emphasized. "Although it leaves much to be desired in the way of coverage."

He swallowed loudly as he took her in. "Yes, it definitely does."

His eyes were large and filled with something...adoration?

"Jesus, Skye, you look hot."

"Hot? I don't think I should look hot. Aren't I a bit old for that?"

He shook his head, never taking his eyes from her body. "Not here. You're like twenty years old here."

"Huh, that will take some getting used to."

She looked down at the dark green top, then turned around to see what she looked like from behind.

"Why do I feel like one of those scantily clad characters from those video games Alex plays?"

"Because you look like one."

"Is this necessary? I thought they were all prim and proper here after seeing that nightgown."

"Yes, the less material, the easier it is to wield your magic," Elspeth's voice said from the doorway. She cast an angry glance at Mark. "I'm assuming you two are done now."

"Did you enjoy the sounds, Elspeth? I warned you to leave."

"Nothing I haven't heard before, especially from this room. Noah is here to collect you, Markhem. Skye, you're coming with me."

But I just came with Mark, and I'd prefer to come again with him, she thought, then felt the blush as her brain caught up with the dirty thought. What had come over her?

"Pull yourself together, Markhem, and let's go. I'm not happy you made me climb all those stairs." Noah stopped and gestured to the bed. "Did you two? About time. Although it's going to be a beast getting him to focus now, Skye."

Mark grabbed his shirt and threw her a wink.

"I'd think you'd be happy; this is better than having me pine for her the entire time."

He brushed past Elspeth, and their bantering continued down the stairs.

Skye missed him already, and wondered if there would be another chance for them to be alone. Would he share her bed when the day was over?

"I haven't been in this room since that last night," Elspeth said, looking around.

"You knew my mother?"

"Your mother was my closest friend."

Skye was surprised. There was so many things she didn't know about the woman she'd called mother.

"It's one of the reasons she chose me to go with you and raise you."

"She chose you?"

Elspeth gave her a small smile, running her hand along the back of a chair, lost in memory.

"Yes. I argued against it and told her she should go, but she was always duty driven. I remember that night as if it were yesterday. It was me, Lyra, and Alina, Markhem's mother. The news had just been delivered that your father and Markhem's had been lost, Markhem having witnessed it." She paused, her expression falling sad. "It had been brutal. Camin blasted through their ranks, slaughtering so many of them. The Mage Warriors were blindsided, distracted by a diversion Camin had created, drawing them away quickly. Lyra had been inside strategizing with the full mages, or she would have never left her Elite. The two groups always fought side by side. But the other Mage Warriors thought differently, letting the distraction draw them away and leaving their Elite vulnerable.

"Lyra and Alina were devastated, as were we all. Alina had stayed with Lyra to help while Markhem's father, Fedhem, went with yours. Only when she went to find Markhem, discovering him on the castle wall, did she realize the two men had been killed."

"Mark saw it happen?"

"I suppose so. Although he never talked about it. Alina brought the news back to Lyra. The four of them were close, like brothers and sisters, a bond between them. The fall of the Elite command left an opening for Camin, his power strangely stronger than it had ever been. He was able to take down two of the Mage Warriors next, and that's when Lyra brought me and Thomas in."

"They both sacrificed their children," Skye said softly, her heart breaking to think that Mark had seen his father murdered.

"For the good of our kingdom and the realms. Camin had already laid siege on our neighbors to the west and the east. If she hadn't cast the spell that tied all the magic to your binding, then the world may have been lost."

She paused before turning to Skye.

"I raised you strict. I know it was hard, but I knew what you faced should we ever return home. I knew you needed to be self-reliant, thoughtful, but fierce. There was never a moment that I didn't love you, Skye, as if you were my own child."

She let her fingers drift through Skye's hair. "Every day I looked upon you was a reminder of my friend. You're very much like Lyra. You have her spirit, her fight, her hair, even her facial features. Your eyes, however, look just like your father's. When we first left, we mourned them—those we had lost, and those we had left behind. We knew what they faced, that the magic would fade. Looking upon you was a painful reminder of what we'd sacrificed."

"I'm sorry," Skye said, the tears behind her eyes mirroring the ones in Elspeth's.

"Sacrifices must always be made for the good of the kingdom."

"And calling Mark my cousin?"

"Was a sacrifice we chose to make."

"Why? What harm would it have done to let us love each other?"

"It is rare that a Mage Warrior and an Elite fall in love, but when they do, it's unbreakable."

"And that would have been so bad?"

"It would have been a distraction, a vulnerability for Markhem."

The confusion must have shown on Skye's face, for Elspeth continued. "Markhem comes from a powerful line of Elite. In fact, he was thought to be the strongest yet. It's one of the reasons he was sent with you and why we raised him so close to you. He is your protector. His blood is pure Elite, traced all the way back to the first of his kind, his line always mating with others of his kind, always the two strongest. He needed to be your protector, not your lover. He needed to train away from your unknowing eyes, to hone his skills, to prepare himself to take command when we returned. There has never been a time when one of his line has not commanded the Elite. It was not only your destiny that awaited you here, but his as well."

"And Sam?"

"Was my doing. Mark argued vehemently at first, then he saw the truth. Sam was necessary to continue your façade of safety. It was too late for you and Mark by then, anyway. We had clearly established that you were related. Sam was a necessity. We all saw that, including Mark."

"Sacrifices must be made," Skye mumbled. Sighing, she asked, "So what now?"

"We train you. Your power is unlocked, but you have no sense of it. Camin will return, and you are our last defense." She gestured to the chair. "Sit. Your hair needs to be up."

"My hair? Why can't I just pull it up?"

"Because we do not wear ponytails or messy buns in Chenthom. Now sit."

Skye obeyed, just as if she were still a child. Her mother's fingers ran through her hair.

"I'm sorry I was hard on you when I found out. I suppose you sacrificed just as the others did. You always treated me with love, even if you were a bitch sometimes."

Elspeth laughed. "I wasn't your friend, Skye. I was your mother, and I took that seriously. I still do."

Her fingers stopped their weaving for a moment. "I will always be your mother, Skye. I raised you as mine in Lyra's memory, and I loved you as mine."

"I love you too, Mom."

She stared into the fireplace as her mother pulled at her hair.

"What was she like?"

"Lyra?"

"Yes."

"She was wonderful. Beautiful and strong. Her hair was just like yours. It flowed down her back when she left it loose. She was smart and funny. I remember the day she met your father. They were young, both only about ten. It was the first time she was introduced to the youngest of the Elite. She told me afterward that she'd gone right up to him and claimed him that day. Just went right to him and kissed him. There was spirit in her, and your father adored her. They were perfect together, but I've been told Mage Warrior and Elite matches always are. The only ones I'd seen before them were her parents."

"Her parents?"

"Yes, your line is special, like Markhem's. It traces back to the first of the Mage Warriors and the Elite. Every marriage in your line has been the two, and everyone has produced a powerful Mage Warrior. That's why you were so special, Skye." Elspeth moved in front of her. "Beautiful. Gods, you look just like her."

A glint shone in Elspeth's eye. Then her softened demeanor changed. "Enough chitchat. You have work to do."

Elspeth moved her hand, and the wooden staff with black engravings appeared. Then she muttered something, and a long navy-blue cape cloaked Skye. A gray one appeared over her mother's dress.

"Wait, why do you get to carry a cool staff and go fully clothed?"

"Because I am but the undercurrent to your storm. You do not need anything but your will to direct your powers."

"Okay, but the skimpy clothes?"

She shrugged. "Battle requires movement, and you will need to remain unburdened from cumbersome threads."

"Jesus, Mom, you sound and look like you just stepped out from a *Lord of the Rings* set."

She laughed. "Fantasy, Skye. This is your new reality."

MARK

S o, you finally claimed her," Noah said as they made their way out of the tower.

"Claimed? That sounds a bit barbaric, even for your standards," Mark replied.

"That's what they say when a male Elite or a mage takes a mate. At least in our kingdom. In others, I've heard they use it anytime a mate is chosen."

"That sounds just as barbaric."

"Remember where we are now, Markhem."

"I don't remember much of our world. I was young."

"Well, it's backwards in every way but the magic."

"I don't think it would be wise for you to tell Skye that I claimed her," Mark said.

"Ha, no, she might bristle at that term."

They made their way through the back of the castle, out through the tunnel to the barracks. He remembered walking the same path with his father. The walls had seemed higher then, the space not so tight.

"Are you ready to stake your claim as commander?" Noah asked, stopping at the opening.

"That's a better use of the word. No, I'm not. These aren't my men. They've been under Donakin's command since my father was killed. I didn't even lead our team in the other world."

"I waited for you to take it from me, but you refused, always staying close to Skye."

"I'm not a leader."

Noah laughed. "You were born a leader. You led us even without the title. It's in your blood. These men have awaited your return. They all knew Donakin's command was temporary until Fedhem's heir returned."

"And he's going to just let me walk in and take that title from him?"

"No, you'll need to fight him for it. Show that you are Fedhem's son. Then he will willingly hand it over to you. The Elite are never as strong without one of your line in command. The times we've lost one and an heir was too young to stand in, like in your case, we were weaker. We need you at the helm, Markhem. Now go claim your destiny."

Mark took a step, but Noah grabbed his arm. "After you shed the human clothes and don your uniform."

"You made me walk all this way to send me back to the Elite wing?"

"That I did. I wasn't sure if you remembered your way around. Think you can find your parents' quarters?"

His parents' quarters. His heart stopped, a wave of emotion drifting through him. He nodded, and as if sensing his feelings, Noah put a hand on his shoulder.

"Take your time. I hear they left it intact for your return."

Noah jogged off, and Mark made his way back down the tunnel and to the Elite wing. He passed a few young Elites, who stared in awe at him, on the way, but he ignored them, focused on the door furthest down the wing.

He paused when he reached it before hesitantly opening the door. A flood of memories rushed back: his parents' faces, his father's booming voice, his mother's soft smile, the love they'd both showered upon him. The room was similar to Skye's, smaller only by a fraction. The commander of the Elite was treated on the same level as the Mage Warriors—another form of royalty.

Mark started a fire in the large fireplace and sat on the fur before it, watching as it kindled. How many times had he sat upon the fur of the beast his father had defeated when Mark had been small? His fingers drifted through the softness of it, imagining that he could still hear his parents' voices as they laughed together across the room.

Skye had lost her parents to the war as well, but she was blessed that she had never known them—never experienced her mother's embrace, never seen the look of pride in her father's eyes. A part of him felt sorry for that, but the other wished he were the same, so the burden of loss wasn't so great.

He'd mourned them when he'd been sent to the other world, pushed their memories far away as he had his love for Skye. But now it was all flooding back and he didn't know how to stop it.

"You know your father would scold you for letting your emotions control you." Mark heard a voice that he hadn't heard in decades say.

He looked up to see his mother's brother in the doorway.

"Uncle Petrian!" he exclaimed, rising, and greeting the man, who gave him a large bear hug.

"Let me look at you, Markhem. Gods, you look just like your father. Only my sister's hair managed to outfight his good looks."

"It's good to see you, Uncle."

"You have no idea. It's been far too long." Petrian glanced around the room. "I haven't been in here since we lit the pyres for your parents. It stirs too many memories."

"That it does."

"I suppose you'll be living here now or...will you be staying in the mage tower?" he asked with a gleam in his eye.

"Wow, that didn't take long."

"Word travels fast around here. Who's wow?"

Mark laughed. "It's an expression. What are they saying?"

"That you and the Mage Warrior have mated."

"Christ, that term makes us sound like animals."

His uncle stared at him. "What did they do to you in that world? What language are they speaking with all these strange expressions? We choose our mates, and if it so happens, an Elite claims his Mage Warrior. If the warrior is male, then he claims his Elite, and they are mates. Gods, do we have to re-educate you, boy?"

"I'm not a boy, and no, you don't need to re-educate me, although it would seem there's quite a bit I've forgotten."

"So it would seem." His uncle's eyes evaluated him. "You do realize this is a first in your line?"

Mark sighed, the burden of his heritage weighing heavy on him once again. "Yes, I suppose it is, but I think there are more pressing matters than my legacy."

"If she has a child, that child will be a Mage Warrior," he said, pushing the subject.

"She already has a child, and I don't think the thought of her having another has crossed either of our minds. It's not the sort of thing one does at our age in the other world."

"Yes, I've heard she has a child from another man. You let that happen? Attraction between a Mage Warrior and an Elite is rare, but when it happens, it cannot be denied."

Mark rubbed his hands down his face. "Try telling that to Elspeth and Thomas. It was not my choice, nor was it hers. Now, Uncle, I have a lot to do. As pleased as I am to see you, the last thing I need at this moment is a lecture on all the things that went wrong in the other world."

"I'm sorry, Markhem. You're right. You have your legacy to claim. Donakin awaits you in the training grounds just as the rest do."

"Great, an audience."

"You will best him. This is your army."

"Donakin has trained every hour of every day since he was a child. He fought against Camin under my father. I trained as a child and have never seen battle. Since leaving, I've trained for mere hours a day, sneaking time in when I could. How am I to best a man like that?"

His uncle smiled. "Because you are the son of two of the strongest Elite. It is in your blood. It is in here." He pounded Mark's chest. "Now, let's get you ready."

He went to the wardrobe and pulled out a uniform—the white and green crisp as if it had never been worn. But Mark knew better.

"Father's?"

"Yes."

Mark fingered the soft material, a melancholy settling over him.

"Your parents loved you, Markhem. My sister was torn over sending you away, but it was the right thing to do. You were needed there and now you have returned. You have claimed your mate. Now go claim your title."

MARK WALKED onto the training field, memories of seeing his father in action fresh in his mind. His uncle strode alongside him. The uniform fit perfectly and with it, Mark felt powerful, and ready to take his father's place and accept his destiny.

As he walked, the sparring stopped, all eyes following him. They immediately knew who he was. He favored his father's image too greatly for the seasoned Elite not to recognize him.

"Markhem of Strantril," Donakin greeted him.

"Donakin," he returned with a nod.

"So, you're back to take command of the Elite."

"They are rightfully mine."

"Mmm, so they are, but you know I can't just hand them over to you."

"Of course you can't. Although you were only to lead them in the interim."

"Still, it wouldn't look good if I simply stepped aside for some child who has yet to prove himself."

"Fair enough."

Donakin pulled a silver disk from his belt. "I hear you've brought the Mage Warrior home and that her magic has returned." He tapped the disk and a long two ended curved weapon formed. "With her magic, so returns our true power." He stroked his finger along the weapon that glowed a bright blue as magic coursed through it.

"So it would appear," Mark replied, pulling his own weapon out and activating it just like his father had taught him, reaching out to feel Sky's magic, the connection only the Elite had to it. As it formed, the tingle of power coursed through him, memories of that same feeling as his father had trained him emerging.

"I also hear that you've claimed the Mage Warrior, mated with her."

"Does nothing escape notice around here?"

Donakin laughed. "Not when it comes to a Mage Warrior. If it's true, that would make you as strong as your father, maybe stronger. Mage Warriors, when they even look at our kind, only ever mate with the second in command. Doesn't that make you my second?"

"Not this time." Mark struck an offensive pose. "And I really don't like that term."

He struck at Donakin, who blocked his blow, striking back quickly. The years of training in the other world fortified him, making his moves precise and swift. If Donakin had thought him weak from his time away, he was wrong. The weapon hummed in his hands; the force of each strike compounded by the magic behind it. Mage Warrior magic strengthened all Elite, giving their weapons a unique power and advantage.

Any thought that Donakin would make it easy on him disappeared as the fight ensued. Donakin was strong. He'd fought alongside Mark's father, trained with him, learned with him. Everything Mark knew, he knew.

With each blow, the ground shook from the warrior magic that bled through their weapons. Time seemed to drag as sweat dripped down Mark's brow. For a moment, his weapon responded differently, the magic changing from a tingle to a warmth that seemed to spread within him as if the magic had latched onto him. Thrown off guard by the reaction, Donakin struck him, and Mark flew through the air, landing hard on his back with a grunt.

Momentarily stunned and still trying to comprehend the sensation, his mind wandered to another memory. His father's voice echoing through his mind.

"For those rare Elite who mate with a Mage Warrior, the connection is stronger. A part of their magic is imprinted on their mate. When the Mage Warrior is close, that magic makes them into a weapon that has no match for any other Elite. They are to be feared and respected."

"Have I bested you already, Markhem?" Donakin asked, his shadow falling over him.

Mark jumped to his feet, feeling that enhanced sensation and knowing Skye must be nearby.

"Not a chance," he gritted.

"Then show me what you have, and let's finish this."

Spinning his weapon, Mark grabbed a second from his belt and activated it. The thought occurred to him that no one ever wielded two weapons at one time. The mage magic that imbued them was too much to control in two. Those who had mated with a Mage Warrior, however, could, making them a threat no other Elite could defeat.

Donakin raised his brow. "So, it's true."

"I'd say it is," he answered, spinning both in his hands then attacking Donakin.

The fight was over with the first few strikes. Donakin was barely able to block attacks from both sides, each blow pushing him back until he could do nothing more than yield when the final blow landed him breathless on the ground.

No one but a pure blood from his line would ever have been able to fight an Elite mated to a Mage Warrior. They were legends in the Elite, a rarity that placed them in the highest rank just under those in Mark's line. And now he held a combination of both rare Elites within him.

He triggered his weapons to return to their original size, then extended a hand to Donakin, helping him to his feet.

"You will make a formidable commander," Donakin said, placing his hand on Mark's shoulder. "Your father would be proud."

He turned to the Elites and announced, "I yield command to Markhem, son of Fedhem. Who will follow him alongside of me?"

There was a resounding chorus of "ayes" from the men and women, but Mark's attention was focused to the east, where he sensed Skye. He wasn't certain how, but he had a strange awareness of her presence, a heightened connection to her.

His uncle came up to him and slapped him on the back. "Well done."

"Thank you, Uncle."

"I hear the Mage Warrior has begun her training."

"Is it true what they say?" Donakin asked. "Did your strength increase with her closeness?"

"In a way. It was like a part of her magic swept through me. It was the strangest feeling."

"I'll be damned. Then you will need to stay close to her when we face Camin again. You are her weapon just as much as her own magic is," Donakin said.

"He's right. Skye's parents and her mother's parents were a force that could not be stopped. It was only by Camin's treachery that they died," Petrian added.

"I didn't know that about Lyra's parents. I thought they'd gone to settle in Presmit like the elders do when it's time to step down for the younger generation."

"No," Donakin said. "They were still young enough to fight. Camin stole Geran to the Fettered Forest where Avantha couldn't reach him."

"Mage Warriors have no power over shadows," Mark said. "I remember Mother saying that."

"Yes, that's why they are weaker at night and why Camin attacks at night."

"What happened?"

"She couldn't reach him, and without her close by, Geran was no match for Camin's magic. He tortured and murdered him. They found his body days later on the outskirts of the town of Crenzit, which sits closest to the forests. Avantha was distraught and sought out Camin on her own. Weakened by her grief and disoriented without her mate, she was easy prey for Camin."

"He killed her?" He heard Skye's voice.

She was standing next to Noah. Elspeth was storming toward her, irritation distorting her features. Donakin and the others bowed, recognizing Skye's uniform, as well as the magic she now exuded—power Mark now saw sparkling in her eyes. He couldn't help but smile; she looked beautiful. Someone had done her hair in braids that piled atop her head. He vaguely remembered her mother wearing hers the same way.

"Well?" she asked, and Mark realized they were all staring at her in wonder.

"You don't interrupt an Elite training, Skye," Noah scolded.

"They weren't training, they were talking. And something was calling to me, like a weird sensation."

Mark looked down at his hands, remembering the same sensation. "It was me," he said. "We're connected."

Elspeth drew a breath. "I'd forgotten that."

"What does that mean?"

"That your magic is now tied to Mark. You must fight as one just as you live as one. You are mates in every sense now that he's claimed you," Elspeth said.

Mark cringed, knowing exactly how that was going to go over.

"Claimed? Mates?"

"They're just terms they use here, Skye," he said quickly.

"They're very serious terms, Markhem," his uncle said.

"Mark didn't claim me. We claimed each other, and how is that anyone's business?"

"The fate of the kingdom can lie in the mating of a Mage Warrior, especially one of your heritage," Noah said.

Mating? she mouthed to Mark.

He shrugged.

"It sounds like we're animals," she grumbled. "Whatever. Go back to the story. The woman, who was she?"

"Your grandmother," Petrian said.

"She was a Mage Warrior?"

"You come from a line of Mage Warriors, remember?" Elspeth said.

"I'd forgotten. There's a lot to take in here. Her husband—"

"Her mate was an Elite. Apparently, they're inseparable," Mark said.

Her mouth formed an 'oh.'

"So Camin killed him to get to her?"

"It's a weakness, and Camin saw the opening," Elspeth said.

Mark's heart dropped. The strength he'd had earlier fleeing.

"What did Camin do to her?" she whispered.

"They found her mutilated body at the edge of the Fettered Forest."

There was a silence as the severity of her death settled on them all.

"It was the first time Camin had killed a Mage Warrior. The moment we realized Camin was a real threat," Noah added.

Mark recognized the look in Skye's eyes, anticipating her reaction before she backed away.

"Skye," he said, trying to call her back, hoping she didn't show any vulnerability in front of the Elite. She turned and walked away. Elspeth went to follow, but he stopped her. "Let me."

"Markhem, you have a team to lead. You can't run after her," Noah said.

"The hell I can't. Everyone back to training now!" he commanded, then stormed after Skye.

She was a quick walker, and he caught up with her close to the tunnels. He grabbed her elbow and dragged her in, away from prying eyes.

"Hey!" she yelled, trying to pull her elbow from him. "Mark, let me go."

"No. What are you going to do? Run away? That's not in your nature, Skye, until recently," he added, thinking of how she'd run from the house that morning.

"What am I supposed to do? I don't belong here. This is not my world, not my fight." She tugged at the tight tunic, accentuating her breasts, and he had to force himself to focus.

"Not my clothes, even. None of this is me."

He grabbed her by the shoulders. "All of it is you, Skye. It always has been, you've just been blinded to it. There is no going back and if there were, the only thing that awaits you is imminent death."

"That's all that awaits me here. I am not my mother."

"You could be. Imagine what you'll become if you embrace who you really are, Skye."

Her eyes were wide with fear.

Sighing, Mark brushed a stray strand of hair from her face. "Look, all of this is new for both of us."

She started to argue, but he stopped her with a finger to her lips. "I know this is my world, but I was ten when we left. The majority of my life has been the same lie you've lived. Now I, too, have to step into my parents' legacy, a legacy I don't know other than from stories I've been told and the few memories I have of my father. That was fifty years ago. I'm just as scared as you are, maybe more because all of this means I could lose you if we don't do it right, and that scares me more than anything else."

She took his hand, running her finger along it, her eyes watching the movement.

"My legacy is so much more than the magic and the power. It's intertwined with yours now, isn't it?"

She looked back up at him, her eyes a deep navy.

"Yes, it is," he answered honestly.

"So, when we gave ourselves over today, we gave more than our bodies. We gave our souls—our very existence as individual people?"

He smiled. "No, Skye. I would never want to lose that part of you that makes you special. You're distinct from me."

"But my heart isn't, and because of that, our souls are linked. My grandmother died because of her broken heart. My mother gave up her life, and her magic because of hers."

"We don't know that. She was saving you, saving the kingdom."

"The love of an Elite and a Mage Warrior is inseparable, that's what they said, and...and I feel that now. I sensed you, Mark. It was like I could feel your presence."

"I know. I felt your magic. It's connected to me now. Like I said, there's no turning back."

"You promise to stay by my side?"

"Always."

She pulled the collar of his tunic. "You know, you look quite handsome in this outfit."

He arched a brow. "Changing the subject on me?"

"Not at all. I just thought that if I'm going to march back onto that field, I'd better get another kiss from my mate."

He cringed. "That word mate. It—"

"Has a bit of sexiness to it. And when you say it while wearing that uniform, it's even sexier."

"Well, if you'd prefer, I'll name you as my mate and claim my dominance over you, then."

He saw the spark of desire in her eyes.

Not the best time, Mark, his mind screamed, but his body ignored it as he stepped closer, pushing her against the tunnel wall.

She exhaled a startled breath, which did nothing but encourage him.

He kissed her open mouth, his tongue tasting the sweetness of her as her tongue met his. He wanted her again—to feel her bare skin against his, the soft supple breasts, the firm hips that were currently situated in his grip. Images of her from earlier filled his mind, sending him craving more as his hands found their way up her shirt to her breasts, her nipples taut and hard.

He grinned as she moaned. "Take me here, Mark," she said in a feral voice.

But he heard footsteps, the reality of where they'd chosen to relax their guard crashing down upon him. Quickly he pulled his hand down and straightened her shirt, praying he could calm himself before the owner of the footsteps was upon them.

"No," she complained, but he stopped her with a hush and stepped away from her.

"Oh no," Alex said, as he came into view. "So, it is true. Why is it every time I see you two, your hands are all over each other?"

"We're not touching each other," Mark said quickly, feeling the need to defend them.

"That's not what it sounded like. Damn, that had me turned on for like two seconds until I realized it was my mother!"

Skye's cheeks grew crimson.

Alex put his hands on his hips. "So, this is what I have to get used to? I feel like I'm going to need some intense therapy after all of this. First, my mother is some powerful magic wielding warrior, then she's from another world, now she's in love with my uncle. And trust me, I heard that there's more that's occurred since we've arrived. The word mate seems popular."

"That word," Mark growled.

"We're not related, Alex," Skye explained.

"I know, Mom. And I'm not blind. It's obvious you two have had the hots for each other for a long time. I think even Dad knew. I'm just glad you're not related, because now the thought of you two drooling over each other all these years sits a little better."

An awkward silence followed.

"Mom, why do you look like one of my sexy game characters?"

Mark couldn't help but laugh. "It's her training uniform."

"Really? And your, um...Mark, you're okay with this, as over-protective as you are? And, Mom, seriously, that's a lot of skin."

"Trust me, I know."

"Why are you down here, Alex?" Mark asked, desperate to change the subject. He felt like a teenager being scolded by a parent and wasn't sure how the roles had swapped.

"I was trying to find either of you, and someone pointed me in this direction. This castle is so cool! I tried to video call Kenny, but there's no reception here."

"You seriously tried to call someone from another world?"

He shrugged. "It was worth a try."

"Hey, you two," Noah's voice called from the tunnel opening. "Elspeth is about to lose her shit out there."

"Okay, we're coming," he answered.

"Is she really coming, or do I need to deal with a full mage tantrum? I've dealt with Elspeth when she's in one of her moods and it's not pretty."

"I am. I just need a moment," Skye said.

Noah stepped closer to them. "Try not to take your moments in front of others from now on. You are a leader here. Some of those men and women remember Mage Warriors, and they will not follow you if they don't believe that you are here to fight with them. Some of them have never seen a Mage Warrior, and you just gave them a sorry, disappointing show of who you are."

Mark saw the anger in her eyes.

"You don't know me. I'm not from this world, and I'm trying my best to adapt in the hours that I've been given to adjust to this new life," she said.

"This is your world, so adapt faster. And I do know you. I have guarded you since the day we left this world, watching every move you've made, every decision, every event in your life down to each twirl of your hair to the bite of your inside cheek. Every one of the Elite who gave up their lives in this world to protect you knows you. Now stop being a whiny human and show us it was all worth it."

He turned and walked away before she could say anything.

"Dang, you just got scolded, Mom."

"Shut up, Alex," she said, storming after Noah.

"You sure you want to handle that, Uncle Mark—I mean Mark."

He laughed. "Definitely, and you can still call me Uncle Mark, Alex."

"Yeah, but won't that seem strange when you two finally get married?"

Mark stopped at the thought.

"You are going to marry my mother, aren't you? You love her, right?"

Mark eyed him. "When did you get so wise?"

"It doesn't take a genius to read the two of you, especially after Dad died. It was like some door was opened, but neither of you could pass the opening, always dancing around it. You do love her, right?"

"Desperately. I just never thought of the reality of marriage or any of this, really. You know I would have married her in a heartbeat when we were young if things had been different."

"And now?"

"I'd marry her today if we didn't have death looming over us."

"Maybe you should, just for that reason."

"Eager to marry your mother off so quickly?" he asked as they grew closer to the others, the idea Alex had presented swirling in his mind.

Alex stopped. "I'm eager to see my mother happy again. You make her happy. You always have."

There was sadness in his eyes.

"You know she loved your father. He was my friend, and I was the one who introduced them. I would never have hurt him, nor would she."

"I know that, and I think he knew that. But why bring him into it? Why make her marry someone else?"

"I wanted her to be happy, to have a life, and to be safe. Your father provided all of that for her."

"And you wouldn't have?"

"I would have, but not there. That label they assigned me the day we left here made it impossible for that to happen, and if I had kept her to myself, well, it wasn't fair to her when she didn't know the truth."

"Was it fair to you, Uncle Mark?"

"Nothing's ever fair when it comes to war and sacrifices must be made. Besides, she had to marry your father, otherwise we wouldn't have you."

Alex laughed. "Good save."

Mark ruffled his hair and looked over to see that Skye and Elspeth were gone.

"Go. You need to be with the mages so you can learn."

"So I was told, but these guys look cooler."

"It's not in your blood, kiddo. Magic marks you. Go and keep an eye on your mother for me."

"Yes, sir," he replied before running in the wrong direction.

"Alex!" he called. "That way." He gestured in the other direction and laughed as Alex made a U-turn.

"Ready to get your head out of your pants and back on your shoulders?" Donakin teased as Mark approached him and Noah.

"At least his gets used. When was the last time you had a woman?" Noah teased.

Mark didn't like the idea of his relationship with Skye being used as a taunting device.

"Last eve, if you must know. I found a nice whore in the village. She's quite good with her tongue," Donakin responded.

They laughed, but Mark rolled his eyes and walked off.

"You've had too much of that political correctness shoved down your throat, Markhem. Learn to let that go. We're back home now," Noah teased.

"Doesn't mean I have to treat women any differently than I have, Noah."

"Does Skye know about all those women you treated right?" Noah asked, causing Donakin to howl.

"I'm sure she does, and if she doesn't, she'll hear it from me and not you. Now get to work and train these men before I demote you both."

Noah grumbled and moved out with Donakin. Mark watched the men train, knowing he'd have to tell Skye eventually, certain she didn't know just how many women he'd slept with over the years in a vain attempt to replace her. Not one even coming close. Most one-night stands that never led to anything more because he'd only wanted more with her.

He ran his hands over his face and focused on his men, clearing away the thoughts of her as he'd conditioned himself to do over the years.

It worked until he heard, "Commander, what's happening?"

He turned to see the green of his uniform pulling away in a mist, a dark gray left in its place. The same was happening to all the other uniforms.

"Skye," he said, then turned toward where he knew she was training in the distance.

"The Mage Warrior." He heard the whisper through the men. There would be no refocusing them now. They were all too curious to see what most had not witnessed in half a century; some never having witnessed it.

"Take a break, everyone!"

His eyes watched as the green of the grass in the field faded to black.

"I don't remember that happening," Noah said, his voice heavy with concern.

Mark met his eyes. "That's not normal?"

"I don't think so."

"Shit," he said, sprinting away, running past the others who, upon seeing him, began to run as well. The green of the forest in the distance began to peel away as he approached the mages. He came to a halt upon seeing Skye in the center of the space, Elspeth and Trent trying to break through to her.

She was glorious. Waves of green swiveled around her, giving her skin a haunting glow. Her eyes were a rainbow of colors with green dominant. They looked far off in the distance, like she was seeing something none of them could. He ran to Alex as the final color seeped from the trees, their tops bending from the strain, a strange crunch echoing around them as it faded. The green made its way to her, swirling around her like a tornado.

"Skye! You need to stop, you're bleeding the color. It's too much!" Trent yelled.

"What's happening to her?" Alex asked.

"I don't know."

"Mark, look." His uncle grabbed his shoulder and pointed to the sky where the blue was now pulling to Skye, leaving an unnatural gray, massive black storm clouds filling its place through the now colorless trees. The hairs stood on his neck as a chorus of feral growls and screams echoed in the distance.

"What is that?" Alex said.

"The shadow realm," Noah replied shakily.

"But that can't be," Mark said, his mind denying what his eyes saw.

Massive claws began to make their way through the tree line.

"Elite to the ready!" he commanded.

"Mages, defend!" Trent yelled, his eyes falling to Mark. "Markhem, stop her!"

Mark knew it was critical. Magic had only just returned to the mages and Elite. Fifty years without it would leave them rusty, the newer ones untrained. So many new ones, the majority of their elders killed in the mage wars by Camin.

"Christ," he mumbled, running closer, the vortex of color that surrounded Skye pushing him back.

"What's happening?" he asked Trent, yelling over the noise, his eyes watching as the remaining brown in his uniform pants and the blue in Skye's cape drifted away.

"I've never seen anything like it. She's bleeding the world of color. We can't break through to her. You might be able to. She needs to feed the color back slowly or who knows what damage she'll bring."

"Jesus, Trent, how am I supposed to do that? You're the one with the magic."

The crack of trees breaking in half caused them both to look back.

"The shadow realm approaches. If she bleeds any more color

from ours, the divide between the realms will fall. You are connected to her now. Stop her."

His heart was pounding. He expected a threat from Camin, but this? The collapse of the divide between worlds? He couldn't comprehend the terror it gave him.

He looked at Skye, a glorious, destructive force. Her eyes were changing; the green dominance had succumbed to blue and was now being overtaken by red.

They were out of time.

He pushed into the vortex of color, forcing his way through as it ripped at his clothes and skin until, finally, he was in the eye of the storm with her.

"Skye."

Nothing.

"Skye!"

There was a slight halt to the swirl of color in her eyes. He grabbed and shook her.

"Skye, you need to stop. You're destroying the world. You need to stop bleeding the colors!"

He didn't know what to do. She wasn't moving. The funnel continued to swirl, a line of brown mingling into the mix.

"Markhem, stop her!" the voice was faint but desperate.

He grabbed her and kissed her, not knowing how else to break her trance and praying he wouldn't be futilely opening his private side to everyone around them, although that seemed to have already happened. Magic tingled over her skin and lips. At first, she remained stiff and resolute, then she softened against him, her lips responding as her tension released. The colors continued to flow around them as she returned his kiss.

"Mark," she said, the color in her eyes morphing to the deep blue he loved.

She looked around.

"Oh my God." The colors froze, a cylinder of hues static and awaiting her command.

"Shh, calm down. I think you need to release the colors now."

"How? It feels like they're attached to me."

A roar echoed across the air.

"What was that?"

"Mark, she needs to release the hues now and you need to get out of there!" Elspeth yelled.

Skye clung to him. "Don't leave me."

"Skye, let him go! You'll kill him, and if you don't release the hues, it will kill all of us!"

Fear filled her eyes.

"You can do this," he said, holding her hands and trying to hide his own fear.

"I don't know how," she responded, her voice quivering.

He wanted to take her from here, to make her safe again, to protect her from this madness.

"Mark!"

"Magic is who you are, Skye. It knows you, even if you don't know it. Trust it. Listen to it. I'll be on the other side, waiting for you."

He pushed his way through the static hues easier than he'd expected, feeling a sear of heat upon his skin as he did so. He glanced to the west, the forest still dark, the terrifying creatures beyond awaiting the last hues to fade.

"Everyone, away and duck!" Elspeth yelled. "We don't know which direction she'll release it, and it will destroy anything in its wake. This kind of power is cataclysmic." She said the last sentence under her breath, but Mark caught it.

He remained where he was. He'd promised her he'd be right beside her. The ground quaked, the world quieting. Then the colors pulled into her, her eyes blazing like a phoenix, her skin a blending golden hue.

His body hit the ground with stunning force as a body tackled him. He pushed Noah from him in irritation, then rolled quickly to rise but Noah demanded he stay down.

"Stay here, you idiot!"

Just as he said it, Skye released the colors. The deafening sound of rushing wind filled the air as a massive force of color flew from her body. It careened into the forests beyond, some hues escaping backward, sending part of the castle crumbling away to dust. The rest hit the forest, lighting it up in a brilliant blaze as squeals and cries from the shadow realm fled. When the light faded, the forest was nothing but a pile of ash—the colors all settling back to the remaining world.

Mark turned to see Skye's knees buckle, her body collapsing. Moving quickly, he caught her before she hit the ground.

Trent and Elspeth rushed over with Petrian and Alex, but Noah grabbed Alex to hold him back.

"What the hell was that?" Mark asked through gritted teeth. "I thought you were training her."

"We were. She's... I've never seen anything like that."

He brushed his fingers along her face. She was so still he worried she wasn't breathing until he saw the gentle movement of her chest.

Elspeth was staring at her, fear in her eyes as Trent hovered over them wringing his hands.

"What are you not telling me?"

She tentatively touched Skye's hand, her own shaking. In the background he heard Donakin directing the others away. Whatever was wrong was not for prying ears.

"She's unlike any Mage Warrior I've seen."

"Why?" He tried to think back to what he knew, but he'd been so young.

"She bled the colors."

"Isn't that what they do?"

"In a way," Elspeth answered. "But they only take some of the hue—that's all they're able to take. The color fades like it's been in the sunlight too long. No one bleeds the color completely. It's not possible."

"But she did."

"Yes, and in doing so, she weakened the barrier that divides the worlds. No one has that power, not even Camin."

"Then that's a good thing, right?" he asked, afraid to hear her answer.

Her eyes were sad. "If she can't learn to control it, then no."

"What will happen if she doesn't?"

"The veil between the worlds will collapse and the shadow realm will overtake us."

"What's the shadow realm?" Alex asked.

"The world of the Death God and his shadow gods, our version of hell."

SKYE

Skye's head was throbbing. She rolled over with a groan, slowly forcing her eyes open. She heard the crackle of the fire as her eyes adjusted to the dim lighting of a room. Blinking, she saw that she was back in her parents' room. How had she gotten here?

She pulled herself up, a light blanket slipping from her shoulders.

"Whoa, don't get up too quickly," Mark said, rushing from a chair across the room.

"What happened? How did I get here?"

"I carried you here after you nearly collapsed the veil between worlds."

"I did what?" Memories of color formed—colors that had wrapped around her like a warm blanket as they intensified until they had overtaken her consciousness. She remembered him there in the storm, the stable force. Her protector. The rest was gone.

"Here." He propped some pillows behind her. "Your moth— I mean, Elspeth brought some food up for you since you missed dinner. I can't guarantee it's warm, but it's good."

"It's okay, you can call her my mother. She raised me. And she's the only mother I know."

He brought a wooden tray over, and her stomach rumbled. At the sound, she placed a hand over her rebelling stomach. It seemed like ages since she'd eaten anything. As she dipped the homemade bread into what looked like a rich stew, she asked, "What happened, Mark?"

"No one really knows. In fact, even Trent is bewildered and scared."

"Of me?" she asked, savoring the taste of homemade food.

"Of what you can do."

"I did what they told me to do. I opened myself up and called the colors to me."

"Well, that's apparently where the issue lies."

She gave him a questioning look and pushed the tray aside.

"You're not hungry?"

"Don't change the subject, Mark."

He took the tray away, then came to sit next to her, reaching a hand up and brushing it through her hair. Someone had undone her braids and waves now hung in the strands.

"You're not like any Mage Warrior they've seen before."

"Go on."

"You're terrifyingly powerful. You bleed color from every-thing rather than dimming it."

"I don't understand."

"They had to explain it to me as well. Color is your power. It fortifies you, like the words of a spell. Mage Warriors pull color forth to wield it like a weapon, then it returns to its source, its original host still holding its imprint. They draw one color at a time, the strongest mages sometimes can draw a few colors. We didn't realize it at the time, but when you brought us home, you summoned every color. And you don't just take the brilliance of it, you take its essence, leaving nothing but a shadow."

"And that's bad?"

"Apparently. Only the shadow realm survives in a such a state —colorless and bland."

"Shadow realm?"

"Let's see. How do I explain this?"

He brushed his hand over his face, and Skye could see the nerves. What had she done to make him so nervous?

"Like the human world, we have a heaven and hell equivalent."

"Wait, they're real?"

"Shh. Listen. The radiant gods dwell in the upper realm and are led by the Upper God. Bright and colorful, awaiting the souls of the people. The Death God and his shadow gods dwell in the shadow realm. There is a pocket in between the living realm and the shadow realm where our souls are given passage to either realm, depending on how we are judged. The goddess of shadows, the Death God's mistress, guides the souls that are judged as deserving to the upper realm. Those deemed unworthy are left with the Death God."

"It sounds like Greek mythology to me."

"Every culture has its version. In the human world, it's all conjecture. Here it's real. Beyond the shadow realm lie the other realms. Like the human world, they are each protected by their heaven and hell, the gatekeepers between the worlds on either side. The veil between the realms must never be broken."

A chill ran through her. "What happens if it is?"

"Chaos. If the divide that separates the shadow realm, the veil, falls, the land of the dead, demons, and other things that haunt your nightmares run loose among the living."

"That's horrifying. Is it possible to continue breaking the veil?"

"No one knows. It's never been a possibility until now."

"So, in theory, I could release hell on earth, then collapse world upon world, destroying us all?"

"Christ, when you put it that way, it's even more terrifying."

"Wow, you're great at assuaging my fears."

"Sorry, it's just...well, seeing you like that was scary. You had no idea what was happening as the shadow realm barreled down upon us."

She looked down at her hands. "I don't remember doing that," she whispered.

He took her hand, and she welcomed the assurance of his touch.

"What do I do, Mark?"

A knock at the door halted the response he was still trying to find.

"Come in."

Alex's face peered around the door.

"Mom! You're alive!"

"Of course, I'm alive." She gave him a big hug as he jumped on the bed to reach her.

"You've got the sweetest room. This thing is great compared to mine."

"Only Mage Warriors get royal treatment," Mark said.

"No one else?"

"Well, commander of the Elite does, and I'd wager Trent has a pretty big room as head of the full mages."

"Huh, something to strive for."

They laughed, then chatted for a while. Alex asked a ton of questions that Mark obliged until Skye emitted one too many yawns, and Mark ordered him to let her rest. She had no idea how late it was, but her eyes were heavy.

"He's okay, right?" she asked as Mark made his way back to sit beside her.

"He's fine. He adapts quickly, and your father has him next door to him."

"Isn't my father with my mother?"

"Facades, Skye. It was all facades."

"They're not really a couple? Not married?"

"No, just friends doing their job."

"Ugh, is there any part of my life that was real?"

"I'm real."

"Not completely," she pouted, remembering back to the years of yearning.

"My love for you has always been real, Skye."

His words lifted the tension from her body, and suddenly, everything else fell away.

"I know."

"You should get some rest."

"I'm not tired anymore."

He arched his brow, a sly grin forming.

"What would you like to do? There's a chess set in the cabinet."

"Help me out of his contraption," she said, gesturing to the shirt she still wore.

"I don't think that's going to help your chess game."

"I guarantee it won't."

He drew closer, and she raised her arms as he removed the shirt, slowly undoing the straps before lifting it above her head. Tossing it to the side, he let his hand drift along her breasts, sending tingles through her body. He pulled the pillows out from behind her and brought his lips to hers as she drifted back, clutching his arms.

His lips made their way down her neck to her nipples where he teased them until she was moaning with pleasure, then he let his tongue wander along her stomach, his hands pulling her free from her pants as his mouth kissed every inch of her leg. When the pants fell, he brought his lips back, his fingers drawing a line along her thigh until he reached her underwear, which he slowly removed with his teeth.

Skye giggled and squirmed in anticipation, watching him remove his shirt, his eyes never leaving hers. He rubbed his hand up the inside of her leg until he found the spot that sent her wriggling, his mouth finding it, his breath warm against it. Waves of arousal careened through her as his tongue did things she'd only read about in the erotica books she sometimes found guilty pleasure in.

Just as she thought she could take it no more, his mouth made its way back to her stomach, her body aching for him. She pushed at his pants, and with his help, freed him quickly. The oncoming orgasm hung on the cusp within her as his tongue traced her nipples before he finally obliged her tugging hands and penetrated her.

A pleasured cry escaped her, his mouth meeting hers to smother it. With every move, the wave within her grew until it crested and crashed down upon her in ripple after ripple that sent her clinging to him tightly.

As she descended from her height of pleasure, he continued to move within her—the feeling doing nothing to calm her quakes. He pulled her leg back up, holding it as he drove deeper, a grunt escaping him. Her senses returning, she drew him down for a kiss, her tongue exploring his mouth, dancing with his. She let her hands wander along his body, taking in every inch of defined muscle that lay upon him. A confused look crossed face as she pushed him back and flipped him.

"Mmm, that's unexpected," he mumbled, kissing her.

"I think you'll find there's quite a bit unexpected about me," she replied, nibbling his lip. She let her hands drift along his chest as he gripped her hips, thrusting his pelvis to meet the motion of her body. She lifted herself, a move that elicited a sad moan from him until her mouth traced the contours of his stomach. Her breasts ran along the swollen part of him that she knew longed for release before her mouth found it, licking the taste of her from him. His groan threatened to take her over the edge again, her thighs twitching at the sound. She lowered her mouth over him, the feel of him reminding her how much she'd longed to spend her nights tasting him and feeling him inside of her.

She moved lower on his shaft, wrapping her hand around his base as his hands pushed gently on her head, fingers entwined in her hair. Her mouth brought him closer to the edge until she could feel he was ready. Tracing his length with her tongue, she lifted her mouth from him.

"You're killing me, Skye," he groaned.

She came back up and licked his nipple, then his neck. Before she could position herself over him, his hands gripped her arms roughly and he flipped her to her back, entering her in one powerful thrust that caused her back to arch at the intensity. His mouth found hers, his kiss hard and demanding, the ferocity of it increasing when she brought her legs up and around him, forcing him deeper. His rhythm quickened and for one intense moment they were one—her breaths matching his, her hips harmonizing with his. The intensity brought her to her peak again as he finally released, her own climax joining his. She held on to him through the storm of sensation that was flooding her, losing herself to it and not wanting it to pass.

Eventually, his body stilled, Skye's remaining pleasure rippling through her as her muscles slowly relaxed with his. He dropped his head to her neck and collapsed on top of her, his lingering breathlessness sending a shiver of desire through her.

He rolled from her body, and they laid together, catching their breaths.

After several minutes, she heard him whisper, "Is that what I missed all those years? God, is that what you were doing with Sam all the time? I shouldn't be jealous, but damn, I really am."

"Don't make yourself out to be the innocent one. How many women did you have to sleep with to be so good at doing that?" She pointed to his mouth.

"Kissing you?" he said with a playful wink.

"You know what I mean." She turned to her side to look at him, his eyes focused only on her breasts until she brought his chin up.

"Sorry, can't help it." He turned to face her and traced the curve of them. "I've imagined them for so many years I can't help but stare."

"And you're changing the subject."

"Perhaps. But do you really want to know how many women I've slept with? How many men have you slept with?"

"Not as many as you."

A guilty look overtook his features.

"Let's not talk about this anymore."

"Mark. It won't bother me."

"I don't know, Skye. I really don't. You were married. I had needs, too, and there were plenty of willing women. None lasted though, you know that. Most were one-night stands, and when they didn't replace you or remove my need for you, I took them home. There were a few who were repeats, a way for me to get some consistent pleasure. I am a man after all. I have needs, and you weren't available to satisfy them. I never claimed to be a saint."

"I knew you had others, but I can't say I ever liked that you were such a playboy."

"Ha, far from it."

"We both have a past that was forced on us. I suppose I should be thankful for your past. Those women clearly taught you a few things."

"Now, why do you assume I didn't naturally know what I was doing? You just assume I wasn't already good in bed?"

She laughed as he pulled her closer, leaning his forehead against hers.

"I love you, Mark. I don't ever want to be separated from you again. Promise me that."

"I promise you." He brushed her hair back, tucking it behind her ear. "When this is over and Camin is defeated, marry me, Skye."

Her heart fluttered so hard she wondered if he felt it. "Yes, definitely."

He kissed her deeply, his love for her coming through in that one small move. They made love again and she drifted to sleep entangled in his protective arms.

SKYE WAS BLINDED with vibrant colors. She squinted against them, raising her hands to shield her eyes, but her hands kept getting tangled in a weblike consistency. She drew her eyes down to look at them—layers of color encased them. She tried shaking them free but with each move the colors themselves reverberated, hurting her eyes more.

"What the hell?" she mumbled. "I don't want this. I miss my grays and blues, my dull shadows."

She pulled at the webbing, pulling and pulling until the light began to fade, the webbing falling away. As the final glow of color disappeared, the world became imbued in the familiar dullness she'd missed.

She breathed a sigh of relief, her eyes adjusting to the cool world around her, the blues and grays that had colored her life. A calm settled over her and she began to walk, wondering where she was, the terrain unfamiliar. It felt like she was walking nowhere but somewhere at the same time. Emptiness surrounded her.

Stopping, she looked around. What was she supposed to be doing? Why was she here? She continued further until the world began to blur. Looking back, she found her vision clear, but looking forward blurred. Raising her hand, she touched a barrier of sorts, pliable yet unbreakable. The blue below her hand cleared, and she saw color again, muted below the strange barrier, but visible to her. She could feel it calling to her power.

The room she viewed looked familiar, then she realized it was the front room of her house. Broken glass lay upon the floor, and the front door was nowhere to be seen. Snow had drifted in, covering the floor. She drew her hand back, fear passing through her. With the fear came the sensation that she wasn't alone.

She turned but saw nothing in the shadows. Her heart continued to pound, and she walked slowly back toward where she had come from.

The landscape changed, the open space feeling suddenly claustrophobic as it lifted to form hills and trees. A growl echoed, and in the distance, she heard a screech. That's when she detected the undercurrent of noise—constant, desperate screams that sliced at her soul.

She ran, but someone stepped in front of her. Her eyes, used to living in the darkened world, noted his blonde hair, the hue lighter in the dim colors that surrounded him. His eyes looked gray, but she couldn't tell distinctly if that was their real color or her sight. He was tall, and as he moved closer to her, he towered over her. She wasn't petite, and at five feet ten inches, she held her own with most men, but this man seemed massive, taller than even Mark's six two frame.

She stepped back, but he grabbed her, his hands hot against her skin. She tried to call her power, but with no color, she didn't know how. A strange smirk took over his lips. He lifted one hand and for a moment she thought he would let her go. Instead, he roughly shoved her hair back, his finger grazing her birthmark, leaving a lingering tingle.

"Mage Warrior. You've wandered far."

"Camin," she whispered, her voice shaking.

"My reputation precedes me. Now what to do with a helpless Mage Warrior?" His hand ran along her cheek, and she pulled back, but he grabbed her face before she could break free. "You shouldn't be here, and now you've left me in quite the predicament."

She struggled, and he let her face go, but his grip on her arm tightened as he pulled her closer.

"What should I do with the weak Mage Warrior who wandered into the shadow realm?"

"The shadow realm?"

He laughed. Then his face turned serious. "You can traverse the shadow realm. No one but I can do that. So, it would seem you are powerful after all. Pity, you're still so weak. Unaware of your full potential and vulnerable. Shame, you would have been a challenge to fight, unlike the rest of your lot."

"Skye!"

Camin looked up from her at the sound of Mark's voice.

"Skye!" She heard him again.

"What are you?" Camin asked.

"I don't know."

His eyes gleamed. The screams rose around her, a cacophony of sound that drowned Mark's voice out. "No one walks the shadow realm but the dead."

"You do."

He let out a cruel laugh. "I lost my soul long ago. I have nothing left to offer this realm that the Death God does not already have. You, however, have everything."

A growl sounded from behind her.

"I think I'll watch as they tear you apart, then perhaps I'll hunt down the owner of that voice and kill him, too."

"No!"

"And there's a son, isn't there?"

Her fear turned to anger, and she reached for her power again, seeing his eyes move to her birthmark. She could see the light from it in the darkness.

"Foolish child, Mage Warriors can't wield in the shadows."

She sensed the connection to something and reached for it; the hues flowing to her, the dull blues of this world encircling her, causing Camin to jump back and release her. His face wore an expression of shock and astonishment.

"I don't think I'm an ordinary Mage Warrior," she said, throwing him back with her power.

She listened for Mark's voice, the screams receding.

"Skye, wake up!"

Air filled her lungs, and she opened her eyes, the dark of the room surrounding her, flickers of orange and yellow from the fire casting a welcome glow that reassured her she was safe.

Mark breathed a sigh of relief and searched her eyes.

"What the hell was that?" he asked. "I couldn't wake you and the colors...they were swirling around like a storm. And then, this." He gently touched her arm where an ugly black bruise had formed in the same place Camin's hand had been.

"Camin. He's almost here. He walks the shadow realm, and he's coming for me."

MARK

N o one walks the shadow realm," the king said, pacing the room.

Trent was standing in the corner, his brows knitted in concern. Elspeth sat in a chair with her head in her hands. Mark had summoned them as soon as Skye had woken.

There had been a moment where he'd feared she wouldn't wake, feared he'd lost her. He'd watched helplessly as she'd tensed, her movements having woken him. The bruise had formed then, deep and vicious, a distinct handprint gripping her somewhere beyond his reach. When she'd finally woken, all he'd wanted to do was hold her close, but then she'd spoken those words, and he knew they needed to act quickly.

How had a night that had been the most pleasurable of his life turned into this nightmare? She'd been amazing, bringing him an ecstasy he'd only ever imagined. Only ever imagining with her. It had been too good to be true, reality returning to shred the images of her body on his, the feel of her touches, the persuasion of her mouth, the taste of her. All of it now lost to the fear that pummeled him—the threat that he could lose her again..

"We've always suspected Camin had the power, that that's

where he'd run to," Trent said, bringing him back. Mark was thankful the room was dimly lit, and the darkness hid the sudden swelling in his pants.

Focus, Mark.

"But it was just a dream," Skye muttered.

Mark was standing behind the chair he'd seated her in and lifted her arm, pushing the sleeve of the light gown up to reveal the bruise.

"This doesn't happen in dreams, Skye. You were there with him. I don't know how, but you were."

She looked at him, her blue eyes rich in the lighting. She looked beautiful and fragile in that moment as the flickers from the fire played upon her hair. The light pink of the dress she'd donned deepened the brown highlights in it. He dropped her arm, letting his fingers trace the material, his eyes lingering on the swell of her breasts. It would have been a romantic moment, save for the impending threat of death that sat upon them.

"Haven't you two gotten that out of your systems yet?" Noah asked.

"Why did I wake you again?"

"Because you need my expertise. Although, to be honest, I don't know that any of us are of help in this matter."

"Mark pulled me out. It was his voice that freed me from the dream."

"How did you escape Camin? Mark's voice pulled you from the dream, but did it pull you from Camin's clutches?" Elspeth asked, finally lifting her head.

"Well, no. Not exactly. I used the color, extended it, and forced him back."

"There's no color in the shadow realm," the king said. "It was part of the shadow gods' strife that they live in the shadows of life."

"There are shades of color, and I summoned the blues."

"That's impossible. Mage Warriors can't summon in the shadows or in shade—it's their only weakness."

"But I did pull the shaded hues. I brought them to me and pushed him away."

Elspeth and Trent looked at each other.

"She is beyond what we know of the Mage Warriors, Elspeth. We can't train what we don't understand," Trent said.

"Wait, you're giving up on training me?"

Mark heard the fear in her voice. Trent was right, full mages had no right training a Mage Warrior. Distinctly different schools of magic guided them.

"They can't train what they don't know, Skye," he answered for them.

"Our power lies in the physical, in the spells. Mage Warriors draw power from the metaphysical, from something we can't even begin to comprehend. That's why they are so rare. They were secretive, they trained separately, even lived separate from the other mages. You need a Mage Warrior, not a full mage."

"But there are no other Mage Warriors," Skye said. "They're all dead."

"They are..." Mark started, his mind grabbing hold of a thought, "but maybe their secrets aren't."

He turned to Noah. "Go wake my uncle and bring him here."

Noah shot him a dirty look. "I'm your lackey now?"

"No, but your commander has given you a direct order. Are you refusing to obey?"

Noah grumbled and huffed out of the room.

"I fail to see how Petrian can assist in the matter," Theodore said.

Mark had to remind himself that he and the others in the room were in the unique position to address their king as Theodore, a privilege only a rare few were given and one that did not extend beyond closed doors.

"I agree. And who is Petrian? Is he really your uncle?" Skye asked, looking up at him.

"Yes, he's my mother's brother. My mother and yours were inseparable, and so were our fathers."

"That's true. Your mother and I were friends, but she and Alina were like sisters. The Elite and the Mage Warriors had a bond that pulled them to one another," Elspeth said.

"I thought they were combustible? Like oil and water?"

"Oh, they could be, especially as couples, but they were also bonded tightly. They were too close not to be. The sole purpose of the Elite is to fight beside and for the Mage Warrior, the relationship is one that only death breaks. The force of the Elite is tied to the strength of the Mage Warrior, and they will fight to the death to protect their warriors. They train together and practically live together—their wings are attached for that reason.

"The ferocity of the Elite and the Mage Warriors is what usually makes them incompatible as mates, with only rare exceptions. Same with Elites mating with Elites. Their personalities are too similar, the fire within them too strong."

Skye rose and stretched, her move emphasizing her curves below the soft material of the dress. His mind wandered to the skin below, aching to lift the dress and bend her over.

"That's why when they do mate, it forms such a powerful bond. The magic of the Mage Warrior enhancing the Elite mate, intertwining around the connection so that they are unbreakable," Trent said.

Mark drew his eyes from her body and met Trent's. Trent shook his head as if he'd read his thoughts. "It's a wonder they managed to keep you two apart for this long."

"Trust me, it wasn't easy," Elspeth answered sourly.

Mark had the urge to strangle her but resisted.

"So, what does Petrian offer?" Theodore asked.

"Yeah, I'm confused on that part, too," Skye added.

"My mother and yours were friends from the time they were

children, our fathers joining that friendship. The four of them did everything together. I can barely remember a time when your parents were not with them. Petrian is my mother's older brother. He was part of it by default. He was very protective of my mother, almost to a fault. In fact, I was surprised to find he hadn't died on the battlefield with her. If anyone knows the secrets of the Mage Warriors, it might be him."

"It's worth the chance," Elspeth said. "He's right. In fact, Mark, it was your mother whom Lyra asked to go with you first. She refused, too loyal to the kingdom, to her duties as an Elite, and to her Mage Warriors. She wanted to die proud like your father, fighting to protect Lyra."

"So, she asked you instead? But I thought you were her closest friend? Why don't you know the secrets?" Skye asked.

"Ah, she was *my* closest friend, but I could never come between the sisterhood she shared with Mark's mother. They were best friends, and I was fine with that. Lyra let me into a lot more of her life than any full mage could expect, but I was not privy to the inner workings of their power, or even their group. You see, we group mages in classes, and it's within those classes that we live. We do not share our secrets with those outside."

"Mages have a class system?"

"Oh, yes," Theodore answered. "It's very strict and rarely do they venture outside their houses unless it's for official reasons."

"God, this is so confusing."

"And not pertinent to the matter at hand," Mark said just as the doors opened and Noah walked in with Petrian.

Petrian bowed to the king, and then to Skye, who seemed appalled by the move.

"Why does everyone keep doing that?" she asked.

"Because, my dear, you are royalty as high as the king himself," Petrian said, going to her and taking her hand, then bowing and adding a kiss to it. "My lady Skye, it is an honor to once again be in the presence of a Mage Warrior. Your carry the beauty of your mother, but your eyes hold a piece of your father."

Skye appeared speechless, and Mark couldn't help but chuckle at her first reaction to his suave uncle.

"Markhem, to what do I owe the honor of being in such esteemed company?"

"Always one for formalities, Uncle."

"Always. Just because I am a brute on the battlefield does not mean I cannot be a gentleman off of it."

"Does that work on the women?" Noah teased.

Petrian gave him a wink. "Guaranteed."

"Uncle, you were close to my parents and, by default, to Skye's. Is there anything you can tell us about the Mage Warriors and their ways?"

Petrian studied him for a moment.

"We need your help. My powers aren't normal, and no one understands them. Only another Mage Warrior would," Skye said, finding her words.

"Yes, they are very special. Your mother was the strongest in her line, but what you did yesterday is beyond anything she ever did. You want to know my secrets? Ones shared with me in confidence by your mother?"

She nodded, and he gave her a gentle smile.

"I must insist then that everyone, but you and the Elite, leave us."

"Leave you?" Theodore asked.

"Yes, your highness. Forgive me for the imposition, but there are some things that are shared only between Mage Warriors and Elite. They are secrets we are sworn to protect."

"So, there is more to them than we see."

"Yes, your majesty."

"Very well. If it will help her master her powers, then so be it. Elspeth, Trent."

There was something in the way Theodore glanced at Skye

that gave Mark pause. He wasn't certain if it was the fact that she was the reason he was being asked to leave the room, or something more. The look was laced with hesitation, and Mark guessed it had more to do with what had happened in her dream. The abilities she'd described. He kept his eyes on Theodore as the three of them left, unsure why an unsettled feeling had come over him.

When the door shut, Mark looked questioningly at his uncle, his mind drawn from the king to the mysterious request to clear the room.

"When the battle ended, our numbers were few, so we prayed we could go on. The losses were devastating."

He took Skye's hand, and Mark saw the tears in his eyes.

"The Mage Warriors were gone, our friends, our family. My sister." He dropped his head. "I lived for Alina. She was the light in my life, the joy, and Camin stole her from me." He looked back at Mark. "I wanted to die that day beside her. Thought I would." He removed his hand from Skye's and lifted his shirt to reveal a wicked scar that ran from his shoulder to his sternum. Skye let out a cry, drawing her hand to her mouth.

"I did not die that day, and now that the two of you are home, I thank the gods that I did not. You are the future we fought for that day."

He pulled himself together, the Elite strength taking over the humble man. "Now, you want to know the secrets of your mother and those who walked with her and before her?"

"Yes, please."

"Markhem, is Noahem your second in rank?"

Mark looked at Noah. "I hadn't really thought about it."

"Decide now. Donakin or Noahem."

Mark thought about who he wanted by his side as Noah crossed his arms.

"Donakin will be crushed," he said.

"Donakin was always third in rank. It was your father, Skye's father, then Donakin," Noah said.

"Damn. Yes, Noah is my second. I trust him with my life."

"Good, because he is your back. When you fight, he fights, as you die, he dies. Just as it was with your father and Skye's."

"Let's keep the dying off the table for now," Mark said. "Why does it matter?"

"Because what I'm about to show you is privy only to the top two Elite and the Mage Warriors. There were perks to being close to a sister who was best friends with the leader of the Mage Warriors—Lyra made exceptions for both of us." He winked at them, then headed out of the room. "Follow me."

Noah looked at Mark with the same confused look he was sure his own face held.

"Aren't we following?" Skye said, taking his hand. The feel of her fingers intertwining through his grounded him.

"I suspect so," Noah said, trailing after Petrian.

"Do you have any idea what he's talking about?" Skye asked as they followed.

"None," he responded, squeezing her hand tight.

"Good, I thought it was just me."

They followed Petrian through the halls of the castle, winding their way around until they reached the divide to the Mage Warrior hall where Skye's tower room and the Elite wing lie. The two were separate but connected.

Petrian stopped in front of the closet sized wall that divided the two routes.

"Did you lose your way, Petrian?" Noah asked.

"Not at all, but I can't lead us any further. Only Skye can."

"Oh, okay. Which direction do we need to go?"

"Here," he said, tapping the wall.

"That's solid stone, Uncle. What are you playing at?"

"Not a thing. Observe." He motioned for Skye to move forward, then said, "Pardon the intrusion," and brushed her hair back where it covered her birthmark.

"Now move closer and turn your neck."

She looked back and mouthed. *Is he crazy?*

Mark was tempted to think so. He hadn't seen his uncle in fifty years. Had the toll of the war and his losses gotten to him, pushed him over the edge? Was he a threat to Skye at all?

As Petrian went to touch her birthmark, the protector in him surfaced. He snatched Petrian's hand, Noah tensing next to him, and shoved him against the wall. If his uncle was a threat to Skye, he would not hesitate to kill him.

SKYE

Skye watched in shock as Mark attacked his uncle. Part of her was in awe at his strength, noting the clenched muscles, the sudden wash of testosterone that filled the air. It turned her on, but she shook the feeling off, noting how her own power seemed to be drawn to it as if his fighter tendencies called to her own warrior magic—the two in sync. She was a sudden mix of tingling magic, fear, and pleasure.

Noah tensed with him. Petrian's demeanor changed, the gentleman morphing to a soldier ready for battle. This was a glimpse into the true nature of the Elite, why Elspeth had said they were volatile.

"You think I would hurt her, nephew?" Petrian growled, fighting against Mark's grip.

"You give me cause to wonder," he returned through clenched teeth.

"Keep your overprotectiveness in check and save it for someone worthy of it. I would never threaten a Mage Warrior, particularly not your mate. Remember who we are, Markhem. She is a part of all of us. The Elite and the Mage Warrior cannot be without each other, not to our full potential. Trust me, I mean her no harm."

Mark relaxed, releasing his grip on his uncle, and Noah stood down.

Petrian rubbed his arm.

"That's quite a grip you have. I see they trained you well while you were away." He turned back to Skye. "Since your mate may attack me again if I touch you, please lift your hair, then move your birthmark closer to the wall."

She looked at Mark, who nodded. He had relaxed, but she noted the taut muscles and the protector stance he still held. He was her protector, and it made her feel safe knowing he was there, watching out for her as he always had.

She complied with Petrian's request, lifting her hair, her eyes still on Mark's. She noticed the subtle flare of desire in them as a few loose locks fell from her fingers, his eyes trailing them down her exposed neck. Turning back to the wall, she situated her neck so that her birthmark faced it. At first nothing happened, but then there was a warm sensation followed by a tingling where her birthmark was. A sparkle of violet reflected across the wall, and she heard a creaking sound.

Petrian motioned for her to stand back and upon doing so, she bumped into Mark, whose arms wrapped around her waist, his other hand taking hers and pulling it so that her hair cascaded down her neck and shoulders. He drew his fingers through her hair, and if not for the sight before her, she would have been completely overcome by the feel of it.

"Holy shit," he mumbled.

The creaks continued, and the piece of wall grew, spreading to form a doorway that sprung open. Petrian put his arm out to gesture them forward. "Welcome to the warrior's lair."

Mark went to move in front of her, to be the first through, keeping her safety his only priority.

She stopped him.

"I think I'm meant to enter first, aren't I?"

She looked to Petrian who nodded.

She took Mark's hand and stepped through. With each step, a sconce came to life, lighting a room that was large yet cozy. She marveled at it, hearing the creak again as the magic hid the room once the others came through, like it knew how many were with her.

Her eyes took it in—a combination of a lounge and study, a large table in the center, books that lined the walls, soft velvet chairs to the side. She could feel the history of it, the power that had once been here, the presence of the Mage Warriors who had once called this home. Her mother had been here, likely laughing and enjoying moments that perhaps she couldn't show outside of these walls, a side of her that wasn't the warrior she was expected to be.

"They met here?" she asked.

"Yes, this was their sanctuary, a space away from the politics and the expectations that lie on the shoulders of both Mage Warriors and the top-ranking Elites. I was told that the room connects to the sanctuary within each kingdom, a meeting room of sorts for every warrior. You see, there weren't many of them, perhaps two, maybe three in each kingdom. There was a fellowship between them all."

"Did the other Elite know? The opening is right in the middle of the wings," Mark asked.

"Some, but they understood it was to be left alone, the secret guarded from the other mage ranks and even the king himself. It's been that way through the ages."

"Amazing," Noah said softly, clearly as stunned as she was. "I had no idea. Why didn't I know about this?"

"Not every Elite was privy to it. Only those who were fortunate enough to see it open to a warrior. Those who did stumble across its opening were bound to secrecy, so it was not common knowledge, but it was known by a few."

"It's as if it was waiting for me." She ran her finger along the table. "There's no dust, no spider webs."

"It's an enchanted room. I imagine that's part of the enchantment. No servants were granted access, and no Mage Warrior I've had the pleasure of knowing liked to clean."

She couldn't help but laugh. "So that explains it."

"That's what you're going to blame your lack of dusting skills on?" Mark teased.

She shot him a playful look. "Petrian, what do you expect me to find here?"

"The secrets to your power. If they're anywhere, they're in here, in one of these books, perhaps."

Noah pulled a book from a shelf. "This is going to be tedious, like searching for a needle in a haystack."

"Well, there are four of us. Grab some books and let's see what we can find," Petrian replied.

FOR WHAT SEEMED LIKE HOURS, they poured through books, each throwing out random facts as they did, none of those facts providing answers. Skye's head was beginning to hurt from information overload. She lifted her eyes from the book and rubbed her temples. Mark rose to stretch, grumbling about needing coffee and feeling like he was back in college.

"Mmm, coffee would be really good about now," Skye agreed. "Too bad there are no Keurigs hidden in here."

"What's a Keurig and what's coffee?" Petrian asked.

Mark went on to explain the wonders of coffee and brewing, while she and Noah continued the search.

"Here," Noah said suddenly. "I think I've found something."

They went silent, all turning toward him.

"'It is thought that the most powerful of the Mage Warriors can bridge the realms. Several have come close, one even speaking of dreams in which the demons from the shadow realm plagued him. He emerged from his sleep with scratch-like markings down his chest, his bed clothes torn and bloody. The only ones to ever state this terrifying ability hail from Eliam's line.'"

"Eliam?" Petrian asked.

"That's what it says." Noah's voice held a strange edge to it.

Skye felt tension settle in the air. Mark's face was etched with the same concern she observed from Noah and Petrian, all given insight as to who the person was—all but Skye.

"Who is Eliam?" she asked, not sure she wanted to know.

"He was the first Mage Warrior, your ancestor. Your line is the only one that comes directly from him. He bore a son, and he, too, held the gift, as did every one of his descendants. Upon his twentieth year, more Mage Warriors were called by the gods, their powers appearing. And so, it has been since the beginning of your line. Only one each generation is born a Mage Warrior, their birthmarks appearing and shimmering at their birth, the others are all called, their birthmarks appearing as the power manifests in childhood. No one has been called since the last warrior was killed."

She swallowed loudly; the revelation holding a pressure that her line needed to continue with her, that another child would need to be born since Alex was only a full mage. The thought was followed by a terror that what she'd experienced in the shadow realm could have been worse. She rubbed the bruise on her arm. Could Camin have killed her? Mark waking to find her dead body next to his? It made her fear sleeping.

"Does it say anything about being able to control it?"

Noah flipped through a few more pages. "No, nothing."

"Damn," Mark muttered.

Skye rubbed her arms, a sudden chill coming over her.

"I think it's time for a break. It must be well into morning by now. Mark, I'm sure the other Elite are looking for their commander," Petrian said.

"Donakin can lead them through drills."

"They need their commander, especially since you are new. You need to assert your dominance before there is confusion."

"Go," Skye said. "He's right. You need to go. I want to stay here. I'm missing something. I can feel it."

"I'm not going to argue," Noah said, rising with a stretch. "This book stuff is tedious. I'm ready to go work out."

"Come along, Markhem," Petrian said, coming up to him and placing a hand on his shoulder.

"I'll be there in a minute. You two go, I'll catch up."

"Don't distract her," Petrian said with a wink.

He and Noah walked back to where the door had been.

"How do we get out of here?" Noah asked.

"You walk out. Follow me."

They disappeared through the wall, and Skye's mouth dropped.

"This is some crazy shit, Skye," Mark said, rubbing his eyes.

"I feel like I'm in a *Harry Potter* movie."

He laughed. "But with adults and not kids?"

"Something like that."

He pulled her from her seat and brushed her hair back from her face.

"I don't know how I feel about leaving you here, Skye."

"I'll be fine. It's a sanctuary, right?"

He pressed his forehead against hers. "Maybe."

"Are you worried about me being here by myself or me not being by your side?"

"Both."

His lips trailed her hairline, making their way to her mouth and kissing her. She gave into it, letting all else fall away but the feel of his hand in her hair, his body against hers, his arm pulling her in flush against him. Her heart pounded in a matching rhythm to his. She was lost to him and knew if they weren't in such a sacred place, she would have given herself over to him again. The temptation of that pleasure begging for her to do so.

She drew her lips from his, bringing her fingers up to trace his face, memorizing each definition of it: the strong jawline, the firm, thick cheekbones, the square chin, soft lips.

"I love you, Skye. I held it in so long that I never realized how deeply I loved you."

The pressure of tears built behind her eyes. Placing her hand on his cheek, she reached up to kiss him once more.

"I love you, Mark, and finally saying it feels so good that I will keep saying it over and over to make up for all the times I kept those words to myself, locked away."

He brought her closer, his arms wrapping around her. As she rested her head against his chest, she felt safe, tucked within his protective embrace. The muscles she knew would kill for her. She snuggled in closer, breathing him in, wanting to stay safe in his arms forever.

He kissed her hair, then released her, the move leaving her with a sudden sense of loss.

"I should go. If I don't, I won't be able to make myself leave."

She nodded, rubbing her arms against the loss of his touch.

"Don't stay here too long, Skye."

"I'll try not to, but I don't know what I'll find."

"Be careful. I have no way to get to you." He backed his way to the doorway. "This goes against everything in my nature."

She gave him a small smile. "I know. You are my knight in shining armor, waiting to rescue me, aren't you?"

"Something like that," he replied before giving her one last desperate glance then walking through the magical doorway, disappearing.

A sudden loneliness, an emptiness, overcame her with his absence, and she stared at the space where he'd been. She'd loved him silently for so long that now that she had him, and he was finally hers, she didn't want to let him go.

Hesitantly, she drew her eyes from the doorway and looked back at the room. It was spacious yet comforting, and she imagined the memories it held of her mother and father spending time with their friends, laughing freely with Mark's parents.

What had they looked like? Sounded like? What things had they laughed at? Had her parents been as enraptured with each other as she and Mark were?

She wondered about the past she'd never known, wandering further into the room until she came to the end of it, a strangely bare wall compared to the others. The others held bookshelves and games, different items, while this one held nothing.

She put her hand up, but nothing happened. Out of instinct, she pulled her hair back to reveal her birthmark. Violet shimmered through the air and settled on the stones, which sparkled. She held her breath as the wall disappeared and a tunnel appeared before her. It too shifted, melding to reveal another room, the wall in that one melting away to reveal yet another, and so on until after five shifts, the stone connected. Five tunnels had collapsed into the former room, bringing the rooms together to create one massive sitting room. Six in total, now connected.

A large fireplace, big enough to walk into, sat at the far end. As she approached, it roared to life, and she inadvertently jumped at its suddenness. Shimmers of violet still sparkled in the air.

She took in the room, suddenly overwhelmed by the memories it held, the people lost, the weight of the history she carried, the expectation.

"What am I doing?" she said. "I'm just a widowed mother from Connecticut. I'm not a mage, I'm not special. God, this is ridiculous." She pushed her palms against her forehead to calm the oncoming panic attack. Breathing through it, she brought her hands down and opened her eyes, only then noticing the letter with her name on it on the mantle of the fireplace. It had twine wrapped around it and a book behind it. She walked over and picked them up, tracing her fingers along the black lettering of her name.

Sitting on a chair in front of the fireplace, she tucked her legs beneath her and untied the twine. Hesitantly, she unfolded the letter.

Skye,

My beautiful girl. You were only mine for a short time, but my heart belongs to you as it did your father. Your father adored you. Our little girl with no name. He knew as did I that your name had yet to be whispered, that it would not be ours to give, that against what the others said, you would simply be our little light. He was right.

I saw you last night as I walked the shadow realm in search of that connection to the realm where I'd sent you. Skye, the name Elspeth chose for you, beautiful and perfect, for you are limitless like the sky above.

You are special, and you are alone. The others have all fallen. Our power wanes from my spell, locked away with you, severing from us as it binds deep within you. I fear this night is my last night, and I will be reunited with my beloved Berrett.

There are things you will need to know that Elspeth cannot teach you. Your gifts are different from any Mage Warrior, even me. Our line is already unique. The ability to transcend the realm veil, to walk amongst the shadows, to reach through to the next realm runs strong within our blood. It is a secret that must be preserved. The other Mage Warriors do not have this ability. None must ever know, especially the king. Do not transcend the shadow realm until your powers are strong enough. Light and color do not exist there, and danger walks amongst the land of the shadow gods.

The shadow gods and their leader, the Death God, do not like us trespassing in their realm. Do not risk it.

Your magic is unique. The colors not only come to you, but they also bleed for you. It is that way with our line. The power has increased with each generation, the old teaching the new how to control this so we do not break the veil between worlds. You will not have me there and this saddens me for you had the power even as a babe. I saw it as you took your first breath—the blues in our room faded, clinging to you, swirling around like a protective aura.

The blues never did return. Your father burned those items so no one would discover our family secret.

You must learn to control the pull to the colors, to ignore the need to bleed them from existence, or I fear with your power, the veils will collapse. I will not be there to guide you as my mother guided me. I can only give you this book, written as the first few of our line experienced the phenomenon and documented it. Each generation has added to it—the knowledge of our line, the secrets of it now in your hand.

I fear the betrayal we faced will remain a force with which you must reckon, and I pray that you know that you have the strength.

Your father and I gave our lives for this fight. I have lost all that I treasure in life; my beloved Berrett, my friends, and you, Skye. Know that it is all worth it to know you remain alive and safe.

My love will always be with you.
Your mother

A line of ink followed the end of the *r* as if a tear drop had fallen in that spot. Skye let the letter drop to her lap, her hands still clinging to it, tears welling. Her mother had risked the shadow realm just to glimpse her, to hear her name, to know she was safe. She had known her life was ending, known Camin would remain a threat.

"She has my powers," Skye said aloud.

All of her line had held them. Her ancestors had bled the

colors. They'd wielded greater magic than the other mage classes. And none had been strangers to the shadow realm.

What did it all mean? And what was she supposed to do with all of it?

Finally, she released the grip on the letter and looked at the book. It was worn, the leather with a seal burned into the cover. She traced the shape of it, wondering what the seal represented. Then she opened the book and began to read.

PAGE AFTER PAGE, Skye learned the history of her family—the changes in their magic as the line continued, the irresistible attraction each had to their Elite mate. Some of the writers were male, some female, all adding to the story. The power to bleed the colors had slowly developed a few generations in, the colors fading more until finally the wielder bled them. There were tips to controlling it and as she came upon each, she would stop and practice. Fearful at first, she'd concentrated on one item at a time until confident enough to focus on the entire room. As she practiced, her magic became a natural part of her, no longer feeling alien, forced. It flowed through her until finally she felt it as a constant, like a second skin, tingling within her.

There were tips and warnings about the shadow realm, but she didn't dare attempt to venture there, the memory of Camin's grip on her too fresh.

On and on, Skye read until the book was almost finished, and she came upon the now familiar writing of her mother. The entry was more personal than the others, and Skye wondered if it hadn't been a purposeful decision, her impending death driving her to write it.

It chronicled her own struggles with her magic, her abilities, her step into the role of leader of the Mage Warriors upon her mother's death, her instant attraction to Skye's father, and the desperate need that drove her to his arms.

Skye's fingers touched the page tenderly. Her mother had loved her father with the same ferocious passion that she'd always had for Mark. Through her mother's eyes, she saw what it would have been like if they'd been allowed to explore their relationship early. Her parents had fallen in love as children, just as she and Mark had.

She rested her head as she came to the final words, the last her mother had written.

Skye is the future, the hope of our line, of all Mage Warriors.

"Nothing like a little pressure," she mumbled.

Her eyes flickered to the table where the book Noah had been looking at sat open still. Rising, she walked over and began thumbing through it, the words now making more sense with the history she'd read. She walked into the room, reading more, unconsciously using her magic, drawing the warmth of the colors, and letting them comfort her.

She was lost in it until a yawn accompanied by a deep growl of her stomach pulled her attention away. She wasn't certain how long she'd been locked away, but given her sudden tiredness, she thought it must have been long. Mark was likely worried about her.

With that thought came a yearning for him, for his touch. She missed him after only a few hours, as if she were now co-dependent upon his presence.

She put the book down next to her family book and stretched. She needed food, Mark, and sleep, not certain which order would be the most satisfying. Fingering the book, she wondered if it was best to leave it here, hidden. She was the only one who could access the room. It was likely best to leave it. Packing it up, she took it back over to the fireplace, laying it on the mantle where she'd found it—her mother had thought it a safe place.

She held onto the note, irritated that her dress had no pockets and missing her jeans. A sudden melancholy overcame her for the luxuries of her world—coffee, music, movies—not that she'd had any time given her current yearning for Mark. She couldn't imagine choosing binge watching over binge sex. She did miss bathing and wondered if Mark would indulge her in a bath. Butterflies tumbled through her at the thought of him joining her in that bath.

With that thought in mind, she decided to tuck the note into the book for safe-keeping, then turned and walked away, hearing the room unfold behind her, and hoping Mark was waiting for her on the other side of the door.

MARK

Mark paced. He'd been pacing the hallway for hours, waiting for Skye. What was she doing? Why had she been so long? He'd exhausted his men, running them through drill after drill until they were bone weary. It was the only way to keep his mind from Skye. He craved her, longing to feel her again. It was so bad he'd had Noah run practice fights with him.

Still, there'd been no sign of her. Dinner had come and gone. He'd even gone back to his room and changed, allowing a few minutes to bathe and missing the convenience of showers. Wishing Skye had accompanied him as he'd settled into the spring that lay deep below the Elite wing. He'd been thinking he needed to bring her there, imagining his hands washing her, then taking her in the water, when a few of the youngest Elite had joined him. He'd forgotten the idea of privacy was not a popular one with the Elite. They were a brotherhood, whether male or female it made no difference. There were the rare few, like his parents, who had an undeniable attraction to one another, still others who simply experienced the pleasure of one another's bodies, but they were rare. For the most part, they looked upon each other as family, brothers and sisters, bathing together, changing with each other, training, bleeding, and dying together. Sexuality was not a factor, defending their Mage Warrior was.

He, on the other hand, had been raised in the world where men and women did not bathe together, unless there was a sexual reason behind it. He'd grabbed his towel and covered up before they noticed his arousal, thoughts of Skye still on his mind.

Now he waited for her, his arousal long ago replaced with concern. What if she was hurt? If she'd tried to use her magic and something had happened? There was no way to reach her, and he hated that. He'd only been a distance away from her a few times in their life, otherwise, he'd stayed close, moving nearby, opening his practice close to her, following her to the states when they'd moved. Always near, always watching, always protecting.

The air stirred, and he turned to see her emerge from the room.

"Skye," he said following his sigh of relief.

She ran to him and jumped into his arms, kissing him fiercely. All worry, all thoughts of yelling at her for being gone so long fled as her tongue explored his mouth, seeking his out.

"I want you," she whispered, and his arousal returned.

"Did you find anything?" he asked between her kisses.

"Lots, and I'll tell you after you take me."

God, it was an open invitation that he couldn't resist. He held tight to her waist as he walked with her in his arms, heading down the hall of the mage wing, then attempting to climb the stairs while she continued to distract him. She pulled on his shirt, and he dropped her, his hands rising to give her the action she was looking for.

"Damn, woman, can't you wait until we're upstairs?" he half-heartedly griped.

"No," she replied, biting his lower lip, and tugging on the buttons of his pants.

His desire took hold, and he yanked her dress, ripping it over her head and exposing the nakedness below.

"Jesus, have you been like this all day?"

"Mhmm, I don't like those granny things they have here."

He kissed her as her fingers pushed at his pants, finding their target and encasing it. He moaned, his hands touching her, exploring her as if he hadn't done so the previous night. She pulled her lips from his to kiss her way down his chest, pushing his pants further down. Her soft breasts brushed against him until her mouth found him and she took him in, the warmth of her mouth bringing him to ecstasy. He groaned as her tongue moved along his length, then around his tip before she plunged back down on him. He wanted to pull her back up, to push her against the wall and drive into her, but her mouth was too enticing. It seduced him in ways he'd never thought possible. Each time she'd gone down on him, it had been like nothing he'd ever experienced; there was a possessiveness to her moves and with each plunge of her mouth she claimed him. He ran his hands through her hair, resisting the urge to push her head down as his pelvis bucked up in reaction, sending him deeper into her mouth. He could do no more than concentrate on the feel of her mouth as it encased him. Nothing else existed. All care that they were in the middle of the staircase fled, his mind left with nothing but the pleasure of her mouth. The muscles in his legs tightened as she brought him closer to climax.

He squeezed his hands tight in her hair, knowing he was likely pulling it but unable to stop himself as the rush hit him and his climax peaked. His pelvis pushed forward, and her mouth drank him down, his knees buckling as the thought of what she was doing further heightened his release.

She let her tongue drift back over him, taking time to suck once more on him—a move that forced a grunt from him before she rose. He grasped her shoulders, a wave of weakness going through him, his knees shaking. She didn't stop, didn't give him time to recover, her tongue licking its way up his body, her hand squeezing him, teasing what was left of him, taunting it as her lips met his. He was still semi-hard, still ready for her. Shoving her against the curved stairwell, he kissed her neck, then licked her breast, pulling her nipple between his teeth. With her moans his firmness returned, her hand still covering him, pulling and kneading. He let his hand drop, his fingers finding the depth inside her, the immense moisture that awaited him. She moaned again as he moved his fingers deeper, sucking her nipple, the tautness only further exciting him.

A strangled groan escaped her as his thumb made circles over her clit, his other fingers continuing the movement within her, her body tightening around them. Just as he sensed her getting close, he withdrew his fingers, tasting her sweetness on them before flipping her. He wanted to be inside of her, to feel her pulse around him as she came. He pushed her hard against the stone, his hand touching her again, ensuring she remained ready. Then he pulled her hips back, spreading her legs before he plunged into her. Her hands locked against the stone wall, and she pushed her ass hard against him, thrusting him deeper. Squeezing her hips, he moved her so that her motion met his, the rhythm picking up speed with her cries, her body shuddering as he continued to hold tight to her, feeling her clench around him as her climax tore through her. It felt almost too good, but he slowed his rhythm, knowing he wanted more. He brought his hands up her body, cupping her breasts and rubbing her nipples until they were so hard the feel of them brought him closer, his need climbing. He was holding himself back and the urge to come was like an angry storm tearing through him, waiting for release. He wanted her to join him, wanted to bring her to climax again, to feel her body weaken while she tightened around him.

She threw her head back in a sensual cry, her hair spilling down her back as he moved a hand between her legs, applying a pressured movement to her clit as he squeezed her waist tight with his other hand, driving himself harder into her with every cry she emitted. Each bringing him close to the edge until as her body shuddered again in his grasp, his own orgasm hit him like a wave that drowned him below so that all he could do was hold her tight through the onslaught, his cry of pleasure echoing in harmony with hers.

When the quivering of their bodies calmed, he dropped his head, his eyes catching the quake of her arms that were still pressing against the wall. He tried to catch his breath, wrapping his arm around her waist and licking the trickles of sweat from her back.

Straightening her up, he felt her muscles give in, his own threatening to collapse. He brushed her hair back and traced the outline of her birthmark, tracing his tongue along it and feeling her shiver.

In one quick movement, he had her in his arms, the move eliciting a squeal as she was airborne suddenly.

"Are you taking me hostage?" she teased in a breathless voice, her eyes heavy with desire.

"I am taking you to your room where I am going to ravage you until we're too tired to move, then I will take you again in the morning all in an attempt to catch up on at least six months of our lost years."

Climbing the final stairs, he opened the door and threw her on the bed. Giggling, she propped herself on her elbows. He took every beautiful inch of her in as her eyes got their fill of him. Then he climbed atop her and made love to her, passionately slow, taking his time to memorize each curve, each freckle, each spot that brought her to pleasure, knowing he could never make up for the time they had lost but he would have fun trying.

Knocking roused Mark from his heavy sleep. Skye's body was tangled with his, and she nuzzled deeper into his chest, grumbling as he tried to move. The door opened roughly, and Noah entered, his hands full of the clothes they had discarded on the stairs.

Skye peeked her eyes up and Mark covered her partially exposed breast, thankful that she was lying against him.

"You two seriously couldn't wait until you were in the room? You're lucky it was me and not Alex who followed your trail of clothes."

"Morning to you as well, Noah," he said as Skye did a cat stretch next to him, the curve of her body under the sheets turning him on. He couldn't get enough of her; it was like an insatiable hunger he'd never experienced.

"Markhem, you need to get your ass out of bed and go lead your men."

"Oh, but he was going to take a bath with me," Skye whined.

"That's the last thing he needs; stop distracting him. You take your own bath, then eat. Elspeth thinks you haven't eaten in two days. Mage Warriors need to eat. We can't have you weak. When you're done, report to Elspeth so we know what kept you so busy yesterday, and I don't mean your mate here."

"He sounds like an old man," she whispered, and Mark had to stifle a laugh.

"That's because I am an old man and you two are acting like a couple of teenagers."

"Isn't that kind of what we are?" Skye asked.

Noah raised his hands in frustration and stormed out.

"It's not good to goad him," Mark said, drawing her in.

"It's not good to wake me or talk to me before I have my coffee. God, I miss my coffee and my toothbrush." She covered her mouth and breathed to test her breath, scrunching her nose. "Oh, that's bad."

He pushed her hand aside and kissed her. "I love you, morning breath and all."

Her stomach rumbled loudly.

"And howling stomach," he added. "When was the last time you ate?"

"The other night when you brought me the stew."

"The stew you barely ate? Damn, Noah's right. You need to eat. I remember my mother once saying the Lyra ate like a horde of men after she'd been wielding. It drains your energy."

"Are we sure that's the magic and not you?" she teased, her hand exploring his menacing firmness.

"Mmm," Mark moaned. "I'm not taking blame for that one with that insatiable appetite you have."

He let his fingers drape across her breasts, feeling her nipples respond to his touch.

"I do feel quite insatiable," she said in a throaty voice that did nothing but enhance his need for her. She gave him a seductive smile. "I think breakfast can wait as can your Elite and everything else beyond these bedsheets."

He pulled her on top of him, her hair draping across his chest. Pushing a few strands behind her ear, he sighed as she enveloped him, her head tilting back in pleasure.

He wanted to tell her she needed to go, to take care of herself, that they needed to focus on the coming threat, but he didn't. Instead, he latched onto her hips, pushing himself further into her, then leaned up to meet her open mouth, knowing he was a prisoner of his unending desire for her. He continued to make love to her until, as her heavy navy eyes met his, the intensity left him shaking from its power, the mix of emotion and physical release breaking him. She came in that moment, sending shocks of pleasure through him as she tightened around his own release. He held onto her and she clung to him, the waves spilling through them both until there was nothing left but a small current that drifted with their heavy breaths.

She brought her head up, the blue of her eyes slightly lighter, and smiled a contented, relaxed smile—one he realized he hadn't seen from her since they were kids. Before the seriousness of their love for one another had caused a distance, before he'd been forced to pass her into the arms of another man, before he'd taken countless women to replace a need that could never be erased, before life had become complicated and the titles they'd been assigned had become barriers that could not be surmounted.

He smiled back, running his fingers along the shape of her face, hesitating on the corner of that glorious smile.

"You're beautiful, Skye. I've thought that every day but was never allowed to say it. I will never stop now. You are the most beautiful woman, and you will continue to be the most beautiful."

"Even when I'm all wrinkled? Do we grow wrinkled here?"

He laughed. "Yes, but not for a very long time and yes, I assure you, you will still be the most beautiful woman to me, even covered in wrinkles."

He laced his fingers through her hair, bringing her face to his, and kissed her.

"Now, we have no more time for this. As much as it pains me, you need to get moving, as do I."

She pouted her bottom lip, which he proceeded to nibble.

"That won't work," he said. "Besides, aren't you worn out yet? Seriously, I've never met a woman who has the stamina of a man like you do."

"It's been pent up for a very long time, Mark. Now that I don't have to pretend my fingers are yours, it's much more fun," she replied with a wink.

"Jesus, that's not going to help me." He rubbed his hand across his face, then proceeded to move her from his body, ignoring the erection that was threatening to rise again.

He sat on the side of the bed, trying to compose himself, but she pressed her breasts against his back, kissing his neck. She really was insatiable, and he loved that about her. The idea of exploring more of her body, of finding her other hidden pleasure spots for days on end, was tempting. Too tempting.

He grabbed her and pulled her onto his lap.

"You, my dear, are naughty and manipulative."

"That's a bit harsh. Naughty is fine, but manipulative?"

He arched his brow.

"Okay, maybe a little bit. I can't help it, Mark. It's like I'm a new person, like I'm twenty again and in love and happy, like I don't have a care in the world."

"But you do, Skye. We both do. Noah's right, we need to move. Camin's coming and you're unprepared. I have a legion of Elite who are fresh and inexperienced; only a handful of experienced members left. The rest were taken out by Camin and his forces."

"I'm prepared now. I know how to use my magic."

"You found something?" He'd been so preoccupied with her body that he'd forgotten about where she'd been the previous day.

"I found a lot."

He picked her up, then tossed her on the bed, trying to ignore the bounce of her perky breasts.

"Hey!"

"I'm getting dressed while you tell me what you found. And... I really hate to ask," he said, pulling his pants on, "but can you pull the blankets up? As much as I adore you naked, I don't think I can concentrate on your words with your breasts out."

"Sounds like a man's problem, not mine."

"Don't pull that on me. You're too irresistible to be like that and I can't go down and lead those troops with a massive erection."

"I can relieve that again," she practically purred.

He threw the blanket over her and grabbed his shirt.

"Fine, fine."

"Thank you. Now tell me what you found and how it helps us."

"You know you're quite sexy when you get serious."

"And you are quite the child trying to distract me."

"Is it working?"

He gave her a look and crossed his arms.

"All right. I see you're immune to my charms when you're in serious general mode."

"Commander."

"Whatever," she said with a laugh.

He was trying hard not to smile at how cute she was.

"I found a book and a letter, both from my mother."

"Your mother?"

"Yes." She proceeded to tell him about reading the book, a history of her family and its magic. Then about her practicing and eventually understanding her magic.

He sat in the chair in front of the fireplace, moving it so he could face her, thinking it through, taking it all in.

"Secrets, even among their own," he pondered.

"They feared the reaction of the others, of the king. The power of the Mage Warriors already surpassed the inherited power of position the king held," she said. "Warriors had always sworn to protect and serve, never questioning the lead of the king as head of the kingdom. But if the power of our line was exposed, there was fear that the mere magnitude of what we could do would lead to persecution. Think about it."

"You hold the power to bring down the veils that separate realms, to destroy our existence, to walk among the shadows in the shadow realm," he said, disliking the possibility of any of those things happening, especially at Skye's hands.

"All terrifying things. Although from what I gather, they could walk in the shadow realm but were not safe there. Nor could they do what I did. I found no record that anyone had drawn color from the shadows. If anything, they feared the realm as much as anyone else, only entering in necessity or by accident, like I did."

"This is huge, Skye, and if you really have mastered your abilities, then there might be a chance for us."

"I don't know if I've mastered the true extent of what I can do, Mark. I can control it, direct it. I feel it now, as if it's a part of me, but without a teacher, I don't think it's everything. And..." She hesitated. "I think I'm different."

"How so?" he asked, concerned by the tone change in her voice.

"I'm not sure, but my mother hinted at it. She said I'd bled the color from all the blue things in the room at my birth. Like that wasn't normal. The journal suggested that with each generation, the abilities were growing, changing."

"Huh, I wonder what that means for you."

"I really don't know."

He studied her, seeing her vulnerability in that moment—the strong, confident woman he knew replaced with a woman who had weaknesses, who could be hurt, who was vulnerable due to what she didn't know and...those she loved. He and Alex made her vulnerable, both an opening for her to be hurt, for Camin to strike. He rubbed his hand over his face. He would need to keep Alex close. He was being trained by Thomas, Skye's father. He'd have to find a way to bring him closer. Watching both him and Skye, protecting them both.

"Damn," he muttered, standing. "I need to get to work, and you need to find Elspeth and Trent. Tell them all you've learned, secrets be damned, they need to know what they're dealing with."

He kissed her, and against the yearning, pushed her hands back from his chest, knowing if he gave in, he would never leave her side, dooming them all.

MARK

Heading through the tunnels, Mark ran everything Skye had told him through his head. Lost in thought, he didn't hear Noah come up behind him. Noah grabbed his arm and shoved him against the wall, catching him off guard.

"What the hell are you doing, Mark?" Noah shouted.

"Wondering if I should punch you or harass you for using the word hell when it doesn't exist here."

"Don't be a smartass. Just because you're commander now doesn't mean I don't still pull rank as your elder."

"What do you want, Noah?" he asked, pushing away from him.

"I want to know what you're thinking. Why are you letting your dick cloud your judgement?"

Mark clenched his fists, restraining his anger.

"Screw you," he said, walking away.

"I'm serious, Mark," Noah said, grabbing his arm. "You need to get your head out of your pants. I get that you and Skye have been separated—"

"Your doing and Elspeth's."

"Pointing blame makes no difference at this point."

"No? Seriously? You kept me from her for fifty years. Then you blast me for wanting to be with her. Do you have any idea how hard it was to be forced from her for that long?" He was yelling, his anger and frustration spilling over.

"Yes, I do. I haven't seen my wife since the war began. She's staying with friends in Drenton, where she's been since Camin's first attack. My duty came first, it always has. We all sacrificed to make sure Skye survived far from Camin's clutches, to ensure the Mage Warriors remained."

"I'm sorry, Noah."

"Don't be. I signed up for this; she knew that, knew the sacrifices. And I didn't sacrifice as much as you, none of us did. You lost your parents, you lived a lie, and you had to watch the woman you love live the life you wanted with another man. None of us came out of this unscathed. All of us, however, have a responsibility to see it through to the end. That means you keep your dick quiet, pull your head out of your pants, and off Skye's body long enough to lead the Elite and let Skye defeat Camin once and for all."

"That's what I was trying to do before you rushed me. Do you think I want her hurt? That I want to lose her again?"

"That's how you're acting."

"Screw you, Noah."

"Your parents gave their lives, as did Skye's, to protect her legacy and the kingdom. What are you willing to sacrifice? Your life? Your love? Her?"

Mark didn't know what to say.

"There will come a time when that choice may have to be made. Be the leader your parents thought you were; let her be the one that her parents and yours believed in. Make the sacrifice and don't let their deaths be in vain."

Mark stared at Noah, his mentor, his trainer, his friend, the words playing through his head, the thought of losing Skye, of having to sacrifice her, heavy in his heart. He gave Noah a nod, then headed out of the tunnels.

He ran the men and women of his infantry through drills, sparring them in pairs, testing his own skills in the process, blocking all thoughts of Skye from his head until mid-morn when Elspeth interrupted his concentration.

"Where is she?"

He huffed at the interruption. "Who Elspeth?"

"Skye!"

"I'm not her keeper—"

"The hell you aren't. Where is she?"

He put his weapon down and glared at her. "She was going to get food and bathe after I left her. If she went somewhere else, I don't know. As I said, I am not her keeper."

"No, he is not. Just because he's my lover doesn't mean he owns me."

He turned to see Skye approaching them. Her hair was still damp, piled upon her head with her curls interweaved through a blue ribbon. She looked so much like her mother in that moment, the memory of seeing Lyra with his own mother emerged, the same hairstyle the same blue ribbons bringing out Lyra's brown eyes—the only noticeable difference between mother and daughter.

She wore the tight training pants that accentuated her curves, but this time, she wore a shortened style of tunic instead of the leather halter she'd worn the first day. The tunic still showed an abundance of skin, her stomach exposed where it ended above her navel and the pants set right above her hips. It tied down the back, lowered at her breasts, the material accentuating them with its tightness. Its royal navy sleeves cusped her forearms, the color bringing the depth of her blue eyes out so that they almost looked like the night sky.

She was talking, answering Elspeth's questions, but he heard none of it, his eyes drawn to her lush lips, thoughts of the prior night on his mind, threatening to send him over the edge. Noah elbowed him and he dragged his eyes from her, only then realizing how tightly he was gripping his weapon, his pants uncomfortable where his hard-on had developed.

"You managed to master your powers in one day?" Trent asked, having remained quiet all this time. He'd followed Elspeth on the hunt for Skye.

"I think so. At least, almost mastered."

"Show us," Elspeth commanded.

"Here? In front of all these people?"

"Do you think Camin will pause to clear the battlefield in order for you to cast a spell?"

"Point taken. Fine."

She quietly waved her hand, and he noticed the color around her shift, ripples of light blue sky above running through her fingers. The sky itself seemed to dim, its hue growing muted as the bands of its original color drifted around her. She pushed her hand forward and his weapon hummed, the depth of her power fortifying it. He could feel his connection to her magic as he gripped the middle and drew it forward. It glowed a bright blue. The others all drew theirs, their eyes wide upon seeing the glow.

"The softer hues empower the Elite. The more vibrant," she released her hold on the sky's color and as it grew brighter, she drew the red from Elspeth's cape, "are my weapons." The red danced through her fingers, but she stopped the flow just as the cape was on the edge of turning gray. "The trick is to be conscious of its life force and know when it's giving its all to you."

She moved her hand, the red forming the shape of a dagger that she then aimed at a training dummy, bursting it into count-less pieces that blazed with its fire before the red hue scattered back to the cape. That small piece of magic, a destructive force that brought them all to realize just how dangerous she really was.

She touched her shirt. "And the deep shades—well, those hold the dark powers, the ones closest to the shadow realm and the shadow gods. Each of the warriors in my line has a color we favor, some black, some gray, some like me, blue. That color draws the veil and allows passage but, if drained too far like I seem to have the ability to do, will break the veil and allow a crack that the bleeding of any other color will enlarge until it cannot be undone."

"Like you did that first day," Elspeth whispered.

"No, I never cracked it; the opening only pulled inward, bending but never breaking it because I didn't start with the color that connects me to that realm—blue."

"So, we were safe even with all that chaos?" he asked.

"Hardly. If you hadn't pulled me out, the realms would have collapsed upon each other."

"One way opens the gates of hell, the other—" Elspeth started.

"Destroys them along with everything else in its path."

"Good gods," Trent said.

"And did you figure out how to enter the shadow realm again?" Elspeth asked.

"Yes, but I didn't try. I was afraid I'd be stuck there without anyone to pull me out, without Mark beside me."

"Then try now," urged Trent.

"Are you mad? What if she does get stuck there?" Mark argued.

"Her body was here and only her spirit went to the shadow realm. That's what you said."

"When she was dreaming, but what if that's only when she's dreaming? What if she's really there when she's awake?" he asked, his fear climbing.

"She's vulnerable either way, Markhem," Trent said. "There were bruises on her arm when she was dreaming. What happens in the shadow realm happens in reality."

"Then she's not going," he said, crossing his arms.

"You don't make the decisions for her."

"I'm her protector, I get the final say."

Upon his last word, he heard her mumble and, as his eyes moved to her, she disappeared. She'd done it, ignoring his concern, tuning everyone out. She had gone, risking everything to test the theory. His theory had been right. She was beyond his reach, lost somewhere in the shadow realm, the realm ruled by the shadow gods themselves, the Death God at its helm, someplace he could never fathom ever reaching her.

SKYE

Skye had had enough. They were arguing, as if she weren't there, as if they made the decisions for her, and she had no free will, even Mark. Mark, who had spent the prior night bringing her to the extremes of pleasure, the man she craved with a hunger she couldn't satisfy. Thoughts of his touch sent shivers through her.

She'd spent the morning bathing in the most luxurious bath, the scented water warm on her skin, calming the bruises she had on her knees from when she'd gone down on him in the stairwell. It had been worth it; the pleasure overriding the sting in her knees. His touch, the feel of him inside of her, God, even the taste of him. The mere thought of it threatened to bring her to climax.

After she'd calmed herself and cleaned herself, she'd found her way to the kitchens, where the servants had argued with her attempts to eat there. After finally winning the argument and insisting they not move her to the dining room, she'd chatted with them, enjoying their company until she was full. On the way to the tunnels, she'd found Alex, only then realizing how she'd missed him. They'd talked as they'd walked until the other full mages told her Elspeth and Trent had gone to the Elite fields in search for her. Irritated that she'd gone the wrong way, she'd given Alex an embarrassing hug and kiss goodbye in front of a very pretty girl who looked about his age and toddled off to find the others.

Unfortunately, she'd set off a firestorm and now stood in the middle of a debate. It was her decision to make, not theirs. She vacillated for just a moment, worried about her ability to travel to the shadow realm intentionally, then, frustrated at the others, she thought about what the journals had told her. Closing her eyes, she pictured the blue hues and called for them, just enough to warm her and to calm her, then she opened herself to them, letting them overcome her senses until the bickering went quiet. Silence surrounded her and when she opened her eyes, she knew it had worked. She'd transported herself to the shadow realm. She didn't feel as she had in the dream, that she was separated from her body and instinct told her she wasn't. She looked around, unsure what to do now. How did she get back? Did the others even know she was gone?

Fear snuck up on her. Was Camin here? Would he find her again?

Her eyes darted around nervously, at first missing the bright colors of the living world but then adjusting to the warmth of the familiar dark tones she'd spent her life in, their presence calming her. On she walked through a field of darkness, then into a forest of looming black trees that creaked in an unseen wind. As the black of the forest enveloped her, she wondered if she should have stayed in the open field then thought it didn't much matter; it was still shrouded in darkness. At least in the forest were gradients of those colors, deeper blacks, shadowed grays, blue undertones that lived below the blackness.

She felt like she was being watched, and the words from the journal came back to her. *The shadow gods do not like us trespassing in their realm.*

Mark had said the shadow realm was like hell or the underworld, a place where the souls were taken to decide their fate, the guilty ones imprisoned there for an eternity of torment. But she saw no souls, heard no screams.

"Why is it so quiet?" she whispered.

"The souls of the dead are not permitted to wander past the gates." She swirled to find no one to which the voice belonged. Her arms had broken out in goosebumps, her heart hammering.

"You should not have risked our wrath. We do not think highly of those who can transcend the veil between realms."

"Yet you let Camin move freely," she replied, suspecting the voice belonged to one she did not wish to see.

"Camin traded highly for access to our realm. What will you give?"

"What did he give?"

The air turned bitter cold, and from the shadows, a long black figure emerged. Its legs were thin and bent like those of a cat standing, its body broad as a man's, its arms, long black tentacles that melded with clawed hands. Skye inadvertently took a step back as her eyes fell upon its face. Terrifying didn't seem the sufficient word for the face of death itself.

"Child, I am simply a gatekeeper. Death, you will find, is the true horror." A strange, gargled laugh emerged.

Skye couldn't draw her eyes from it. The face was flat like an ant's but with defined features like a man that would distort—one moment holding fright, the next anger, the next pain, and so on. Morphing to all but happiness.

"Gatekeeper?"

"I have come to give you a warning. The Death God favors you although we do not know why. We shadow gods allow you entrance because of that favor."

It stepped closer to her, and it took all her strength not to crumble to the ground in tears.

"Camin seeks you. We have kept him here as long as we can, now he shall be set loose. You are ready."

"Ready for what?" Then a thought hit her. "You want me to bring down the veil?"

The face morphed to horror, and she stifled her scream as its clawed hand grabbed her arm.

"To bring down the veil between the living and the dead—the demons we hold at bay—would be the end of both realms, of all realms. Chaos would ensue, the veil beyond into the other worlds would fall. No child, you must preserve the veil, leave it bound. Camin seeks the power but only you own it. Be sure to never unleashed it. Now, do not trespass in our world again. Camin will find a way free this day and the final battle will begin."

Instinctively, she called for her power, seeking out the hues. The black hues answered, the blue shades below them giving way and heeding her call, swirling around her.

"Well, well, yes, now I see why you are favored by the Death God."

It dropped her arm, but the pain continued to make its way through her.

The thing disappeared, the pain eating her until she could take no more. The hues faded from her hold, a scream tearing through her throat as she fell to the ground, writhing in pain. The feeling made its way to her neck, seeming to condense on her birthmark, the sensation intense until within seconds, it abated. Her breathing returned, and she slowly opened her eyes to see the daylight of the living world. The warmth of the sun did nothing to remove the chill that still sat in her bones and her eyes closed again to it.

She heard her name being called, then the rush of feet and the warmth of Mark's arms as they embraced her.

"She's freezing." She heard him say.

"Here," her mother said before something covered her skin, a cloak.

"Skye?" She heard Mark's voice after a few minutes.

"We should take her in. Her skin is so pale."

"Mark?" she managed, reaching her fingers up to touch his face, forcing her eyes open. He couldn't contain his startled reaction, and she creased her brow, wondering why he'd given her that response.

She grabbed at his shirt, the urgency of what she'd discovered fueling her, although she was suddenly exhausted.

"He's coming," she whispered.

His eyes grew serious. "Skye?"

"Camin. He's coming for me. The shadow gods are releasing their hold on him and he's coming."

The world spun, darkness overtaking her. She could hear him calling her name, his voice growing fainter as she passed out completely.

There were voices arguing, hushed, and worry tinged. Skye groaned, her head hurt and there was a throbbing where her birthmark lay.

"Skye," Mark's voice cut through the others, and she felt the warmth of his hand on her cheek. She blinked away the fuzziness, his face coming into focus. His eyes were laced with concern.

Giving him a warm smile, she tried sitting up, but he kept her down.

"Not yet. I'm not risking you passing out again."

"I'm fine, just tired."

"We need to know what she discovered, Markhem." The voice belonged to the king. She turned to see him and the others in the room.

"Where am I?" she said, rubbing her head and sitting up against Mark's wishes.

"It's still prominent," Elspeth murmured.

"What does it mean?" asked the king.

"What is everyone talking about, and why do I feel like I missed something important?"

"It's we who missed something, Skye." Mark tentatively touched her birthmark, as though fearful of it. The prior night he'd been kissing it, eliciting a pleasured cry from her as his tongue had swept over it, but now he feared even touching it. She dropped her eyes, knowing she couldn't see it, but still drawn to his fingers. He moved his hand to reveal blue markings that bled from the place where her birthmark lie. They shimmered like a night sky, with countless stars within it.

The markings formed a shape, but at her angle she couldn't see the shape.

"It forms a Scynthe," he said.

"A what?"

"It's the sign of the gods, the Death God. The crescent moon within a golden sun is the symbol of the Upper God. The crescent moon within an endless tangle of night webs is that of the Death God and his shadow gods," Trent said, his expression so serious it frightened her.

"The gods mark us with only our birthmarks, always the same for each rank. Never have they included the full sign of the gods."

"I met one," she said, her voice shaking.

They stared at her.

"A shadow god. He...well, *it* seemed quite perturbed that I was there."

"Perturbed," Mark muttered. "A shadow god told you he was perturbed." He rubbed his hands over his face. She hadn't seen him this stressed since the day she'd married Sam. Did he think he was losing her again?

"Tell us exactly what happened," the king said.

She gave her account of the meeting while he paced the room; the others nervously shifting their stances, all except Mark, who sat on the edge of the couch she was on, gripping her hand tightly.

When she finished, there was silence. A long, drawn-out

silence in which she could feel Mark's worry turn to anger. In the back of her mind, she remembered the letter saying the king shouldn't know of her ability, and she wondered why. What was the danger in him knowing?

"So, they kept Camin there, barring his entrance back into the world?" Elspeth asked, interrupting her thoughts.

"Yes, I got the impression they were pissed at him, like whatever he's bargained his soul for, he hasn't done."

"And what would that be?"

"I don't know."

"They want this realm, to own it, take it back from the Upper God," Trent said.

"Back?" she asked.

"Yes. This world was once overrun by demons and beasts of the night, things that walk your nightmares. Much like in Greek mythology, two brothers rule the gods, Carzent, the Upper God, and Derrant, the Death God. Derrant had driven back his brother, leading a world of madness until Carzent finally defeated him. Instead of casting him out, he made him god of the dead, locking him in the shadow realm, the gateway of the dead and this world's hell. It was a peace treaty of sorts, it rid this realm of the destruction, containing Derrant but still giving him a powerful role, the passing of the dead through his kingdom to the upper realm or to be tied to the shadow realm to live eternity cursed by the deeds sown in life. Derrant's followers—those gods who had rallied with him—were cursed to the shadow realm as shadow gods. Their blessings as radiant gods, those who follow Carzent, were stripped along with their titles and the shadow gods were created. There they rule with Derrant as the leader."

"So, destroying the veil would give Derrant back this world," Mark said, the anger still evident in his voice.

"No, no, I'm sure that's not what they want," she countered.

"One encounter in the shadow realm makes you an expert on the shadow gods now?" he snapped.

His words and the vindictiveness of them stung. She didn't know what had gotten into him.

"No, but it said the chaos created from doing so would be uncontrollable. It's something else."

"We need to find out what, soon. Camin could attack you at any moment," Trent said.

She thought about all she'd learned. The events of the past few days. The demons that Mark had told her had torn at the very fabric between the realms.

"They need me. That's why they've helped Camin. They were testing me, watching to see what I could do. They don't want me to shred the divide because that would bring the realms tumbling into each other in a way that would crush the very fabric of existence. So, they waited, knowing I needed to be stronger, to understand how to avoid that and control my abilities."

"To what end?" Trent asked.

"To rip a fracture in the veil and only a small one. That's all they need."

"To make a doorway between the realms. They could come and go as they please, twisting our world slowly without the Upper God even realizing it."

"I don't like this. She can't fight Camin. That's what they want now. She slips up, an opening is created, and Camin kills her. We need to hide her," Mark said hurriedly.

"There is no hiding her. The shadow gods know she's here, Derrant knows, and they are releasing Camin. There's no stopping the oncoming storm."

"We need to prepare for battle," the king said. "Trent, Elspeth, ready the mages. Markhem, the Elite. I'll ready our troops." He looked at Skye, but she wasn't certain what to make of his expression. Was it fear or worry? If it was fear, she didn't think it was for Camin's arrival, but rather for what her magic could do. Was that why her mother had warned her in the letter? Fear was a powerful enemy. Would it bring mistrust and with it, danger? She hid her worry as he continued. "This battle is yours. We will do what we can to protect you, but the battle is in your hands. We are but noise in the background."

"Sire, Camin is bound to return to the Fettered Forests first, to rally the wizards, the creatures that reside there."

"Yes, that's true. I'll send scouts—"

"There may not be time. I'll go with your permission, sire," Elspeth said.

He nodded. Skye watched as a staff appeared. She pounded it on the ground and in a mist of smoke, she was gone.

"The rest of you move." He walked out swiftly, followed by Trent.

Noah looked to Mark, then said, "I'll give you two a minute, but then you need to prepare. The Elite need both of you."

The door closed loudly behind him. The room was dark, no windows lined it, only candlelight sending shadows across the walls.

Mark looked away from her.

"I've known you long enough to know when you're angry," she said.

"Angry isn't quite the word."

She waited for him to continue, but he didn't.

"That's not fair, Mark. You can't be mad at me and not tell me why."

"Not fair?" He looked at her, the hazel in his eyes dancing in the candlelight. "You jumped into the shadow realm with no regard for my opinion, no thought of the risk, no thought of what could have happened, and you say I'm being unfair?"

He rose and began pacing the room.

"Christ, Skye, I had no way to protect you. None of us did. You can't do this alone; that's why you have an army of Elite to protect you."

"I didn't know that would happen, Mark."

"You didn't even stop to think that it could happen."

She rose, but he stopped her, pushing her down, pinning her back with his body, his hands on the back of the couch as he leaned over her.

"I'm sorry, Mark."

"I could have lost you, Skye. You could have been trapped there and I had no way to reach you. They could have killed you, kept you, tortured you."

"But they didn't."

"It doesn't matter. The only times Mage Warriors are vulnerable is when their protectors are not with them. You cannot go alone anywhere until this is over."

"You can't force me to live with you as a shadow, Mark. I'm not a child."

"In this world, you are. My father, your father, died because the Mage Warriors they were fighting with left their side. It cost them their lives and those of the two Mage Warriors. This is not a game. We are tied to you, to your magic, to be your shield."

She softened, understanding now why he was so adamant about it. The same action had lost him his father. She trailed her fingers down his cheek, feeling the tension beneath them.

"I can't promise you, Mark. You are not meant to follow me to the shadow realm—that is my gift to bear for whatever reason. But I will not venture elsewhere without you, without your shield."

He dropped his head to hers. "I was scared, Skye, terrified I'd lost you."

She picked his head up, finding his lips and kissing him, feeling the vulnerability in him, the frightened boy below the strong man.

"Shh, I'm here. You didn't lose me, and you won't."

He kissed her back, hungrily, as though she'd been lost to him for another fifty years. Her body reacted, warmth spreading through her as his hand pushed below her shirt, brushing the skin along her breast.

It wasn't the time, nor the place, but the hunger he had for her fueled her own. She tugged at his shirt, wanting to feel his muscles against her skin. Breathlessness overcame her, and his hand pushed at her pants. This wouldn't be a long lovemaking session. It was a fiery, need driven release and the thought excited her, her mind going to their encounter in the stairwell. God, she wanted to taste him again, but knew they didn't have time.

Her pants freed, his fingers found her again, and she tipped her head back as they searched her, exploring to test her wetness and finding it. He sucked at her breast, shockwaves coursing through her. Her own hands shoved at his pants, not wanting to wait any longer to feel his length, her body writhing with pleasure. He grunted as she set him free, her hand gripping his length, stroking him until his hand grabbed hers, the moisture from her sliding along it. He tilted her hips and thrust himself into her. They moaned together, his hand pushing her ass closer to him, sending him deeper. His hand grabbed hers, clinging to it as she moved her hips in rhythm with his, his mouth finding hers again. Her body was an explosion of pleasure and as if sensing her own need, his fingers found her nipples, his mouth following.

She pulled her leg high around his neck, her hands pushing him down further, plunging him deeper until she cried out, his mouth moving up to stop her cry. He pulled her up somehow, so that they were seated, never leaving her, the motion continuing even as she sat upon him. With her legs tucked beneath her, she had the power. She slowed her movement, each rise extended to bring the most pleasure, each fall the deepest reach. His fingers found her pleasure spot, his mouth encasing her nipples again, his free hand pushing against her on her back so that her breast filled his mouth.

Desire pummeled her, and she quickened her rhythm, feeling him grow thicker, knowing he was close, but God so was she. The wave crested, hanging in status until it flooded her with ecstasy, her cries unable to be contained as his mouth continued to suck and pull, his hands gripping her hips, continuing the motion she could no longer do, her body too weak with the onslaught of her orgasm. Finally, he grunted, his thrusts slowing to hard tense ones, his hands gripped so tightly on her that the pain weaved through the remaining waves of her climax, heightening it.

His body stilled, his head dropping to her chest, and she could feel the waves of residual pleasure going through him, her own body still out of her control. They stayed that way until the tide receded and they could move again.

Still breathless, she kissed his head, running her hands through his thick auburn hair.

"God, what you do to me, woman."

"Mmm, I could say the same about you."

He picked his head up and looked at her, his thumb wiping away a trickle of sweat from her brow. He brushed her hair back, tracing the new markings around her birthmark.

"We should go. I'm surprised they gave us this much time," he said.

"Likely scared they might walk in on something they couldn't unsee."

He laughed as she crawled off him, stopping to lick the mess of their lovemaking from him.

"Don't start that, Skye. There's no way we'll leave this room if you do."

She took him in her mouth, feeling him react, teasing him with her tongue until his softness had fled. Letting it roll around his head, then down his shaft before taking him all the way. Groaning, he protested again, pushing at her shoulders but she didn't stop, the feel of him in her mouth too pleasurable, the smell of their sex intoxicating as his erection grew. His hands dug into her hair, and he gave over to her. She knew Camin could attack at any moment, but she suspected he wouldn't. He would gather his army, knowing she'd had time to gather hers. He would attack this day. The gods had freed him, but it wouldn't be at this moment. She would take the small amount of time she had to enjoy herself.

As her tongue explored the depths of Mark, his hands teased her nipples, grabbing at her breasts and squeezing them each time she took him in completely until no longer able to concentrate, his head fell back, his hand pushing her head down as his pelvis lurched up, his full length going deep into her mouth. She brought him to climax again, his juices filling her mouth, this newly awakened part of her claiming it—claiming her control over him, over his desires, his body. Slowly, she pulled her lips back, catching the remaining drops of his manhood, letting it linger on her tongue before swallowing it. She trailed her mouth up his hard body until he grabbed her roughly by the hair and kissed her, as if to take claim back, assuming his dominance on her.

"I own you," she said seductively.

"Mmm, I'm tempted to concede to that notion if this is what I can expect. I had no idea you were this demanding."

"I had no idea you tasted so good," she whispered.

"You need to stop before I take you again."

"You do this to me, Mark," she said, nibbling on his earlobe. "This has never felt so good. You do something that makes me only want you inside of me."

"Jesus, Skye. All right. We need to go, or I swear I will take you again and this time it will be rough and demanding because you are driving me nuts and making me hard again. It's like I have no off switch with you."

"I might like it rough—"

He rose, picking her up and planting her on her feet.

He wobbled a little and she could tell, despite his soft but still lengthy erection, that she'd left him weak.

"Get dressed now before the Elite rally and pull a mutiny on me."

She pouted her lip but obliged, noting how his eyes followed her body as she covered each part. Her own watched as he tucked himself away but couldn't hide the swollen lump within his pants.

She caught his eye.

"Not sure how I'm going to hide that. You're torturous, Skye."

"I know," she said, trying to figure out how to fix the ripped shirt she held. He grabbed her waist and pulled her close, his hands caressing her breasts, pinching her nipple as his mouth found hers. He brought his head down, kissing her breasts, his tongue dancing along them, licking them, sucking at them. She clung to his shoulders as his hand dug below her waistband, finding her again, his fingers pushing deep, one, then two. Pleasure exploded through her, his tongue and fingers driving her mad. Then he pulled his hand back, tugging her nipple with his teeth, and stood back, licking his fingers slowly before grabbing his shirt.

Her knees were shaking, and her body was aching for its final release.

"You're not the only one who can tease, Skye. If I have to go out there with a hard on, you can go out there like that."

"But I finished you off," she complained, feeling like a child.

"Hmmm, that you did. Oh well, I'll save the rest for later."

"I'll just finish the job before I leave," she threatened.

"Now that's a dirty trick," he replied.

Raising her brow, she brought her hand to her breast, letting her tongue slide seductively across her bottom lip.

"Damn you," he mumbled, watching her hand move down her pants, her eyes rolling back as she met the moisture. She let her head fall back and closed her eyes, thinking of him, feeling the swell again.

"Dammit," he grumbled.

He moved back to her, pushed her across to the wall and pressed against her, kissing her passionately, his hands pushing hers away, his fingers replacing hers, grinding into her, her breath exhaling at the force. He was fast and powerful, stroking across her clit with his thumb as his fingers continued to plunge. His moves brought her to climax, releasing her need quickly, the sheer fire of his actions pushing her to the edge a second time, the anticipation of it causing her entire body to shake until he released her need. Pleasure drowned her again, her knees weakening as he withdrew his hand before she could catch her breath. He gave her a quick kiss, and walked away, licking his fingers.

"Get dressed, Skye, and don't tease me again or I'll make you come so hard you'll be begging me to stop."

A shiver of excitement tingled through her, the door closing softly behind him. Her knees gave, and she slipped to the floor, closing her eyes, the remaining quivers sweeping through her until she could breathe again.

AFTER FINALLY PULLING HERSELF TOGETHER, Skye emerged from the room. She'd managed to use her magic to mend the shirt, pulling the hues from the room to form the damaged material. Thinking of her magic only on a grand scale, she'd missed the subtle delicacy of it, the ability to do smaller tasks with it.

Making her way through the tunnels, she sensed something, a subtle shift in the air, a change in the pressure. She switched directions, heading out through the Elite wing, into the main castle, winding through the corridor once again as if she knew every part of the castle.

As she was heading to the main door, she heard Alex.

"Mom!"

She turned to see him jogging happily toward her. A girl had been at his side and she lingered behind. Alex gave Skye a big hug, which she readily accepted.

"What are you doing out here, Alex? I thought you were in training?"

"I was, but Trent summoned all the mages and told those of us who are training to go back inside. Clover here was giving me a tour."

She moved closer to them, and Skye looked at the pretty girl with freckles, her ginger hair emphasizing the brown eyes. She bowed to Skye, a move Skye didn't think she'd ever grow accustomed to.

"Please don't," Skye said.

"My lady?"

Alex laughed. "That's so strange."

The girl looked confused. Skye wanted to stay and talk, to learn more about this girl who had garnered Alex's attention, but that strange feeling came over her again.

"Alex, you and Clover need to find Mark. Tell him there's something happening. That I can feel it."

She walked away, leaving them, drawn to that feeling which had turned unsettling to her. There were guards stationed at the door. They bowed and protested slightly when she insisted they let her through, but obliged. At the opening of the doors, the sensation grew. Magic, her own magic, sensed it. The colors were on edge, gravitating toward something. She continued into the sprawling courtyard. Passing more guards.

She had yet to leave the castle with the exception of the training fields, so she had yet to see it from this vantage point. It was glorious. She turned to take it in, its structure towering above her, sprawling as far as the eye could see. It was like something out of a movie, with stone that rose in towers, a flag of red and white flying high at the top of one of the towers. She felt small, staring up at it and very out of place. Stuck in a world she didn't understand, one in which she didn't know her place, yet one she was being forced to defend.

She swiveled around, surveying the guards who lined the

front of the castle and those around the wall that stood erected at its outskirts. Guards stood atop, overlooking the kingdom. Was it like the movies? Was there a town beyond those gates? One that now stood in the path of danger?

She ran toward the gates, past stables where horses could be heard, their screams rising as she passed them.

"My lady, you can't go beyond the gates at this time; it's not safe." A guard stopped her. She noted how his eyes drifted to her exposed skin and cursed the lacking outfits assigned to those they called their strongest warriors.

"I need to see what's beyond the castle. Does a village line the outskirts?"

"Aye, one does."

Her heart raced as the sensation swept across her skin again.

"Something is coming." *Camin,* her mind screamed. "You need to evacuate them, get them to safety. Is this all you have stationed out here?"

He gave her a funny look.

"Shouldn't you have more to guard the castle?"

"You guard the castle, my lady. You and the Elite. We fight alongside and protect against average threats, but we do not wield magic. It is you who fights."

She gritted her teeth. Why did it have to be just her?

"Let me through. I need to see the town."

"That's not a wise idea."

"Let me through," she commanded a second guard who stood in front of the gate, and he pushed the heavy door open without hesitation.

"Do not tarry, my lady. I will leave it open until you return."

"Thank you."

She stepped out, seeing the town sprawled out in the distance. It looked as any town in every fantasy movie she'd seen, a shopping district of sorts, small shops, carts for vending, a street that likely was busy with people on any other day, but today, those shops were closed. The houses further on were all shut tight against the oncoming war. As she drew closer to the center of town, she felt the sensation again, only then noticing the black mist that drifted from the town.

She lifted her hand to call the hues, wondering why they were there, separated from their hosts. Everything stilled, even her breath, then a force grabbed her, knocking her to her feet and dragging her down the empty dirt street. The skin on her back tore open with the motion, but she was too shocked to feel the pain. The force pulled her through a wooden door that shattered from the impact of the magic that gripped her body. Pain seared through her arm as it took the force. She'd raised it to protect her face, and something had broken, something other than the door. She bit back the cry when her body stopped. She was in what looked like a woodworker's shop. The windows were all covered with the black hues she'd seen marking all but the space where the shattered door had stood, black and shadowy.

Camin emerged from the shadows, his brown eyes dim in the darkness, his dark blonde hair matted and dirty. He didn't look crazy. In fact, with a shower, he would have been a handsome man, not the typical bad guy.

"You're still weak," he said. "They gave you time, locked me there, thinking I didn't know what they were doing. Yet you remain weak."

He came closer, stooping down next to her until he was close enough to see the rim of gold surrounding his pupil. He pulled a strand of her hair out, letting it glide across his fingers, a strangely tender act.

"You look so much like her, yet you are nothing like her. She was strong, confident, powerful. Her magic was a part of her. So beautiful, yet so lethal." His eyes were distant for a moment, lost in memory, then they narrowed. "You have her beauty, albeit marred by Berrett's eyes, but you are not Lyra, nor will you ever be as strong as she." He lifted her with his power. "They have sent a child into the den of wolves."

He threw her, sending her crashing through the window, glass slicing her skin, her body hitting the ground hard as the sunlight blinded her. She scrambled to her feet, fear engulfing her, adrenaline encouraging her. As confident as she'd been in discovering her magic, the book, all of it, the fear overshadowed it.

A force hit her like a strong wind, sending her into the air, imprisoning her in a tornado of power. She smashed through another window, this time feeling the glass that embedded in her leg before she landed with a hard thump.

"All the power in the world and you can't even defend yourself." He reappeared in front of her. "You need a proper teacher, but they give you their second—the full mages."

He was standing over her, and no matter how she tried, she couldn't will herself to move as he continued to talk. "Typical of this kingdom. Did they tell you why the wizards are banished to the Fettered Forests? Do you know the imperfections of the façade? No? They told you the glory of the kingdoms and forgot the suppression. Do you not wonder why the Mage Warriors live like royalty? Why the other mages live below them? Why the classes exist? Why Mage Warriors, just as wizards once were, are treated as gods yet still chained to the king's rule?"

"No," she managed when she finally found her voice.

"No. Because those secrets must be kept. Ask questions and you may not like the answers you find."

"Skye!" She heard Mark's voice from the distance.

A corrupt smile overcame Camin's face, and he stooped next to her again, sniffing.

"I smell your fear and your mate. I can smell him on you. You are claimed. Pity, if you ever learn your true potential, you and I could have made a glorious couple."

"Skye!" Mark's voice was growing closer.

"Tell me, mage child, how long have you lived in the shadows?"

"What?"

"Only a rare few can enter the shadow realm. I am the only one ever to control its shadows and only after a hefty price from the Death God. You control them with no hesitation, while you hesitate in the world of color. You are curious."

He stood as Mark and Noah burst through the door.

"Let this be your warning. Find the answers before I seek you out again. Otherwise, everything you love will be at risk and I promise you will not live next time."

He disappeared in a swirl of black hues. Mark and Noah moved as though they'd been frozen for that moment. Mark ran to her, Noah searching for any remaining sign of Camin.

"Jesus Christ, you're a mess, Skye. What did I tell you?" He was yelling, but she detected the shake in his voice, the quiver of fear in it. "Noah, he's gone. We need to get her back. The novice mages can patch her up."

He put his hand on her cheek, tracing a cut with his finger.

"He threw me through the window. I'm okay, just a bit banged up."

"She's not ready for this, Mark. No matter what Trent and Elspeth say."

"You're right. We need to find a different way to defeat him."

"He surprised me, that's all. I can do this." But she heard the doubt in her voice, the lack of confidence, as did Mark.

"Mark, we need to get her back now." Noah had moved closer and was pointing to the ground next to her leg, where a puddle of blood had pooled.

"Is that mine?" she asked, growing woozy.

She felt Mark lift her as everything fell away, her eyes closing to the heaviness that had overtaken them.

MARK

Mark paced, an action he was becoming all too familiar with.

"Pacing isn't going to help the situation, Mark," Noah said.

The situation. How had they gotten into this situation? He'd left her after bringing her to ecstasy again, after she'd done the same for him. He hadn't been able to resist. She turned him on in ways no woman ever had, in ways he couldn't have fathomed her doing. He'd imagined that if they'd ever been allowed to express their love for each other, it would be intense. The fantasy had been in his mind for half a century, so it made sense that finally being able to touch her, to kiss her, to feel her, taste her would be an incredible experience, but this...this was addictive. He couldn't get enough of her and the things she did to him, the things she let him do to her, were like the most amazing wet dream ever.

That last time he'd pleasured her, he'd barely been able to make himself leave, the wetness of her on his fingers, and her cries of pleasure as she'd come had been almost too much. It had taken all his will not to tear her pants off and take her there, pounding her against the wall.

Calm yourself, Mark, he told himself, knowing this was not the time nor the place for such thoughts.

He focused on what had happened after he'd left her, not entirely sure what had occurred. He'd calmed himself. Although he'd still received a knowing look from Noah when he'd arrived on the field. They'd been drilling the troops, ensuring everyone was prepared, and that weapons were present, minds focused, and bodies sharp. Only a handful of the Elite had been present for the last war, Camin annihilating their numbers. These men and women had never seen battle, nor had he. He'd been biding his time as an eye doctor for the past decades. He had no idea what he was doing, but he did know what to expect. He'd looked out upon the war, listened as his father led war strategy discussions, as Skye's mother had argued or agreed with whatever suggestions he'd made. He'd watched as they'd prepared, hanging on his father's every word.

He was ready, mentally and physically, as was Noah, who had served below Mark's father.

As he'd stood, thinking through it all, two guards had come to him, telling him of Skye's words, of her wandering into the bordering town, the one that had been evacuated the prior day, that now lay empty of anyone who could help her if she ran into trouble. Alex had come to him a few moments later, babbling about how she'd sent him to say something was coming. Mark wondered if Alex had written her off and taken his time, preoccupied with the pretty girl who remained in the distance as he'd spoken to Mark. He'd address the delay later, after Skye was healed, or perhaps he wouldn't. It would only serve to lay guilt upon Alex's shoulder. The boy was still adjusting, not truly understanding what was at stake.

Upon Alex's words, he and Noah had run the expanse of the castle, knowing the time had been long from her initial conversation with Alex and the guards, knowing the delay had put her at risk. He'd noticed the trail in the dirt road, the fresh track of what looked like a body being dragged, heard the glass break but had been unable to determine where it had come from. His heart beat uncontrollably, adrenaline fueling him as they'd discovered the broken door, the blood drops on the floor of the shop, the splatters of it on the broken window, then again on the ground where her body had fallen.

They'd found her, watching in horror as Camin stood over her, talking. Something had stopped Mark so that he'd been unable to move until Camin had disappeared. Having to watch as Camin had been so close to Skye had been disarming and fear had flooded through him until the hold released and he'd had her in his arms. She wasn't prepared for Camin, nor was he.

Now, he waited as the novice mages tended to her wounds. She'd lost a lot of blood from the gauge on her leg, and he thanked the gods he'd made it back in time, cursing himself for not taking a horse to find her. Too many years in the human world had left his instincts dulled with the privileges of human life, never having to think in terms of necessity.

The wait had seemed endless, Noah keeping him company, keeping him sane as the hours ticked by.

Finally, the doors to the infirmary opened and a mage novice ushered him in. Noah stayed back to give Mark his time alone with Skye. The novices had prepared the infirmary for the impending battle. Beds lined both sides as they had been when he'd been brought in to see his father's dead body, the bodies of the other Elite lining the room at the time, the cries of pain insufferable. He had clung to his mother's hand, holding back the tears as he'd been told to. He was a commander's son, next in line to lead the Elite. Tears were for the weak.

Now the beds lay empty as he walked the same steps he had that night, past the last bed and the room reserved for the Mage Warriors and Elite commanders. As the door was opened, he saw his father's body below the blood-soaked sheet, felt the intense squeeze of his mother's hand as she gripped it, pushing her own unending sorrow away, for she was an Elite, expected back on the battlefield once her respects had been paid.

He blinked the image away, seeing Skye's pale face looking at him instead, a guilty smile upon it.

"I'll leave you two alone for a few minutes. She is not to get up yet, the healing is still occurring in her deeper wounds."

The novice left, and Skye hurriedly whispered, "The novices are healers!"

He sat on the side of the bed, thinking how childlike her wonder was. Brushing a strand of her hair back, he said, "Yes. They are gifted with the more docile, domestic abilities."

"But healing? That's huge!"

"Maybe. Now tell me why, after you agreed to stay in my sight, you decided to wander past the gates without me?"

That guilty look presented itself again. "I don't know...something called me."

"Yeah, Camin called you," he said through gritted teeth, unable to contain his anger.

"I don't know what it was. Whatever it was, my magic was interrupted."

"Magic you can't even use."

"I can, Mark."

"He could have killed you, Skye. You weren't able to defend yourself. I'm telling the king you're not ready and I'm taking you far from here."

"No, Mark. I can't leave. Camin will destroy the kingdom."

"He'll kill you and after what I saw today...seeing your broken body...I'm not going through that again. I'm not risking it."

"He didn't kill me, though."

"But he could have, and he hurt you badly."

She reached over and took his hand, tracing her fingers over his. "I don't think that's what he wants."

He tensed, and she must have noticed, for she spoke quickly. "I'm serious, Mark. He has an agenda, but I don't think killing me is his intent, otherwise, he would have done it today."

He took a moment to think on her words. She was right. He'd had the time—the perfect opportunity to kill her. Why hadn't he?

"Okay, I'll bite. What are you thinking?"

"Why are there ranks of mages?"

"That's the question you ask? I give you free rein to convince me not to hide you away somewhere and you ask me the history of the mage classes?"

"Yes. Why the classes?"

"There's an order. Like I said, the novice mages have the basic abilities, domestic magic, healing—"

"Healing is a basic ability? Can I heal?"

"No, only the novices can, and medicine—as humans would call it—is considered a domestic magic."

She rolled her eyes.

"If you're not going to take this seriously, I'm not going to tell you."

"Fine, tell me about the full mages."

"Full mages are spell casters. Their magic is physical, manifested only with spells they cast or in actions through their staffs or wands."

"So full mages can't wield magic without some sort of conduit?"

"Correct."

"And Mage Warriors use the hues of their world to fuel their magic. They don't need a conduit."

"Yes. Their magic is also the deadliest. It increases with each rank."

She twirled a strand of hair, chewing on the end of it. An act he found intensely adorable.

"What's the connection between them?" she asked.

"Connection?"

"They're all connected. They must be, each a bridge to the other."

"Skye, what is this all about?"

"Camin said I need to ask questions. He implied that things aren't as they seem."

"Camin? The bad guy? The enemy of all the kingdoms?"

"Why is he the enemy?"

"Because he waged war on the kingdoms. He killed my parents, Skye, and yours."

"I think he once loved my mother."

He found that surprising, having never heard anyone suggest such a thing. "That would imply he knew her."

"Yes, that's how I understood it. I think there's a lot more to this story that we don't know, Mark."

The door opened too soon, and the novice mage returned.

"She needs to rest now."

"Rest? There's a war brewing, there's no time for her to rest," he argued.

"She needs another hour at the least, or her deeper injuries will not completely heal."

"Can't I talk to him for a little longer?"

"No, my lady—"

"Please don't call me that. Skye is fine."

The novice looked taken aback, the lesser ranks never addressed Mage Warriors by their first name. Only higher-ranking mages like Trent and Elspeth had that privilege.

"What's your name?" Skye asked.

"Madeline."

"Madeline, are there any libraries dedicated just to the novice mages or to the full mages?"

"No, my—Skye," she corrected as Skye shot her the mom-look she often gave Alex. "But we do have a section of the learning library dedicated to our magic, as do the full mages."

"What's the learning library?"

"It's the library we all use as we're being trained, Elite and mage alike," Mark answered. "It contains the books of our history, our science, anything needed to teach a youth to use magic to their full potential."

"I must insist you sleep now," Madeline said.

"I can't sleep," Skye protested. "I'm too awake."

Madeline placed her hand on Skye's head and Skye yawned, her eyes growing heavy.

"Are you doing that?" she asked groggily.

"Shh, rest just a little longer."

Skye's eyes fluttered shut and soon her body relaxed, succumbing to the sleep magic.

Madeline eyed Mark. "I take it you want to stay with her?"

"That would be nice, but I need to run out and speak to Noah first, then I'll return to her."

She nodded before leaving the room.

Mark looked at Skye again, thinking of how easily she'd been put to sleep. Why were the novice mages ranked as having lesser magic? Skye was right, the ability to heal was a strong ability. He'd just witnessed the girl put Skye, a Mage Warrior, to sleep in seconds. Why were their powers locked behind the castle walls and not used for the good of the people, or on the battlefield for that matter?

He rose, stopping to kiss her on her forehead, taking her in again—the beauty of her, the fragility that frightened him. Then he headed back out to find Noah, who was right where he'd left him.

"How is she?"

"She'll survive. She thinks Camin has his own agenda."

"Yeah, to take over the kingdoms."

"No, something different."

"Did they not fix her head? Does she have a concussion, and they didn't realize it?"

"I'm serious, Noah."

He looked around before pulling Noah into a corner, away from prying ears.

"She's asking questions about the rank system. Camin told her to question it."

"Why?"

"I'm not sure. She also thinks her mother knew Camin."

"That's unsettling."

"So, you're not aware of that?"

"No, but Lyra was older than me. There is much I don't know about her. Your uncle would know. If anyone knows, it would be him. But, Mark, the rank system has been in place for ages. Why the question about it now? And I thought we'd determined the shadow gods are the real reason for these attacks."

"Maybe each of them has an agenda. Maybe Camin's has always been the reason for the fighting, the wars, and the addition of Skye has fueled the shadow gods for their own purpose."

"I'm incredibly confused. So, both Camin and the shadow gods want Skye for their own use?"

"Exactly. The Death God and his shadow gods are using Camin to get to her. I wonder if they even know of his agenda."

"So, you mean to tell me the war was never about overthrowing the kingdoms?"

"Perhaps not."

Noah wiped his face, letting his hand linger on his chin.

"How do we know this isn't all a ruse? That he's not misleading her?"

"We don't, but she's right about one thing, he didn't kill her. He had the chance, and he left her alive."

MARK

Feeling as if he were going cross-eyed, Mark closed the book and looked at Skye, who was surrounded by a stack of books. He had waited for her to wake and, as soon as the novices had cleared her, led her to the learning library. Here they'd sat as she poured through every book she could reach and every one she made him reach.

"Skye, there's nothing here. I swear, all I do with you is read through books."

She peeked around the stack. "All? I do remember us doing a bit more than reading earlier today."

She winked at him, running her tongue across her lips.

"You know what I mean," he growled in a low voice as his body reacted to the move.

Her foot came up, rubbing against his pants.

"Now that's just not fair," he said, stopping it.

"I never said I played fair."

"Ha, no you don't. Why don't we go someplace private, and you can show me how unfair you can be?"

They were tucked in the farthest corner of the library, hidden behind shelves of dusty books that no one ever used. Skye had asked to be left in privacy and a Mage Warrior's command was always heeded, no matter if it was meant as a command or not.

She rose and walked to his side of the table, pushing his book stack aside and leaning against the table.

"What are you doing, Skye?"

"Playing unfair."

She pulled his shirt, urging him from his chair and bringing him to her.

"I don't think this is the place," he whispered as she brought his hand to her breast, the soft skin of it pushed above her dress, causing his heart to beat faster.

His body reacted again, her hands reaching down to feel his growing erection.

"God, Skye. You were just in the infirmary."

"But I feel so much better now." She drew him closer, kissing him, his resistance fading.

He slipped his hand below the material, cupping the swell of her breast, his resolve shattering as her nipples firmed in his hand. With his other hand, he lifted the material of her dress until her nakedness greeted his hand.

"You really need to wear some underwear," he breathed, stroking his thumb against her, silently thanking the novice mage for making her change into the dress before leaving.

She freed his hardness from his pants, and he moved his hand around her, lifting her so that she sat on the table, the books falling around them.

Entering her, he pulled her ass closer, pushing himself deeper. She shoved his shirt up and moved his hand from her breast, pulling the scoop of the neck down enough so that they sprung free, pressing them against his skin, the softness of them arousing him more. The thought of getting caught, the sheer recklessness of their actions, moved him to climax faster, the moistness of her only succeeding in the effort.

She was breathless, yet continued her demanding kisses as if all she wanted from him were his hard, quick thrusts, each one emitting a soft moan from her. As the need for release became too great, he clung to her, the rapture hitting him hard. He pushed into her a few more times, slow and deliberate, as the remains of his climax swept through him. It was the first time he had come without her, and part of him missed the accompanying quivers of her body. He withdrew and peeked around, relieved that no one had discovered them. Tucking himself away, he stopped her from pulling her dress up, his thumb rubbing along her nipples, delighting in how they rose to attention for him. He brought his mouth to one, pulling the firm nipple into his mouth and meeting it with his tongue. His other hand caressed her left breast, playing with her nipple until it was hard enough to crack glass.

He dropped his hand below her lifted dress, continuing the assault with his tongue on her breasts. Her body shook as his fingers slipped into her, the remnants of his orgasm still filling her, making her seductively wet, his body reacting like it hadn't already been sated.

"You make me so hungry," he said, draping his tongue up her neck to her mouth, while his fingers dove into her, his thumb rubbing against her clit, his thigh spreading her legs wider.

She threw her head back, her back arching, his mouth dropping to her chest, her muscles tensing, hands gripping the table so tight he thought it might crack. Finally, she tightened around his fingers, her body convulsing as he continued to torment her. He heard her stifled cry as she bit her lip to stop it. As the final tremor settled, and her muscles relaxed, he pulled his fingers free and pushed his pants back down, too hard to resist the slickness that lay spread wide for him. He plunged into her again and she gripped his back tight, her body beginning to tense again as he pounded hard, her feet hooked on the ledge, a position that left her wide enough for him to go to his full extent. Ripples of her prior orgasm were still flushing through her, and he could feel her rising to another one, his own body reacting at how easily she came for him.

He wanted to go slow, knew he'd go longer after having just come but the threat of being discovered turned him on so much that he reached his climax fast, Skye breaking with him this time. Her fingers dug into his back as they rode the wave down.

He held her close, feeling the energy drain from his body with the final tremors of her body below his.

"We really need to get back to a bedroom," he whispered. "This fast stuff is great, but I want to make love to you for hours again."

She kissed him, pulling his shirt down and then pushing him back so that he exited her warmth.

"Although," he said, pulling his pants up, "I don't think there's anything left in me.".

She slipped her hand down them and played with him until instinct took over again.

"There's plenty left in you and it's all mine." She pulled her hand free and hopped down, her dress covering her again, all but the breasts which still draped free. He reached out and grabbed one, rubbing her nipple until it grew hard again, then pulled the material up to hide them.

"Is it the place that makes it so hard to not crave you?" she asked.

"No, it's the last several decades we've craved each other and are now making up for."

"I could get used to this," she said, then a strange look crossed her face before she pulled her dress up, reaching her hand below it then bringing it back out, sticky with his juices. He gave her a smirk as she licked her fingers.

"I think I'm in need of a bath and a dress change," she said, using the material to clean the rest of her legs.

"I don't think that's very ladylike, Skye."

"I keep telling them I'm not a lady."

She turned back to the books and put her hands on her hips. He had to shake the dirty thoughts from his head so he could concentrate. She drove him mad with need, and each time she filled it, the need rose again, an unquenchable thirst.

"What does he want me to find?" she muttered.

He put his arms around her waist and leaned against her, knowing she could feel the erection that was throbbing again.

"I don't think he wanted you to find what we just explored."

She giggled. "Don't tell me you're frisky again."

"You do something to me, Skye, something you've unlocked that I can't cage again."

She reached her hand behind her and squeezed his erection. Visions of bending her over and taking her from behind filled his mind.

Focus, Mark.

"Did you find what you needed?" A voice startled them both.

For fear of being exposed for the arousal that filled his pants, he couldn't turn, but thankfully, Skye quickly turned to talk to the novice mage who tended the library. She'd been there forever and looked her age, her long life clearly beginning its descent to her passing.

"Not quite. Are these all the books you have on the differences between the rankings?"

"Yes, dear. What exactly are you trying to find?"

"Similarities, something that connects us," she answered.

"Magic is the only thing that connects the classes, but the differences within that magic are what keep us separated."

She walked away and Skye stood, chewing her finger and thinking on her words.

"I'm missing something—something that's not in these books."

"Maybe it's just a wild goose chase. Maybe he's playing mind games with you, Skye."

"No, I don't think so." She turned back to the table, running her hands along it before hopping onto it and sitting again.

"Is that a hint?" he asked.

Laughing, she replied, "Have the mages always lived here in the castle?"

"Clearly not a hint," he mumbled before answering. "No. Long ago, thousands of years ago, the mages and Elite had their own kingdom."

She seemed surprised at the knowledge. "Really? Why were they merged with this kingdom?"

He shrugged. "I really don't know. I was never much for history and a lot of it has been lost over the years, anyway. It's been an insanely long time since the kingdoms were merged."

"Who would know?"

"Really?"

"Yes, there's something wrong. He implied I need to look at the classes, find out where I come from."

"Petrian is the only one who might know and the only one I would trust to not have this get back to the king."

"Why would the king care?"

"I'm not really sure. I remember my mother once telling me that some things were only for our ears, that we had to watch our tongues."

"Strange, and why would Petrian know?"

"He's a huge history nerd. He may not look it, but he will bore the pants off you if given the chance."

"Funny, he struck me as more of a Casanova type than a nerd."

"Oh, he is. I've always been suspicious that he lures women in with his knowledge or maybe he does literally bore the pants off them."

She laughed, and he held his hand out to her.

"You sure you want to go down this path with me?" she asked.

"Certain. I'm on whatever path you take. Besides, my heart

and my position are sworn to you. The Elite commander never questions his Mage Warrior."

THEY SEARCHED the Elite wing for Petrian, only to find he'd gone with Trent to the town of Merant. It was the closest town past the bordering town of Henire, which was currently empty and partially destroyed by Camin's stunt earlier that day.

Merant lay about three miles beyond the castle. Mark had given a few of the Elite a day of rest, believing Skye's theory that Camin wasn't ready to strike yet. That Camin was giving her time. Although now that Camin had attacked her, Mark was regretting that decision. Complacence never led to anything good. He'd ordered them to be on guard, but some, like Petrian, had left the castle grounds.

"We'll need to change if we're going into Merant, plus you need clothing you can ride in."

"Ride?"

"Horseback."

"I haven't ridden a horse since we were kids in Skye and...oh. Is that why my parents insisted I master riding?"

He nodded. "You'll be fine. I haven't ridden much since then either, although Noah insisted riding remained as part of my training. It's been a few months, though."

"You went riding? As training?"

He winked and started walking toward his room.

"Go change into something better suited and less conspicuous. Grab a cloak as well."

He ignored her complaints and continued down the Elite wing.

When he'd changed into a pair of brown riding pants and a white tunic he'd found in his father's belongings, he waited for Skye at the intersection between the two wings. It seemed strange wearing his father's clothes. He and his father were the same build, but the memories attached to the clothing weighed heavily on him.

As he waited, he stared at the space he knew was the secret Mage Warrior lair, wondering why it was secret, why even the king did not know of its existence. Was there more to it than they'd originally suspected?

He stood pondering it. His parents and Skye's had all secretly met in that room. Skye had said Camin had known her mother. Had his parents known him as well? Had Petrian? There was a history he'd been too young to be aware of, one that possibly held some of the answers Skye was looking for.

As if knowing she was in his thoughts, she came around the corner. She wore a tight pair of brown riding pants with boots that rose to the top of her calves. His eyes traveled their length, imagining them without the pants, although the pants made no effort to conceal her curves, nor the fact that no underwear lie below them.

He swallowed, his eyes drifting to her shirt. She wore a blue tunic with long loose sleeves; the neck dipped low, a bit of skin from her breast peeking out. Over the shirt, she'd donned one of her mother's training shirts, the brown leather tight in spots that helped emphasize the opening at her chest. She'd left her hair loose, the thick dark auburn locks falling down her back. The blue of the shirt made her eyes stand out strikingly.

"I got tired of all the exposed skin, so I found this in what must have been my father's clothes."

"So, you did. I will say you left just enough exposed to torment me and every other man within a mile of you," he said, skimming his fingers along the dip in the neckline.

"Don't we have horses to ride?" she asked with a lift of her brow.

"That's a lead in for a really cheesy sexual line that I'm not going to fall for, no matter how my mind wants me to."

"Come on, lover boy." She wrapped her arm through his.

It was then that he noticed the blue cape she'd brought in her other hand.

"Seems your mother had a penchant for blue as well," he noted.

"Yeah, there's a lot in her wardrobe, as well as my father's. Did I wear a lot of blue?"

He'd forgotten everything had looked blue or gray to her before her true sight had returned.

"Yes, almost everything you wore was blue. Strangely enough."

"Huh, I wonder why I'm so drawn to it."

They continued to walk toward the main area of the castle.

"Look, there's Alex!" she excitedly cried, moving to go to him.

He pulled her back, thinking this wasn't the best route, something nudging him that the fewer people who knew what they were up to, the better.

"What are you doing?" she asked as he dragged her back into the hallway.

"Leave him, he's fine." Alex was talking with the same girl with ginger hair that Mark had seen him with earlier, laughing at something she'd said. He looked happy. "It's better if he doesn't know what we're doing. It might be best if no one else knows."

"Mark?"

"Just a hunch. Come on, let's go through the tunnels and use the horses stabled near the Elite wing."

He pulled her with him, and they made their way back toward the tunnels. When they got to the stables, they waited for a stable hand to saddle the horses. Mark directed her to put the cloak on, glad it was one that didn't have the king's insignia on it. He knew he was being overcautious, but something was needling him. Something told him they were meddling where they weren't supposed to. Otherwise, the answers Skye needed would have been in those books.

Just as he'd suggested, Skye remembered how to ride. They made it through the front gates; the guards letting them through on the premise they were on a training mission for Skye. Then they rode through the debris from Camin's attack on her, and out to the countryside. Skye pulled her horse to a halt, her eyes surveying the open land.

"It's so beautiful, fresh and untouched."

He let his eyes take it in, realizing how right she was. After so long in the other world, surrounded by great cities and sprawling suburbs, he'd forgotten the glory of their true homeland. He looked back, surveying the castle looming in the distance, grand and towering, the reality of their new life coming back to him. The afternoon sun was beginning to lower above them, and he hadn't realized it was so late in the day.

"Let's go," he said, urging his horse to a fast trot.

After about a half an hour of riding, they came upon the town. Mark urged her to pull her cape up and cover her head. He did the same. Word travelled fast and Mage Warriors were like gods to those outside the castle walls. They were likely myths brought to life with Skye's return. She was too striking to go unnoticed, her clothing too distinctive to belong to just anyone.

He led her inside after tying the horses. She tried to take his hand, but he pushed her away.

"Discreet, Skye. This isn't your local bar. We don't know who could be in here watching."

"Since when are you so mysterious?"

"You forget, I was young when we left, but the Elite begin training as soon as they can walk. I have years of training with the sharpest of commanders leading me."

He scanned the room, finding Petrian in a far corner, Trent next to him but with his cape drawn. Mark hadn't seen Trent since earlier in the day and wondered why he and Petrian were hiding in the back of the tavern. Had they been together all day?

"Come," he said, putting the thought aside and leading her further in.

Petrian tensed as they approached until Mark dropped his hood back to show his identity.

"Markham?" He looked between them. "Skye?"

Skye stayed quiet as he ushered her into the seat closest to Trent and furthest from the room.

"Why the secrecy?" Petrian asked.

"Same reason as Trent, prying eyes and listening ears." He refrained from asking about Trent's reason for secrecy, thinking if he had a reason, it was best left discussed at a later time. They had more to worry about.

Petrian's expression grew serious. "What's happened?"

"Camin attacked Skye earlier." Petrian and Trent both reacted, but Mark stopped them. "She's fine, as you can see, but we need some answers. Skye needs them."

Petrian eyed him. "You're leaving something out."

"I wandered beyond the castle gates. Camin lured me out. I lost the fight and ended up in the infirmary."

"You went beyond the gates? Without your Elite? Without Markhem?"

"Trust me, I've heard it from Mark already," Skye said defensively.

Petrian's forehead creased with worry, but Trent spoke this time. "Camin attacked you, bested you, and let you live?"

"Yes," Mark answered for her. "Which is why we're here. Skye thinks there's something he wants her to find. Answers that aren't easily found."

"Did you try the libraries?" Trent asked, taking a sip of his ale, tension clear in the grip on his mug.

"I don't think answers found in the library warrant a hooded appearance in a tavern," Petrian said with a hint of edge to his voice. "What is it you're looking for, Skye?"

"I want to know about life before the kingdoms merged."

Trent nearly spit his ale out and, for a moment, Mark wondered if it was safe to include Trent in the conversation. Was there a risk? He hadn't gone with them to the other world. He'd been here, working for the king, an outsider to their small group. Mark wished he'd grabbed Noah to accompany them. He could have asked Noah's opinion.

"Have you been putting this in her head?" Petrian asked.

"No, Camin did. Skye thinks Camin knew her mother."

Petrian leaned back and Trent pushed his hood slightly so they could see his concerned eyes. He glanced at Petrian.

"They did know each other," Petrian said in a whisper. "Camin was once part of the Mage Warrior ranks. He grew up with your parents."

"Why didn't I know that?" Mark asked.

"It's not talked about. He's a stain on the ranks, and they prefer to leave the legacy of the Mage Warriors clean."

"He grew up with my parents?" Skye asked.

"Trained side by side with your mother. He was in love with her, but she loved your father. The attraction of their blood was unbreakable; he knew this."

"But he still pursued her?"

"Pursued? What makes you think that?"

"I don't know," she murmured.

"No, he swore his allegiance to her, to your father, to protect her as best he could."

Mark was confused. "But he killed her."

"Yes, he did. It's a long story, a sad one," said Petrian. "Camin lost his way, began experimenting with dark magic, the side he inherited from his father's blood creeping out. They had taken him in as a youth, knowing he was Swalda's son, gave him a chance, but the wizard's blood made its way in, corrupting the magic he'd inherited from his mother. They'd suspected it might happen, suspected his magic was a strange combination of warrior and wizard magic, but that the dark magic of his wizard blood would overshadow his warrior blood. And it did."

"He got caught practicing the unsanctioned magic, and they kicked him out," Trent said.

"Unsanctioned magic?" she asked.

"Wizard magic, shadow magic from the shadow gods. You see," Trent said, "a Mage Warrior's magic comes from the brilliance of the light, the colors that make our world. The shadows make the shadow realm, and magic from the hues of that realm is forbidden magic."

Skye squeezed Mark's hand under the table. She had used the colors of the shadow realm to escape. He knew exactly what she was thinking.

"Wizards live in the shadow hues," Trent continued. "Their strength is in the darker shades, in the colors of night. They have magic similar to both the warriors and full mages. They can move themselves from place to place like a full mage would, but without a conduit. They use the hues but not the light hues like the Mage Warriors prefer. Instead, they use the shadow hues, close enough to shadow magic to be a concern. That's why they were banished to the Fettered Forest."

"Shadow magic?" Skye asked.

"Yes, it is long lost magic. It comes directly from the shadow realm. It was only ever seen in Digremile but was lost to them when the Death God cursed them ages ago. Talk of shadow magic is forbidden and anything close to it, like wielding the shadow hues, is seen as a defiance of the law, hence why the wizards were banished."

Mark could see Skye was confused. There was a history to their world that was rife with the stories of old magic, but there was not time to take that path now. It would only derail the purpose of their secretive visit. Instead, he steered the conversation back to the wizards.

"The wizards once lived in the kingdom?" he asked.

Trent looked around, but it was Petrian who answered. "It's best if we take this conversation away from non-caster ears."

He pulled a few coins out and placed them on the table, motioning them to get up. "Trent and I will meet you on the edge of town shortly; it's best if you leave separate from us."

He and Skye did as directed and waited for them after getting their horses.

"What's going on Mark?" she whispered.

"Apparently you've stumbled upon something that only we casters are privy to, or perhaps we're not meant to discuss."

"What's the distinction? Why are you considered a caster when you don't wield magic?"

"Because we can control magic, only the Elite can handle the power of a Mage Warrior and direct it for our own use. Even full mages can't do that. We're like a conduit for your power, but use it for your protection."

"That's why you bear the mark."

"Yes, our birthmark, like yours, identifies us as Elite. Non-casters have no birthmark and again no connection to magic, and they outnumber us greatly."

"At one time, they did not," Trent said, coming up to them, his gray dappled mare pulling against the reins.

"Why are you asking questions, Skye?" Petrian asked, drawing up next to her.

"There's something Camin wants me to know. He said I needed answers, that I needed to understand why the wizards live outside the kingdom, why I can walk and wield in the shadows."

"Those are dangerous words, Skye. Do not ever let any non-caster know that you have that ability," Trent warned. "Your powers are untapped and untrained. It is the only thing that might protect you from the reaction to those words or it may damn you. Fear of the unknown is a wicked sword."

"Noted," she said, her voice soft.

"But Theodore knows. He was there when she passed out

that day. Elspeth knows as well," Mark said, hearing the concern that layered his voice, the same that was now assailing him internally.

"Elspeth is fine. She will not jeopardize Skye's safety. She is the least of your concerns. Theodore is another matter, but the questions about the past pose the bigger threat than does her ability to walk the shadow realm."

It had grown dark and as their horses moved further from town, Petrian steered them from the main road to a small patch of trees where they could not be easily seen.

"Would someone mind telling me why there's so much secrecy to my questions?" Skye asked.

"Because, my dear, you are stirring the warnock's nest," Petrian said.

"Warnock?"

"Miserable things, worse than hornets," Mark told her, remembering the sting of one as he'd run along the creek behind the castle training grounds.

"You see, mages and the non-castors have not always been allies. Long ago, the mages and Elite lived in the kingdom of Kantenda, far beyond the Fettered Forests." He pointed to the west. "The kingdom encompassed the forests and beyond to the Dranth mountain range. The non-castors resented us, jealous of our abilities, fearful of them. We were no threat, we were peaceful, keeping to ourselves. There was no rank system, no differences between the types of magic other than casting names. Each level mage was considered crucial to our kingdom. Mage Warriors were still respected but not treated like royalty, with one exception—your line. Your line ruled the kingdom. It was pure, always continued through mating with the strongest of the Elite. The Elite were our warriors, guarding the kingdom, not left to simple guard duty for the few Mage Warriors. They were feared throughout the kingdoms for their strength and skills. It was supposedly a glorious time."

"What happened?" Mark asked, surprised he'd never heard any of this.

"Theodore's ancestor. He sparked fear in the non-casters and kidnapped our king's daughter."

"Kidnapped? How is that possible if we have magic?" Skye asked.

"Ah, Mage Warriors are born with the mark but do not come into power until their fifth year. The Mage Warriors of your line do not come into power until their third year of life, when the birthmark takes on its color. You were an exception to that," Petrian said.

"How do you know—"

"I was close to your parents Skye, remember that."

"So, they kidnapped her and?"

"Brought our kingdom to its knees. He threatened to kill her if the kingdom did not bend. Your line only bears one warrior offspring, other Mage Warriors who are called do not bear Mage Warriors; the calling is random. The king's line, being the only pure line, is tied to the power of every mage, no matter rank. The non-caster king knew this somehow," Petrian continued.

"Kill the ruling Mage Warrior, drain the power?" Mark asked.

"Yes. Why do you think the Elite are all entrusted to protect only a handful of warriors? Why the commander of our kingdom and his second are charged with the lead Mage Warrior, that of Skye's line?"

"I never thought about it."

"Theodore's predecessor had the advantage; we succumbed and were enslaved to the kingdom. No one says that, but it's true. We use our magic for their king, to protect their people, our own used for domestic uses, healing, casting protection spells, war."

"Why haven't we tried to escape?"

"Most are blind to it, the history blurred, the ability to live within the castle walls too tempting, the royal treatment of the Mage Warriors too enticing," Petrian said.

"There was one once who tried," said Trent. "Camin's mother, she was cast out, dropped in the darkness of the Fettered Forest, her abilities muted by the lack of color. Camin's father found her, forced her to bear him a son, then killed her, dropping her body at the castle gates. Her death was a harsh warning to anyone else who questioned the order."

They were silent as they contemplated the cruelty of both sides.

"But you said Mage Warriors don't have Mage Warrior children," Skye said, breaking the silence.

"That is true and Camin remains a mystery to this day," Petrian said. "It was thought that something in his wizard blood called the Mage Warrior powers. His marking was not Mage Warrior, but he wielded the hues just as the warriors do."

"Wizards have their own marking?" Mark asked, not remembering any wizard history in his studies. It was a topic most preferred to avoid.

"Yes, it is the opposite of the Mage Warriors, distinctly opposite. It holds the same shape as the crescent moon but turned backward and the color is black. When triggered, it does not emit the soft purple shimmer that Skye's does."

"Were the wizards ever part of the kingdom?" Skye asked.

"Interesting question," Trent answered. "I imagine they once were, but that part of our history has been forgotten, convoluted with their terrible deeds."

"Yes, I don't remember them ever being part of our kind, none who were assimilated into the existing kingdom. Camin was the only exception due to his mother's heritage," Petrian said. "The rest stayed hidden in the forest. The occasional few who dared wander to the kingdom were pushed back to the forest long ago so that in time they remained there."

"Perhaps they were. Perhaps they were the only ones who fought back," Skye said, causing them all to halt their horses.

"You think the wizards were once part of our people?"

"Yes," she answered confidently. "I think they refused to comply, or perhaps they fought back."

"And their own king turned his back on them to save his daughter," Mark finished. "Jesus, Skye, do you know what you're saying?"

"That those people that we're fighting are our people, they always have been. They may not be the monsters history has made them out to be. That's what Camin wanted to show me."

"None of this can get out, Skye," Trent said, concern in his voice.

"Why? What does the king hold over our heads now to keep us enslaved?"

"Our lives," Petrian said. "This world is new to you, but the ways that are in place have been in place for thousands of years. If you upset the balance, it will all crumble."

"It looks to me like it was already on the brink of crumbling before I entered the picture."

"Skye," Mark said, agreeing with Petrian that she needed to keep silent until they knew Camin's agenda. "Please, you can't do anything about it yet. We're all vulnerable and highly outnumbered."

"But we have magic."

"Yes, but is it enough to keep the novices alive? Their numbers are greater than your one. We need to find out why Camin wanted you to discover this. And don't forget, his agenda and that of the Death God are separate. We need to take this cautiously."

"Fine, we wait, but that doesn't mean I stop asking questions."

She urged her horse forward, leaving them to stare at her, leaving him to contemplate what they'd gotten into and how he was going to keep her safe now that she had entered a completely unexpected battlefield.

SKYE

Skye had woken early, well before the sun rose. Her naked limbs were still tangled in Mark's, his hand still cupping her breast even in sleep. They'd made love twice before the long day caught up with them and sleep overcame them. She'd stared at Mark, taking in all the features of his face that she knew by heart, the relaxed, contented expression that lay upon it. Unable to resist, she'd made her way down his chest to where his morning firmness had already taken shape. She'd gone down on him, taking him in, letting her tongue glide along his length, his thickness filling her mouth. He'd moaned in his sleep and the waves of need had poured through her. As he woke, he grew thicker, the cusp of his climax rising, his hands burrowing in her hair, pushing her head further, his moans intensifying until he had spilled into her, her lips pulling all the juices from him as he bucked in pleasure.

After he'd recovered, he'd taken her, flipping her on all fours before taking her from behind, his hands tight around her hips, making sure to give her breasts the attention they needed to bring her close to her own climax. He'd pulled out when she was close, his tongue finishing the job, the pleasure exploding through her, then continuing as he'd entered her again, a second orgasm building intensely until she came again with him, their bodies tightening with the force, the ecstasy of it sending shock waves through her.

Now as she sat on the bed, dressed in the same clothes she'd worn the prior day, her mind wandered to the bath they'd taken, the images threatening to make her want more. She tried to focus as she watched him pull a shirt over his head, covering those firm muscles that she loved to rub, the same ones that pressed against her soft body when they made love. He tugged it down and met her eyes, raising an eyebrow as if he knew her thoughts. Walking over to her, he ran his fingers along her neckline, letting them slip under her shirt, her nipple reacting as the warmth of his hand engulfed her breast, his thumb sliding gently across its peak.

She sat up on her knees and pulled him closer, kissing him, letting the kiss linger as though it were their last. Something deep within her telling her that today would change everything for them.

"Hey," he said, releasing her breast and bringing his hand to her face, "What's wrong?"

She gave him a small smile. "Just stealing one more kiss."

His hazel eyes studied her, seeing into the deepest parts of her soul. She brought her fingers to his face, tracing every inch, re-memorizing it.

"Everything okay?"

She nodded, unable to shake the feeling, but also unable to voice it, to put the possibility of losing him into words.

Instead, she kissed him, letting her kiss speak for her, sending her feelings through that one small act. His arms embraced her, pulling her and lifting her from the bed so that she was standing against him, his embrace protecting her from whatever was to come.

Their lips parted slowly, and he lowered his head against hers.

"You're scaring me, Skye. Is there something you're not telling me?"

She shook her head.

"Skye—"

"I'm sure it's nothing, just a feeling. I think ..." She hesitated, not wanting to put her fear into words, afraid doing so would make them real. "I think Camin will strike today. Be careful."

"Me be careful? After the wreck of a state he left you in the other day, it's you we should be worried about."

She smiled. "Good point."

"You need to fight back this time, Skye, or he will kill you. If he doesn't, his army will. Now, since you seem extra concerned today, I'm going to put the troops on high alert and set perimeters around the castle grounds."

There was a hasty knock on the door, and Noah barged in.

"Thank the gods you're dressed. Camin has taken the Nenochin Kingdom. It fell in the night. We just got word."

"Where is he now?"

"We don't know. He has wizards attacking to the east of us but the message didn't mention him."

"East? Apendia? They're no threat to him. He left them alone during the war. Why attack them now?"

"They have a new queen, Crimson. Her father died during the war. She's young, untested like Skye. She's been pestering Theodore for a glimpse of Skye since we returned. She has a strange fixation with mages, but Theodore won't let her near you. He's suspicious of her."

"What kind of fixation?"

"From what I've been hearing, she uses their magic for her own pleasure."

Skye's lips formed an *oh*, the word not coming out but the images filling her head. She'd never thought of using her magic with Mark. What they did was intense enough, but it did make her wonder.

"I've also been hearing she can be quite manipulative. Now, mind you, this is all hearsay I've collected since we've been back."

"I'm confused. I thought Theodore's kingdom merged with the mage kingdom. Why would she have mages?"

"Someone's been doing her homework," Noah said, looking behind him then shutting the door.

"It did," he whispered. "The other kingdoms grew jealous and demanded they get a share. Full and novice mages were sold to the other kingdoms, and each was given two Mage Warriors. The Eltander Kingdom was the only one that refused to take the full and novice, but they did take the Mage Warriors."

"Wait, they were sold like slaves?"

Noah cringed, but didn't deny it.

"And the Mage Warriors and the Elite?"

"The Mage Warriors were gifted. They were treated as royalty just as they were here. The bulk of the Elite remained with the original queen here in our kingdom, with only a few sent to guard the Mage Warriors in each of the other kingdoms."

"The queen we kidnapped."

Noah's eyes grew serious, then he looked at Mark.

"Keep her in check, Markhem, before she gets herself killed."

"It's a hard thing to do. She's quite stubborn."

"Only a few of us know the history, Skye, it is imperative that you do not let anyone hear you discuss it."

"I'm getting that feeling. You said the Eltander did not buy the other mages?"

"No, they were close to our kingdom, their race related to ours; they don't have magic per se but they have certain abilities. They are similar to what the humans call elves, but without the ears and long flowing hair."

"They have their own abilities?"

"Yes, but nothing like those of our people. Theirs are more spiritual, mental, you might say. Their magic is too weak to fight.

It was that way when our kingdoms merged and so it was when Camin attacked."

"How do you know all this?" Mark asked. Skye could sense the suspicion in his voice.

"There are a few of us privy to the history, some passed it on orally, as was my case, some like I suspect your uncle, based on whose circles they travel. Your mother would have known, she comes directly from the royal line, there's no way it didn't pass on as a warning to each born into your line."

"But it wasn't in the journal she left me."

"It wouldn't be," Mark said. "That sort of story would be handed down orally. Having it in writing would be risky."

"Treasonous," Noah said.

Treasonous? What kind of world had she stepped into? It had appeared so inviting and wonderful, the draw of royal treatment. All of it was a façade, covering the terrible reality beneath.

"Does our kingdom still exist?"

"We are one kingdom," Noah said, "and it would be wise to never forget that."

"Does the old kingdom still exist?" she asked, crossing her arms.

"No, it's only ruins now. I snuck out there once when I was a child, after my gran told me the history. The towns were laid to waste, a pile of rubble stood where I suspect the castle once stood. There's nothing there now, I'd wager, but the same. But, Skye, you need to keep your questions guarded. If raised in the wrong company, the consequences will be swift."

She shuddered at the thought. "Duly noted," she said, slowly chewing her thumbnail. "I should find Elspeth, tell her my strange feelings about today."

"Feelings?"

"Skye thinks something is going to happen today. I'm putting the Elite on high alert. Will you inform the king so he can have the guard ready?"

"Of course."

He gave a quick nod to Skye and was gone, heading down the tower stairs.

She walked to the window, her hand holding Mark's until she could no longer reach, and it dropped to her side, like a foreshadowing of something to come.

"What are you thinking, Skye?"

"That I don't know what I'm doing, that I want to be back in my old life oblivious to all of this..." As she said the words, she realized that her former state had forced her to be without Mark. It hadn't been ideal, and she would never take it back if it meant losing him. "Well, not all of my old life."

He placed his arms around her waist and leaned his head into her neck, giving her a soft kiss. "Good save."

"I feel like a princess locked away in her tower," she said, looking down at the ground below.

"Only you're not locked away and I'm here with you, Rapunzel."

"True," she said, laughing. "I'm glad you're here."

"Me, too. My body is extremely glad it's here."

She bent her head back and laughed. "Only your body?"

"All of me," he whispered.

She turned, so that she was facing him, and searched his hazel eyes. "You don't regret getting into this mess with me?"

"As long as you're part of the mess, I'm content where I am." He kissed her nose. "Now, as much as I want to devour you again, we should really go, especially with Camin turning his eye to the kingdom."

"Duty calls," she said, her mind drifting to that strange feeling again. She shrugged it off, hoping it was nothing but her imagination, before taking his hand and leaving the tower with him.

SKYE

Skye watched as Mark directed the Elite, commanding they stand guard in specific places around the castle walls, side by side with the king's guard. She stood with Elspeth; Trent having gone to round up the full mages. Their magic would be needed if the same force directed at their neighbors to the east turned on them. The last they'd heard, Apendia was holding its own against the onslaught that had met their kingdom earlier in the day. Trent seemed to think it bought them time, but Mark had disagreed, insisting that reinforcements be in place.

"This is nerve-racking," she said to Elspeth, biting her thumbnail.

Elspeth pushed her hand down. "Don't bite your nails, Skye."

"Aren't you nervous?"

"Of course I am. I know what Camin and his army are capable of. I was on the battlefield in the last war. But that doesn't mean the others need to know I'm nervous. You are an example Skye, don't let them see your fear."

Mark caught Skye's eye. He winked, and she gave him a slight smile, noting how handsome he looked; he was in his element. She'd always thought he wasn't meant to be an eye doctor, that his calling was for more, perhaps the armed forces or the police. Not an eye doctor. Had he taken that job just to care for her? His father, the man she'd called his father but now knew had been an Elite before a drunk driver had struck him down, had been her eye doctor as a child. Had he really been a doctor or just posing as one to care for her, to ensure the spell remained in place? Had Mark done the same, just another part of his role as protector?

Trent approached him, and Skye drew her eyes from Mark, sensing something in the air. Nothing caught her eye upon looking around, and no one else seemed to notice. She stepped toward the castle wall, past the guards distracted with strategic talk, through the passageway she'd passed the day Camin had attacked her, drawn to something once again. Something no one else could see, just beyond to the edge of it, her senses tingling. There was something there, unseen, until a black mist drifted through the air. Still, no one else seemed to notice. Only her. The black hue pulled from something, the feel of it on the air tainted with something she couldn't quite make out.

Camin was coming. Her magic flared, sensing more than just Camin. There was a different magic in the air, a darker one that made her recoil. Wizards?

Mark had talked about them as if they were the scourge of this land. The stream of black stopped, an eerie silence falling across the town, the air stilling. Goosebumps layered her arms, and she shivered. Every instinct told her to run, but she was frozen, hanging on the edge of the oncoming storm.

"Skye!" Mark's voice boomed behind her, but in that moment, the world exploded. Building and dirt flew into the air in a wave. A body hit her, and Mark landed atop her, having thrown her to the ground, her magic instinctively pulling the white from a nearby sign that flitted above them and forming a shield. Debris pummeled them, but the shield kept them safe.

"What the hell are you doing out here?" he yelled, yanking her away as the debris settled. "You stay with us!"

He pulled his weapon out and she could feel its connection to her magic.

He kept dragging her back as a group of Elites took position around her until they were back at the gates.

"Where are they?" Noah yelled.

It was still too hard to see and the fact that nothing had happened increased the tension.

"Mark, what about the people in town—"

"They've been evacuated, before Camin's first attack, or did you not notice how empty it was that first time?"

"I was a bit preoccupied."

He pushed her behind him. Fear swept through her, but then chaos erupted. The castle wall peeled apart brick by brick, flying toward them but shattering before they could hit their mark.

Elspeth and Trent stood on either side of them with more full mages, all of them breaking the stone. As the wall shrank, men walked through, wrapped in cloaks as black as night, the feel of their magic making her skin tingle as she adjusted to it. It wasn't quite corrupt but different, the opposite of what her magic felt like to her.

A panther-like creature jumped to the top of the wall, mauling two of the guards. Skye brought her hand to her mouth to stifle the scream as blood splattered the wall.

"Elite, prepare!" Mark yelled as the beast was followed by more, each scarred and snarling, foam dripping from their mouths, their eyes blood red.

"Elite! Target only their weak spots or they will grow!" Noah cried.

The creatures leapt and the weapons of the Elite flowed with power, sparks streaming from them, rainbows flaring with their motion.

Mark turned to Skye, grabbing her by the shoulder. "If you're going to use your magic, now would be the time." His eyes were hard, the commander in control, the lover buried far from her reach.

"I'm scared, Mark. I don't know what I'm doing."

His eyes drifted past her as they caught sight of something, his brow furrowing.

"Dammit!" He spun her. Alex stood staring in awe at the battle. "There's your incentive. What the hell is he doing out here?"

The ground exploded next to them, sending them through the air. Mark leapt to his feet and Skye, drawn to the sight of a creature whose eyes were set on Alex, let her magic take hold, feeling the draw of the colors pulling the black from the creature's pelt then the red from its eyes as they turned to her. She rose, still guiding the colors to her, its attack now aimed at her, survival its only focus. It threw itself at her and she snapped her wrist back, yanking at the colors. Mark screamed her name, his weapon reaching out to slay it, but it was dead before he reached it. Its lifeless, gray body fell to the ground as the magic in the air drew to Skye.

The blacks and reds from the creature circled her, and she aimed them at each wizard she saw, sending the charged hues toward them with stealth and pain. Her hues encased their bodies, tightening around their necks. Their attack stalled as they battled her magic. She pulled the white from the clouds above, changing it, then directing it to the Elite and to Alex, forming a shield around him.

The colors called to her, seducing her to take more, but it wasn't the bright colors, it was the deep rich of the blacks, blues, and grays—the colors she'd known all her life. The ground shook, breaking her concentration. As the remains of the wall collapsed, those wizards still standing freed themselves of her magic and returned to their attack.

An army of beasts and men tore through the debris. The outer existence of this world, those banished to the Fettered

Forests by her predecessors and driven back as Camin had licked his wounds, were returning with a vengeance. Elite weapons sparked with the magic she'd infused in them, driving back the onslaught, the king's guards in the fray, battling the best they could against powers beyond their understanding. She saw Mark run toward her, his weapon flying past her face, the wind of it tingling against her cheek as it impaled a man behind her.

"Now would be the time to show those new skills," he said, passing her and yanking the weapon from the man's chest. Blood layered the man's body, and she froze, terrified of what she was dealing with, of the chaos around her, the threat to her life and those she loved.

"Move, Skye," she told herself. She gave herself over to the magic like she had before, this time calling the green from the trees in the distance, the grass, and plants of the gardens beyond. As she did, Noah and Mark fought to protect her, cutting down anyone or anything that came close. If she hadn't been so focused, she would have watched the graceful dance they were enacting.

The greens encircled her, and she studied them, calling to the deeper shades, letting them overtake the brighter ones. Forest green and deep sage pulled to her, and she forced her arms out, sending it like a rain of daggers through the frenzy, willing it to miss her allies and target her enemies. Screams and howls filled the air before the color of the forest and gardens returned to their full vibrancy. While the green hues were in motion, she called to the browns of her Elite's uniform pants, careful not to weaken the owners. The browns felt lush against her skin, almost tempting her to lose herself to their touch before she commanding them to do her bidding. She aimed the hues at the troll looking creatures, directing the colors to freeze them as if a tomb of cement had captured them. Then she squeezed her hands, the brown obeying her command and compressing, the beasts exploding into chunks of stone before the browns returned.

"No!" a booming voice shook the land. "Mage Warrior!"

She turned to see Camin across the land from her. She'd surprised him with her power. She could see that. She also saw how close he was to Alex, who had not heeded Mark's warning and stayed to watch, hidden but still vulnerable, even with the shield she'd given him.

Out of her periphery, she saw Mark slowly inch toward him; he had seen Alex as well.

"Camin, your fight is with me," she yelled, hoping to hold his attention. "Stop your attack!"

"You think a few days with your magic gives you dominance over me? I told you Mage Warrior, you have weaknesses. The downfall of every Mage Warrior is their attachments." He put his hand out and a black void appeared behind Alex.

"No!" she yelled, commanding every hue to attack him. He took a step back in response, fighting free of her magic, the vortex still pulling at Alex.

"You are weak, your powers untrained, unskilled, erratic. You are no match for me."

The hold on Alex strengthened, and she called the white hues to grab him, fighting the grip Camin's magic had on him, but losing. Mark jumped, pushing Alex forward, her magic loosening Camin's hold on him. Alex fell to the ground as her magic dragged him away, but she didn't take her eyes off Mark, the force of the vortex catching him.

"No!" she screamed again, her eyes fixed on his as her magic hit him too late, his body dragged into the void, the blackness shrinking before finally disappearing.

"Only one is needed to bring you to your knees," Camin said, laughing. "You were told to find the answers. Keep looking." He disappeared in a puff of fog as she unleashed her fury, pulling the black hues from every one of his catlike creatures and the capes of the wizards, the sky above turning black as the hues circled her, the cats collapsing, the wizards vanishing, those who managed to escape the crushing grip of her magic.

She let it loose along with a primal scream that shook the foundation of the castle, collapsing the remains of the castle wall and bursting the eardrums of those around her. She collapsed to her knees, her power drained, exhaustion, fear, and desperation succumbing to the intense sadness that engulfed her.

"Mom!" Alex's voice broke through the onslaught of emotion, the only voice that rose above it.

She turned to him. His clothes were turning an ashen gray, everything around her doing the same. Even in this state, her power roared. She calmed her breathing, unclenching her hands, only then seeing the circle of hues that she'd pulled back to her after initially releasing it. Slowly, she let it drift out, like the tears that were damned behind her eyes, dripping one by one as the colors returned.

Alex ran to her and hugged her. He held her tight, just as he'd done at Sam's funeral, the boy who'd been forced to be a man at such a young age, caring for her once again as she fell apart against him.

All around them lay the devastation of the battle, while the devastation within her festered like an open wound. Noah came and took her from Alex.

"Skye, do you know where he took Mark?"

"He took him...he was going to take Alex but Mark—"

"Skye!" Noah yelled, shaking her. "Where would he have taken him?"

"She doesn't know," Alex said. "How would she know?"

"Because she's talked to him on several occasions now. Where would he have taken him?"

"I don't know," she answered, but in the corner of her mind she knew. The shadow realm where the shadow gods lay in wait for her, waiting for her to free them. "The shadow realm," she whispered finally. "He took him to the shadow realm."

"It's real?" Alex asked. "I thought it was just a myth, like heaven and hell?"

"It's very real, just like heaven and hell are for the other world," Noah said.

Alex's mouth dropped, but Skye tuned their talk out, staring at the spot where Mark had been, where now nothing stood, leaving a strange emptiness in her soul.

People bustled around them, rushing to help the injured, walking through the space where she stared, but she paid them no heed.

"Come." She heard. "Let's bring her inside. I think she's in shock."

She thought it was the king's voice, but she didn't turn to look. As they led her inside the castle, her eyes remained fixed on the spot until it was completely out of view. Even then, her neck craned, eyes turned as far as they could, vacantly staring.

SKYE

The drink left a bitter taste in Skye's mouth, but it was warm and gave her a sense of calm, the blind anguish she had locked away softening.

Elspeth stooped in front of her.

"How are you feeling, Skye?"

"Like someone has torn my heart out and ripped it to shreds before pushing it back in."

"We suffered losses today, but they could have been worse. You fought well," said the king.

"People still died, and Mark is gone. I didn't fight well enough."

"We'll find him," he said.

She laughed, a pained hollow sound. "No, we won't. I will. I am the only one who can."

"That's the spirit. Elspeth round up the full mages. I want the courtyard cleared and the wall repaired. The novices are busy caring for the injured."

"I'd like to stay with her, sire."

"Noah and Alex can stay with her. You're needed outside."

He walked from the room, and Skye couldn't help but think

of the stories she'd been told. The false façade of freedom was breaking, the king in command, the mages doing his bidding.

Elspeth squeezed her hand and rose to follow the king.

"Mom, we should get you to your room so you can rest," Alex said.

She shook her head adamantly. The last thing she wanted was to be where she and Mark had made love, where the scent of him still lingered, the memories of his touch still present.

"Why take him?" Noah asked.

"He was going to take me," Alex replied.

"But why? Why not kill you? That's Camin's way. He doesn't take hostages."

"It's a lure to get me to the shadow realm. The Death God wants me there to open a doorway and he must do his bidding. Whatever deal he made with him has forced his hand and he's out of time. Taking Mark gives him more time. It's a guarantee I will enter the shadow realm to find him. This satisfies the Death God and his shadow gods and gives me time to finish finding out what Camin's own agenda is."

"You truly think the war, this battle, the attack on the other kingdoms is all due to something other than a madman's quest for power?" Noah asked.

"Yes."

"That sounds mad, Mom. You know that, right?" Alex said.

"Yes," she answered, her mind drifting to what she had learned. "What if Camin wasn't the only one fighting a war?"

"Skye?"

"What if the two were tied to one another?"

She rose suddenly.

"Alex, I want you back with the new mages. Stay there, do not look for me and do not repeat anything you just heard. Noah, I need to go back to the warrior lair. Where is Petrian?"

"He was injured; the novices are healing him."

"Damn, okay. I'm going by myself then."

She turned from them and made for the door.

"Alex, do as she instructed. Skye!" Noah called after her, grabbing her as she entered the hall. "What are you doing?"

"I have a hunch, but I need to get back to my mother's journal. I must have missed something."

He trailed after her. "You're not going without me."

"Let me be, Noah."

He grabbed her arm again. "I'm not leaving you. With Mark gone, I am commander, and you are under my protection now. I will follow you whether you like it or not."

She yanked her arm from his grasp. "Fine. You Elite are stubborn."

She ran to the place where the Elite and warrior wings divided, then revealed the entryway like Petrian had shown her. Noah followed her through, and the entranceway shimmered closed behind them. The torches roared to life, the chill of the room fading.

Walking further in, the room opened, the connecting warrior rooms from the other castles revealing themselves. There was no need to use her birthmark to initiate this action, the room recognized her now.

"What the hell?" Noah said.

"The realms are all connected by mage magic."

"There are only three realms left Skye. Kantenda fell to this kingdom as you know, Digremile fell during the last war and became part of Crimson's kingdom. Nenochin fell to Camin earlier and Theodore is already talking about claiming it. It was the smallest and weakest of the kingdoms."

She looked up at him, surprised. The connections made six distinct rooms that merged into one. Could all six kingdoms have had their own lairs, the six connecting when warriors were present? Or when it was necessary? She walked over to the mantle, where she'd found the book, letting her finger drift along the wood, worn with time. Her eyes picked out the differences, the aged feel of this part of the room, then the subtle differences in each section that had combined with it.

"This is part of our kingdom," she said in a hushed tone.

Noah came closer.

"They remembered...and if they remembered, then perhaps..."

"That's treasonous Skye."

"Is it? To want your kingdom back, to want your freedom? To cling to the old ways that were stolen from you?"

"Skye, what you're suggesting that the Mage Warriors, that your mother, was plotting against the king."

"Maybe Camin wasn't alone, Noah."

His eyes were serious as they studied hers. "We need proof. We need something that tells us you're right before I go any further with that assumption."

She scanned the journal her mother had left but found nothing. Closing it, she looked around, knowing they would have hidden it well but unsure of where to look.

"Gods, I knew your mother. Your father was my commander, Skye. If what you're thinking is true—"

"Then there was more going on in this room than we thought."

Did Petrian know? she wondered. He must have, but he'd wanted her to discover it on her own, just as Camin had.

Camin, who had been her mother's friend, who had likely sat in this room with the others.

She stopped as a thought hit her. Could the battle have been a unified one, fought outside by Camin and inside by her parents and their friends? But how could that be? They'd sent her away, and the very spell used to save her had depleted all their abilities. Camin had killed her father and Mark's, then killed their mothers. How could he have killed them if he'd been aligned with them? There were too many holes in the theory.

Her eyes fell upon a small indentation in the wall. Moving

closer to it, she brought her hand up to trace the familiar symbol of her birthmark.

There was another hidden room behind that wall. She knew it instinctively but wasn't certain she wanted to go further.

Mark, her mind whispered, urging her forward. She pulled her hair back, the light of the torches hitting it, sending violet sparkles across the wall. This time, instead of a new room appearing, the wall slid open, a dark corridor now ahead of her.

Noah grabbed her and pushed her behind him.

"Is that necessary?"

"I don't know where this leads or what lies beyond that darkness. Do you?"

"No, but I don't think it will hurt me. This was a Mage Warrior sanctuary, remember?"

"Nevertheless, I go first. Mark will kill me if I let anything happen to you."

At the mention of Mark's name, her heart clenched. She missed his presence more than she ever had before. Noah walked ahead of her, the glow of his weapon lighting the dark space. At the end of the corridor, they were forced to turn right, stairs leading them to another room, one that lit with magic torches as she entered it. One by one, they lit until the room was bright; the contents illuminated.

A large table sat in the center of the room. Maps and notes spread across it, scattered as if they were still in use. Skye knew better. They had last been used the day the final Mage Warrior fell, her mother with Mark's mother alongside her. With no one left to fight the fight, the memory, the purpose was left to the dust that now coated the table's contents, the spiders that skittered into the corners.

She shivered. God, she hated spiders.

Why had this room not been covered with the magic that kept the others clean? Was it under a separate spell? Perhaps not every Mage Warrior was privy to what went on in this room.

Noah searched through the maps, looking over the scribbled writing that lie on parchments beside them.

"You were right. They were rebelling."

She joined him, picking up a map with Fettered Forest written elegantly atop it. Her knees were weak, and her mind confused. What did it mean? What was she meant to discover?

"Why did they all die? If they were fighting for their freedom with Camin, why did he kill them?" she asked.

"I don't know. That's still a huge assumption to say that Camin's intentions were good. He killed every Mage Warrior in the kingdoms."

Something nudged at the back of her mind. "Which kingdom fell first?"

"Nenochin, but their kingdom was small compared to the others, their defenses weak. They were never fighters; they were quiet, peaceful, so it was always a mystery why Camin started his attacks there. They conceded quickly once their Mage Warriors fell. The heir to the throne survived, and they rebuilt."

"Until recently?"

"Yes, the recent attack has left them crippled. Theodore will claim the kingdom if he hasn't already. They're too small to be any threat against his army."

She chewed her thumbnail, wondering why Camin would start with such a small kingdom, one that didn't seem like it had been worth attacking. She ran her finger along the map. "There was another kingdom that fell, correct?"

"Digremile. They never recovered. Their people fled to the countryside and eventually fell under Crimson's rule, becoming part of her kingdom, Apendia."

"That's strange. Why would that be?"

"Hers was the closest kingdom, so it was natural that they would. Her father was still king, but he was very ill at the time."

"So, she gained people and land."

"Correct. Digremile was left devastated; their queen killed

without an heir. Their line was a cursed one, cursed by the Death God ages ago and fading. It was only a matter of time before they fell. That left us, Eltander, and Apendia. Camin turned his advances on us and the rest, you know."

"But Crimson lost her Mage Warriors as well, right?"

"Yes, she sent both to fight. One fell during the battle here, the night your father and Mark's father were killed. The other... well, I don't know. We were gone by then."

"Was I the only child?"

"Yes, Mage Warriors are rare births and no other had carried the mark in decades."

She chewed her thumb, wondering what all of it meant, her eyes drifting to the map again.

"I need more. There are too many questions, and I can't fight for Mark until I have the answers. Camin sent me down this path for a reason."

"What are you suggesting?"

She picked up the map. "I take a trip to the Fettered Forest."

His eyes went wide. "Are you mad?"

"No, quite sane actually."

She folded the map, looking for anything else that seemed relevant before heading back out.

"Skye, you can't just waltz into the Fettered Forest. You'll be killed."

"I have no choice."

The room closed behind them. She grabbed her mother's journal and a brown satchel that lay across a chair, placing the journal and the map into it before heading out of the sanctuary. Night had fallen, and the corridor was empty.

Noah took her arm. "Skye—"

"I'm going, Noah. I'm leaving now and you can't stop me. The answers I need are in those forests and until I have them, I cannot get Mark back, nor can I keep the Death God at bay."

He sighed. "Fine. But I'm going with you."

"No—"

"Yes. With Mark gone, your protection falls to me. I will go with you whether you like it or not. I know how to get us there. We'll need supplies first. It's a four-day journey even by the fastest horse. Meet me at the Elite stables and don't let anyone see you."

"But Alex—"

"Will be safer remaining ignorant of your whereabouts. Now go wait for me at the stables."

He ran off, and she prayed she was putting her trust in the right person. She didn't know Noah, had never met him until the day her life had turned to a shit show.

Could she trust him? Could she trust anyone?

Mark had trusted him, and she trusted Mark.

The shadows in the hallway seemed to grow, as if reaching to her. Turning quickly, she ran to her tower to grab a cloak and some supplies. Then she made her way through the shadows to await the next move in this crazy, real-life version of a fantasy game.

MARK

Darkness engulfed Mark as he tried to open his eyes. His head pounded like he'd been knocked unconscious. Where the hell was he? As much as he tried, he couldn't get his eyes to adjust to the darkness. He remembered something pulling him forcefully and seeing the fear in Skye's eyes, their blue a lush navy, then nothing. With the thought of Skye, he became frantic. Where was she? Had Camin hurt her? What had happened after he'd blacked out?

He scrambled to his feet, bumping his head on what felt like branches. His eyes couldn't make anything out. Reaching for his weapon, he discovered it was gone, as was the knife he kept in his waistband.

He stumbled forward, tripping over tree roots, then hands were on him. Long nails that scraped at his skin and knees that pinned him down.

"Someone's awake," a female's voice said, the words slithering out in a snake-like fashion.

A soft light illuminated the space and Mark pushed the creature from him quickly, jumping to his feet, only then realizing it was a woman. She crouched, licking her lips, beady black eyes looked back at him. She may have been pretty once but her short blonde hair was knotted and matted with grime. Barely anything covered her body. A small piece of cloth was tied around her back to cover her breasts, and a loose ripped skirt fell just to the top of her thighs, leaving nothing to the imagination.

"Back, Femin, our prisoner does not need you fawning over him."

Camin emerged from behind the light, staring Mark down. "Go find your sister and play with her for a while."

She rose and Mark was surprised by how tall she was, her long legs lithe with muscle. She strode to Camin and draped her long nails down his chest.

"Will you play if you won't let me play with him?"

"Go, Femin."

She turned, looking back at Mark. "Shame, he looks like fun." Her face morphed, her eyes turning a deep shade of blue, her hair lengthening before changing to a lush brown, her face now Skye's. Her clothing disappeared, and Skye's naked body stood before him. He stepped back, his heart leaping, his mind reminding him it wasn't her, but the mere image causing a response.

"Oh, yes, we could have some serious fun."

She licked her lips and trotted off, her image returning not to her previous state but to a red-skinned demon with a tight ass and small waist. As she rounded the corner, he could see the side of her pert, full breasts, her long black hair partially covering them, and the two small horns that protruded from her head.

"What sorcery is that?" Mark demanded.

"Femin is a demon. She and her sister are shapeshifters. It's how they lure their prey."

"A demon?'

"Welcome to the shadow realm, Markhem."

He glared at Camin. "Why am I here, and what did you do with Skye?"

"You are here as bait. The shadow gods want her, the Death

God is fixated on her, and so, she will come for you. And when she does, she will have no choice but to do their bidding."

"And what is that?" he asked, as if Skye hadn't already figured it out.

"To unleash their beasts on the world and slowly reclaim it as their own. But you already knew that. She's sharp, like her mother. That same mind, same beauty, all but those damned eyes she inherited from Berrett. If not for them, it would be like Lyra herself were still alive."

"She won't do their bidding."

"Oh, I disagree. For you, she will do anything. In fact, she travels to the Fettered Forest at this very moment, finding the answers she seeks."

"She wouldn't..." But he knew her well enough to know she would. She was impulsive, inquisitive, stubborn. If she thought there were answers there, she would go no matter the risk.

"You know as well as I do that she would."

"What is it you need her to find?"

"The truth."

"And what is the truth?"

"Something she will discover on her own."

"You killed countless people, destroyed kingdoms, murdered her parents. She won't help you."

Camin stepped closer to him, getting right in his face, but Mark didn't budge.

"You are but a child. Nothing you have been told was seen by your eyes."

"I saw my father killed; her father with him. I saw the blast that took them from us. I screamed as my mother found me and held me back, ushering me away. That was not told to me."

For a moment, he thought he saw remorse in Camin's eyes, but that didn't seem possible.

"She will find the answers before she faces the Death God. Only then will she understand her true power."

"And until then? I'm to stay here willingly?"

"Make no mistake, you are my prisoner. I have done many terrible things in my life. Holding you captive is the least of them."

The light extinguished, and a force pushed Mark back to where he'd woken. He heard the limbs of the tree creaking, sealing him into his prison.

SKYE

True to his word, Noah arrived with food and water as well, as a myriad of other supplies. He saddled two horses swiftly and quietly, then they took off.

He led the way, sneaking them past an unsuspecting guard who was too involved in a servant girl to notice them. Skye could hear his grunts and the woman's cries of pleasure as they snuck through a small side entrance and cautiously urged the horses through. Her mind slipped to Mark and their last lovemaking that morning. If she'd known, she would have stayed in bed longer, delighting in his touch, letting him take her over and over until neither would have had any strength left.

Now he was gone, and all she was left with was the lingering memory of those touches. Was he still alive? Was she right? Was Camin only using him as bait? Would this detour end his life or save it? She prayed she was right, and that this was the path Camin intended her to follow.

They stayed north, guiding their horses through the barren countryside once they'd left the surrounding town. She remembered going west when they'd gone to see Petrian, and so, that night while they were resting, she asked why no towns were further north than those that lie closest to the castle.

"No one ever settled north, too close to the Fettered Forest. The towns all lay south or west or even east of the castle. Not even farming families settled this far north. Theodore is the front line to the woods and what lay within them."

He handed her a piece of the rabbit he'd slayed and cooked. Thankfully, he'd kept the gruesome part from her eyes, for she didn't think she could have stomached eating the creature after seeing it skinned. Even now it seemed sad, but she knew she needed it to keep up her strength. There were no protein bars in this world.

"I thought the other kingdoms lay to the west?"

"They do, except for Apendia, which lies to our south, and our kingdom is vast. They all are. What you see in movies doesn't reflect the sheer size of a king's rule. Each kingdom is a small country, spanning hundreds of miles."

"Wow, how do they keep an eye on such a vast space?"

"They can't, not really."

She chewed her rabbit, thinking of how different it was here, how out of her element she still felt.

"The lines have always been blurry, but none of the kingdoms ever seemed to mind. Well, before Crimson, that is. Before the war, she tried persuading her father to challenge Theodore over the land that bordered their kingdoms. He ignored her, but I'm sure now that she's queen, she has the same thoughts."

"She's the one who claimed the fallen kingdom?"

"Yes, it gives her the second largest kingdom, second only to Theodore's, as the Fettered Forest falls within his borders now and, of course, if he claims Nenochin."

"What about our kingdom?"

Noah raised his brow.

"The one our people come from, Kantenda," she continued, wondering why he hadn't replied.

He dropped his rabbit but recovered quickly, catching it before it hit the ground, then looked around the empty space where they were camping.

He leaned in closer, saying, "I told you before, talk of the old kingdom is treasonous. You'd be wise to keep your thoughts to yourself."

"Or what? They'll send me to the forest? I'm already heading there. You already snuck off with me. Both of us are in deep shit when we return. Now answer my question."

He was quiet for a moment, and she wondered if she'd gone too far.

"Only a few of us know of our history, Skye, and those who do, do not talk about it openly. You need to understand that."

"I know. I've been warned already. You're not the only one who knows the secrets of our past."

"Who else did you hear it from?"

She stayed silent.

"Petrian," he guessed. "His line is semi-pure. Only those who come from the old families have had the history handed down."

"Semi-pure?"

"One parent is Elite, one full mage. Only two Elite parents are considered pure bloods."

Her face must have shown her confusion.

"Elites can't stand each other in any serious sexual way. They're like oil and water, too aggressive and proud. They need a mate who is not such a thing."

"Did you ever—"

"Ha! I tried my hand at a few of our women. It makes for a fiery night of sex, but nothing more. No, my mate is a novice mage, like most of our mates are."

"You have a wife?" This surprised her, as she'd never seen him with anyone but the other Elite.

"Aye, she's in the countryside with a friend, waiting until this mess is over before she can come home. The king gave permission for her to leave the castle ground when I agreed to go with you."

"Permission?"

"No mages live outside the castle grounds. Her friend is a non-caster. It is forbidden for any mage to live anywhere but under the protection of the king."

"Protection my ass," she mumbled, knowing exactly why they couldn't leave.

Noah gave her a funny look.

"Why don't the Elite mate with full mages often?"

"They're a spoiled, pretentious lot. Snooty."

She laughed. "Snooty?"

"Don't try telling me you never saw Elspeth that way."

"It's a good word for her."

"They think too highly of themselves. Their magic is greater than the novices, used for many special tasks, particularly for the king. Don't get me wrong, their spells keep the kingdom strong and safe, but they are no Mage Warrior even though they think they are. Too much for any Elite to take. Novice mages are humble, soft-spoken, caring. They offset our aggressive natures perfectly."

"It's strange how different we are, yet so connected."

"It stems back to our true nature, or at least that's what my gram always said."

"She's the one who told you of our kingdom?"

"Aye, the old kingdom."

"Where is it? Did this kingdom claim it?"

"No, only its people. The land bordered the Eltander kingdom, and they insisted it become theirs. It was supposedly a request that almost brought war between our realms."

"Can you show me where it is?" She pulled the map out of her satchel and handed it to Noah, who laid it out on the ground.

"You see the Fettered Forest and how far it stretches?"

"Yes, it's massive."

"Well, over here—" He pointed to a section to the east of the woods, the trees drawn less dense. "—is our kingdom, Kantenda."

"We lived in the forests?"

"Not quite, although there were parts of the kingdom that built their houses among the trees. We were people of the land, our castle built into the base of a mountain that cornered our land, separating it from much of the Fettered Forest. We hunted, we fished, we lived as one, or so the myth goes. I don't honestly know how much is true and how much is fantasy created to enhance the theory through the generations."

"What lies here?" She pointed below the forest.

"That's Eltander."

"The ones who claimed the land. The ones who are like elves, having their own abilities."

"Well, well, aren't you a plethora of knowledge?"

"The Eltander were our kin, weren't they?"

"That I don't know. Their abilities were more mental and ours physical."

She chewed at her nail.

"Where do the wizards come into play?"

"Is that what this is about? You want to enter the Fettered Forest to ask the wizards about their history?"

"Partly, but I think there's more to it. There's something that's been forgotten through history, something left behind that Camin discovered, that my parents discovered."

There were so many missing pieces that she still couldn't see a clear answer. She rubbed her eyes.

"Get some sleep, Skye. Put your questions aside and rest or you won't have the energy to find those answers."

She put the map away and made a makeshift pillow with her satchel, Noah pulling a blanket from his bag and covering her with it. Sleep quickly took hold, but her dreams were far from restful.

Four days later, they stood before a looming forest. Their

horses had been too frightened to go near it, so they'd set them free. Skye craned her neck, the trees higher than she could see. Did they touch the clouds?

Rubbing her neck, she looked back into the dense forest.

"Ready?" Noah said.

"Maybe?" she replied.

He turned to her. "Once we step through the boundary, we cannot come back."

She swallowed loudly. "Boundary?"

"Yes, no one leaves the woods—anyone can enter, but magic blocks it from any exit. That's why it's the perfect prison for anyone with magic. There's no escape."

"Who raised the boundary?" she whispered.

"No one knows. But the only ones who know how to escape are the wizards and Camin. His horde leaves with him and returns with him. Are you certain you want to proceed with this suicide mission?"

"No, but it's the only way to save Mark. I know that whatever lies beyond those trees holds the answers I need."

He drew his weapon, its center glowing brightly with her magic.

"Then let's not keep those answers waiting."

"You don't have to go with me, Noah."

"Yes, I do. Mark is your shield, but with him gone, I become that shield."

She nodded, a swell in her heart for the man who was risking his life to keep her safe. Then, taking one last look at the open land behind her, she walked into the forest.

MARK

It had all been a dream. The past days locked away in a prison of roots and darkness, only slivers of what he thought was light creeping through, had only been a dream. As the feel of Skye's lips against his skin slowly roused him from his sleep, he moaned, taking in the feel of her hands gripping his thighs. All a dream, a nightmare really, and he was waking to the dream.

He ran his hands through her thick hair, then felt her touch on his biceps, her breasts smooth against them, her lips finding his and kissing him. But that wasn't right; her lips were still doing wonders below his belt. Her mouth lifted, and she positioned herself above him so that he penetrated her. She was wet and ready, tightly wrapping around him. It was ecstasy. His hands reached up and kneaded her breasts, feeling their firmness as he pulled one hand away to feel the other breasts that were draping over his chest. She continued to kiss him, her tongue demanding as her body arched atop him, her hands draping his legs along with her hair. He blinked his eyes open; something wasn't right. There were too many limbs, too many breasts. God, there were two of her—one riding him hard while the other seduced him.

He blinked again, the darkness still surrounding him, only a dim light enough to allow him sight. The Skye atop him leaned forward, kissing the other Skye, her hand moving deep into the other's womanhood, eliciting a moan that was more of a growl.

No, his mind screamed, his body rebelling, his arousal increasing as the two versions of Skye made out, touching each other, the one still pumping hard atop him.

There aren't two of her, his mind barged in. *It's not her!*

That woke him and he shoved them, kicking the one far away after flipping her from him and punching the other as her form shifted, the red-skinned demon replacing his beautiful Skye. He scooted back, yanking his pants up.

"Get the hell way from me!"

"But you were enjoying it so. You were so close, let me finish you and then you can enjoy my sister," she said, morphing to the dirty blonde he'd seen the first day. The other, who morphed into the same appearance and looked just like her, came to her, reaching her hand between her legs.

"We know you want more," she said between kisses as they both shifted back to the red demon form, both naked with shiny scales on their chests. Everything about them looked like women but for their color, the scalelike patches, and the small horns that protruded from their heads curling so they blended into their hair.

"You tricked me," he complained. "Leave me alone."

"But you want us," the one said as her body shook from the pleasure the other was giving her. It was hot in a strange, messed up way and he looked away as she cried out in what he assumed was a response to her orgasm. He didn't want to know, preferred not to even though his firmness had returned.

"No, I want her, not you, and you played on that fact," he complained.

The one shifted, her body morphing to Skye's again, his damned erection growing further from the thought of her.

"We can be her again and finish pleasuring you."

She licked her fingers, moaning as she sucked them clean, then crawled to him. He kicked her chest hard before she could reach him, sending her flying.

She howled and her sister scrambled to her, licking her breasts and moving her body seductively against her. Thankfully, his kick had caused her natural form to return, or he may have been too fascinated by watching a version of Skye getting it on with another woman.

"Let us leave him. If he doesn't want to play, then he can suffer. The master said we can only play with him, but this one... this one we can have."

Mark didn't know what they were talking about as he watched them morph into two different, beautiful women. A blonde with legs that seemed endless, her breasts too large to be real, the other with raven hair that covered her ass, her green eyes large and sultry. They left his cage, and that's when Mark noticed the naked man bound and gagged outside his prison.

The man stared wide eyed at them, his erection prominent but his eyes fearful. The blonde straddled him as the other untied him, using her teeth to remove his gag. Mark thought he would run, but he didn't, instead falling under their spell. He watched as the man pawed at their breasts, the blonde riding him still, her rhythm growing faster with his groans.

Mark couldn't stop himself from watching, as voyeuristic as it seemed. Even though he knew what they were, his erection was full and throbbing; they were seductive, their bodies writhing with the man's. The raven-haired one was playing with herself as her sister sucked on her breasts and Mark wondered if it would have hurt to have indulged in their façade, his hands wandering to his erection. He was about to give in and stroke himself when he saw the nails on the raven-haired one lengthen, becoming long sharp talons. She slowly brought them to the man's stomach as he came, his body clenching with pleasure, his moans filling the space. In one quick swipe, she opened him from navel to neck, then sliced his neck. Blood poured as his body spasmed in pain and the remaining pleasure of his orgasm.

The blonde cried out in satisfaction, her body convulsing from her own climax. As the man's movements stopped, she climbed from him and pleasured her sister, blood slicking across their bodies as she came. Leaving her sister in the remaining tremors of her orgasm, the blonde turned and dug her hands into the man's stomach, pulling out his organs and eating them.

Any remaining arousal Mark had fled as she fed her sister, the sound of their mouths smacking as they gorged on him, turning his stomach. It was a dichotomy of beauty and horror. He turned to the corner of his prison and vomited; all thoughts of pleasure gone. His stomach heaved violently as the sound continued. The bare minimum of food Camin had afforded him, left nothing to regurgitate.

He wiped the back of his hand over his mouth and stumbled back, daring a look at the horrific scene. Still in their facades, they had emptied the man and were now gorging on his limbs.

Mark gagged again and covered his ears. God, how could he have been seduced by those things?

He remained there for what seemed an eternity before he forced himself to look over again. They were gone, a bloodied patch of ground and bright white bones all that they'd left, the only sign they'd ever been there. They had eaten him, every piece of him, plucking the bones clean.

Mark sat staring at the violent scene, wondering who the man had been and what sin he'd committed to have been given such a death sentence. He'd seen violence in his life, exposed to war and death at an early age, but nothing he'd seen had ever been as disturbing as this. Would they have done the same to him if he'd let himself believe they were Skye? If he'd given over to his need for her, and had let them seduce him? He shivered at the thought and forced himself to stand.

"Pull yourself together, Mark," he scolded himself, only then noticing they'd neglected to close his cage back up. There was nothing blocking his escape.

He moved toward the opening, waving his hand through to see if it was a trick. His hand went right through. He stepped out, pausing, his eyes drawn to the bones. He was in the shadow realm —a small amount of light was all the realm allowed, and he didn't even know if it existed beyond Camin's space. There were creatures out there that likely made these two look like angels. Did he stand a chance outside of Camin's prison? Likely not. If a monster or demon didn't kill him, a shadow god surely would. He thought of Skye, her rich blue eyes wiping away the images of the demon sisters. He missed her. He needed to get back to her and if it meant he'd die trying, then that's what it meant.

Muttering an apology, he grabbed two sharp rib bones from the remains of the poor soul. Tucking one in his waistband, he took his first steps toward what he hoped was freedom and not his death.

SKYE

The darkness of the Fettered Forest surrounded her as Skye stepped through the boundary. For a moment, she was alone, and she questioned if Noah had left her. He stepped through, weapon still drawn, and she let out a sigh of relief.

"No turning back now," Noah said.

She looked back. Instead of the open field they'd stepped from, dense woods lay behind them.

"Guess that's why no one ever escapes."

"No one but Camin and his wizards."

"There's a way out and I'll find it when we're done here," she said, moving forward.

The forest was dense with thick undergrowth. Noah used his weapon to help clear a path, but it was still slow progress, as if the forest didn't want them venturing too far.

It was hard to see, the canopy of trees blocking all but slivers of sunlight. The trees seemed to rise even further from where she stood, so far that her eyes could barely make out their top branches.

On and on they walked with no end in sight and no sign of

anything or anyone. The day dragged into night, and she had no idea how many miles they'd walked. It all looked the same. Were they walking in circles?

"Skye, we should stop for the night. We can't see where we're going."

"We don't have time to stop."

"We don't have time to trip and break a bone or twist a foot, either."

She was about to concede when they heard a low growl behind them.

"Great, our welcoming committee is here," Noah mumbled, bringing his weapon up, then turning, the glow of it meeting a pair of red eyes across from them. Only the creature's eyes were visible, which led Skye to believe its coat was black, just like the large cats she'd killed in the courtyard.

"Now would be a good time for one of your tricks, Skye."

"But Mage Warriors can't pull color from..." She stopped, knowing other Mage Warriors couldn't, but she could. She'd lived in the shadows, in the darkness; she understood it all too well.

The creature eyed her as she brought her hand up to feel for the connection. She'd been so tense she hadn't thought to draw her magic. As it rose within her, she sensed the thickness of the ebony hue, its form emerging upon her connection to it. She drew the hue to her, the creature's eyes narrowing as it took a step away. She pulled at the hues, bringing them to her, sensing the layers of blacks and blues.

The creature whined, and she paused, a thought coming to her. She stepped closer to the creature.

"Skye," Noah said, his voice revealing his confusion at her move.

"Shh."

She loosened her grip on the hues, and the beast stepped back.

"I need you to lead us to your other friends," she said softly.

"I don't think I want to meet his other friends, Skye."

As it took another step back, she tugged at the hues. It bucked, fighting the hold she had on it. Tightening her grip, she pulled the hues closer, feeling them swirl around her. There was power to them, but something else, too—essence. Lowering her hand, keeping her hold still on the creature, she let her fingers drift through the hues, feeling the depth of the ebony, the richness of the blue, the spirit of the creature. The hues went deeper than just color and control. They made up the very essence of the organism. That's why she could bleed them, it bled their life, giving way to the shadow realm, a bridge between life and death.

She closed her eyes and let the colors flow into her body, feeling the beast, its thoughts, its emotion, its life-force, the colors sweeping through her like a soft breeze. Opening her eyes, she looked at the creature, watching as it dropped to a sitting position before bowing its head. She felt its deference to her, the giving over of its will to her.

"That's how Camin does it," she said, walking to the creature and petting its head.

It nuzzled against her, and she let the hues flow back to it. It seemed surprised, and she thought it might attack, but instead, it nuzzled harder against her. She scratched at the softness of its ears and laughed.

"How in the hell did you do that?" Noah asked.

"She walks the shadows. Camin was right—you are special."

Skye jumped, and Noah turned his weapon, moving to stand in front of her.

"If I intended her harm, she would have been in pain before you Elite. I will not harm your warrior."

Skye took in the man who stood before them. His cape, a deep violet, was embroidered with black symbols that ran in panels up the sides. He wore the hood down, his black hair blending into the darkness, his curls highlighted where the thin beams of light touched them from the canopies above. He had a long black beard that was braided at the end with small silver charms interwoven within the braids.

"Elite, I mean you no harm."

But still Noah remained in his protective stance, unwavering.

The man let his hand out, and the cat came to him, lowering its head for a pet. "I see you have made friends with a Noctum. Strangers are never that lucky. They only take to our people and eat the trespassers."

"Who are you?" Skye asked, suppressing the shudder at the thought of the creature eating someone.

"I am your kin. We all are. Come, you both are hungry and tired. We will eat and talk."

He turned to begin walking away.

Skye looked to Noah, seeing him mouthing, *"No,"* which came out in a low hiss.

"Why not?" she whispered.

"He's a wizard; they kill our kind."

The man stopped and turned to them. "If I had intentions to kill, you would be dead. She is too untrained, and you are not educated in the true power you wield through your connection to her. Now come before more beasts converge. I assure you, not all trapped in this forest have benevolent tendencies."

"We follow," Skye whispered, pushing past Noah.

He huffed but obliged.

They walked for what seemed a short time, but whenever she looked behind her, Skye saw only trees as if they were hundreds of miles within the forest. Finally, they came upon an opening and she and Noah froze, both staring, mouths agape, at the city before them. The trees were less, more spread apart, leaving open space below where huts sat, people bustling in and out, children frolicking in the sun that lit the space. Along the trees were the dwellings, wooden bridges sparkling in the tree limbs, just enough for Skye to notice in the remaining daylight, but she imagined they glowed beautifully in the darkness of night.

The tree dwellings were open with light cloth that hung in doorways, the breeze wafting them in and out. The small bridges or walkways were planks of wood laid against each other, each with drawings in black, like those of the wizard's capes.

Noticing her presence, everything stopped, silence falling upon the tree city, no one moving, their eyes upon her.

Whispers began—they knew who she was. Their whispers were laced with excitement and fear.

"We have been expecting you, Skye of the other world, daughter of Lyra. Your mother was expected once as well, but she sadly never joined us."

"Because you killed her. You and Camin," Noah seethed.

"Come, dinner will be ready shortly and we will talk. Not everything is as it seems."

NIGHT FELL QUICKLY as they waited for answers and food. Skye watched the large cats—Noctum the wizard had called them —stroll through the village, sometimes sniffing a small child, but never showing any aggression. It made her regret having killed so many during the attack.

"I don't trust them," Noah whispered.

"They seem harmless."

He turned to her, scrunching his brows. "Harmless? These are the same people who killed your parents, Mark's parents, countless Elite, full mages, and every one of the Mage Warriors. Harmless is not a word I would use to describe them."

Sighing, she took another sip of the fruity drink she'd been given. The man came over, followed by several others who laid food in front of them, large wooden bowls of colorful plants and grains, a wooden plate with strips of meat. It smelled delicious after the past days of rabbit and pheasant they'd been feasting on.

They were handed bowls, then the others left, the man sitting across from them. Three others joined them, all in the same fashion of robe, a woman and two men. The woman had thick blonde hair, curly like the first man's and braided down to the side. Her sharp brown eyes evaluated Skye.

"So, this is Lyra's daughter, Queen of Kantenda," she said tersely.

"Queen?" Skye asked. "I'm no queen."

"You are Lyra's heir. Your line has ruled our people since the magic began, the originating line of all mages."

"All mages?"

"Yes, Eliam was the first Elcant. After his magic emerged, more magic came to our lands so that, in time, all our people had magic or a connection to it as in the Elite. Our magic is tied to your line, and now to you."

"Elcant?"

"You were not always called Mage Warriors. That is the simple tongue of the non-casters."

"You said our people," Noah interjected. "Kantenda never ruled the wizards."

She laughed, a throaty, sexy laugh, the others joining her.

"The non-casters weave their own spells to their advantage. Spells of the tongue to bury the truth of their atrocities."

"Tell us what we don't know, what Camin expected us to know," Skye said.

"You know nothing. Raised in a world that does not hold your past, your power, your possibilities," one of the men said. His hair was a dirty blonde, close to brown but not quite, and his eyes were the brown of the tree trunks. He, too, wore his beard long, braided at the tip.

"That was not her doing," Noah said.

"No, it was her mother's. A sacrifice for the cause she knew she'd lost. We'd all lost." The woman sighed. "There is much the kingdoms would have you believe about our past, our people. All to protect their dependency on our magic. Your mother stripped them of that, took the Mage Warriors, as they are called, from them. No longer to be used as weapons against their own kind. And now you are back, a new pawn. One kingdom holds you; another covets you, planning, conniving to steal you away. A third kingdom prays you will save them, while a fourth prays you will restore them, and a fifth remains shadowed by the Death God's curse. Five kingdoms when once there were six, Nenochin too foolish to know when to listen, too proud to remain allies to Kantenda, and so falling again, never to be restored."

Noah sat back, rubbing his hands over his face. "You act as if Nenochin had a choice, but your people and Camin's brought it to ruins again only days ago."

"They had a choice just as Digremile did and they turned their back on us twice, believing lies that twisted their loyalty to us. They were our allies, but the truth was manipulated, and they fell. When they were rebuilt, their crown disavowed us and as payment for what they saw as our disloyalty, they were brutal to your kind and Theodore foolishly handed them more mages after the war. It didn't matter that the magic had waned; the mages were still tools to use for what magic the kingdoms could leech from them. Crimson, the queen of Apendia, is another cruel one who should hold no mages, her greed too strong, her desire for pleasure too untampered. She will fall to her own doing, but Nenochin needed to be undone."

"Left for Theodore to claim?"

"He is the least of the bad lot, rather it be he than that red-headed queen, Crimson," the woman said.

Noah sighed.

"You are back and with you returns the dilemma, the crux of every mage. The curse of our kind for the gifts we hold. He knows it. Don't you? You see what the non-caster kingdoms have subverted all this time."

"I see nothing but a string of words that have no meaning.

Kantenda, my kingdom, is gone. It was lost long before I was born," Noah argued.

"Not lost, hidden, stolen, ripped in two. Our kingdom once ran the span of the Fettered Forests to the Dranth mountains where the ruins of our capital lie."

"Our kingdom?" Skye asked.

"Yes. Look around. What do you see?"

Skye looked, her eyes taking in the now twinkling lights that lit the walkways above her, the people that mingled through the space below. Magic stirring pots over large flames, magic cleaning, spells of children giddily turning a squirrel into a frog, then back to a stunned squirrel, two others changing their hair black, then blonde, then red. A mother rocking a child in a suspended hammock that had no ties as she laughed with her husband over something he'd said.

She looked back at them. "Everyone has magic."

She smiled. "We are what is left of your people, those who escaped the great round up when our king acquiesced to save our princess, the Mage Warriors diverting attention as the wizards hid as many as we could."

"Wizards are part of our people?" Noah asked.

"Yes. They tried to capture us, but our place was always deep in these forests, with the beasts that dwell here. Over the centuries there have been new beasts, monsters the Mage Warriors were forced to imprison in these woods. The kingdoms attempted to flush us out, and we dealt with the beasts as they came."

"I don't understand. In fact, forgive me, but I don't even believe what you're saying. Wizards are the enemy. You kill, you torture, you killed her parents, my friends. So many lives taken in a battle that Camin lost."

The woman's eyes grew sad. "Do we look like the vicious killers you have been told we are? Ones who sneak into non-caster homes and steal their babies? Words hold power, whether or not they hold truth. The propaganda of the kingdoms was powerful.

"There was once a time when we stood side by side with our people. We were the providers. The Mage Warriors, the leaders; the Elite, the protectors. Everyone had a role, a sense of purpose. All of us equals—our powers seen as a blessing of the gods. Over the years, the enslavement of our people to the kingdoms has demeaned them, stripped them of that pride in their blessing. The novice mages, as you call them, degraded to cooking and cleaning when their magic is the life of our people. It keeps us strong, healthy, and when allowed to flow free it is powerful."

"We have a good life at the castle—" Noah started.

"Do you? Are you allowed to come and go as you please, or do you hide in the corners of inns to enjoy your cup of ale? Did you sneak under cover of night to leave the grounds? Are you aware of the king's guard that hunts for you even now? You have no freedom; you are property of the king. Be thankful you live under Theodore and his line. The female ruler is hard, cruel to her mages, punishments that leave them scarred and submissive to her demented will."

"And the Eltander? They had Mage Warriors," Skye said.

"Only to protect themselves. They refused to take another mage. They are our cousins. Magic flows through their veins just as it does ours. The other kingdoms have no use for their magic—it is too subtle, too unseen, and so they are left in peace, for now. Crimson will turn on them at some point, just as she did on the now extinct Digremile kingdom."

Noah stood and began pacing behind her.

"My mother saw it, didn't she?"

"Yes, and your father. She and Camin were friends. When Camin discovered he had the ability to leave the forest, he went to the kingdom. They took him in immediately, knowing he was half Mage Warrior, his abilities clear even at that age. He lied and said he had escaped his father. He went to see for himself, not believing, thinking it would be a better life. He didn't believe me when I told him. How could he? Then he saw the truth, and he knew I'd been right."

"You're his father," Skye said to the blonde man, only now seeing the similarities.

Noah stopped pacing.

"Yes, I am."

"But you murdered Swalda, his own mother."

The man's eyes grew sad. "Propaganda, distorted truths."

"You left her at the castle gates, dead. There were witnesses," Noah spat.

"No one saw her die but me. I loved Swalda. When they turned her away, dropped her in the forest, I found her fighting a Noctum with what light she could find. I saved her, brought her home to be healed, and fell in love with her spirit. She'd discovered the truth, questioned it and for that she'd been left to die."

"If you loved her—"

"I didn't kill her. One of those monsters they cast into the forest did. She went with Camin to pick berries. He was small. They went with a Noctum but it stood no chance against the beast. We heard her screams. She died protecting Camin. We slaughtered the foul thing. In my anger, I took her body to the castle to show them what they'd done, what their monster had taken from me. I should have buried her here, given her a proper burial, but my pain blinded me. It marked us once again, feeding into the horror stories and marking Camin."

Skye was stunned. Noah dropped to his seat, his eyes fixed on the man.

"Who are the wizards?" he quietly asked.

"We are the adjoined magic to the Mage Warriors, where they cast from light and the bright space of the world, we cast from the dark hues, pulling color where they cannot while they pull color where we cannot. Together we are a harmony that has been disjointed. We were never meant to be separated."

"The warriors and the wizards were meant to be mates?" she asked.

"No, on occasion it would happen, just as the mating of a warrior and an Elite. It is special and rare and produces powerful heirs. Full mages and novices are typical mates. Occasionally, two wizards will fall in love, but as with the Elite, our personalities are better paired as companions."

"Wizards cast in shadows," she said. "That's how Camin walks the shadow realm."

There was a change in their demeanor, a tightening of their frames as she said it.

"No one walks the shadow realm, and no one controls the shadows. That is shadow magic, long lost to this world with the curse of the Death God. We walk the shadows of the forest, the hues of darkness. We have always lived in them—that's why we went unnoticed that day, why we were able to help so many flee, to raise the barrier that protects us. No one enters the forest because no one ever returns."

"But Camin—"

"Camin struck a bargain. When your mother made her desperate play, they all knew the magic would fade as she tied it to you. They knew Camin would be hunted. He was being blamed."

"He attacked the kingdoms—you all did," Noah argued. "He killed Lyra's husband."

"No, Crimson ultimately did," the woman replied.

"What? But her kingdom, Apendia, fought with us against Camin," Noah said in shock.

"That is what she wanted everyone to believe. Only a few knew the truth."

"My mother was working with Camin," Skye said as the pieces began falling into place.

"Yes, they were trying to lead a rebellion. We fought on the outside, the Mage Warriors and a few others on the inside."

"My parents, Mark's parents."

"All friends with Camin."

"The secret study. It was a meeting room. You were right, Skye."

"It was supposed to go smooth, starting with the Nenochin kingdom. Their king knew, but it had to look like a battle had been fought. Crimson interfered, sending troops and her Mage Warriors. Unbeknownst to your mother, they had told her of the plans. As I said, she had a hold on them. Her Mage Warriors turned on us, killing their own and making it look like Camin had done it. The Nenochin kingdom were our allies, and they destroyed it, killing its king and crushing the kingdom, doing their queen's bidding. When they withdrew, the remaining heir believed that we had brought about the misery of her people, the truth further manipulated by Crimson and her lies.

"We told Camin we should give up the fight, but he didn't, knowing the others were waiting. Instead, we headed to Digremile, another disaster, and to Theodore's kingdom. In Digremile their warriors were poisoned, Camin was blamed, and the kingdom turned on us. We had no choice but to defend ourselves. With its warriors gone, Digremile fell. It is a burden we shall forever bear, crumbled by our mistakes, never to be rebuilt. The curse of the Death God hung over their kingdom from eons before, causing their final demise, but our transgressions sparked it."

"You had a choice. You could have fled," Noah said, rubbing his head as he leaned his elbows on his knees.

Skye could see the frustration these revelations were causing him. She herself was having trouble understanding how the truth could have been distorted to such a degree.

"No, we still had hope. Lyra awaited us. But when we arrived, Crimson had sent her Mage Warriors again. They'd feigned the death of one in Nenochin, all of us unaware that she still had two. They killed your father, making it look as if the blast had come from Camin. Then they turned on the others. They had been the distraction that separated the warriors from their Elite. One was killed this time, his body found with your father and Markhem's, Lyra recognizing him. Still no one questioned; the truth buried with the dead, the lies twisted, the blame placed upon Camin." Camin's father paused, wiping his hand over his face, his emotion raw after all these years. "No one questioned how my son could have killed them as he was killing their Elite. It was a disaster. Your mother knew, she knew the truth, so she made the final play, the one they'd discussed as a last resort. Stripping the power, tying it to you, mage and wizard. Hoping it would free the mages who would no longer be seen as useful."

"It backfired," Skye said.

"Yes, it took time for the spell to take hold. The fighting continued."

"Fighting that killed countless men and women," Noah said angrily.

"Do not think it was only your side that took losses. It was not meant to be this way. We would never have fought our own kind unless out of necessity. As the magic waned, Lyra went to Theodore and pleaded for him to end the war, to free them finally and let them return to their own homeland. He refused and sent her back to the battlefield. He called on Crimson, who sent her last Mage Warrior and her Elite. Her Elite were weak, corrupted—only Markhem's line was ever meant to lead them. They were never meant to be split between commanders, warriors, between kingdoms. Lyra snuck out that night to meet Camin. I was with them," the woman said. "Our power was depleting from her spell. She told Camin to give up the fight; they'd lost too many lives. He refused, stubborn just like his mother. We were ambushed. Crimson's warrior murdered Markhem's mother and, in her rage, Lyra killed the rogue warrior, the few Elite with him we killed."

A heaviness sat over them along with a silence.

"We were trapped—everything Camin and Lyra had hoped for had gone wrong. Lyra knew there was nothing left, nothing more for her to fight for. She could return and suffer Theodore's wrath, powerless to fight back alone or she could be free.

"She chose her freedom, begged Camin to find you, to protect you. She was sure you were the answer. She begged him to draw back, to wait until you'd had time outside of our world, enough time in a life free of constraints before he brought you back. Then she took her life. Camin was devastated. They were friends, and he'd wanted nothing more than to see her here, living her life free with Berrett and you, but that dream had shattered. She knew it, as did he. And so, he took blame for her death, we withdrew and he—he—"

"Sold his soul to the Death God so that he could walk the shadow realm and keep an eye on me," Skye said, a heaviness in her chest.

"Yes. He was gone a very long time and one day he returned, saying it was time, that your power was breaking free. The war began again. You see, he knew Theodore held the connection to bringing you home and he would use it when threatened, which he did."

"The day of the accident," Noah said. "Camin must have felt the pulse of your magic."

"We all felt it."

"But how is it his magic returned and no one else's did?"

"Camin is linked to you with the spell. He didn't know Lyra had done it, but she did. When your magic flared that day, it was a call to his and his awoke."

"Like a safety net, a guardian to make sure..." She stopped, unsure of what it would have been for.

"To ensure you did not fall into Theodore's hands. Unfortunately, you did and now you remain weak, untrained. Camin is the last of the Mage Warriors. He may be half wizard, but his mother was a Mage Warrior, and he was blessed with her magic, a rarity, as your line is the only pure one. He is the only one who can teach you to reach your full potential."

"And my mother trusted him that much?"

"They were all friends when they were at the castle together. Camin loved your mother, but he knew her heart belonged to your father. There was no stopping that, but he could never stop loving her. Eventually she died. He fights in her name now, for you. But with no one left who knew what the true fight was for, he has become a monster, something to be feared, just as we always have been."

Skye stared into the fire, trying to grasp it all. Piecing everything she'd learned together. Realizing the betrayal her mother had mentioned in the book hadn't been Camin's, it had been the Mage Warriors from Crimson's kingdom. She'd known, had trusted Camin enough to see the truth.

Noah dropped his head to his hands. "Why didn't any of us know?"

"Lyra and the others didn't want you implicated. Fedhem was your commander. He couldn't risk a divide in his troops, and he knew there would be hesitance, those who doubted, even as they followed his lead. The intention was for Camin to attack under the pretense that he was taking the crown. Theodore's kingdom is the strongest. If he could have overthrown him, then turned the Elite, the full mages, everyone who did not know, then we stood a chance against Crimson."

"That's a lot to risk."

"We had nothing to lose."

"But they did," Noah said. "And they lost everything."

"Not everything," the woman said, looking at Skye.

"Is there anyone left who knows the truth?"

"A handful. Elspeth, the woman who raised you, knows as does the man who posed as your father and the one who posed as Markhem's."

Skye was stunned.

"That's why she refused to tell you about your power. That's why she took the lead. Why she kept you and Mark separated. She knew, and she didn't want Theodore getting you until Camin had time. She knew the spell linked you both, knew if you were with Mark, there was a chance it would wake your powers too early. Damn, how could I have been so blind all those years?" Noah said.

"They wanted you blinded. It was safer for you, for all of you. Theodore is kind to his mages, but his kindness has limits. My wife's banishment made that clear. How many others were dropped into this forest for questioning, never to make it past the beasts that roam it?"

"Crimson is not kind. She tormented her mages into submission, bad enough to turn them against their own kind. If she had suspected a rebellion within her own ranks, she would have killed them all," the woman said.

Noah raised his head quickly. "She wants Skye. She's been at Theodore since the day we returned."

"Of course she does. Mage Warriors are true power, magic the non-casters cannot have but can control by the very society they created when they stole their freedom. She must never get her hands on you, for if she does, it will mean death to us all."

"Why?" Skye asked.

"Because you walk the shadows. You walk both worlds, harness the colors of both, something no mage has ever done. You hold the power to bring this world to its knees."

A chill tore through Skye, fear gripping her.

"Why do you say that?" Noah asked.

"Did she not bring the barrier of the shadow realm closer to our world? You saw her take the life of the Noctum that day we attacked. Camin was testing her again and that time, she showed us all the true nature of her power. No one bleeds the life-force. Only wizards wield the shadow hues, only Mage Warriors the light hues. To have dominance over both is an anomaly that is awe-inducing, but to also have the gift to bleed life from our world, to cave in the barriers that divide the realms, that is unimaginable and terrifying."

Skye didn't know what to say as a shiver went through her. She didn't want that kind of power. She'd never wanted any power. Her breathing grew shallow, and she was overwhelmed, lost in a flood of emotion from Mark's disappearance, to the long trip here, and now to finding the truth.

"Skye," she heard Noah say, but she was too lost in the fury of emotion to look up from her hands.

"Skye!" he yelled, shaking her roughly.

She broke her gaze, jarred to look up. A swirl of red surrounded her. She heard crying, her eyes seeing the blonde hair of the woman now a dull gray, the red bleeding from the violet in her robe that was now a mere blue. The cats were on their sides, the black bleeding from them as it was from everything else.

She took shallow breaths and calmed herself, slowly guiding the hues away from her, listening as the cries ceased, a breath of relief coming from the woman.

Scrambling up, Skye looked around at the frightened faces.

"I never asked for any of this. I never wanted it. I don't want it! I just want my life back, my boring old life where I lived in the shadows, and they gave me comfort. I can't be this person you need me to be."

She ran off, across the small forest village and into the dense woods, tears streaming as she tumbled and fought against the tree limbs and thick vegetation layering the ground. Finally, too tired to run and fight any longer, she sat against a tree stump, bringing her knees in tight and hugging them as she cried for everything she'd lost—that which she'd known and that which she'd never known. She cried until exhaustion finally won and she slept; the forest encasing her; the shadows protecting her.

MARK

The shadowy world was frustrating. Mark wished he had his cellphone flashlight to offer something more than the gray haze that seemed to encompass this realm. At least they'd given it an appropriate name. His eyes were adjusting, but only enough to make out shapes. He still tripped and stumbled on things he couldn't see. He'd made it to what seemed like a clearing at one point, only to slide into a murky substance which he had to fight against to keep from being pulled under. He stuck to the wooded areas after that point.

He wasn't certain they really were woods. The trees seemed to grow in odd directions, sometimes parallel to the ground, other times from above, their limbs tangling in his hair, scratching against his skin.

He stopped and leaned against a relatively normal looking one, a patch of open space before him, a misty moon above, although he wasn't certain if it was a moon or a sun, there didn't seem to be a difference here and with the constant haze it was hard to tell.

"Well, well. What do we have here?"

He turned at the low voice. It sounded feminine but at such a deep range he couldn't say for certain until he saw her. She was naked. *Does anyone wear clothes in this realm?* he wondered as he took in her dense snakelike skin that shimmered in hues of black and what looked like it could have been forest green save for the poor lighting. Behind her, a tail flicked back and forth before slithering around her overly voluptuous breasts. Her serpent-like black eyes were curious, her full red lips curved into a sly, seductive grin. She had hair of the same shade of green that ran down her back, spikes like long horns protruding from it.

"I think we have a lost soul, a fresh one," she said, stretching her long fingers out to touch his chest, the ends of them curved like serpent fangs. He took a step back, his feet landing with a squish in a muddy substance, whatever lay below the surface of the deceivingly inviting open land.

"Not fresh, dear, alive."

A male dropped from an upside-down tree. He was tall, extremely tall as he towered above Mark's six two frame. Only then did he realize the female was standing at his own height.

He, too, wore no clothes which left his well-endowed member hard to miss. Although Mark averted his eyes quickly, it was not quick enough to avoid noticing the full erection. God, he hoped that was for the woman and not for him. He wouldn't have been offended but complimented by it, if it weren't on a seven foot massively built demon who looked like he could tear Mark to shreds with one hand.

"A living soul found its way into our realm?" the male said.

"Can we play with him?" The female wrapped her tail around Mark, yanking him closer to her, her large breasts pressing against him. She smelled like a sour swamp, but he didn't dare push away. These were demons of the shadow realm, and unlike Camin's demon seductresses, it didn't look like these two would play nice with him.

He wished he had the rib bones still, but he'd lost them when the corpse of a strange rabid looking animal collapsed into the muck after he'd killed it with them. Judging from these two, they wouldn't have made a difference.

A long, forked tongue darted from her mouth and ran along Mark's cheek and neck, his skin tingling oddly where it touched.

"Oh, he's yummy. I can feel his pulse," she said, dipping her nose to his neck and sniffing. "He smells of life."

"How did a living creature pass into our realm?" the male asked, pushing Mark back, his fang-shaped finger against his heart. "The only ones unlucky enough to find themselves here are those the shadow gods allow us to steal, a rare treat."

"Well, that's a long story," Mark answered.

"I don't have time for long stories," the female said, her sharp fingers grabbing his crotch. Would there be any time in this realm where someone wasn't trying to get into his pants? It may have been flattering if they weren't demons and he hadn't had Skye.

"Trana, you prefer this insignificant mortal to me?"

She let Mark go and turned to the male.

"Nothing could replace your prowess," she said, her tongue reaching to the one that had exited his mouth to meet it. Mark held back the gag, then saw her hand enclose around the demon's erection, her claws plunging into it. Mark's hand went to his own, in instinctive protection, feeling the pain it must have caused, but the male only groaned in pleasure. He pulled her close, their mouths closing around each other, tails doing a ritual of their own.

Mark took a small step back but hit the mud again. He was trapped unless he could somehow sneak around them.

As if they'd forgotten he was there, they began fornicating. He looked away, chastising himself for his own slight erection as the male suckled her breasts, her cries of pleasure echoing like banshee cries around him.

He slipped to the side, but a tail whipped around and threw him to the ground. The female flipped her body and land atop him, her eyes slits of green.

As he tried to scoot back she straddled him.

"We're going to play," she purred.

Mark could only imagine what her version of play encompassed, and he cringed as she ground against him them leaned into him. Her mouth was dangerously close to his when her body was lifted from him, the male entering her from behind.

She arched her back, her breasts falling against Mark, pinning him as her body moved with the rhythm. He had no place to go. Her long tongue snaked out to meet the male's as he leaned against her, grabbing her breast, and pulling her back against him. Mark was like a voyeur, forced to observe their strangely erotic dance.

With her body raised from his, he scooted some, trying to go unnoticed, but her tail snaked its way under him, emerging over the hardness he couldn't stop even with his fear holding him hostage. It snaked into his pants, gripping him, pulling him as the male groaned again in pleasure.

"Where are you going, pet?" she said.

Her tail pulled his pants down, and in one quick move, she enveloped him. He tried to scramble away, but she held him in place. The male stood over them as she moved her body to a rhythm Mark's body couldn't resist. He was horrified but turned on at the same time. She pushed her breasts against his mouth, the male still standing above them, watching and tugging at his erection.

"Take it, suckle me," she demanded, her tail squeezing his ribs tight. His mouth opened in response, and he took her breast in unintentionally, the fullness of it, the hard nipple doing nothing to stop his strange uncontrollable need to come. A sweet juice filled his mouth, his tongue moving to lick it, his mouth sucking at her breast automatically. It was intoxicating, relaxing him. He wanted more, his hands pulling at her other breast as she groaned in ecstasy. Her body pulled back, the juice still dripping from his mouth and fingers. He licked his fingers clean as the male moved closer, filling her mouth with his massive erection. She took him, her head moving in rhythm with that of her body, the male shoving himself hard into her, grabbing her head and dictating the movement.

Mark had never been so turned on, his arousal growing to a precipice, the need to climax intense but still not ready as the male came, his juices dripping from her lips and rolling down her chest. She turned back to Mark, her eyes predatory, the male backing away, still grunting as he stroked out a few more streams of his climax onto her chest. She leaned down and thrust her breast back into Mark's mouth, the fragrant nectar now mixed with the taste of the demon's essence. He drank, clawing at her for more as her body moved against him. The need to come burning through him like an ache that would not cease.

She drew back, and he reached for her breast, squeezing the liquid from her nipple and trying to catch it in his mouth. She pushed him, holding him down with her hand and riding him hard, the intensity within him peaking to a point that it was painful but still not tipping.

The male came behind her, rubbing her breasts as she leaned further back, their tongues dancing, her body pumping until her orgasm clenched tight around him, so tight his hardness ached, the need to join her pleasure so high that he grabbed her hips, pulling her down for more.

"Haha, my dear, yet another pet," the male said, excitement layering his voice.

"And this one is so alive," she said, lifting herself from Mark before taking him in her mouth, her forked tongue dancing against his skin as she rose.

"No," he complained, pulling at her to finish him.

"So alive, it's like a drug," she said, licking her lips. "You, I will keep."

She kissed the male before dropping above Mark again, placing her breast in his mouth. The nectar filled his mouth, all his pleasure senses rising along with the unquenchable lust for her.

"Finish me," he begged.

"No, no, pet. You must want it badly and you don't, not yet." Her tail trailed his erection before forcing his pants up.

She rose. "Bring my pet but separate him from the others. I don't want them pleasuring him. This one is my favorite. I do believe I'll take him again today."

"Please take me now," he begged again as the male picked him up and dragged him along.

"Don't wear him out too quickly, Trana. The living aren't as pliable as the dead. You'll kill him too fast if you take him too many times without giving him rest."

"But you know you get to take me each time I take one. Don't you want to share in that?"

"Trust me, I will take you as often as you give me, but I know how you covet your toys."

"Fine, perhaps I'll indulge in another tonight."

Mark understood none of it but the devastating fact that she wouldn't be pleasuring herself with him and that there would be no release for the overwhelming need he had to climax in her. Tears fell as if he'd lost the love of his life, his body aching for her.

"You are cruel, my wicked one, and I love that about you," the male said as they strode deeper into the darkness and further from his freedom.

MARK

Dreams plagued Mark's sleep, dreams that ventured from the erotic to nightmarish. Ones filled with screams that set one's soul ablaze with fear, ones that left him wanting and craving. In those dreams, he drank the nectar of the gods as pleasure tortured his body, driving him mad, leaving him exhausted, sleep keeping him in its grasp. He craved the nectar; he craved his keeper.

Through the fog came the screams, the cries of terror. He thought there were others with him, but the fog kept him from seeing them. He could hear them when they were chosen, he and the others begging to go, to taste the nectar, to finally have the release they ached for. It was constant, never ceasing, always on the cusp of orgasm, but never satisfying it.

He lay there, the dreams one of terror this eve, screams that ripped through the silence, then just as he was becoming aware of them, of their implication, the nectar filled his mouth, her breast soft against it as she touched him. It was brief, but enough to send the urge through him.

"Quiet, my pet, your turn is next. Tonight will be your last. You will finally have the release you seek."

Her hands played with him, teasing him, but then she was gone, and the ache returned, the fog growing heavy, taking him away from the reality. His only thought, the release awaiting him.

"Mark." His name came as a whisper. With the fog too heavy, his head fell again. He was dreaming of her but as his eyes flittered, the image changed, her body transforming, face flickering in a shine of sunlight, blue eyes that broke through the fog.

"Mark," she whispered, her hands touching his face.

Skye. The memories surfaced, fighting through the heavy fog, pushing aside a sense that now seemed false.

"Skye," he whispered back, kissing her, but the magic faded, the feel of her gone.

"Mark!" a man's voice said sharply, nudging him hard.

He blinked his eyes open, fighting their heaviness, the groggy feeling threatening to pull him under. The man yanked him to his feet, a foreign feeling, as if he hadn't woken in days, maybe longer.

"I need you to wake long enough to get out of here."

Mark looked around, eyes open for the first time. Bodies were strewn in a cage beside him, men laying with their hands on their erections, writhing like they were atop a woman. Then he looked closer. Men and women filled the space, all trying to reach a climax, none successful, some so frantic about it they were clawing themselves alive, blood upon their organs. Bodies, blood, and fornication everywhere. His own cage was empty save for him and he felt a sense of relief that he wasn't among the mutilated bodies.

"You are living, kept segregated from the tormented souls for your living essence. Now hold on," Camin said.

He would have tried running, save for the heaviness in his limbs and head and the horrific scene before him. Instead, he grasped Camin's arm, watching as he pulled the black from the cage, the darkness swirling around him.

"No!" He heard a shrill screech, the tail of the demon snapping the bars moments before the scene disappeared and Mark found himself back in Camin's space. Camin pushed him so hard that he landed with a thud. Suddenly, his head was throbbing. He felt like he'd gone without caffeine for days. It was dull and heavy, hammering constantly.

"Here, chew this," Camin said, throwing a soft leaf at him.

Mark picked it up, eyeing it suspiciously.

"Eat it. It will dampen the effects of the nectar. Why would you run? You were safe. Instead, you run straight to the den of a succubus demon?"

"Safe? I was safe? Those demons tried to seduce me, then ate a man after fucking him!" he yelled, standing, but quickly sitting again as the room spun.

"They wouldn't have hurt you. They're a hundred times safer than a succubus!"

"A succubus? What's a succubus?" he asked, the term vaguely familiar to him, his headache increasing.

"Demons that lure you in with sex, enslave you with their addictive nectar, and then feed from your pleasure and your soul, draining you until nothing is left. They are particularly fond of living things because they can torment you longer and feast off your dead soul once your body gives out."

"I wasn't lured by a succubus," he said, fighting the onslaught of memories, the demon body, the nectar that flowed from her breast. He chewed on the leaf, trying to contain his anger at the situation.

"The drug will wear off in a few hours. It will take a few days to free yourself of the need for it."

"Skye," he said, guilt hammering him.

"It's nothing to be ashamed of, there's no way to escape it, no matter how deeply you love another. Their spell, the nectar, it erases it all, encompassing your reason and all you are until you want release so badly that you beg for more, begging and pleading for it with your last breath."

"You speak as if from experience."

"I've been in their lair, been under their spell. When I first came here, one captured me. Captured...I went willingly. There's no way not to want them. There are three things that drive every realm: love, pleasure, and pain. All are things demons feast upon, and succubi excel in both pleasure and pain."

"How did you escape?" he asked, his head clearing more as the fog lifted.

"Like you, I had help. You see, my soul was already claimed, marked by the Death God. The succubus got greedy and paid the price. One of his minions freed me. I had a purpose yet to serve. The succubus was paid a visit by one of the shadow gods who turned her spell on herself, leaving her with a hunger that she still suffers to the day, drinking her own nectar, pleasuring herself, feeding on her own soul until she will one day wither to nothing from her unquenchable thirst. The Death God does not play games."

Mark shuddered both at the story and at the thought of what he'd done. "God, I need a drink."

"It will not erase the memory. Be thankful you survived to fight the memories."

"Did I really..." The thought brought bile to his throat, and he turned, vomiting liquid that burned its way up his throat. He stared at the puddle of nectar that had been feeding him while under the enthrall of the succubus.

"Seems to be a habit of yours," Camin said.

Mark wiped the back of his mouth with his hand. "Your creatures ate a man in front of me. They're just as foul as that succubus."

"They need to be fed. The Death God allows me to drag men in who are destined for this realm. I take them right as they are ready to cross over. The girls feed on a treat that keeps them contented."

"Contented?"

"They are valuable. Quite satisfying if you let them be. They would not have harmed you."

"You think I should have indulged in two demons who ate a man in the throes of his orgasm? That sounds tempting."

"You indulged in a succubus who drugged you with her breasts as she pleasured herself with your body and fed from your soul. I think my offer is the better one."

Mark grumbled and chewed on the leaf.

"Besides, they are useful. They are the eyes and ears in a world that has only fangs and claws. And they know how to satisfy a man, especially if you take them both at once."

"To each his own. Why are you not caging me again? Does this buddy-buddy talk mean I'm free?"

"Not a chance. I need you to bring Skye here."

"So, I'm bait? And you think I'm fine with that? That I'm going to let you lure the woman I love into your trap?"

"Yes, and I see the leaf is working."

"Yes, it's working, although it's not erasing any memories. In fact, they're growing worse." Had he really begged for the demon, pleading for her? He felt depraved and embarrassed. How easily his love for Skye, one that had prevailed through everything, was erased in a matter of minutes.

"Once their tail touches your skin, you're lost. There's something on the tip that enters the bloodstream. The nectar seals the spell and keeps you in the state. There was no choice, no matter how much you love her. That's their power—seduction."

Mark wiped his eyes. "Why should I trust any of this? I'm your captive. You're trying to kill the woman I love."

"Yet I saved you, kept you alive and fed."

"Left me with a pair of homicidal deviant demons."

"Says the man I just pulled from a succubus den, clutching his hard on and begging for more in his sleep."

"Don't remind me," he said, running his hands through his hair.

"I'm not trying to kill the Mage Warrior."

Mark stared at him in disbelief.

"It's time you learned the truth, just as she now is. She'll be here soon, and she will need your strength and trust."

"If she forgives me for cheating on her with a demon."

"That's the least of your problems. You've slept with other women, have you not?"

"How is that any of your business, and how do you know that?"

"The same way I know you were named as cousins to keep her magic clamped down; the same way I knew her name was Skye before I met her."

Mark studied him, his eyes looked sincere, the brown of them almost black in the dark of the shadows.

"Talk. It can't get any worse than what I've been through the past few days."

"You might want to stay seated for this and let me get you that drink."

His tone didn't bode well and, as he rummaged in the corner for a drink, Mark tried to imagine what could be worse than what he'd experienced, other than having to explain how he'd been the sex toy of a female demon for days, drinking some kind of drug from her breasts. That would be a fun conversation.

Camin handed Mark a glass of wine, which he chugged before holding his cup out for more. After the third glass, he put his cup down, crossed his arms, and said, "Tell me why Skye is so important to you and why I should let you hand her over to the Death God."

SKYE

kye stood across from the female wizard, whose name she'd
discovered was Bridget. For days she'd trained with them,
learning spells she should have learned from her mother.
Mastering and owning them. All the while, Noah stood guard,
still leery, watching in case anyone turned on her.

Where she'd thought she'd understood her magic after
reading the journal, she realized she'd barely scraped the surface.
Wizards and Mage Warriors used the same magic, they simply
manipulated different sides of the color spectrum.

She'd worked with Camin's father, learning control, the
ability to sense the life-force as she had with the Noctum, but
through everything, even the inanimate world. Understanding
that as she touched that force, she had claimed all she should. Her
power was stronger than anyone before her, and she needed to
recognize that the life-force was a gate, locked for all other mages
and wizards. Only she had the ability to bleed it, to use it for her
own and kill the living. It was a terrifying thought, and she knew
she'd done it that day in the battle, the lives of the Noctum taken
when she'd bled them of their lifeforce.

Bridget stood, evaluating her. Skye had trained with all the others, but this was the first with her. Skye was growing tired of training; she wanted to find Mark. Although they assured her Camin would not harm him, she had a strange feeling he'd been in trouble. The prior night, she'd dreamt of him, calling for him through a thick fog filled with cries of pleasure and pain. It had smelled sweet and foul at the same time, a smell of bodies, sex, and sweat. She'd called for him, and finally heard his voice, felt his touch on her skin. For a brief second, the sun had shone, and his hazel eyes had been there, filled with fear and confusion, blurry as if he were drugged. As he'd recognized her, they had cleared, his love for her shining through until the fog had stolen him away and she had woken.

"Your mind wanders today," Bridget said, bringing her from her thoughts.

"Something's happened to Mark. I—I can feel it."

"Camin will protect him until you arrive and play your part."

"No, something's happened. He's not with Camin, he...I don't know how to explain it. He's in a dense fog, confused, drugged maybe? There were screams and this weird mix of smells like bodies." She ran her hand through her loose braid.

Bridget's eyes grew concerned. "Would he have run from Camin?"

"Given the opportunity?" Noah said. "Definitely."

"If he escaped Camin, then he is in trouble. The shadow realm is the realm of the Death God and his shadow gods. They are cruel, and the demons who serve them, who feed from the souls the gods keep, are vicious. They can be seductive, and they will covet a living soul like Mark's."

She swallowed, her knees shaking. "I need to get to the shadow realm. I went there once; I can get there again."

"No, you're not ready. You need to complete this next step—"

"No more steps. I can't stand another day without him, knowing he could be in trouble—"

"Please, this one more day and you will be ready. No one

walks into the shadow realm and lives to leave but Camin and he sold his soul to have the ability. He sold his soul for you. The least you can do is give him this one more day."

She dropped her eyes, remembering what they'd told her the prior night. "He made that choice."

"For Lyra and for you. He promised Lyra he would help you. That he would ensure you would not meet the same fate as the other Mage Warriors. She wanted you to be the one to lead all of us to freedom, a return to our kingdom, to the lives we once led."

"Me?"

"She saw your power early. She knew you would be the one. Camin watched you through the shadow realm to ensure you were capable. And he believes you are. You lived in the shadows your entire life. You are the bridge between wizard and mage, the one who can walk the shadow realm, the living realm, and the upper realm."

She stepped back, her hand coming to her chest. Her mother's words coming back to her. *The colors not only come to you, they bleed for you.* She'd recognized it, the blues had faded. She had stripped the life-force the day she was born. She'd watched her in the shadow realm with Camin the day she'd known she would sacrifice her life.

Tears filled Skye's eyes. "I'm not that person. What if...what if she put her faith in the wrong person?"

Bridget smiled. "She didn't." She took Skye's hand. "Draw the shadows."

Skye furrowed her brow. They were standing in the forest where, before, she'd always trained in the more open space where color was more accessible.

"You don't need color. There was a reason the spell left you only blind to color and not completely blind. That spell would have rendered any other Mage Warrior blind until their power returned. You see, it was designed to clip the power of the Mage Warrior. The ability to wield the color of the light hues."

Skye pulled her hand back and called the gray of the shadows, the black beneath them. They came to her, swirling like a comfortable cloak around her skin.

"You are the bridge."

Fire stirred within her, anger at all that had been stolen from her, from the people she loved, the parents she'd never known. Even Camin, who had taken the title of enemy that was handed to him so that others could be free. She reached beyond the forest edge, calling for the colors, the reds, the gold of the sun slivers, the green of the grass, calling them to her.

Bridget backed up as the hues gathered, swirling with the shadow hues. Skye had taken only what she needed, enough to feed them, to let them dance along her skin as they stopped the familiar swirl and she called the shadows home, then the colors, letting them cascade over her like a brilliant dark cloak. At first, they stung, but eventually, they soothed, settling upon each other until they were like a rich haze against her skin. She called the navy that lay within the black of the forest, letting it dance in her palm. That was her home—blue, the color that drove her, that was the foundation of her power. With her other hand, she tore at the hem of her shirt, ripping the material and holding the fractured edge out, commanding the hue to find it. It danced as it met the torn edge, then grew in force, its color strengthening. It tingled along her skin, playing with the sheen of colors she wore. In a frenzy, it morphed her clothing, taking the piece and extending it to a lush blue cloak that fell upon her shoulders. The gray that surrounded her flared before etching itself into the cloak, settling upon her skin once it was done and fading from sight. She could still feel the hues resting there, waiting for her command.

She brought her eyes up, meeting Bridget's wide ones, the woman's mouth hanging open in surprise.

"I know the shadows. I have walked them my entire life. The shadows are where I take comfort—they are my home, my core. You're right, my mother was right. I am different and I can walk the shadow realm with ease because it's part of me. I wish to see my kingdom before I face the Death God and bring Mark and Camin home. Can you take me there?"

Bridget brought a shaking hand up and moved closer. "The hues, where did they go?" she whispered.

Skye reached for them and let them surface, sitting upon her skin. Bridget let out a small gasp.

"No one holds the hues," she mumbled.

"No one but me." She looked at Noah, who appeared just as traumatized. "My training is done. We see our homeland and then I go to the shadow realm."

He nodded as Bridget picked up the edge of Skye's cloak. Along it, embroidered in light magic, were symbols that included the birthmarks of each mage level, the Elite, and the wizards. Her fingers traced a moon, the iridescence clinging to her fingers in sparkles as she brought them back up.

"I need to get the others; they will want to go. It is rare that any of us venture back to the homeland."

Bridget disappeared in a drift of black smoke. Skye had learned that the wizards traveled in a fashion similar to full mages, but without the need for a staff or conduit, their magic closer to the Mage Warriors. Portals that she and Camin could create, however, were beyond their skills.

"Who are you?" Noah asked, staring at her.

"Skye. The same Skye, but with more understanding. With open eyes. Look at your weapon."

He looked down and pulled his weapon out. It was glowing with the same hues that now lay within her. They swirled in the handle in a continuous motion.

"This is the way we should have been, my line. But fear kept them from claiming the powers as they should have, fear of the shadows, fear of becoming the balance between mage and wizard."

"Is that what you are now?"

"Yes, and more. To lead, one must understand all roles. I heard that in some leadership training I had once. It's the same here. My line ruled our people but clung to the Mage Warrior gifts, when within us was the capability of every gift."

"No," Camin's father said as they all arrived. "Within you. Your mother had the capability of our magic, as did others in your line, but you are something different. The hues are part of you, the magic within you fully awakened so that it connects to all five orders of magic. You were meant to rule us, to bring us back."

"Home," she said. She called the hues forth from within her, then those from their robes and more from the shadows. She thought of the realm Petrian and Noah had described on the other side of the Fettered Forest. *Take me there*, she commanded to the colors.

The hues swirled and bucked before them, forming a portal that stood alive with magic. Without hesitation, she walked through. The air escaped her lungs with a force as she emerged to see that she was standing atop an overgrown pile of white rubble. The portal dissipated in a gray mist-like smoke once the others walked through.

"You did it," Bridget said.

Skye looked around. Before her stood the ruins of her family's home, her people's land. Now that her connection to her magic was deep, she felt the tie to the home that had been lost, its proud people domesticated, used as tools and weapons for the very people who had destroyed their land and stolen their identity from them.

It had been generations removed yet beneath the overgrowth and the ruins lay the skeleton of a grand city. A foundation, one they could rebuild with their magic, the magic that tied them to one another, to their homeland.

She breathed in deeply, letting the essence of her homeland fill her lungs.

"Noah," she said. "I want you to return to Chenthom. Find

Elspeth, Thomas, and Trent, as well as Petrian. Spread the word. This time, we will all know what was taken from us. Confirm the stories, raise the Elite."

"But Skye, if Theodore—"

"Theodore does not have the power, nor does the queen to the south. Her warriors are dead, as are all the others—all but me. We have the numbers, we hold the power, they must be made to believe this."

"And us?" Camin's father asked.

"You are our allies, but no longer can you be asked to fight. It has cost you too much already. This time, the cry for freedom must come from inside, from your brothers and sisters."

She called to the white of the stone, pulling it to her, letting it flow through her until she sensed the touch of the shadow realm, the edge of the stone's life-force. Then she stopped, letting it fill her until the others stepped away in fear. Releasing it with a graceful sweep of her hand, she watched as it reattached to the stone, only this time with her magic imbued in it. The stones moved, multiplying, bonding, rising until a glorious castle stood before them. A beacon of hope that shone with a sparkle in the sun's beams.

The others stared at the structure.

"Gods, Skye, what are you?" Noah asked.

"I am a mage. Now they will know that our kingdom is still here, waiting to be reclaimed by the mages, wizards, and Elite that once lived here in peace and prosperity."

She touched the stone, feeling its warmth. "And my parents' lives and all those who fought with them will not have been lost in vain."

She took her hand away and pulled her hood up.

"You're leaving, aren't you?" Bridget asked.

"I have a date with the Death God, and I need to find Mark and Camin. I will bring them home, both of them."

"But the shadow realm—"

"The shadows are my comfort. I have lived in them all my life. That is how I wield all hues. They are my weapon and my shield as much as the colors of day are, maybe even more."

Camin's father removed a trinket from around his neck and placed it over hers. Skye touched the navy amulet, which deepened at her touch before she looked to him.

"Camin gave it to me for safekeeping when he left for the shadow realm. It was your mother's. She gave it to him the night of her death so that you could have a piece of your family—of her, and your father. Camin said I would know when to give it to you."

There were tears behind her eyes, and she hugged him tightly.

"Thank you. I will bring your son home, I promise."

He drew back, giving her a nod, his eyes watery.

"Skye," Noah said. She met his worried eyes. "You can't go in there by yourself."

"I have to. I'm the only one who can."

"But Mark—"

"I will find him, and he'll understand why you couldn't follow me. Your place is here. Start the revolution so that when I return, I can finish it."

He pulled her in for a hug, squeezing tightly.

"Promise me you'll be careful."

"I promise."

He released her, and she took a step back, pulling her hood up. Internally, she was terrified, but she knew she needed to find Mark and end this. The final play with the Death God and the kingdoms rested upon her shoulders.

She drew the hues from around her, the bright colors, and formed a portal for Noah. He gave her one last look before stepping through, the portal closing behind him. The others nodded to her then disappeared, leaving her alone in a land that should have been foreign to her but one that felt like home.

After a few moments of reflection, she reached inside and

summoned the dark hues, pulling at the ones that lie around her, the black of the rotted woods, the gray of the stones, expanding them, before opening her eyes and letting them surround her. She accepted them, opening herself to the hues and the shadows they held. Sending them out to the sky, she watched as they spread, darkening the clouds, covering the sun, the shadows abounding. Last time, she'd been unprepared. This time, she wanted the Death God to know she was coming. She summoned the shadow hues to her, bleeding them, feeling the disruption in the shadow realm, the bending of the veil between the realms, the straining of the demons and creatures within at her insolence. Finally, she let it go, succumbing to the darkness and entering the shadow realm for the last time.

MARK

Mark stared at Camin in disbelief. He'd listened attentively, his mind and everything he thought he knew in chaos. Now that he was done talking, Camin awaited Mark's response. It took him a few minutes to recover.

"So, you want me to believe that you're actually the good guy and all of this has been an attempt to free our people from a slavery they don't realize they're in?"

"Did you realize you were under the succubus's enthrall?"

Mark groaned. "Point taken. How do you expect me to believe this?"

"I haven't killed you. I didn't kill Skye."

"You beat the shit out of her and nearly killed her!"

"She needed to wake up and ask questions, to see our world through her outsider eyes and not those you and the others were redefining her with. Frankly, I'm surprised Elspeth didn't say anything to her."

"How could she? You were attacking Skye at every turn, and she barely had control of her powers. She nearly crushed the realms, almost tore down the veil the first time she really used her magic."

"Did she now? Is that what that was? That must have worried the Death God."

"Apparently. But isn't that what he and his shadow gods want her to do?"

"No, they need an opening, a way in that's easier, bigger. Now they rely on me and a few demons who can traverse both realms. They are few and weak. They want to feed their hungrier demons with living souls like they once did before the other gods forced them into the shadows."

"Skye was right."

The ground shook and the air in Mark's lungs seemed to be sucked from them as everything around them stretched. The shaking turned violent, the air becoming thick with an excited frenzy of howls and shrieks. The hairs on Mark's neck stood.

Camin's two demons fell, scrambling to their feet in a frantic move. They'd entered during the story, eyeing Mark hungrily before Camin had ushered them away. They'd been playing with each other in the corner, a distraction Mark had forced his eyes from before Camin's story had engrossed him too fully to notice.

"Skye," Camin said. "She's coming for you."

Mark's heart beat incessantly in fear and excitement at once. "She can't. She needs to stay there. The Death God—"

"Will be no match for her. That was not an accident, that was a warning."

The two demons sniffed the air, then ran from the space, spooked by something.

"Should we be worried by that or...Skye, maybe she's found us already." He ran to the entrance, only to stumble back in as the succubus demon flicked her tail at him.

"Shit," he mumbled, scrambling toward the corner.

"You stole my feed, my special toy," she growled at Camin.

"You can't kill me, my soul is taken," he said quickly, and Mark could see him calling the hues.

"Wizard," she hissed as her tail darted to him, quickly knocking him over before he could cast a spell. He rolled away from its tip but not fast enough, and it grazed his cheek.

"Dammit," Mark muttered, looking for any way to defend himself. His weapon—where had Camin put his weapon? The succubus didn't seem worried about him, crouching over Camin and holding his fighting body down.

"You may be marked, but I don't have to feed from you to torture you or to play with you."

Mark searched for any sign of his weapon. The entranceway was wide open. He could escape and leave Camin to his demise. He looked back over to see the demon forcing his mouth open, her nectar spilling from her breasts. Camin's fight fled as she pushed her breast further into his willing mouth, throwing her head back with pleasure, her lower body grinding against him.

Camin had risked his life to save Mark, he couldn't leave him. His eye caught the reflection of the demon in his weapon, seeing it propped behind them deep in a corner. He'd have to go through the beast to get it, which was not a possibility.

Remembering his presence, her head snapped toward him, her breast freeing from Camin's mouth, his tongue reaching out to get more of the juice. He was lost, his hands grabbing at her. Mark would get no help. As she moved from him, Camin begged for her to return.

"Shh, my pet. I have one more to capture, then we will have games all night."

She rose to Mark's height, and he couldn't help but be turned on by her, her naked body strutting languidly to him, hips swaying, the nectar dripping from her breasts, his mind not completely free of its spell.

Wake up, Mark, he told himself, pushing an image of Skye in her place. From the corner of his eye, he caught the movement of her tail just in time. Jumping into a roll, he avoided it, using his skills to quickly make his way toward Camin and his weapon.

Camin grabbed at him, pulling him down.

"Submit to her; she's all we need now."

She turned to them, and Mark fought Camin, pushing him away and reaching for his weapon, his fingertips just about to touch it when she grabbed his ankle and yanked him back. He struggled to escape her grip, the tail tightening around his legs, stretching to his hips. He was still shirtless, too much exposed skin to avoid the tip if it went higher. Kicking, he tried to keep it lower, but it crawled its way up, rubbing against his crotch, trying to tempt him, but this time, his adrenaline was high as he fought for his life.

"You and I have some unfinished business," she hissed, her forked tongue easing toward him.

"Shit." He cringed back, waiting for it to slither across his skin.

Her head darted up, and she looked toward the doorway.

"What do you think you're doing to my boyfriend?" Skye's voice came from the hooded figure standing there.

"Another plaything," the demon hissed, her tail releasing Mark, her body lifting as drops fell from her nipples across his chest. He tried scooting back, but her tail grabbed his leg again. As long as it didn't touch his skin and the droplets stayed out of his mouth, he'd stay sane, unlike Camin, who was thrashing in the corner.

"I don't discriminate. Women are just as tasty, especially living ones."

Skye dropped her hood, her blue eyes bright with power swirling within them. The markings on her robe sparkled in the dark, her hair, thickly braided, fell to the front, the sparkles shimmering beneath it. She looked beautiful and deadly.

"I don't want to play and he's not yours."

She raised her hand as the demon whipped its tail from around Mark toward her at lethal speed.

"Skye, don't let it—" He never finished the sentence.

The color bled from the demon without hesitation; its tail flopping to the floor as Skye killed it, the body collapsing in a shriveled form, the hues swirling around Skye before she sent them out in a force against the wall of Camin's shelter, the foundation exploding until she brought her other hand up, pulling hues quickly from the treelike structure. Mark watched in awe as it repaired itself, the pieces whole again.

"Mark!" she yelled and ran to him, collapsing in his arms.

He held her so tightly she yelped slightly.

"Sorry," he said, "I just—"

She cut him off with a kiss and he pulled her close again, not wanting to let go. Camin's cries caught his attention and he drew away, holding her face briefly, not truly believing she was there.

She was there. She couldn't be there, or they would use her, even kill her. He didn't know what fate awaited her. He stood, dragging her with him.

"You need to leave now. Go before they discover you."

"Shh," she said, pulling his hand back to her. "I'm not going anywhere. I know who I am. I know what I'm meant to do now."

"But the past—"

"I know, all of it. I can do this, Mark. I understand now—my part in all of it. I need to face the Death God and his shadow gods."

Camin howled in the corner.

"Christ." He grabbed a leaf from the plant Camin had taken one from earlier and forced it into Camin's mouth.

"What's wrong with him?"

"Her." He pointed to the gnarled up remains of the demon.

"Is she the reason you're shirtless, or should I be concerned that you're leaving me for Camin?"

He laughed. "That is a very long story, and trust me, I am never leaving your side again."

An angry roar echoed through the dwelling, and the doorway ripped open further.

"What is that?" she whispered.

"That would be her mate. He's a big boy, a bit of a perve too, so I'd really prefer you to be far away from him."

"Part of that long story?"

"Yeah," he answered as the male entered the space, roaring at his mate's body.

"Skye, whatever you did to her, please do it to him now. Trust me when I say she was the gentler one," Camin said.

"Nice of you to join us," Mark grumbled.

"Yeah, please tell me I didn't—"

"Save it for later," she said, stepping forward.

"You will pay, but not until I feast upon your body and your soul mage!" the demon bellowed.

"Yeah, no, only one person gets to feast upon this body. I don't like to be shared," she said.

Before he could respond, she grabbed his hues. He backed away as they stripped quickly from him, but too late as she bled them completely and his body crumpled next to the female's.

"Now that's impressive," Camin said. "Terrifying but impressive."

"Gross," she said. "Both of them feel like a locker room full of horny men. The pheromones are almost overwhelming." She looked at Mark, raising an eyebrow.

"I told you. A story for later."

She cocked her head, furrowing her brow, and he dropped his gaze, still not sure how to tell her he'd spent days lusting for and fornicating with the dead demon at her feet, her male getting off as she took him. He shivered, a chill running through him.

"May I?" Camin said, taking the focus from Mark.

"What?" she asked.

"The hues, may I take them since it's clear you don't need or want them? They hold power and the shadows down here are dim, lifeless. I cannot extract the navy hues as you can from the realm, only black and gray."

She nodded and released the lighter hues that swirled around her, Camin syphoning them. They skimmed along his skin until they settled and disappeared.

"You can do that, too?"

He nodded. "It comes with the mark of the Death God. With it we can harvest the hues and retain them as a demon would harvest a soul." Skye pursed her lips in a sour expression as he continued. "Any hue down here I can feed from as food is scarce here, but the lighter ones are hard to find."

They looked at each other, an odd silence following. To Mark's surprise, she walked over to Camin and hugged him. Mark knew Camin was still loopy from the effects of the demon, but he caught himself before falling, and hesitantly wrapped his arms around her.

"I'm sorry you've had to go through so much, that you had to be blamed, to take everyone's fear and hate, to keep the truth silent."

"It suites me," he replied. "I'm rather good at being the bad guy."

She backed out of his arms. "Not anymore. Now, we're getting out of here after I deal with this Death God thing you ensnared me in."

"In my defense, he and the shadow gods ensnared me."

"Hmmm, I suppose since your soul is part of the package deal, I'll forgive you."

She turned and walked back to Mark. Camin gave him a confused look, but Mark just shrugged as Skye studied him, walking around him, then running her fingers along his birthmark. He bit his lip, her touch like ecstasy, especially there.

"As much as I love you shirtless, it's too much of a distraction."

She walked back, pulling hues from Camin's clothes and Mark's pants, the hues wrapping around him until fabric appeared on his stomach. The hues continued to weave at an unbelievably fast pace, only ceasing when a shirt had formed.

"Fantastic. You are full of surprises, young one," Camin said as the last stich fell into place.

"You have no idea," she said, stepping over the lifeless bodies. "Death God! I am here! Bring us to you and tell me your bidding!" she yelled.

"Skye, are you mad?"

"She just might be mad enough to win," Camin said right before a cloud of black smoke transported them so that they stood before the Death God and his shadow gods, awaiting their fate.

SKYE

Skye drew the breath that had stuck in her chest when the smoke had moved them. Mark stood beside her, Camin at her other side. She couldn't believe she'd found them. She'd found Mark. Saved him from that foul female demon who'd looked like she was trying to seduce him. Had she? He'd told her there was a story. He looked worn, exhausted, shirtless. Why had he been shirtless? Her mind wanted to think there was an innocent reason for it, but his guilty look and the way he'd relied on saying there was a story for later told her there was more to it.

He was a grown man. They had only just begun sleeping together, neither stating they were monogamous, although the constant I love you's and the talk of marriage when this was over had led her to believe they were.

Had a demon seduced him? The one she'd killed was gorgeous in a snakeskin covered kind of way, her breasts many sizes fuller than Skye's and there had been something quite seductive about her, even with the creepy tail.

Let it go, Skye, she told herself as the smoke dissipated around them. They were in a massive room with no end to it. Demons stood along the side of a wide staircase, black clouds swirling at the top. Some were touching each other erotically, and she couldn't keep from watching one huge demon who was getting off on two females, his body in the throes of his orgasm as he covered them with his juices, their mouths opening to catch it as it splashed across their faces and breasts.

"Good gods," Camin muttered.

"You dare summon us, warrior?" a deep voice boomed, a strange mix of man and animal, drawing her attention away from the sight.

"You require my services, do you not?"

The floor shook, the clouds becoming blacker, the shadows in the room disappearing as darkness covered them completely.

Mark took her hand to move her back, but she resisted. She truly didn't know what she was doing and was beginning to doubt winging it was the safe bet anymore.

"You will open the doorway to the mortal world and set our minions free?"

"Why not just break the veil?" she asked, knowing the answer.

"No! The veil must remain."

"But with the veil severed, you can take the mortal world back, show your brother that you are triumphant."

"Skye, what are you doing?" Camin asked urgently.

She had no idea, but she was going with it.

The cloud dissipated and a massive, terrifying beast rose from a throne that looked to be made of bones. He was every bit of what she'd envisioned the devil to look like, but worse. This was the Death God, Derrant, they'd called him. The ruler of the shadow realm. On either side of him stood several other massive men or what looked like men, except for the strange markings that decorated their faces and bodies, almost like tattoos but with movement as if the soul of every sinner was etched into their skin, suffering in eternal agony while they fed from the souls. She had to stifle her reaction as she realized that was exactly what they were.

The Death God descended multiple stairs in one step, dragging two women behind him. They were chained to his hands, but they didn't seem afraid. Instead, as he stopped at the bottom, they slithered along his body, touching him as if every touch brought them closer to orgasm. Their hands were everywhere. He snapped a finger, and they drew back, touching each other instead. The chains fell away, yet neither moved to take their freedom.

Skye averted her eyes, then elbowed Mark, who sharply looked down. The god laughed, the sound rumbling through the space.

"A little pleasure will not hurt him, Mage Warrior. Pleasure of the flesh is the only kind we get down here."

She remained silent, her mind racing to determine her next move.

"So, you threaten to break the veil between worlds?"

"That wasn't exactly what I said."

"To break down the veil of one realm is to fracture them all. Even I know the chaos that would cause."

"What if I could do it without touching the others? Fracturing only your veil—"

"Would piss my brother off and give me a pleasure I have not felt in eons." He remained quiet, his red eyes studying her intensely. "The control and power it would take to do so...now, that is tantalizing."

"I'll do it, but only on two conditions."

"Two? You ask much for a mortal."

"You ask much, assuming I want your kind in my realm."

"Your realm? You are bold, child."

"Two conditions."

"And what would those be?"

"The three of us return free to our realm, and Camin's soul is freed from your service."

The god crossed his massive arms that looked to be the size of two buildings.

"You wish me to break the contract he has been marked with?"

"Yes, he fulfilled his end. I'm here. I'm doing your bidding. In fact, I'm doing more than your bidding. I'm giving you free rein via a doorway."

"You are bold, given that I get much pleasure here in my realm, and your three living souls will please me and my demons for many centuries. You, in particular, will please me. The other two I will send back to another succubus since you killed their sister and her mate. I'm sure they will be treated likewise."

"That is within your power, but it will not give you unlimited access to the living souls of my realm."

He drew her to him with his power, morphing closer to her in size. His hideous form changing to a tall, muscular man with thick wavy blonde hair and intense blue eyes. The Death God in mortal form, a stark contrast to what he'd been moments ago but still to be feared, no less.

"No!" Mark yelled, but he and Camin were thrown back, two minions grabbing them.

Her heart hammered in her chest.

"I smell your fear," he whispered as his hand reached under her cloak and stroked her breast.

She heard Mark fighting behind her.

"Do we have a deal?" she said, trying not to flinch.

His hand moved further, rubbing her nipple. She bit her tongue against the sensation, the warmth it sent through her, the flare of desire in his blue eyes. She had to remind herself that this was the Death God, that he'd been a monstrosity moments before. His nail gauged her skin, and she bit back the cry.

"You would taste fresh. I could make you my slave and take your body every night and every day until you beg me to kill you. I could make your lover watch."

"That won't get you your living souls."

He squeezed her breast, and she held in her reaction to the mix of pleasure and pain.

"Both options are tempting." He pulled her closer, his arousal prominent against her and she prayed he took her option, imaging the horror of being forced to sleep with the god of death, his massive erection tearing her apart with each thrust.

"Pity. You smell tasty, and I bet your screams would hasten my pleasure."

He pushed her away.

"Then you will free us, release Camin's soul from your mark?" she said hastily, trying to ignore the shake in her hand as she pulled her shirt down.

"And you will bring down the veil and allow the true gods to take the land of the living?"

Those were the words she'd been waiting for.

"Yes, it would be my pleasure," she said seductively, hoping it would keep him distracted enough to not notice what he had said.

He laughed. "Oh, I will fuck you one day, Mage Warrior, regardless of what your lover thinks. Go, before I change my mind. If the veil is not down as soon as you are returned, I will call your soul back to me."

She momentarily wondered how he had that control, but then a burning flared through the spot where his nail had cut, and she looked down at the angry red gash on her chest as it turned black with the mark of the Death God. "Only when the veil falls will it fade. Until then, you belong to me. Now go!"

In a cloud of black smoke, the room disappeared, and they were outside, the smell of fresh air upon them. With the sun setting in the distance, its final rays spread across the land.

"God, Skye, what have you done?" Mark said, moving her hand to see the mark, the brand of the Death God.

Skye saw the fear in his eyes. She was just as scared as he was, but she couldn't show it. She'd played with the devil, literally, and she wasn't certain how she would win.

"I think that might be the least of our problems," Camin said, causing her to tear her eyes from Mark.

They had landed in the Elite training grounds, and she had no doubt the Death God had been strategic about where he'd returned them. It appeared as though every Elite was present, all drawing their weapons.

Where was Noah? Her eyes scanned the faces, but she didn't see him.

"Elites, stand down," Mark commanded. "There is no threat here."

Donakin came forth, the Elites seeming confused but not lowering their weapons.

"I didn't want to believe it when the king stripped your command and named you and the Mage Warrior as traitors to the kingdom. But here you've brought us proof."

"Donakin, stand down."

He pointed his weapon at Mark's throat.

"You know you took command from me and didn't even name me second after the years spent leading in your place. I don't think I'll stand down."

Skye felt Camin draw his power. "No, Camin. This is no longer your fight," she whispered.

"We don't have time for this," Mark muttered and in one swift move, Donakin was on the ground, his weapon in Mark's hand.

"Skye, do your thing."

Trent appeared with the king, and she heard guards echoing through the tunnels.

"He did this to ensure you lose and become his," Camin said. "Then he can force you to open a doorway any time he wants, target the veil, he'll own you and the magic."

"Over my dead body," Mark grumbled.

"So, the traitors return. Seize them Elite!"

They looked to the king and then at Mark. Only a

commander could lead the Elite. They trumped even a king's command.

"We're not traitors," Skye said defiantly, "and we're running out of time."

"You will be sent to the Fettered Forest, and he will be sent to the dungeon with the others who tried to start an uprising with their lies."

"They aren't lies," Skye said, noticing the mages were coming closer to see what was happening. "Your ancestor stole our princess, my kin, and forced us all to do your bidding. We have lived under your control for too long." The mark began to burn, and she knew she was running out of time. "I know some of you know the story, that it has been passed down. Our kingdom awaits and with it the freedom to live outside the castle, free from his control, and that of the non-casters!"

"Seize them!" Theodore ordered, his guards having arrived.

She pulled at the light from the fading sun, knowing she needed the day hues if she was going to beat the Death God. Then she pulled it within her before sending it to fuel her Elite, letting it drift over their bodies first, so they could feel the power, the connection to her magic. Their weapons glowed brilliantly, humming with her magic.

There was a moment as the guards were drawing closer when she questioned if it would work. Would they honor their bond to her and the Mage Warrior magic over the command of the king? To her relief, they took formation around the three of them, weapons drawn and aimed at the king's guard. From the guard she summoned the green of their uniforms, putting her hand out as it streamed through her fingers before pushing it to Trent and the other mages who had gathered, full and novice alike. The strength, the conviction of her words imbued within it.

Trent turned on the king. "I've waited a long time for someone to bring about the truth. None of us will stand down."

Her mark burned painfully. "You're almost out of time, Skye," Camin said.

"Mages, Elite, I need your fight, your allegiance, your bravery. All of you, even novices, you were meant to be as one with every mage. Today we join in one last battle that is pounding upon the veil to be freed."

"Are you mad?" Theodore yelled, fear in his eyes.

"Perhaps, but if I don't do this willingly, The Death God will force me to do it and then there will be no chance of survival for any of us. You and your non-casters should take cover, they enjoy living souls. We will protect you, but only with our freedom and recognition of our kingdom and my claim as queen."

Theodore stared at her. "I will do no such thing."

She turned her back and lifted her hands. "Then die."

She waited, giving him the few seconds she had left.

"What you ask is impossible!"

"As impossible as bringing my kingdom to ruins and enslaving my people, selling them off like cattle?"

There was no time left. Her mark burned painfully. She called the hues, the same dark ones she'd called the first day she'd almost cracked the veil. She began with the blues, then the browns and the reds of the natural world, being sure not to touch any mortal hues.

She could feel the fear from Theodore and his guards. The full mages drew their magic in defense of what everyone knew was coming.

Theodore let out a huff. "Fine!"

"Fine, what?" she demanded as the hues circled her.

"Skye?"

She heard the worry in Mark's voice, but ignored him. "Fine, what?"

"I acknowledge the kingdom of Kantenda again and your claim as queen."

"And the freedom of our people?"

"Yes!"

She glanced back at him, seeing the fear mixed with anger in his eyes.

"Guards, I would suggest you get your king to safety. My people and I will protect you, but you'd best move with haste." She looked to Elspeth. "I need him flanked. He is not to be harmed."

Elspeth commanded a handful of mages to go with the king.

Skye turned her attention back to her magic and serving the Death God's purpose. She pulled from the shadows the sunset had cast, bleeding them, hearing the screams of the demons, the thunderous cry of the shadow realm as it pushed against the veil for release. Time seemed to freeze as the mortals around her screamed in terror, the king being ushered to safety by his guards and the mages Elspeth had assigned; the Elite turning their weapons toward the bulging darkness, mages drawing their magic.

Hell broke loose, the veil shattered with a crack that echoed piercingly through the sky. She waited for just enough time to feel the mark fade, her end of the bargain met, before reaching for the lighter hues. Mark pulled her to the ground, stopping her action, as a winged demon soared over them, chaos erupting with an insane frenzy, the world growing dark. Her hope of saving them all fading with the encroaching shadows.

MARK

She's gone mad, was all Mark could think as Skye brought the veil down, inviting the Death God's demons into their world. She struggled below him, but he was afraid to let her up, afraid the Death God would steal her away.

"Mark, let her up," Camin yelled, fighting a small demon that was trying to bite his neck.

"Please, Mark, I'm not done."

He pinned her arms down. "Not done? You just unleashed Armageddon. What more can you do?"

"Please, before the sun sets completely."

He looked up to see the setting sun, only a fraction of blue left within the sky. It was then that he understood. She could break any veil, she had the power to walk any realm, to bring down any realm.

He released her, helping her up quickly, only to find himself face to face with a massive demon whose muscles were the size of Mark's head.

"The master wants his magic," it growled.

Mark drew his weapon.

"Not gonna happen," he said. He felt Camin beside him. "Do what you have to do, Skye, before it's too late."

"I've got your back," he heard Trent say, but couldn't turn from the beast.

"Actually, you might come in handy," Skye said, her hand lifting, the beast's bright red color fading, crippling him. Mark sliced him down the middle, a fountain of blood spewing from it. She stole the color, and as she did, the demon turned to ash.

"Demons have blood?" he asked.

"Not their own—blood of their victims," Camin said.

His stomach turned, and he looked back at Skye. The red hues were gone, but a reddish glow sat upon her skin. She was reaching for the sky, the orange and pink hues from the setting sun bleeding away, the remaining light blue fading. The ground shook as she pulled the remaining color from the world, then a tail whipped by him, slicing her neck.

"No!" he screamed as her hand drew the last light from the sky and the second veil shattered.

He caught her as she fell, blood spilling from her neck.

"No, no, no!"

The world exploded around him, the radiant gods and shadow gods battling above them.

"Brother!" A roar shook his very bones, but he clung to Skye as her eyes grew glossy.

He heard yelling and a commotion around them but stayed focused only on her, watching helplessly as her life faded. Sprinkles of gold and black from the gods above rained down upon them.

A haze of white seeped around her neck, its magic buzzing against his skin. He drew his eyes from her to find novice mages encircling them. Elite and full mages stood in protective stances around them as they healed her. She'd been right, they were meant for more. They were as powerful as the other mages, hidden in domestic duties, their true talents wasted.

Skye coughed, and he looked back down at her, the wound gone, the blood the only sign she'd been wounded. She rolled to her side and coughed, blood coming from her throat.

"She'll be all right," one said, then they returned to using their gifts for the battle, just as Skye had said they should.

"We good?" Noah asked, stooping next to them.

"Noah!" Skye said with a gurgle.

"Spent a bit of time in the dungeons but it looks like I made out better than you," he said with a wink.

There wasn't time for Mark to ask why his second in command had been in the dungeons and not guarding his Mage Warrior, but he had no doubt there was a good reason and that Skye was behind that reason.

She gave Noah a big hug, leaving a bloody imprint on his dirty, rumpled clothes.

"Is that mine?" she asked as a demon crashed into them.

Mark helped Skye up, only wanting to hold her, to take her from the mess that surrounded them, but knowing she somehow needed to end it.

"Any more to your plan?" he asked as he and Noah ran her to a safer spot.

"Not really, I'm just winging this as I go."

He stared at her. Her eyes were wide with fear. Blood still lay splattered upon her skin and clothes, and it was hard to look at her without his own fear surfacing.

"Jesus, Skye, you don't know what you're doing?"

"No."

"You're finishing this. That's what you're doing," Camin said, approaching them.

His face was splattered with blood, his blonde hair matted with it.

"You walk both domains, but the shadows are your home. Only a wizard can work with shadows, but you own them as if you were one of the gods themselves. Finish this before they spread to the other kingdoms."

"How is she supposed to stop a fight between the gods?"

"With my magic," she said, looking at her hands.

The world was growing dark, the moon only slightly risen, the sky colorless, as was everything. She'd stripped most of it, and the shadow realm had enveloped the rest.

She stepped away, staring at the gods as the two brothers battled like the world below didn't exist.

"Skye, don't," he said, reaching for her, but Camin blocked his hand.

"Trust her," he said.

"She is our queen for a reason," Noah added. "You know, I learned an interesting tidbit when we were with the wizards. Did you know the myth says that the first Mage Warrior came from the union of a god with a mortal?"

He forced his eyes away from Skye and looked at Noah, who smirked and shrugged. Camin nodded.

"The blood of the gods runs through the ruling line, but only in her have we truly seen it."

He looked back at her as she freed the hues within her, her body glowing as those of the radiant gods, brilliant and captivating. For a moment, even the gods took notice. A flare of gold fled her, lighting the sky, attaching to the remaining sliver of sun. She pulled the inky color of the sky to her, leaving the powder blue, the moon sitting within it, giving the impression that the world was still between day and night.

The dark hues swirled around her, and the demons screeched. Then she drew them, not enough to kill but enough to warn, and they turned, fleeing back to their realm. One came behind her, a succubus, its green and black, snakelike skin dull as she held onto its color. Its tail lifted but Skye's hand snapped toward it, freezing its motion, bleeding its life-force. As its body crumpled, the demons howled, more skittering away.

The shadow gods turned on her, but the radiant gods took a stance before her as the Death God's brother grabbed him by the neck then boomed at Skye.

"Finish this!"

She called the shadows from the shadow realm, the hues flooding to her from beyond the fractured veil, the shadows eclipsing her before she sent them hurdling toward the shadow gods. The hues dragged the gods back to their realm. The Upper God pushed his brother, sending him stumbling back into his realm.

"You will stay in your realm with your filthy demons and leave the other realms alone!"

The Death God growled angrily but didn't move. "This realm is mine, brother! One day I will remind you of that! I will return to the shadows, but I will not go alone. She's mine, no matter whose blood runs through her, or perhaps because of whose blood runs through her!"

A shadow snaked quickly toward Skye who stood defenseless, all the radiant gods having returned to their realm when she'd sent the final demons and shadow gods away. Mark ran toward her as the shadow struck like a cobra, the Upper God sending the Death God falling back into his realm, the veil rebuilding but not in time. The shadow struck, but Mark didn't make it in time. Camin, however, did, the shadow grabbing him instead, yanking him through the closing veil.

"No!" Skye screamed, running toward him, but Mark snagged her, holding her as she fought.

"You are so much like your mother," Camin said before the veil closed around him, the world quieting, the color returning to push the veil back to its rightful place.

Skye's feet gave under her, and Mark held her up, his arms tight around her waist. The Upper God looked down at them.

"You would be wise to avoid the shadow realm. Our reach does not extend there, and my brother holds grudges. If he ever discovers the truth about you, he will stop at nothing to claim you. Even one light in that world is enough to give it strength."

He disappeared, the fractured veil to his realm healing, the world returning to its natural stasis. She had done it. She had freed Mark from the shadow realm, bested the Death God, and brought freedom to her people.

Before them, the Elite and the mages slowly bent to one knee, pledging their allegiance to their true queen, the woman he loved, the woman who had faced the Death God, the shadow realm, and emancipated her people from a tyranny that had enslaved them for millennia. The daughter of the gods.

She turned to him, her blue eyes large and glorious. Below the wisps of hair that had freed from her braid, her birthmark shimmered. Where before it had shown as a violet sparkling against her skin, now he could see a trace of gold within it, like the power of the gods themselves.

He slid the wisps back, brushing his fingers across it, feeling the shiver of pleasure it caused her. She was still his Skye, a more powerful, titled Skye, but she was his and she always would be.

EPILOGUE

SKYE

Skye stared at Mark as he finished his story. She wasn't sure how to react. Jealous that he'd had sex with the demon? That he'd enjoyed it? But it hadn't really been his fault. Angry that he'd cheated on her?

She rose from her seat and straddled him, feeling him respond below her. His arms wrapped around her waist, and he attempted to bring her closer, but she pushed back.

"So, you have a thing for demons now?"

"Hardly. Are you jealous?"

"Of a sexy demon with large breasts that secretes intoxicating nectar? Should I be? Was she that intoxicating?" she asked, drawing her finger up his chest.

He moved his hand under her shirt and cupped her breast, letting it slide free of the material. Caressing it, he brought his lips to it and licked her pert nipple, sending a shiver of anticipation through her. God, she'd missed his touch. He sucked at it while his other hand slipped to her other breast and rubbed her hardening nipple with his thumb, each glance across it warming her lower body more. Below her, his arousal grew, pushing against a dampness that was increasing steadily.

"Definitely not as intoxicating as you," he said, dragging his tongue across her neck.

"Hmmm, then perhaps I'll forgive you."

He stopped and raised an eyebrow, his hand slipping down the back of her pants.

"Perhaps?"

"You still pleasured yourself to another woman's body."

"Technically, she pleased herself with my body and she wasn't exactly a woman."

His hand had slid to the front of her, and she moaned as his fingers found her dampness.

"I suppose wc weren't truly official at the time," she said, her voice hoarse.

"And we are now?"

"I seem to remember,"—she crawled off him, pulling his pants down before shimmying from hers. She dragged her tongue along his length, tempted to continue, the feel of it almost too inviting. Rising, she found his mouth again, kissing him—"you saying we would marry after the mess was over."

"Ah, I did," he said, lifting her hips to line himself up and entering her. She cried out, her back arching, his mouth finding a breast again. "I don't remember proposing the formal way that day."

She drew back and stopped her movement.

Laughing, he pulled her closer. "Marry me, Skye."

"That's better," she whispered. "But do you really think it's the best time?"

He bit her lip and forced her hips to move again.

"I mean, we're just rebuilding the kingdom. Camin is trapped in the shadow realm—"

He stopped, his eyes turning lethal.

"You will not set foot in the shadow realm again."

"But we have to save him."

"No, you don't. He knew what he was doing. He didn't give

up his life to save yours just to have you hand it back over to the Death God."

"You're jealous of what he might do to me."

"Damn right I am."

"You got to sleep with a demon, I can't taste a god?" she said teasingly.

"That's not funny, Skye."

She kissed his neck and lifted her body, knowing she'd let the moment pass, sensing how his desire had been replaced with jealousy and protectiveness. Slipping down, she wrapped her mouth around his waning erection, enticing it to grow again.

"That's not fair, Skye."

She didn't stop, ensuring she had him extremely aroused, her mouth feeling the throb of his need for release as his hands played with her hair. Finally, she rose, pulling him from the chair.

"We have things to worry about," she said, pressing against him, the muscles in his chest and arms tensing as he picked her up. "A mad queen to the south, a furious king to her north—"

"All of it can wait," he said, laying her on the bed and kissing her stomach.

"And I vaguely remember you promising me dragons."

His tongue found her spot, and she drew her legs in at the force of it before he came back up, nuzzling her neck and thrusting into her, pulling her leg around him so that they were one.

"I promise I will show you dragons and I will marry you before we deal with anything else," he whispered against her ear.

She drew her power, pulling the cool hues and letting them encase their bodies as the heat from their lovemaking intensified. He was right, everything else could wait. As long as she had Mark, the world could burn down around her.

COMING SOON

Skye and Mark will return in The Coveted Hues of Skye
Spring 2023

ABOUT THE AUTHOR

J. L. Jackola discovered her passion for writing in grade school when she wrote a short story that earned her a spot in a local writing workshop. She has been creating fantasy worlds ever since. When she's not weaving tales, she can be found logging miles in her running shoes, watching movies with her family, or curled up with a book. She resides in Delaware with her husband and three children.

To learn more, visit her website at
www.jljackola.com

www.ingramcontent.com/pod-product-compliance
Lightning Source LLC
Chambersburg PA
CBHW030359200726
48286CB00015B/1716